D0247207

For Mum

*A woman whose glass has always been half empty
but who has topped it up at possibly the
lowest point of her life.*

I'm so proud of you.

WITHDRAWN FROM STOCK

Chapter 1

Was it love? It certainly made her feel all tingly, although perhaps that was more to do with his magical fingers than the irrevocable connection between two people destined to spend an eternity having buttock-toning sex and finishing each other's sentences. Currently those naughty fingers were tracing a delicious trail up her arm, over her shoulder and drawing tiny circles on her neck.

She shivered, despite the blistering August temperatures. The air-conditioning had struggled all week at work, but away from the office and enjoying a lazy Sunday afternoon in the quaint Suffolk market town of Tattlesham, the hot sun soaked into her skin and bathed her in joyful expectations of the coming months.

'Do you realise that skirt is see-through, you little minx?' said Gareth. 'Especially when you stand with the sun behind you.'

Maisie sat up abruptly and glanced down at her legs. She was lying on the freshly mowed recreation ground behind the town hall feeling slightly tipsy. Gareth had provided a picnic of sorts (Prosecco and a packet of Hobnobs) and Maisie determined next time she'd be in charge of refreshments. She had a delightful wicker basket at home; she could make tiny sandwiches, bake fresh white chocolate and raspberry muffins, perhaps provide a selection of cheeses, and, of course, bring proper glasses. It was embarrassing drinking from the bottle but Gareth seemed unconcerned.

She smiled at her boss – a man she'd admired from behind the Apple Mac for so long that her neck had adopted as its default position the slight angle necessary to view his delicious face without it being obvious. Suddenly, her tidy, ordered, quiet life had changed. The whirlwind that was a proper romantic relationship brought with it an infuriating chaos but also gave her much-sought-after company. And anyway, she had time to domesticate him.

Hopefully, all the time in the world ...

Chapter 2

4 months later

'I suppose it could have been worse,' said Maisie, as she unwound her mile-long knitted scarf, and finally liberated the chunky bright green coat buttons straining across her ample bosom. 'There were no unpleasant scenes and no hysterical screaming.' Largely because the screaming and shouting had been conducted in her head.

Nigel peered over to the door, watched as she disappeared back into the hall to hang up her coat, and waited patiently to hear more of the tale.

'Actually, that's not true.' Her golden curls bounced up and down like slinky springs as she returned to the room. 'Finding Gareth in the basement was a decidedly unpleasant scene.' She shrugged. 'So I now have no boyfriend and no job.' Her sun-soaked expectations of the summer had curled up in a dark corner and were shivering with cold.

That afternoon, she'd been sent down to the archives to research the names of chief brewers from years gone by as the brewery looked to relaunch a historic ale. Entering the basement, she heard the huffing and puffing often associated with lifting down heavier box files from high shelving, but as she got closer, there were an awful lot of squelchy noises that didn't fit the scenario. The naked bulb hanging from the high concrete ceiling failed to light the back row adequately and, as she turned the corner, she recognised the Hollister polo shirt she'd bought Gareth for his birthday. He was not only showing the new girl from HR around the archives but also giving her a guided tour of his tonsils. Maisie's world stopped for that moment. She squeaked and dropped her notebook, Gareth turned and flushed traffic-light red, and the young girl slid out from under him and made for the fire exit.

Maisie brushed the unpleasant memories from her cluttered mind as she sat primly in her upholstered armchair. Time to move on, she told herself, and bit back treacherous tears.

Nigel took another nut from the ceramic bowl in front of him and popped it in his mouth. They made eye contact across the low-backed sofa where three aubergine satin cushions were set at precise forty-five-degree angles. The question he hadn't asked hung in the air between them.

'I could hardly stay. He's my boss. *Hashtag awkward*,' Maisie said, in her defence. 'It's fine. Another job will come along. I might even look for something different. Four years in the same office has been suffocating. You have to pick yourself up and embrace new things.'

Nigel looked momentarily worried, probably because the bowl in front of him was empty, more than an overriding concern for her crummy job and relationship statuses. He shuffled through the tummy-high sawdust, lay on his back and stuck his stumpy legs in the air. Never one for convention, he slid underneath his wheel to place his tiny limbs on the exterior of his well-nibbled exercise device, and a low droning rattle began as he scampered like mad, almost as if his tiny life depended on it.

Maisie Meadows wasn't a *why me?* kinda gal. Gareth's betrayal and her subsequent resignation were both upsetting but not insurmountable. However, as she placed a silver cracker across the solitary white dinner plate, she acknowledged this wasn't how she'd planned to spend Christmas Day – alone. The original plan, Christmas dinner with Gareth at the local gastropub, had been struck through the calendar with such force the pen had ripped the paper. So, it was just her and Nigel, and he would remain in his cage until after the meal because she didn't trust him with her Brussels sprouts.

Cutting herself off from Wickerman's, she had also inadvertently cut herself off from her social life. She no longer wanted to be with the mutual friends she'd shared with Gareth, and because her absolute best friend and sister, Zoe, was as far away from Maisie as she could geographically be, she had no one to discuss her Christmas wish list with or share a laugh about her unrealistic New Year's resolutions. As if in response to her thoughts, there was a scuffling from the corner of the room. At least she had Nigel.

An expensive Merlot breathed next to the hob, where she steamed a single portion of vegetables. A chicken breast fillet wrapped in maple-cured bacon – like an oversized pig in a blanket – roasted merrily in the oven with four crispy roast potatoes. There was already a half-drunk glass of pale cream sherry on the go and, as she sipped it, the leathery fruitiness added to the festive aromas swirling around the room.

It wasn't as if she didn't have family. Goodness – she had more than enough to go around. Both parents were still alive and kicking, although should they ever find themselves alone in the same room, the kicking would be seven shades of something unpleasant out of each other. And she also had three older siblings. Problem was, she couldn't even remember the last time they were all together. Part of it was logistics – they were scattered across the globe – but most of it was more ... complicated.

Several years ago, she received separate Christmas dinner invitations from her parents. Not prepared to undertake the forty-mile round trip to keep them both happy, nor to accept one and refuse the other, an amicable solution was reached that had endured ever since. Christmas Eve with Mum (because she did the most fabulous stockings and even at twenty-five Maisie refused to relinquish the tradition) and Boxing Day with Dad and whichever lady happened to be hanging adoringly off his jaunty elbow at the time.

Her smart strawberry kitchen timer buzzed to announce her Mini-Me banquet was ready, so she stood it back on the worktop in a line of matching red appliances. (The kitchen was the first room she'd painted when she moved in the previous year; a study in monochrome with accents of scarlet – she'd even persuaded the landlord to go halves on a beautiful black and white chequerboard floor.) Ten minutes later, she sat down to her seasonal feast, flicked out the pure white linen napkin and let it drift gently down to her knees. 'Merry Christmas,' she toasted into the air as she sipped the sweet, plum-flavoured wine and then promptly burst into tears. There's only so much positivity a person can muster in the face of such life-changing circumstances, especially when emotionally lubricated with a couple of glasses of sherry.

In recent weeks, the television had bombarded her with

images of picture-perfect, happy families gathering to share banquet-sized meals of gastronomic perfection. The culinary aspect she could do standing on her wavy blonde head, but where were all the people she cared about? Because there had been a time, many moons ago, when her life had mirrored these saccharine adverts, long before the Meadows family members were scattered to the four winds.

The last family Christmas she could remember, Maisie had been six. Mum had woken at silly o'clock because the ostrich-sized turkey had to go in at half five and then she'd busied herself with table-laying, present adjustment and tree titivation. She always maintained once she was up, she was up. With all the crashing and banging drifting up the stairs, a bleary-eyed Maisie stirred to find Father Christmas had been. Her pillowcase was stuffed with exciting, oddly shaped parcels and the pine-green fabric stocking at the end of her bed was overflowing with sweets and treats. She stumbled her slippered feet downstairs to show everyone her Sylvanian Rose Cottage – which proved what she'd said all along – she *had* been a good girl this year. (No one knew about the hair-pulling incident at school. Not even Santa, apparently.)

Everywhere she looked there were delicious piles of food. The sideboard was covered in bowls of nuts and crisps, the fridge was bursting at the hinges, saucepans overflowed with pre-prepared veg, and the whole back worktop was loaded with bottles of wine and spirits. But most exciting of all, presents cascaded from underneath the Christmas tree like a water-fall of cheery wrapping paper. (This year, she'd only poked exploratory holes in a couple because she was a big girl now and had learned through bitter experience that anticipation was part of the fun.)

Dad was doing silly dances in a Santa hat and naked-lady apron to the loud music throbbing from the kitchen. Lisa, her eldest sibling, who had been her usual sarcastic and grumpy teenage self all morning, was unusually human by lunchtime – having found some festive joy from somewhere. Her brother, Ben, sat upstairs, contentedly bashing away at his drums. The beats echoed through the house, and even though they weren't in time to Mum's cheesy Christmas CD, it was all happy noises and general jollity. Maisie's morning was spent either sneaking small fistfuls of salted peanuts from the sideboard or flat on her tummy arranging and rearranging Rose Cottage, only getting shouted at once by Lisa, who tripped over her sprawled legs when she came through to flop in front of the television.

Both sets of grandparents arrived in time for lunch, showed great interest in all Maisie's presents (Granddad even playing board games with her) and then fell asleep en masse in the armchairs after the Queen's speech – the only truly boring bit of the whole day. Later, the elderly contingent was roused for tea but decided to go home early. Maisie guessed all the excitement and post-dinner brandies were too much for them. Daylight ebbed away, and Zoe, older than her by five years, played with her instead – which was a first as she usually whined that Maisie was too babyish to play with. As Mum laid out another magnificent spread of food that everyone was too full to eat but still managed to devour, Dad took his parents home. Granddad had given up driving when his eyesight started to deteriorate but they lived locally and her dad told Maisie to save him a caramel square as he winked and slipped out the front door. Two hours later, he burst back into the house, laden with surprise presents for everyone and a huge bunch of flowers for Mum. The day was so full on that it seemed to Maisie it had ended almost as soon as it had begun. Lisa disappeared to bed uncharacteristically early, shortly followed by Maisie, who was full of delicious food and totally content. It was, she fondly recalled, how a Christmas Day should be ...

Pulled out of her reverie by the buzzing of her mobile on the kitchen worktop, Maisie put down her nearly empty wine glass and walked over to the counter.

'Merry Christmas, baby doll.' It was Zoe Skyping across a vast expanse of ocean and continents.

'Merry Christmas.' Maisie leaned her bottom on the edge of the worktop, her heart temporarily lifted by Zoe's beaming face. 'What are you still doing up? It must be midnight there?'

'I suddenly realised I hadn't spoken to you, but now that I come to think of the time zones, you're probably in the middle of a romantic Christmas dinner with that hot bloke of yours.'

'Not at all. I've always got time for you.' It wasn't necessary to bring the mood down with Gareth's tongue-thrusting exploits.

'I miss you.' Zoe reached a hand out to the screen and Maisie mirrored it with her own. 'It seems ages since your visit.'

The three-week trip to South Australia was one Maisie would never forget even though it nearly bankrupted her. Despite the memorable art gallery, the adorable pandas at Adelaide Zoo and the winery tour in the Barossa Valley, spending intensive, quality time with her sister had only made her miss Zoe all the more upon her return.

'Who are you chatting to?' There was a chirpy voice in the background and a man's mid-section appeared in front of the screen; the yellow cotton T-shirt and dark shorts of

9

her favourite non-family member. The figure bent down and a beaming upside-down face appeared.

'Cheers.' A glass of red was waved in her direction. 'How's it going?' Oliver was like a second brother to Maisie – a slightly less grunty and more interactive one.

'It's good.' It was all the positivity she could muster. 'I'm full of glorious food and about to kick back, pour another glass of wine and toast absent friends.'

'And absent sisters?' Zoe said, raising a Martini glass of something that looked far too colourful to be good for the waistline. For the Meadows family, weight, while not a major issue, was certainly something that tended to misbehave if it wasn't monitored.

'I shall toast them most of all.' There was a moment when the two girls looked at each other on their respective screens, glasses aloft, and neither could readily form more words.

'I promise I'll be over soon,' said Zoe.

'Make sure you are, 'cause I miss you like crazy. Mum still made you up a stocking, you know? Says she'll post it in the New Year.'

Maisie blew the biggest, most heartfelt kiss into her phone, and hoped her sister couldn't see the burgeoning tear in the corner of her eye as she ended the call.

Later, with Nigel scampering over the sofa, cheeks so stuffed with pieces of raw vegetable he looked like he'd eaten two ping-pong balls (or possibly two whole Brussels sprouts) Maisie reflected on her day. Childhood memories were taunting her, probably because most of the Merlot was sloshing around in her tummy and there was no one to play Balderdash with. The gaping hole caused by the shifting tectonic plates of Gareth's deceit was deep and cavernous. The happiest people she knew were those surrounded by family, supportive and ever-present. Surely there was a way she could pull her fragmented family together again to help fill that gap? And, if anyone could gather the scattered Meadows, it was her – largely because she was the only family member everyone was still talking to.

But with two siblings abroad, parents who couldn't be trusted alone together in any room that contained sharp objects, and another sister who managed to generally rub everyone up the wrong way, it was a seemingly impossible task.

Chapter 3

'This way, my dear, this way.'

Maisie swallowed. She was only applying for this position at the auction house because it was close to home and the first job advert she'd seen that was vaguely appropriate, so she tried to calm herself by repeating in her head that it was all good practice, regardless of the result. The suitability of the job was questionable but the location – in a tiny village just outside Tattlesham – was perfect.

The ovoid man beckoned Maisie through the front reception area and into a tiny office out the back. He was like an extremely well-dressed hard-boiled egg in his tweed jacket and contrasting waistcoat. Unable to drag her eyes from the broccoli hair (short back and sides, with a crown of glorious silver curls sprouting from the top of his head) and two highly animated and fuzzy eyebrows, she nearly walked into the doorframe. An old-fashioned leather button-back chair stood behind a cluttered mahogany kneehole desk and, for a moment, it was as if she'd stumbled into a Dickensian novel. The man was even wearing a maroon silk cravat, for goodness' sake.

He followed her startled eyes as they swept the higgledy-piggledy scene before her. A thin shaft of light cut across the room, originating from a small window high up the back wall, and dust motes danced through the beam. A ceiling-height glazed bookcase dominated the side wall, bursting with reference books, and a wobbly stack of the *Antiques Trade Gazette* stood on the floor – several empty coffee cups balanced precariously on top. Used to a bright, open-plan office, full of light and clean surfaces, this crowded space was anathema to her.

'Do, pray, excuse the mess. Part of the problem really; too much to do and not enough time to see each thing through to its proper conclusion. We really do need a purge of the accumulated detritus.'

The man beckoned for her to take a seat and he stuck out a plump hand as he finally introduced himself and shook hers vigorously.

'Johnny.'

'Maisie,' she replied and cleared her throat. 'The advert said you needed someone with marketing experience to help update the website and promote your online presence?' she said, keen to establish the parameters of the job. 'I have several years of relevant experience at Wickerman's Brewery—'

'Yes, yes, you are eminently qualified, dah-ling.' Johnny plucked at his corduroy trousers and pulled them up a fraction at the knee, before launching himself recklessly into his chair. It was on castors and slid back behind the desk, coming to a halt directly in front of her. He's practised that, she thought. 'However, the crux of the matter is that Theodore, my partner ...'

He inhaled and put the fingertips of his left hand to his chest, as if he'd made some dramatic proclamation in a theatre production. Did he expect her to be shocked by this revelation?

If his flamboyant wardrobe hadn't given it away, the way he called her dah-ling, stretching out the word like it was made of elastic, was a bit of a clue.

'... does not see the need for Twitter and the like. He's so old-fashioned in many ways – and terribly behind the times. Do you know, his mobile phone is one of those brick-shaped button things that positively went out with the ark?' He gave an exaggerated roll of the eyes. 'And as I'm a total imbecile when it comes to anything of the technological persuasion, I decided it was about time we employed someone to drag our frenetically kicking feet into the new millennium – albeit nearly twenty years too late ...'

As the interview progressed and Johnny asked a series of probing questions, she reassured her potential employer that social media and company websites were her forte. The eccentric man before her was making her care about this job more than she'd expected.

'Theodore is away at the moment, flaunting himself in front of television cameras across the land, so I have inaugurated a company shake-up whilst he is in absentia. It simply would not do to sit and dwell.'

'I agree. Work can be an excellent distraction,' Maisie said, thinking of her own situation. It wasn't healthy to brood over things you couldn't change, like unfaithful loser boyfriends.

'Lamentably, he will be absent for longer than I anticipated. Apparently, the camera just adores him and he's been asked to shoot some extra episodes.' His eyes fluttered towards the ceiling, and Maisie couldn't help but conjure up a mental image of Theodore as some kind of John Gielgud luvvie, but then chastised herself for perpetuating stereotypes. 'But time and tide, dah-ling, so with that said, let us take a perambulation around the premises.' Johnny wriggled to free himself from the confining arms of the chair. 'Monday is valuation day so do not be alarmed by the proliferation of people. I shall introduce you to every member of our small but dedicated team and if you aren't bored totally rigid to the point of needing CPR after ten minutes with Arthur, you'll do for me.'

As they walked into the biting late January air, an attractive, clean-shaven man rushed past and nearly sent her flying.

'My bad,' he called as he disappeared down a gap in the buildings, leaving a musky scent and a startled Maisie behind. If he was the sort of customer the auction house attracted then working here might have its perks after all. A boozy New Year's Eve might have allowed her to set her Gareth-trampled heart free, but a hungover New Year's Day had brought back the reality of being alone. She longed for the companion-ship and security that Zoe had with Oliver. Being single was all very well until your ovaries started idly flicking through pension options – not that she was anywhere near that stage, but sand still trickled relentlessly into the bottom chamber of her hourglass. She pulled her coat tighter around her body and waited for Johnny, who'd been caught by the accounts lady on his way out of the office.

At the edge of the car park stood an elderly man leaning on a sack barrow next to a young girl clutching a bundle of folders to her chest. Maisie couldn't help but notice a small port wine stain across the girl's left eye and how she turned her face away as Johnny stepped from the building.

Maisie caught the old man's strong Suffolk accent carried by the breeze. '... So, I told her we often have similar things come up and I could keep an eye out and let her know if any appeared, and she said she appreciated that, but it's really no trouble ...' The girl was taking tiny backwards steps, nodding and trying to extricate herself with the minimum of fuss.

'... You know as well as I do that there's no rhyme or reason to what turns up each week,' he continued. 'Sometimes I look at the lots and think my Pamela would snap up some of them dainty bits and pieces in an instant. And there's always weird and wonderful things out the back. Why, only yesterday I helped the lads unload one of them red telephone boxes. Now that's something that would look lovely in a—'

'Arthur, my dear fellow, Ella is obviously busy, and totally inappropriately dressed to be standing about in this most inclement weather.' Johnny turned his head and stage-whispered to Maisie. 'What *is* she wearing? An avocado blouse with that ghastly shade of blue?' The volume of his observation made Maisie feel uncomfortable so she tried to make sympathetic eye contact with the shivering girl, but she was eyes down, staring intently at her elegant knee-high boots. 'Let her go about her work, please.' Half-grateful, half-embarrassed, Ella gracefully picked her way across the pot-holed forecourt and stepped into the front office.

'Sorry, Mr Gildersleeve, sir.' The old man nodded in deference to his boss. Ah, so that was where the company name came from.

'Arthur is our *head* porter,' Johnny announced, his eyeballs inspecting the insides of his upper eyelids, as if to indicate the job title was possibly inappropriate. 'And this charming young lady is Maisie. She's applied for a position in our burgeoning empire and I'm giving her a guided tour of our salubrious premises in an attempt to woo her over.' Johnny really liked his big words. If nothing else, her vocabulary would expand should she take the position.

'Right lovely to meet you, Maisie.' The old man stuck out his hand. As she tentatively reached out, Arthur grasped her fingers, but didn't let go as he began another verbal ramble.

'Coming for a job, you say? It would be smashing to have another bright young thing about. We always seem to have more jobs than staff. Everyone is so busy, with barely a moment to pass the time of day.' There was a small cough from Johnny but Arthur continued, undeterred. 'If you get the job, and I know you will because I can tell by looking at you what an asset you'd be to the company, come to me for anything you need help with. I've picked up an awful lot during my time here and it would be smashing to pass that knowledge on to someone else. Always new objects to research and interesting people coming and going ...'

On cue, the clean-shaved man who'd bowled past her earlier appeared briefly in the doorway, bobbing his head around the barn door looking lost. He must be a customer either dropping off items for sale or collecting things he'd bought in the auction the previous week. He caught her eye and grinned. She felt her cheeks burn hot and looked away but no one seemed to notice her discomfort or the bobbing man.

Two porters, one bearded and one bald, appeared from a huge barn, wrestling with a heavy green upholstered sofa that resembled a bathtub.

'Art *Dee*-co, that is,' Arthur said, nodding towards the sofa knowledgeably and stressing the first syllable. 'Heavier than it looks.'

'Can you get the door to the storage shed?' one of the porters panted.

17

'Don't be stressing. I'll be there presently. And, before I forget,' he said, turning back to Johnny, 'I noticed a nice little Moorcroft vase in the sale – Mrs Collins said back in the summer how she was keeping an eye out for them, so I thought I might let her know. She doesn't make it to the viewings now the weather's turned nasty. What do you think?'

'Yes, yes,' said Johnny. 'Whatever you think best. Anyway, don't let us hold you up, Arthur.'

The two men rested the sofa on the damp concrete path by a large shed and looked over to Arthur, who ambled towards them, rattling a bunch of keys, as if he had all the time in the world.

'Head porter, you say?' Maisie clarified, her forehead creased into a frown, as they walked over to two gigantic farm barns.

'Don't ask, dah-ling. Don't ask.'

Maisie stood in the doorway to Saleroom Two. It was the upmarket version of the larger barn they'd just walked through. Saleroom One held household and modern effects; this was antiques. Both had the large central space divided by trestle tables, strewn with boxes. Larger items, such as furniture, stood around the edge and pictures and rugs hung from the walls.

At the far end stood a glass-fronted cabinet that contained small objects of value, every item proudly displaying a numbered sticker, which Johnny explained was cross-referenced in their printed catalogues. In her efforts to understand the system she looked up the lot number for a pair of silver cufflinks and read the description with a £130–£190 estimate. It seemed a frustratingly vague idea of their value to her.

Having never been to an auction, Maisie was wary of them as a concept. She liked the certainty of wanting an object, knowing its price and being able to purchase it without competition. There were too many elements of chance associated with the random and unstructured nature of bidding for her liking.

Johnny leaned an elbow on the top of the cabinet and ran a hand through his bouncy hair. There was a pause when all she could hear was the echoing footsteps of the porters at the back of the barn.

'Look, I'll be brutally honest,' he said, 'I've only had seven applicants and interviewed three. You are far and away the most impressive candidate and possibly over-qualified for this job. We need marketing skills like yours to help the company grow but you'll also be asked to lift tables, offer practical help on auction days and even sweep up occasionally.' His foot toyed with some dead leaves blown in by the wind, letting them crunch beneath his highly polished shoes.

The advert in the local paper had been optimistically worded: *Growing firm of Auctioneers seeks individual with marketing and communications skills to contribute to vibrant team.* Maisie was beginning to suspect *General dogsbody who knows a bit about computers because we're largely clueless, and who'll probably be asked to clean the toilets if we're a man down* might be a more accurate job description.

'However, I promise you won't have anyone looking over your shoulder or making you account for your movements, and I will genuinely listen to any input and ideas you have. I liked your portfolio, particularly the unusual Wickerman's beer mats you designed for the Felixstowe Beer Festival. You are clearly creative and focused. But more importantly, I like *you*.'

For the first time that morning, Johnny looked slightly nervous; tiny beads of sweat forming on his corned beef-coloured brow. He was wringing his hands together and looking intently at her face. 'So, my darling, I fall procumbent at your alabaster feet, and ask if you are in or out?'

Not quite sure whether being procumbent was a good thing or not, Maisie gazed across the cluttered room of miscellaneous objects, contemplated the joy of a ten-minute commute, and the distinct and welcome lack of potential romantic partners in the workplace.

'In,' she said.

Chapter 4

Maisie didn't regret her impulsive decision to take the job for a moment. It was nothing like working for Wickerman's and *nothing* like Johnny had led her to believe, but that wasn't necessarily a bad thing.

For the first week, she shadowed various members of staff because he insisted she got a feel for the place. With an evil north-westerly wind slicing across the forecourt every time she ventured between the salerooms and the offices, bloody freezing was her overriding feeling. Now she understood why so many of the staff wandered around in fingerless gloves and quilted jackets. But somehow even this lifted her spirits. How much more invigorating than sitting at a desk all day, trying to remember to get up and move every half an hour to encourage blood flow and reduce eye strain.

She realised now that even though she'd worked in an office full of people at Wickerman's, there had been a sense of isolation. Tied to a desk, each person in their own little computer-centric bubble, interaction was sparse. The auction house by comparison was a bustling and varied working environment.

Maisie quickly settled into the weekly routine. Monday, the public dropped off items for sale. Tuesday and Wednesday

Johnny dealt with private appointments or left the site to oversee probate valuations. Thursday was a frantic collation of the lots and production of the catalogue – all ready for the sale on Friday. People were invited to view Thursday evening or early Friday morning. No one, with the possible exception of Arthur, paused for breath. And then on Monday, the whole cycle started again.

Maisie was given a desk and a computer in the back office with Johnny and, in amongst the clutter, she created an oasis of calm and order. By the second week, she was keen to put her marketing skills to good use, and her priority was to tackle the dated brand. Simple was the way to go, with a clean GA monogram and a coffee, aqua and teal palette of colours.

'Oh, you are an absolute darling of the highest magnitude,' Johnny gushed, resplendent in a double-breasted suit of British racing green, with a cheeky silk handkerchief poking out the left breast pocket. They were gathered in the front office-cum-reception – Maisie showing everyone the new logo and gauging opinion.

'Ladies, what do we think? I value and indeed actively solicit everyone's input.' Johnny turned to Maisie. 'They are, after all, the frantically paddling legs under the surface of the water, whilst we glide along like the serene and elegant swans that we are. Ella, stop hiding behind the computer screen. Do you not agree Maisie has captured the very essence of Gildersleeve's? Sophisticated and professional?'

The poor girl coloured up faster than a halogen hob and although Maisie liked the exuberant Johnny enormously, sensitivity and tact were not his forte. She threw what she hoped was a conciliatory smile across the office but the girl didn't raise her eyes and instead chewed nervously on her bottom lip, reluctant to leave her desk. The glossy mahogany curtain of hair that covered the left side of her delicate face swished as she gave a brief nod.

'Arthur's had a slight accident.' The bearded porter ambled into the reception and Maisie immediately raised a concerned head.

'What is it this time?' Johnny sighed. 'Ran over a customer's foot with the sack barrow? Dropped a box of crystal glasses? Or got his wretched foot caught in the storm drain *again*?'

'No, he's excelled himself with this one. Locked himself in the men's toilet cubicle and managed to pull the handle off completely. Apparently he's been in there nearly two hours. Poor bloke is getting a bit agitated,' the porter explained.

Johnny let out a long sigh. 'I know Theodore is terribly fond of him, and it's largely why I feel obliged to keep him on, but really? He should have retired years ago. Why work here when he could be at home, enjoying his retirement, pottering about the garden, and playing bowls? – or whatever it is old people do.'

What business the staffing of the auction house was to Theodore, Maisie couldn't possibly imagine and hoped Johnny's boyfriend wasn't the sort of person who knew nothing about the business but still waggled his oar about in the company waters as he rowed past.

'Perhaps Arthur's wife doesn't want him under her feet all day?' ventured the accounts lady.

'I fear the poor woman more likely craves respite from his incessant chatter,' said Johnny.

Or he needs the money, thought Maisie, rather more charitably than the rest, wondering how no one, including her, had missed the old man for two hours.

Johnny, Maisie and the porter headed to the gents', a

separate brick building with a corrugated metal roof and a brown tile-effect linoleum floor – draughty but functional. A lick of paint and a big mirror would brighten the place up a bit. Perhaps she'd mention it to Johnny later, although she knew she was volunteering herself for another job.

'I'm a daft old bugger. The lock jammed. I panicked, used too much force and the knob came off in my hand, but you can take all associated costs out of my wages and dock the two hours' pay when I wasn't working. I don't want to cost the company money.' His disembodied voice floated over the cubicle, only a pair of scuffed brown Chelsea boots visible under the door.

'Applying that logic, he'd earn about four pounds fifty a week,' the porter mumbled.

'Is the lock screwed to the door?' Maisie called, trying to find a practical solution to the situation as fast as possible.

'Well now, let me see ... Yes, little cross-head screws,' came the reply.

'I'll grab a Phillips,' Beardy Man offered and disappeared, returning with the appropriate screwdriver and thrusting it under the gap below the door.

After much huffing and tutting, it became obvious Arthur couldn't undo the screws with his arthritic hands.

'That's it,' Maisie announced. 'I'm going over the top. Someone give me a leg up. Stand back, Arthur. I'm coming in.'

'Oh, dah-ling, you aren't serious,' said Johnny. And then another stage whisper: 'You don't know what you are going to find ...'

She glared at him and he looked slightly abashed, clasping both hands together and bending forward to help her mount the cubicle door by way of an apology.

One exuberant heave and she was half over the top. She leaned forward, shifting her centre of gravity to help propel herself forward. As her legs lifted, her floaty wool skirt slid towards her waist and revealed her sturdy underwear. Was it better or worse, she wondered for that suspended moment, that she was wearing tights?

'Oh, I say!' exclaimed Johnny from the other side, as her kicking legs disappeared over the top. 'Look away, people. Preserve the dignity of this fair maiden.' She fell awkwardly to the floor, next to a remorseful Arthur, sitting on the closed lavatory seat, with his head in his hands.

Two minutes later and she'd liberated the pair of them to embarrassing whoops from the porter.

'Would one of you take the dear fellow to the back office? There's a comfortable old armchair in the corner somewhere, under a pile of coats. Someone should sit with him for a while and revive his flagging spirits,' Johnny said.

'I'll take him,' volunteered Maisie. 'Come on, Arthur. Let's get you a cup of tea. You could do with one, I imagine.'

Arthur looked over to his rescuer and smiled a watery smile.

'I'm a silly old fool, aren't I? Don't know what my Pam will say.'

'Nonsense,' Maisie said. 'It could have happened to anyone.'

Chapter 5

'Here's the camera I was talking about.' Johnny handed Maisie a large, black digital camera. 'But you might prefer your i-Thingy to upload pictures. A selection of photographs for the catalogue, focusing on our more lucrative items, if you would be so kind.'

'Oh – me? Right.' Maisie was hoping to crack on with updating the website. There wasn't even a section detailing staff members – a must if they wanted to create a friendly, family feel about the business.

'Everyone else is so dreadfully busy today. It won't cause you an unnecessary degree of inconvenience, will it? The lot numbers are already in place, so all you have to do is fly around the saleroom with the speed of Hermes and take some photos of the more interesting pieces. It should be a breeze for someone as capable as your good self.' Johnny's round face broke into a charming smile and his fluffy eyebrows gave a little jump. Flatterer, thought Maisie – feeling suitably flattered.

'I mustn't linger, for I have a probate valuation in Norwich shortly. Deaths and doddery old dears,' he joked. 'Families can't cope with a lifetime of accumulated possessions and are happy for us to dispose of it all – forever hoping there is an undiscovered masterpiece in the attic or some scandalous and valuable correspondence from an illustrious historical figure deposited in the secret drawer of a roll-top desk.'

'And is there, ever?' she asked. 'A hidden gem that turns around the fortunes of the family?'

'Closest we ever came was a little Constable sketch. Fetched thousands. The family were so delighted they quite forgot to grieve.' He winked and slid a gold pocket watch from the pocket of his waistcoat and glanced at it. 'But I must away – the traffic can be such a bore.' He tugged on an outsized dark blue Barbour wax jacket, flung the tasselled end of a banana-yellow silk scarf over his shoulder and floated towards the door like an enormous and colourful hot air balloon.

'And you're still okay with me rearranging things, to get them looking their best?' Maisie asked. She'd been itching to play about with the salerooms and put her marketing experience into practice, but was conscious of overstepping the mark.

'Absolutely, dah-ling. I told you at the interview, you have carte blanche. We are so terribly behind the times. It's why you got the job. I knew deep in my very soul you would be the restorative tonic this business needs.'

Heaving back the huge door to the first saleroom, Maisie squinted to adjust to the dim interior. The day was sunny and bright but, typical of February, the underlying temperatures were colder than the bottom drawer of a freezer in the Arctic. There was a dusty smell, not unpleasant and reminiscent of old hymn books, the church feel accentuated by the loftiness of the barn ceiling and bare walls. Her eyes took a while to adjust to the darkness and then she walked over to the light switches, allowing the artificial blue-white light to invade the space.

Remembering her lesson from Johnny on how to handle the items (ironically, not by the handle) she took several photographs, marking each item off on the sheet as she did so.

She was halfway down the second aisle when a shiver of something rippled through her. The sensation came upon her so decidedly that she almost stopped mid-step. Her skin danced as a thousand tiny pinpricks exploded over her arms. It was a feeling she'd experienced many years before and one she'd all but forgotten about. Bending down, she pulled out a box of household objects from under a trestle table, the prickles moving up her arms like an army of inchworms. As she rifled through the mismatched saucers and dated kitchen paraphernalia, something at the bottom caught her eye and her heart gave a funny little jolt of recognition. It was a teapot, nestled between a yellow plastic colander and a cake tin – and one that was startlingly familiar.

Kneeling on the cold concrete floor, she carefully lifted out the surrounding contents. With one hand about the body of the teapot and the other keeping the lid secure, she placed it on the trestle table and sat back on her heels.

The china was white but the bold abstract pattern was in black, and it was a good size for a teapot, possibly holding five or six cups of tea. The squiggles and shapes that covered one side and crept over the lid were like jigsaw puzzle pieces, but not quite. And then sections of the pattern tailed off down and round to the predominantly white side – as if pieces of the pattern were drifting away from the whole.

Her heart was beating like Ben's thudding kick drum. She knew this teapot of old – she was damn sure of it. There was nothing else in the box that matched it – no china that would imply it was part of a set. But then the one she remembered from her childhood had also been a solitary item. Long-forgotten words floated into her brain – words the owner of the teapot had said to her all those years ago, and her heart began a slow tattoo.

'It isn't a set any more and my darling teapot so misses her companions.'

Chapter 6

How strange that Meredith Mayhew's teapot should come up for auction and Maisie should stumble across it. No, strange wasn't the word; it was disconcerting. Memories flooded back as her thumb traced the pattern around the pot and up the handle. Although not unhappy memories, they sat uncomfortably with her because they took her back to a troubled time in her life nearly twenty years ago ...

Meredith Mayhew had lived next door for as long as Maisie could remember. A funny old dear with tortoiseshell cat-eye glasses either perched on her elegant nose or on her aluminium-coloured shampoo-and-set hair. She always had a neatly pressed collar on her polyester print dress or floral cotton blouse, and there was invariably a string of beads hanging under the collar and around her neck. Sometimes jet black like small, shiny olives; sometimes bright red like ripe cranberries; occasionally, on high days and holidays, iridescent pearls. And, like many older ladies of Maisie's acquaintance, she always smelled of Parma Violets and talcum powder.

There were several years of exchanged pleasantries over the garden fence between Meredith and her mother, often as Maisie tumbled cartwheels across the lawn, or sat cross-legged, threading daisy stems together to make chains whilst her mother hung out a never-ending line of cotton tops, branded jeans and more odd socks than she had pegs for. (*How is that growing family of yours doing? Oh, you know. Eating me out of house and home.* Cue an eye-roll and a flustered expression. *You're always welcome to pop in for a cup of tea. If only I had the time, Meredith, but I never get so much as five minutes to myself …*)

All this changed on a blustery morning in April, as the scampering wind scraped the branches of an overgrown buddleia across the wall outside her bedroom window, even though the day was bright and inviting. A seven-year-old Maisie woke to Zoe perched on the edge of the twin bed, headphones on and staring straight ahead. Competing with the buffeting wind from outside was the sound of someone pummelling on the front door.

'Come on, Bev. Be reasonable.' The voice was pleady and distant.

'I'll give you sodding reasonable,' her mother's voice shrieked from the hall. Bleary-eyed and half-asleep, Maisie stumbled out of her bedroom to witness her irate mother launching a brown leather shoe out the landing window – three black sacks of clothes and books at her slippered feet.

'Owww. That got me across the shoulder. Look what you're doing, woman.' Her dad's troubled voice floated in through the open window and across to a bemused Maisie. What *was* Daddy doing on the outside?

'It was meant to land smack bang across your lying, cheating mouth and break a few of those perfect teeth of yours,' her mother yelled, pulling back a Russian shot putter's arm, pausing to take considered aim, and launching its companion on a similar trajectory. Open-mouthed, Maisie watched as her mother heaved up one of the sacks and tipped the contents out the window, giving the bag a final shake, before it was caught by a gust of wind and carried into the stratosphere.

'And I'm changing the locks. You'll have to find somewhere else to live because you aren't welcome here any longer.'

'Why does Daddy have to live somewhere else?' Still in her Hello Kitty pyjamas, Maisie returned to her bedroom to ask Zoe what the confusing scene was all about – it was Saturday so neither Lisa nor Ben would surface until the afternoon. Zoe wasn't quite a teenager like her older siblings but she was at high school so practically a grown-up. She kissed boys and everything.

'He's got this … friend that Mummy doesn't like. In fact, she's only just found out about her. But it's complicated,' Zoe sighed.

Maisie thought about this for a moment and her eyes expanded as she processed the information and its consequences. Inwardly, she resolved to steer clear of that new girl in her class. All showy-offy and sly. Mummy wouldn't like her at all.

The verbal warfare continued through the open window as her mother stomped backwards and forwards along the landing, scouring the house to seek out all vestiges of her husband. The lawn was now a colourful and abstract display of one man's possessions as the owner chased loose sheets of paper across lawns and pavements. Amused neighbours gathered at the edges of their gardens, intrigued by the spectacle, as he repeatedly begged his wife to let him in.

But the lady was not for turning. Her father eventually scraped together his scattered belongings from the front lawn and drove off in his company car. And Meredith Mayhew, who had remained inside for the duration of the showdown, opened her front door, walked purposefully down to the road, U-turned up her neighbour's drive and gave the front door three sharp knocks. It was opened by, Maisie's sobbing mother, floundering around in a world that had collapsed overnight, and in which she was now bereft of adult companionship.

'The offer of tea still stands. The kettle is on and we only have to talk if you want to.'

'I'd like that,' her mum replied between sobs, and the older lady ushered her down the front path with Maisie trotting behind, determined not to lose both parents during the course of a morning.

Meredith's house was the semi attached to their house. Everything was mirrored. And considerably tidier. And smelled less like stinky socks and overused deodorant. As she walked into the kind lady's living room, Maisie felt all fuzzy and peculiar – a bit like when you had to stand up in assembly and talk to the whole school, and were worried everyone would stare and laugh. She sat on the edge of the floral-patterned sofa, her small feet barely reaching the Chinese rug that covered the centre of the room. Maisie crossed her chubby legs in front of her and then uncrossed them again. They sat in silence for a few moments until Meredith reappeared with a tray.

'Drink this,' Meredith ordered, picking up a curious black and white teapot and pouring a steaming stream of dark brown tea into a dainty cup. The tulip-shaped cups and saucers matched each other, but didn't match the pot – Maisie always noticed things like that. 'It will take the edge off things, Beverley. I promise.'

Unable to drag her eyes from the teapot, Maisie felt the

pricklings become more intense. Meredith looked across at her as Maisie stared, transfixed, and rubbed her small hands up to her shoulders and down to her elbows.

'Are you okay, dear?' she asked, returning the teapot to the tray. Maisie's wide eyes followed her movements, as if hypnotized.

'Um ...'

'Can you feel something?' She bent over the little girl, her voice breathy and excited. 'Gamma used to go all peculiar and tingly whenever she brought out this tea set. She was so insistent it was like a family and should be kept as a whole. "Split the set; split the family," she used to say. It had been in our family several generations, so she was very attached to it. But then it isn't a set any more ...' The old lady looked sad, Maisie noticed. 'And my darling teapot so misses her companions.'

Maisie shook her head but kept her lips firmly pressed together, not wanting to be associated with a mad, old and long-dead relative of Meredith's. There *was* something funny about the teapot, but at seven, she couldn't even begin to articulate what it might be. And with two grown-ups both staring at her, she wasn't inclined to try.

Maisie uncrossed her arms and stared down at her blue T-Bar canvas shoes.

'I think we've all got rather more on our minds than a silly old teapot – no offence,' her mum sniffed.

'Of course. I suppose I always wanted to believe there was something unworldly about the teapot or even that I might feel it too ...' Meredith's voice tailed off and she placed it back on the tray.

Maisie's mum lifted the delicate bone china cup to her

trembling lips, eyes red-rimmed and posture defeated, and half-sipped, half-choked on the scalding tea.

And a silent seven-year-old Maisie tried to ignore the continued prickling sensation, as she watched the pain drain from her mother's face and her hunched-up shoulders relax.

'Wow,' said her mum. 'You're not wrong, Meredith. That tea is remarkable.'

Chapter 7

The saleroom find unnerved Maisie for the remainder of the day. It opened a chapter of memories she'd not allowed herself to dwell on for many years. The divorce had been difficult and drawn-out but the children were shielded to a degree. Ultimately, the Meadows siblings knew they were loved by both parents; Mum's love a daily dose of kisses to heal grazed knees, broken teenage hearts and academic disappointments. Dad's love demonstrated by the fun activities he did with them every weekend, facilitated by his bulging wallet. His magnetic personality made him a delight to be around. But then everyone who came across David Meadows fell under his spell. His monumental charm was used to great advantage at work – hence the healthy finances – but more destructively with the female population of the planet – hence the divorce.

Despite a busy afternoon setting up social media accounts for the company, Maisie felt called back to look at the teapot before she left for home – the blissful ten-minute commute still a novelty. As she wandered towards the centre of the barn, Johnny bumbled in. The pricklings had started as soon as she walked up the middle aisle.

'How are you doing, most magnificent of marketing executives?' he asked, rubbing his hands together and blowing over them, trying to summon a warming flow of circulation from somewhere. 'Found something interesting?' He wandered over to where she was prodding about in the box.

'Yes and no,' she said. 'It's this teapot ...' She lifted it out and held it aloft.

Johnny peered over the steel rims of his spectacles. 'Part of a household clearance from last week. These boxes of odds and sods don't fetch much. Five to ten, at best.'

'But it's so unusual ...'

'Not really. Hip-hop design, probably mid-Eighties – not at all my cup of Darjeeling.' A frisson of distaste rippled through him. 'At home, I'm classic Wedgwood all the way.'

Not wanting to correct her boss, who clearly knew his vintage ceramic onions, Maisie frowned. She thought the teapot was significantly older than that. Meredith had told her it belonged to her mother, and her grandmother before that. It had stuck in her mind at the time because she couldn't imagine Meredith ever being young enough to have a mother, and certainly not *that* mother having a mother.

'I like it,' said Maisie, more to herself than to Johnny. 'My kitchen has a monochrome theme. It would look lovely on the corner display shelf near the window. Everything is black, white or a cheery bright red.'

'Ah, a girl who co-ordinates. Perhaps you won't get on with our Theodore as much as I hoped.' A little sigh escaped from his full lips. 'I've never before met a man who embraced such a mismatch of colours and styles. Sometimes I think he does it on purpose, just to wind me up. As for the teapot – nothing to stop you placing a written bid, dah-ling. Your money is as good as the next man's.'

'I might,' Maisie said, but she knew in her heart she would

because it was destined to belong to her.

'Whilst you're about it, put a bid on these ridiculous and vulgar garden ornaments.' He pointed his highly polished toe at a box of six-inch-high garden gnomes. As she studied them more carefully she noticed they weren't undertaking the usual gnomish activities such as fishing and wheelbarrow-pushing. These gnomes were engaged in more dodgy pastimes; pole-dancing, naturist sunbathing (with alarming anatomical detail) and a variety of other unpalatable, largely naked, pursuits.

'Who on earth will want these monstrosities, I simply cannot imagine.'

Maisie thought it was funny – not only the thought of someone displaying them in their garden but also Johnny's obvious discomfort and abject horror at their very existence.

'Oh, I don't know. You could make a feature of them,' she joked, her face deadpan. 'Or give them as Christmas presents to the people you don't like. In fact, I can picture them dotted along my flower border.'

One of Johnny's haystack eyebrows came out to play. It bobbed above his spectacles and stayed there. 'Really?' he huffed in disbelief. 'Well, it takes all sorts, I suppose.'

Placing her soft leather house shoes neatly outside the door to her tiny spare room, Maisie stepped inside and onto the plastic sheeting. Everyone had a hobby and most people happily talked to others about the activities they engaged in during their free time. Maisie didn't talk about her pastime much. She didn't want to be judged for indulging in something so ... unregulated, but she got far more satisfaction from this than she ever did from alphabetizing a bookcase or ironing the bed linen.

Pulling her long hair back into a ponytail and placing a

one-and-a-half-metre-square board in the centre of the room, she grabbed a tube of vivid violet acrylic paint, took a deep breath, focused, and with a ferocious sweep of the arm sprayed a satisfying run of paint across both board and floor.

It felt amazing.

As she added to her creation, grabbing more tubes and squirting them just as wildly, a glorious array of colours emerged on the floor before her. The greens and purples seeped into one another, wild and untamed, and her heartbeat began to accelerate.

She flicked on her iPod and the docking station speakers pumped loud rock music into the room. A further frenetic burst of activity followed; dripping and smudging, flicking and scraping. A damp rag in her left hand was used to wipe clean the brushes and spatulas and, as she reached the crescendo with a forceful thumbprint on the bottom right-hand corner, her hands.

If the resulting mess hadn't been such a rainbow of colours, the room would have resembled a horrific and brutal murder scene. Daubs of true ochre were on her cheek and spatters of black plum had caught the skirting board. (She'd promised the landlord this room would be totally redecorated should she leave, but then he was so delighted with what she'd done to neaten up the tiny garden that he hadn't made a fuss about her messy pastime.)

Now *that*, she thought to herself, was intensely satisfying. Although the paints had very little odour, she walked over to open the window and let in some fresh air. Her abandoned mobile buzzed and her brother's name flashed up.

'Benjamin Meadows. To what do I owe this unexpected pleasure?' she said, running the back of her hand across her sweaty brow and inadvertently streaking herself with pista-chio mint.

'Sis ...' Whilst not everyone could be as verbose as Johnny, her brother rather took it to the other extreme.

At thirty-three, he was the perennial teenager who'd ambled through life with minimum effort. He didn't have far-reaching ambitions or crave great wealth. He was happy with a Beef and Tomato King Pot Noodle and a four-pack. Luckily for him, his high-school band had picked up a few gigs as he'd drifted through sixth form and things took off unexpect-edly. In their heyday, they'd even opened for Quo and were consistently massive in Bulgaria. Although perhaps not to Ed Sheeran proportions, for the last fifteen years it had earned him a moderate living. Consequently, he'd never had to attend a formal interview in his life and had bypassed the need to get to grips with the structure of a proper sentence.

'How's the tour?' she said, to kick-start the conversation.

'Good.' There was a pause. 'Mum said you'd given Gareth the heave-ho?'

Maisie was one of the few people who understood that below Ben's thick veneer of not giving a flying ferret about the world, beat the heart of a man who noticed things – little things. She wouldn't hear from him for weeks at a time, but when there was cause for concern or even celebration (like the bunch of flowers that arrived the day after she got her A-level results), he came through for her. It was often under false pretences, as if he couldn't bear anyone to know how much he cared, but it was apparent to Maisie now he was checking in to see if she was okay after Mr Two-Timing Pants had betrayed her.

'I felt hurt at the time but he wasn't right for me – I see that now. I trusted him. I gave my heart to him. And he stabbed it with a pickle fork. Fundamentally, I think—'

'Yeah, well, I don't need the gory details or to talk emotions and stuff. Just checking you don't want me to thump him for you.' From across the Channel, it would have to be one hell of a left hook. 'So, up to much?' He'd satisfied himself she wasn't about to launch herself off a high-rise and was making an effort at small talk, but his social skills were nanoscopic.

Maisie swallowed and looked at the paint-encrusted canvas on the floor. 'Oh, you know me. Running the hoover around and combing the grass,' she joked. She couldn't possibly divulge her hobby to Ben. How could she insist washing was hung on the line in colour groups and size order, or that every pen in her desk-tidy at Gildersleeve's was the right way up, when her spare room looked like Mr Creosote had eaten his last wafer-thin mint at her desk? She returned to the centre of the room but there was a squelching sound as her bare foot landed in a puddle of blue. 'Actually, I've been meaning to ask if there's any chance of you popping back to the UK soon? I've decided we need to do more family stuff together.'

He snorted down the line. 'You ARE yanking my chain? It would be like trying to organise a social outing for a pride of lions and herd of gazelles. You can count me out.'

And as a blob of crimson red dribbled down the wall, so did Maisie's hopes.

Chapter 8

Maisie quickly found her auctioneering feet and began to make wholesale improvements to Gildersleeve's. She mentioned the possibility of bringing in a mobile coffee shop to keep the bidders fed and watered but Johnny was one step ahead. Planning permission for a small café at the end of the car park was already in place and work was due to start in the spring.

She embarked upon a serious clean and tidy of the sale-rooms, an area Arthur struggled with, admitting Pam had always done the housework and it really wasn't his forte. Once the barns were more presentable, she experimented with dressing the barn. She laid a dinner service out on a dining table that was in the sale and knew it made both lots look so much more appealing. With Arthur's help, she dragged a sofa and two non-matching armchairs into a horseshoe, placing a glass-topped nest of tables in the middle, and arranged some ornaments on the low tables.

Johnny wandered in, clutching the digital camera, and stopped in front of the homely arrangement.

'Oh, magnificent work, young lady. Why we did not have the perspicacity to think of such an ingenious yet simple idea, I do not know. So embarrassingly obvious now I give it thought.' He stuck out a plump hand to shake hers vigorously.

'I'm glad you approve,' she said, hoping people could now envisage the items in their homes and that would increase their appeal. As an added benefit, it would improve the catalogue photos and make Gildersleeve's look more like an upmarket antique shop and less like a bargain warehouse.

'I do indeed, my little budding Laurence Llewelyn-Bowen. Talking of which, a couple of interesting items came in late this morning and I'd like them photographed. The lot numbers are on the sheet and I'm certain you'll whiz through them in no time,' Johnny said. He thrust the camera at her and words such as 'inspired' and 'marketing genius' tumbled from his lips. *Whizzing* wasn't the word she'd use. It took longer than you thought to take decent photographs but she was again suitably flattered so didn't protest.

Saleroom Two was peaceful and she worked undisturbed, glad of her extra layers as the industrial oil-fired heaters struggled to keep the hangar-like space warm. There were plans afoot to update the insulation of both barns – also scheduled for the better weather – so sturdy thermal knickers and thick black tights under her smart trousers were the order of the day.

As she stood back to get a shot of an Edwardian wardrobe, she heard footsteps echo down the far end and looked across the barn to see a dark figure moving about. Letting the camera hang from her neck by the strap, and giving her hands a quick rub in an attempt to get some blood flowing back into her stiff fingers, she walked up to see if it was one of the porters. Perhaps they could help shuffle the wardrobe forward into the light. She was toying with hanging a Nineteen-Fifties faux fur coat inside and taking the photo with the door ajar, to give it a Narnia-esque appeal.

An unshaven young man, wearing a thick-knit striped woolly hat, and a shabby camel-coloured duffel coat, was behind the glass cabinet. Johnny had left it unlocked as she needed access to a couple of the lots.

'Excuse me,' she called, getting closer now and realising he was sliding the cabinet door open. Some of the most valuable pieces were kept in there; this week they included a selection of Victorian enamel brooches, a couple of pocket watches and a gold sovereign. Exactly the sort of easily pocketable items opportunistic thieves went for and exactly why they had the lockable cabinet. Arthur had told her earlier they'd had a spate of thefts before Christmas. The staff at Gildersleeve's wore many hats and it seemed security guard was yet another they were expected to wear – especially the porters, who prowled the salerooms with friendly smiles but beady eyes.

'Viewings are Thursday evenings and Friday mornings.' Maisie used her PowerPoint-presentation-giving voice – clear and with assumed authority. 'The salerooms aren't open to the public at the moment.'

The figure ignored her, continuing to slide the door back and reach inside. He clearly thought she wasn't a threat. Arthur said the pre-Christmas thieves were so self-assured, no one thought to challenge them. They had the balls to carry a fifty-inch screen TV out the saleroom, with everyone assuming they were either staff or customers. Was this scruffy man brazening it out with her, knowing full well he was stronger and faster, and she was unlikely to try anything physical? Where the heck were the porters? She cast a nervous glance around. They were normally wandering about, moving furniture or stickering up recently delivered lots.

'Morning,' the untidy chap said, several days' worth of pale stubble scattered across his chin. 'Nice selection this week. The half-hunter pocket watch should fetch a bit. I'm hoping to get at least three hundred for it.' He slid the cabinet door shut, the watch still in his hand, and turned to walk towards the back door.

The cheek of the man. Not only was he stealing from them but he was also shamelessly informing her of his plans to sell the items once he'd made off with his loot. Well, not on her watch – pun intended. Maisie lifted the camera strap over her head and laid it gently on the glass top. He continued to head for the back door, and without pausing for thoughts of his size, her gender, or her zero knowledge of any form of self-defence, she launched herself at his back with grunting tennis player sound effects, clinging to him like a baby koala clinging to its mother's back as she scaled the lofty eucalyptus trees.

'DROP THE POCKET WATCH, YOU THIEVING BASTARD!' she screamed, as loud as her squashed lungs would let her. And as an afterthought: 'Help! We're being robbed.' The pair of them tumbled to the ground, the man's knees hitting the concrete floor with an unpleasant crunch. She gave him an elbow in the side for good measure and heard a muffled oomph from the face-down woolly hat. A not entirely unpleasant waft of pine soap and musky after-shave drifted past. Were shoplifters allowed to smell this appealing? Shouldn't they smell of stale alcohol and used ten-pound notes?

It was only as they lay together in a wriggling heap, that it occurred to Maisie he might be armed – carrying a knife or even a gun. But within a microsecond of her piercing yells, the back door of the barn was flung open, a bitter February wind slicing through the air, and several people burst in, including a heavily panting Johnny. His hands fell to his mustard, corduroy-covered knees as he took in the tangled bodies before him.

Her squirming quarry gave up his futile struggles and lifted his head to face the assembled crowd, standing in a concerned semicircle looking down at the pair of them.

'Theodore, dah-ling.' Johnny sounded most puzzled. 'What on earth are you doing to the new girl?'

Chapter 9

Theodore? As in Johnny's partner? *Hashtag Endofpromising career.* Maisie rolled off the man and onto her bottom.

'She hit me! *Really* hard,' Theodore said, as he lifted his head from the floor, the knitted hat now slipped down half over one eye. He put a hand to his head and tugged it back, enabling him to throw Maisie a dirty look. Now she thought about it, he looked vaguely familiar ...

'I ... I thought he was stealing from us,' she blustered.

'Oh, bless you and your misguided company loyalty,' Johnny said, offering his arm to Maisie, who heaved herself from the floor and brushed down her dusty knees.

'*This* is Maisie?' Theodore asked, looking at Johnny and waving a vague hand in her direction. 'The one you were interviewing when I was on my way to the studios last month? You said you'd employed an extra pair of hands, not a bloody guard dog.'

Could this man be the clean-shaven figure who had caught her attention a couple of weeks ago? This man was more stubble than skin. No wonder she hadn't made the connection.

'This is indeed she.' Johnny put out the same burgundy velvet arm to help Theodore to his feet.

'She whacked me really hard in the guts,' Theodore grumbled, rubbing his left side.

'Maisie was multi-tasking, dah-ling – photographer, marketing whiz *and* guard dog.'

'I. Am. So. Sorry,' she said. 'I honestly didn't know who you were.'

'Don't sweat it,' Theodore sighed. Having recovered from the assault he was beginning to see the funny side. He gave a lopsided smile and a tip of the head. 'Even Johnny didn't know I was coming back in to work today.'

'You *work* here?' Maisie couldn't stop her mouth from falling open.

Theodore looked over to Johnny. 'You didn't tell her about me? Bloody hell, mate. I'm only the most important person in the whole company. I'm the media superstar. I'm the draw.' He said all this is a most un-superstar way, Maisie noticed. And yet ... there was something beguiling about this untidy, mismatched young man. Something that drew you in. Was it the moss-green eyes, or that enchanting lopsided smile? He tugged the hat from his head and an indefinable mass of springy, fair, afro-textured hair sprung up like a very small, very thick sheepskin rug.

Or perhaps it was the extraordinary hair.

Not sure whether he was exaggerating for her benefit, or whether he truly was in that much pain, every time Maisie came across Theo (it transpired only Johnny used his full name) for the remainder of the day, he limped like someone with a shoe full of acorns. Mind you, he'd really thudded into that concrete ...

Arthur was on clouds nine, ten and eleven, and unable to conceal his Cheshire-cat grin.

'I didn't think he was coming back until tomorrow so I was really made up when he knocked on my door this morning and asked if I wanted a lift to work. We live in the same part of town, you know? And he's always looked out for me, even before this job came up. Turned out they were absolutely desperate for someone with my skills, even though I thought I was on the proverbial scrapheap. Wonderful really, that I'm still useful to someone, especially as I often say to our Pam that I passed my prime many moons ago. Naturally, I said yes to the lift because I've really missed him. He's such a good boss ...'

'Boss?' interrupted Maisie, who was half-listening, as she tapped away on the keyboard at her now thoroughly organised and totally business-like desk. Unlike Johnny, who still spent five minutes looking for his ringing phone under all the papers, if she needed a spare USB cable or an orange highlighter, she could lay her hands on both in seconds.

She was designing an 'About Us' section for the website – especially as she now needed to add another member of staff. Why the original website hadn't included any details about the employees was beyond her. Her experience taught her it was people and animals that got the most attention in any marketing campaign. And she was beginning to realise it was the people who made Gildersleeve's special so they should be actively promoted along with all its other attractions.

'Well, yes. He's like a sort of manager, I suppose. Deals with all the day-to-day stuff. Didn't you know?'

No she jolly well didn't – she hadn't even known he was an employee until that morning. Johnny was drip-feeding important information about her job – information that could have saved her considerable embarrassment and her manager from unprovoked grievous bodily harm.

Arthur barely paused, not needing any verbal responses from his audience. 'Everything will be rather more ship-shape now he's back. Don't get me wrong, Johnny's a wonder, but we were all so surprised that the *Wot a Lot!* crew wanted Theo – particularly Johnny, who between you and me rather fancied himself as a charismatic, less orange, David Dickinson figure. But they insisted on our Theo – and why wouldn't you? They said he had great visual appeal and the researcher I spoke to thought he'd pull in a younger audience, particularly the females.'

'But isn't he a bit erm ... untidy for television? Don't they want experts in suits with clipped accents and neatly combed hair?'

'Nonsense. Look at them popular characters on the telly, like Columbo?' The reference meant nothing to Maisie. 'The public loves quirky.'

'Johnny's *quirky*. Theo's a bit ... scruffy.' And that was her being polite. She knew it was wrong to stereotype but the majority of gay men she'd come across had been immaculately turned out. Theo's jeans weren't distressed, they were positively traumatised, and the hand-knitted jumper he was sporting was so misshapen, she couldn't be sure which member of the animal kingdom it had been knitted for – possibly a rhinoceros. No wonder she'd mistaken him for a ne'er-do-well, loitering around the back of a dimly lit saleroom.

'To my way of thinking, Johnny is a caricature of himself,' Arthur said. 'And twiddly moustached, eccentric antiques experts are ten a penny. Handsome, young, wiry-haired men full of charm sporting a pair of sparkly eyes – now that's going to get the pulses of the female audience racing.'

And possibly about five per cent of the men, she conceded.

Although Maisie's encounters with Theo had been less than positive, she saw Arthur's point. She could quite understand Johnny being too much of a handful for TV. The flowery language and ostentatious clothes had been done by other so-called experts, and possibly more successfully.

'Theo really knows his stuff, you see? Everyone expects antiques experts to be as old as the items they're valuing but our Theo has nearly fifteen years of experience under his belt. If I had a pound for the number of times clients have come in here and asked to speak to one of the experts, thinking Theo was a junior member of staff ... But oh, those patronising faces soon vanish when they realise he knows what he's talking about. I take my cap off to him, and Johnny come to that. Have you seen the mind-boggling range of things we handle? Everything from pushchairs to antiquarian books. And they have to know about it all – the history, the value and the current market.'

'Ah, there you are, Arthur.' Theo appeared in the doorway and slouched a hip against the architrave, two empty coffee cups dangling from a curled forefinger. The knitted hat was back on, his sheepskin hair wrestled into its woolly confines, and he had a look of nonchalance about him. 'Keeping our resident pit bull from her work?'

'No, no,' Arthur protested, 'I was telling her how much I admired you and Johnny, and how knowledgeable you both are.'

Theo smiled. 'I know, old boy. I'm teasing.'

'Let me take those cups for you, sir. I'll rinse them out.' The cups were removed from Theo's fingers before Arthur had finished speaking and the old man disappeared kitchen-wards.

'I wish he'd stop with the sir thing. It's embarrassing,' Theo said, still leaning at an I've Got Nothing Better To Do And All The Time In The World To Do It angle.

'It's a form of respect,' Maisie said. 'He's from an age where hierarchy mattered more than it does today. It's endearing. Whilst I've got you ...' She efficiently saved the piece she was working on and slid her chair back. 'Can I take a photo of you for the website?'

Theo gave his wonky grin. 'Snap away.'

'What, now? With the hat?' Maisie asked.

'Yeah, sure, with the hat.'

'Oh, okay, if it's your thing.'

'My *thing*? It keeps my head warm. Are trousers and jumpers your *thing*?' There was a slow curl of the lip, as he continued to lean in a lackadaisical manner against the doorframe.

'I meant, if you think more people will recognise you with it on. I want the friendly and informal nature of the company to come across on the website.' She'd expected him to remove the hat, but now she thought about it, marketing Gildersleeve's as a company of smartly dressed businessmen was missing the point. 'It's one of our strengths.'

'You're not going to plaster my mug shot all over social media though, are you? Johnny's been banging on about our inadequate online presence for months but I'm rather more cautious when it comes to the power of the internet. It can make and it can break.'

'Not if you don't want me to. But don't underestimate it as an advertising tool. And posts with people in always garner more likes than those without. We found that at the brewery.'

'Ah, yes. Johnny told me you were a high-flying marketing assistant at Wickerman's. Don't know why you left a cushy number like that to come and work here? The promotion prospects aren't great. And the canteen pretty much consists of that dodgy-looking biscuit tin in reception.'

'It was a personal move.' She shrugged. 'Not every life decision has to be based on material or hierarchical gain.'

Both his eyebrows bobbed up to greet the hat. 'Couldn't agree more. Go on then. Snap away.'

'And you're sure you don't want to um, freshen up?'

'Nah. What you see is what you get. Crumpled shirt and all.'

She pulled the camera out from the low drawer in her tidy and ordered desk and put the flash on to compensate for the low light levels.

'Macaroni cheese,' he said. The button clicked a few times – she wanted to make sure she got a decent shot – and she let the camera drop. Their eyes held for a few moments until it became obvious neither had anything to say. Theo coughed as she bowed her head and began to scroll through the images.

'Anyway, I came here for Arthur and he's scuttled off. I need some help with shifting a dresser.'

'Get one of the others to help,' the accounts lady called from the front office. 'They're younger and stronger.'

Theo twisted his head back over his shoulder. 'No, it's Arthur I need. He's the best in the business.'

On cue, Arthur shuffled back into reception and a wide grin spread across his wrinkled cheeks as he caught the end of the conversation. 'Right you are, sir. I'll be there straight away. I know we were mid-chat, Maisie, but I'm needed by the boss,' Arthur apologised, and Maisie nodded a disappointed but understanding nod.

As they disappeared, Maisie uploaded the photo of Theo and her stomach flipped as she studied his twinkly green eyes and wide smile. She flapped the open neck of her blouse in an attempt to cool a sudden rush of heat from nowhere. Yep, she totally understood where the *Wot a Lot!* researcher was coming from ...

Chapter 10

Staff were required to stay until eight for Thursday night viewings, so there was no time to artistically express her pent-up emotions in the spare room when she finally arrived home that night. After her unintentional assault on Theo, the consequent shake-up of her contented little work bubble and the complicated feelings she couldn't quite decipher for her new boss, she had a burning desire to splash a lot of flare red about and then smear some sharp lines of black through the whole lot.

The following day was sale day. Friday was always the best day at any job but at Gildersleeve's it was more so. It saw the culmination of all the hard work throughout the week, and buzzing staff milling about the premises as items hit higher prices than expected and nail-biting bidding wars played out in the salerooms. Maisie was particularly excited about this week's sale because Meredith's teapot was one of the lots.

After offloading her embarrassing day on to Nigel, she wandered upstairs in search of a book that had occupied her thoughts since she'd stumbled on Meredith's box of miscellaneous kitchenalia. When she was younger, it had lived under her pillow and only when she was certain Zoe was asleep, would she sneak her pink torch out from the bedside table drawer and take both book and torch deep under the covers. She knew the book so well she hadn't looked at it much in recent years, but with thoughts of Meredith flooding her head, it was suddenly important for her to physically hold it again.

It was where she knew it would be, amongst the oversized volumes and nestled between a photography manual and a guide to logo design. Sometimes it was hard deciding whether to sort according to subject matter or size. Or – if she had her way and as impractical as it was – colour.

Flicking through the familiar pages, her hand tracing the images within, she realised the teapot and this book were so inextricably linked, that she simply must be the winning bidder on sale day. After all, it was her curiosity about the teapot that had led Meredith to give her the book in the first place.

'Why does your pot only have a pattern on one side?' Maisie asked Meredith, tipping her seven-year-old head to one side and drawing in her eyebrows as she'd seen her teacher do when she wanted the children to know they had her full attention.

Since Mummy and Daddy had decided to live apart (although Maisie was pretty sure Mummy had done most of the deciding) Maisie and her mum often popped in on Meredith in that delightful slice of the afternoon between walking back from school and the number fourteen bus dropping off her rowdy older siblings – when all peace and order was irrevocably shattered.

Maisie was the baby of the house. Her brother and sisters were born within five years, and then there was a gap of another five before she was even thought of – if indeed she'd been thought of at all. It meant she always felt slightly apart from the cluster. So with a houseful of hormonal teenagers, high-pitched screaming and the reverberating echoes of a drum kit being thrashed to within an inch of its life, Maisie trotted behind her mother whenever there was an offer of tea and sympathy next door. It was either sit in a strange old lady's house and listen to boring grown-up conversation, get caught in the cross-fire of squabbling teenage girls playing tug-of-war with a much coveted halter-neck top, or get shouted at by Ben for walking in front of the PlayStation 2 screen.

Meredith smiled. 'I suppose it does look rather unfinished. Almost as if the person painting it got bored and went off to do something else. But then that's what I like most about it. It isn't uniform or conventional.'

Grown-ups really used ordinary words in the most surprising of places. The only uniform Maisie knew anything about was the mustard-yellow polo shirt and bottle-green jumper she had to wear to school. She felt like a plate of salad in those dumb colours.

'Gamma loved that it wasn't dotted with pink flowers like every other tea service around. And yet my mother hated it for those very reasons. Drab old set, she would say. No colour on the damn thing at all. But things don't have to be colourful to be beautiful. Think of black and white photographs – considerably more atmospheric than colour. And how striking a zebra is when compared to a horse. What do you think, Maisie?'

Even at her young age, she could tell Mrs Mayhew was a retired teacher. She was good at explaining things, would ask Maisie questions that made her think and often actively sought her opinion. Grown-ups normally didn't care what she thought. If they did, Daddy would still be living at home.

Maisie put her best thinking face on to show her neighbour she was adult enough to take this question seriously – this time she allowed her eyebrows to rise up her forehead in a considered manner. Eyebrows, she noticed, did a lot of talking.

'I love Lisa's black and white stripy dress. I think she looks super cool. But colours are fun too. I like Coca-Cola because it's in red shiny cans—'

'Not that she drinks lots of fizzy drinks, Meredith,' her mother interrupted, keen to be seen as a responsible and caring parent by their neighbour.

'But if everything was black and white, like in the old days,' Maisie continued, 'you wouldn't be able to tell things apart.' Now wasn't the time to admit she had lots of Coca-Cola at Daddy's house. In fact, she pretty much got whatever she asked for, on the condition she didn't run back and tell Mummy.

'I do so love a child who knows her own mind,' Meredith said, much to Maisie's delight. 'You are quite right, young lady. Variety is key. It doesn't matter how wonderful something is, if it becomes too commonplace, it loses its appeal.'

'Someone tell that to my wandering husband,' her mum muttered, under her breath.

'So if everyone had your teapot it wouldn't be special any more?' Maisie was trying to follow the logic. Just when she thought she'd grasped something, adults threw something else into the mix.

'Exactly, and according to Gamma, this teapot is particularly interesting for reasons she never properly explained – at least not to me or my sisters. If she elaborated to my mother, sadly that information went with her to the grave.' She stroked the spout, running her finger along it carefully, and let out a little sigh. 'Gamma always rabbited on about finding someone

58

to look after the whole set, but in the end, it passed to my mother and I can't think of anyone less guardian-like she could have left it to. It was divided up between me and my sisters not long after Gamma died. But then I suppose at least it remained in the family even if it wasn't together.'

'You have sisters?' gasped Maisie. Did old ladies have sisters? And if so, were they as much trouble as her own? Lisa, never mind drama queen, was a drama goddess, and kept blaming Mummy and Daddy's quarrel for everything. And Zoe, rather boringly, had turned to exercise – as if she could work through her worries by pumping weights and running around the estate in Lycra. She was now far too busy to play with Maisie.

'Five,' Meredith replied. 'Including me, that made six girls and I'm the oldest. Which is why I was given the teapot. Talking of which, it's time to make a fresh brew. You look like you could use another cup, Beverley.' Meredith swept up the tray of tea-making paraphernalia and returned to the kitchen.

Maisie was left wondering what made the teapot so special. Could you rub it and get three wishes, like Aladdin's lamp? Or could you peer into it and see the future, like a crystal ball? She never did find out but perhaps it was one of those things said to a child merely to get an impressed, wide-eyed look. She'd fallen for all that nonsense before: unicorns and tooth fairies. Thank goodness Father Christmas wasn't one of those silly stories made up by adults – she'd seen him with her own eyes.

A cheery rat-a-tat-tat at the back door interrupted Maisie's memories and her mother, passing by after a late shift, let herself into the kitchen. As she snuck a home-baked cookie from the plastic tub on the side, Maisie entered. They faced each other and both gave weary smiles, her mother stepping forward to tuck a strand of Maisie's loose hair behind her daughter's ear.

'Don't hide your pretty face behind your hair. You'll never get a boyfriend by hiding away.'

There had never been another man for her mother after the divorce; instead she'd launched herself back into the workplace to compensate. She once confided in her youngest daughter there had been a few tentative romantic offers over the years but no one had that dazzling smile, exuded that charming personality, or made her feel her insides would implode with longing as she entertained lustful and wanton thoughts when she was within a ten-metre radius of his intoxicating after-shave.

As soon as Maisie was at secondary school and relatively independent, her mother registered with a handful of job agencies, wondering what on earth she was qualified for with a cavernous twenty-year gap in her CV and no qualifications to speak of. Eventually, she took a part-time job in a local care home and over the years worked her way up to duty manager, having found her true vocation. The plus side of being a highly emotional person was she understood and respected the emotions of others. The old dears loved her, and Maisie's mum, who had survived the horrible teenage years being repeatedly informed by her offspring that she was the worst mother *ever*, was loved again, by a myriad of doddery but tender-hearted residents.

'How are things?' her mum asked, as she slipped her coat off and helped herself to a second cookie. Her shoulders drooped and her face was pale and drawn.

'Good,' but Maisie didn't return the question. It was obvious her mum had *not* had a good day. 'Lost another one?' she asked, flicking on the kettle.

'Oh, sweetheart, sometimes I can't bear it.' Any pretence things were okay was now gone. A salty tear dribbled down her soft cheek and dangled from her jaw. 'Such a darling. Thought she was still eighteen and didn't understand why her mother never came to collect her. Every day she waited in reception, black leather quilted handbag at her feet, wringing her tiny hands together. She was the sweetest, meekest soul you'd ever find. And one of the few residents who wasn't unduly alarmed by our in-house streaker. Honestly, he's going to give someone a heart attack one of these days. Waving everything about and shouting, "Suck on this, ladies – dentures optional."'

She tried to summon some joy from her heavy heart but it had clearly sunk too low for her to reach. Maisie embraced her mother and kissed the top of her head, noticing a few more wiry grey hairs. They gave a marbled appearance to her mum's thick, wavy bob, but she was in pretty good shape for a woman of nearly sixty.

'I don't know why I put myself through it. Every time we welcome a new resident, I can't help but size up their potential life expectancy. It's so heart-breaking – knowing we lose them all in the end.' She began to sob softly as she considered her words.

'I prescribe a good, strong, hot cup of tea,' Maisie said firmly. 'Which reminds me, do you remember that quirky black and white teapot Meredith Mayhew used to wheel out? It's come up at the auction from a house clearance, so I guess she isn't with us any more.'

Maisie's mum looked up and shrugged her shoulders,

mopping the cascade of tears with the hem of her regulation navy blue cardigan.

'I heard she'd passed away a couple of months ago from the lady behind the deli counter in the Co-op. I felt bad because we were close at one time.' She shook her head, moving on quickly from a time of heartache she wanted to forget. 'I'd have attended the funeral if I'd known. But then Meredith wasn't there to miss me. Well, technically she was present – but you know what I mean.'

There was a moment where Maisie's heart skipped a beat. Meredith was dead. That was it then. She'd never be able to tell the old lady what a profound impact she'd had on her life – even inadvertently influencing her career path. Swirling hot water around the pot to warm it, Maisie tipped it away before counting three spoons of loose tea and adding the boiling water. She reached for her red and white spotty mugs and stood back to let the tea brew. Both women liked a strong cuppa.

'Meredith was a kind woman,' her mum added. 'Lived a lonely life though. Must have adored children, because you certainly don't choose the teaching profession for the glamour and untold riches. Always kind to me and I don't know that I ever said a proper thank you.' This melancholy thought caused a further surge of tears. 'I'm not sure I can cope with memories of Meredith on top of losing one at work today. Oh, why does it get me like this every time?'

'It means you're good at your job, Mum. Some of those old people don't have anyone to miss them apart from care home staff. If you're sad, it means you cared,' Maisie said, pouring and passing the tea. Her mother appeared to mull this over as she brought the mug to her lips. Fresh tears hung from her chin, like a row of pear-cut diamonds from a necklace, and one plopped onto her lap. She blew ineffectually at the hot liquid before taking a sip. As it made its journey downward, she sat up straighter and, as Maisie hastily slid a coaster in front of her, placed the mug back on the table. Maisie pulled out a chair to join her mother at the table, giving her an encouraging smile.

'You're right,' her mum said, finding some inner strength. 'I do care. About *nearly* all of them.'

Chapter 11

'Lot 243 – an immaculate condition Moulinex mixer, boxed, with all the attachments. Embrace your inner Raymond Blanc and reject this heinous culture of pre-packaged micro-waveable mush. Do I hear twenty? Thank you, gentleman at the back. Twenty-five, anywhere? I can do two, if it helps? No? Twenty with you, sir ...' Johnny's arm swept the room. 'Going once. Sold.' The gavel was smacked down on the wooden rostrum with gusto. He gestured towards the back corner and did the peery thing over his glasses. 'Number, please?'

A disembodied country accent announced, 'Forrrr. Three. Ni-yern.' Johnny noted the number on his sheet and turned the page.

Johnny had suggested Maisie watch some of the auction – especially as she'd put a written bid on the miscellaneous box of kitchenware. 'All part of your continuing education, dah-ling,' he said. 'And there really is nothing like it. The atmosphere can be deliciously electric, especially if you have two tenacious bidders after the same item. Never mind a pin, you'd hear the downy feather of a recently plucked fowl drift to the floor.'

Arthur had popped into her office to say they were getting close to her lot, so she'd reluctantly dragged herself away from the old-fashioned oil heater roasting her toes, if not the rest of her shivering torso, and walked over. She watched as groups of people drifted in and out, some in expensive dark green quilted jackets and Hunter wellies, some in purple North Face anoraks, jeans and trainers. Maisie initially sat rigid, not daring to move her arms in case she accidentally bid for something expensive and found herself hundreds of pounds in debt. The stuff of sitcoms, perhaps, but Arthur assured her it still happened occasionally.

Settled on a high bar stool recently vacated by a serious-looking man in casual clothes and a brown wool trilby, Maisie was now able to distinguish dealers from the general public. The serious gentleman had been the former, not making eye contact and studiously ticking off items from his catalogue as he walked towards the door, an empty travel mug swinging from his fingers. He was there to do business, not socialise.

'Lot 244. Miscellaneous china and kitchenware. Do I hear ten to start?' Johnny's deep, melodious tones boomed across the cavernous space. This was the box containing the tingle-inducing teapot, so Maisie turned to the front and focused on Johnny as the follicly challenged porter tugged the box out and pointed at it. He was the 'show-er' for the auction – the member of staff who highlighted the item currently being sold.

The barn was uninterested and silent. Maisie didn't need to do anything as her bid would be on Johnny's sheet.

'I have some interest on the books, so I'll start at five. Six, anyone?'

Again silence.

Maisie felt a bubbling in her tummy. Was it going to be this easy to buy the teapot?

'No advance on five? Going once. Sold.'

He peered over his glasses to Maisie and shrugged an I told you so, before updating the paperwork and moving on.

'Lot 245 – an anomalous collection of garden ornaments.' There were a few giggles and murmurs as the porter held a couple of the less embarrassing gnomes aloft. 'I'll start the bidding at ten? Thank you, sir,' and he nodded to his right. Someone in the front row obviously had a burning desire to turn his garden into a saucy sideshow. 'Twelve. Fifteen. Eighteen. Twenty. Do I hear twenty-five? Thank you, madam. With you, sir, at thirty? And thirty-five ...'

When the bidding reached forty, Johnny cast her an astonished look and shrugged, as he waited for one of the eager bidders to decide whether life would be complete without an assortment of sexually uninhibited dwarf-like figures. Good grief! his eyes seemed to say – there are people out there who find such unpalatable objects of interest. She gave an emphatic nod and grinned, despite herself. After all her teasing, they were going to fetch a pretty penny.

'And a new bidder, so it's forty-five with you, madam.'

Maisie's heart started to race. He'd explained how some buyers waited for the initial flurry of bids before stepping in. Three people in the room who wanted a box of garish gnomes. It beggared belief.

'And I have fifty here at the front,' Johnny said. Maisie shuffled her hands under her bottom, to make certain there were no ambiguous hand movements, and looked down at her feet, swinging happily over the edge of the stool. 'Fifty-five with you, madam, at the back?'

She couldn't quite see where Johnny was looking but he caught her eye again, grinning like a loon. Even he hadn't foreseen this level of interest. She smiled and gave the faintest tip of the head and an eye-roll to acknowledge the humour of the situation.

'And sixty?' He swung back to the front. 'No, sir? Certain we can't tempt you? Are we all done then at fifty-five pounds?' The gavel was held aloft as his eyes scanned the crowd. 'And sold. Thank you, madam, this delightful collection of deviant outdoor ornaments are yours.' He did another of his loud stage whispers to a group huddled at the front: 'Each to their own, eh?' He looked across at her again. 'Number, please?'

Maisie's heart, slowing slightly after the excitement of the bidding frenzy, began to race again. He was looking directly at her.

'Umm ...' A high-pitched whine came out. Oh my God. Had she just bid for the damn things?

'Ah, it's okay, Maisie, I already have your number on my sheet.'

Yup.

A few lots later, during which time Maisie could barely look up from her now *not* happily swinging feet, Arthur slid beside her. She'd spotted him moving around the room when she'd first come in, chatting to people as he went.

'Interesting collection,' he said, nodding to the front and clearly referring to her recent purchase. 'Pleased you got them if they were something you wanted. Wouldn't have put you down as that sort of girl myself. I saw you as more flowers and veg – pots of primulas and window boxes of cherry tomatoes – but you never can tell. And I'd never judge anyone for their personal taste.'

'Oh, the gnomes. No, that was a mistake.' Her face was pale and her stomach leaden. 'I didn't even raise my arm.'

Arthur chuckled. 'Well, there's a rum do and no mistake. Poor love. Fancy being lumbered with all them. I'm quite broad-minded but there are a couple of those that made me blush. I daren't tell our Pam. Not her sort of thing at all. She didn't even like it when I bought one of them novelty cork-screws. Made me titter but she's very much a lady and I've always respected that.' He stroked his chin as he pondered her predicament. 'It's an eye contact thing. Did you make eye contact?'

'Well, yes, but—'

'Ah. It's the dealers, see? Don't like other dealers knowing their business. Watch them. They barely move an eyelash but the auctioneer knows they're bidding. Not like the general public, jumping up and down with their printed bidder numbers in the air, ever anxious the auctioneer won't see them and they'll miss out on their bargain Bavarian cuckoo clock.'

As she watched a few further lots, she realised Arthur was right; the extremely tall man beside them successfully bid for a collection of reproduction oil lamps yet barely twitched. But watching his face and Johnny's, she could now see their interaction. Lesson learned, but an expensive and possibly humiliating one.

'Tell Johnny and he'll sort something out. I've seen buyers put things back into the sale the following week and even turn a profit. You did have competition.'

'Please don't say anything. I'd rather not have everyone thinking I was so green I bid on them by mistake.'

'As opposed to them thinking you are a collector of naughty gnomes?'

It was a tough call but she nodded. She would just have to put her marketing skills to the test and see if she couldn't make her money back somehow. She liked a challenge; after all, that's why she took this job in the first place.

'It's right lovely to see someone who doesn't let little mishaps in life get her down. I was telling my Pam that a bright young girl had started at work and what a lovely smile you had – just like a sunrise over the back fields – all glowing and lifty.' Maisie felt a tiny grin spread across her cheeks despite her glum mood. 'And you've got a keen eye. I saw you with that kiddies' train set earlier. It looks smashing laid out on that glass-topped table. Might not be worth much but I reckon it'll attract a fair bit of interest now.'

Arthur was on her wavelength. With the porters previously responsible for arranging the items in the salerooms, she'd noticed a distinct lack of the female touch. And Maisie was nothing if not organised. 'Yes, I—'

'And I thought to myself, that girl knows what she's doing. She'll be running the company before the week's out ...'

'I hardly think—'

'Because this company really needs more female input. The lovely ladies in the office don't get the opportunity to leave their desks much, and when they do they always seem so busy. Always scurrying past me, with no time to talk. I guess they must be—'

'Ladies and gentlemen,' Johnny's voice cut through the chattering hum of the room. 'A little bit too much voluminous babble. May I suggest you take your chit-chat outside if your conversation is vital?' Maisie was pretty certain voluminous was more a measure of quantity rather than level of noise, but Johnny liked his fancy words and seemed to get away with it – his flamboyant vocabulary rivalling his flamboyant clothes.

'That's told them,' Arthur whispered, oblivious he was a

sizeable part of the general level of increased chatter. 'But then, you should have heard him when I first got the job. He was telling everyone to bugger off out of his saleroom if they couldn't behave like *decorous* citizens – don't mind admitting to you, I had to look that particular word up. But he's toned down a bit in recent years. Definitely Theo's input.' Maisie threw him a questioning look. 'Let's just say Johnny's tendency to say what he thinks don't always go down well with the customers. And when he insulted a painting last year, the vendor was in the room, eager to see how much his masterpiece raised. Turns out not only was he selling it, he'd also painted it ...'

Johnny proceeded to rattle through three hundred lots in the space of the morning. Everything from furniture to miscellaneous boxes of goodness only knew what. Often, it was house clearance, and Maisie found it heart-breaking that boxes of personal possessions were sold to people for whom the items held no significance. What of the trinkets bought on a honeymoon to remind the happy couple of their holiday? The book won at school decades ago for academic achievement, its ornate bookplate inscribed with the proud pupil's name and treasured in a bookcase throughout the years? The sepia photographs of Victorian families, stiff and formal, but the names and relationships of the subjects long-since forgotten?

It was the memories attached to things that gave them their greatest value. Sometimes just looking at a possession could move a person to tears, or make a couple reach out for each other's hands, reliving a special memory. And when no one was left to remember, they reverted back to objects with only a material value. It was, she suspected, why the teapot was so important to her. No one else would have those memories – it was merely a teapot – but to her it symbolised a tiny light at a time in her life when things had been dark.

At the end of the day, Maisie paid her unexpectedly hefty bill and wandered over to the barn to collect her goods. Theo and Johnny had their arms about each other so she coughed to make them aware of her presence, but neither seemed embarrassed by the embrace.

'Here she comes,' Theo teased, 'to hang out with her *gnomies*.' She tried not to react as she handed him the stamped invoice. 'If you're going to take them *gnome* with you, you'll need to bring your car to the front – *gnome* pun intended,' he said, smirking. He held her gaze rather longer than she anticipated and her tummy did a double handspring.

'I can manage,' she said.

'All four boxes?'

'FOUR?' She snatched the invoice back and sure enough, *Lot 245: Four boxes of miscellaneous garden gnomes* were listed – any marketing idea she came up with to shift them would have to be pretty damn good. The box containing the teapot made five. Ten minutes later, lugging the last one into the back of her Fiat 500 and trying not to focus too hard on what the blue-hatted gnome was doing to the smaller red-hatted gnome, she slammed down the boot.

Climbing into the driver's seat, she reflected how sad it was that Meredith's possessions had been shoved into cardboard boxes and carted down to the local auction house to be sold for peanuts and scattered to the four winds. Those visits had only lasted a couple of years, until her parents' divorce had been finalised, and the house in Hickory Street, with only Mum, Maisie and Zoe rattling around, had been sold. They moved into a modern box-like flat closer to the town centre and the secondary school. But in those two years, the neighbour who had previously only called a cheery hello over the fence offered a refuge to them both. She'd been an escape from the squabbling of her teenage siblings and company for her mum who, looking back now, must have been so terribly lonely.

And as Maisie turned the ignition key an amusing thought entered her head as she wondered if the collection of gnomes had also belonged to Meredith.

Chapter 12

'Hi, sweetie. Just checking in with the family. Or rather, speaking to you to find out what they're all up to. Ringing everyone individually is so tedious. You can get me up to speed,' Lisa's singsong voice gushed down the phone.

It was Saturday evening and Maisie was in the car park of Willow Tree House about to help her mother with a programme of activities for the residents. For some it would be a quiet hour doing jigsaws whilst others would engage in the more raucous Wii Sports. Maisie enjoyed a game of tennis but only when she could play it sitting down – Zoe's sporty gene seemingly only present in one-quarter of the Meadows siblings.

'We're good,' Maisie replied. 'Any chance of a visit soon? Mum said there's always a bed for you at hers.' Her oldest sister hadn't been down to Suffolk in over a year. Lisa had mentally distanced herself from the family before imposing a physical distance, but even the guilt trips home were becoming fewer and further apart.

'Too busy, babe. Too busy. Absolutely rushed off my feet. Haven't you seen my Insta?'

With her job at a large television studio outside York, Lisa rubbed shoulders with an array of celebrities and attended a wild assortment of glitzy functions that resulted in a never-ending stream of social media posts depicting her successful and exciting life. She had been what their mother called a *spirited* child and that spirit had found a home in the busy and equally dramatic world of television production. 'Besides, you know Mum rubs me up the wrong way. Always asking prying questions.'

'She asks because she cares, Lisa. She's interested in what you do.'

'But she knows there's things I can't talk about; I have to stay professional and all that. You can't name-drop just because Ryan has flown in to film some scenes outside the Minster. You'd lose your job.'

'Wow. Reynolds?' Maisie was impressed. 'Or Gosling?'

'Couldn't possible say, sweetie. And as for Mum, what I *can* share is on the socials for everyone to see. But it's so chaotic up here right now, you wouldn't believe. I barely have time for a toilet break, never mind a day off work, and if I'm not working I'm partying – which is basically the same thing.'

Any hopes Maisie had to see Lisa in the immediate future were dashed. There was a glugging sound as her sister topped up a glass at the other end and Maisie consoled herself with the fact it wasn't an outright no. Perhaps she could travel up to York and pay her sister a visit. After all, if the mountain wouldn't come to the bosom of the family, the family could catch a train up to her.

'So – how are things at the antique shop?' Lisa asked, followed by a slurp.

'Auction house.'

'Same thing.'

Although a large number of antiques went through their

hands, Gildersleeve's was about so much more. They had an enormous yard, for a start, a concrete space behind the two barns where an open-air auction was held for larger items, like timber and architectural salvage. And Saleroom One was practically a huge charity shop full of household paraphernalia and unwanted domestic appliances. You could hardly describe a second-hand toaster as antique. But even if she took the trouble to explain to Lisa, her sister would forget. It wasn't something she needed to remember, like when the new season of *Love Island* was starting, so she invariably switched off.

'I'm finding my feet but I love it. Although, after assaulting one of the managers by mistake I'm lucky to still have a job.' And she told her sister about her run-in with Theo.

'Ooo. Young? Single? Sexy?' Lisa asked.

'Five or six years older than me, *definitely* not single but, yeah, sexy in a Robinson Crusoe kind of way.'

She could appreciate Theo was attractive even if he was unavailable. In fact, if she was honest, she was torn between the massive disappointment that she wasn't on his carnal radar, and relief that there would be no boss-employee romantic shenanigans after the Wickerman's fiasco.

'Shame. Mum told me Gareth turned out to be a non-starter. Actually, that's not true. She said he was a rotten two-timing git, just like our father, who deserved to have his genitals severed from his body and run up a flagpole to see if anyone would salute them. Then she cried a bit and said she hoped she hadn't passed on the genetic predisposition to attract skirt-chasers to you. Skirt-chasers? I mean, where does she get her expressions from?'

That sounded like their mother. The poor woman simply

couldn't let go of the hurt, but it was hard not to smile at some of her more imaginative plans for revenge.

There were a couple of hearty slurps and then Lisa said, 'Men can be such pigs.'

'I'm over it now,' Maisie said, because working at Gildersleeve's had reminded her there were plenty of decent people about. She'd been unlucky and Gareth was an idiot. 'It's having company in the evenings I miss the most. You know? Someone to talk to when—' She was about to offload to her sister when Lisa cut in.

'Great, don't let the bastards get you down. Anyway, gotta go. Heading out shortly to try my hand at speed-dating. Never done it before but sounds like it might be a laugh.' For a woman in her mid-thirties, Lisa certainly lived life to the full, with an almost teenage air about her lifestyle. In their different ways, Ben and Lisa had clung on to the blind optimism and unaccountability of youth and Maisie was slightly jealous. 'Then I'll hit the bars and work my way through a few of bottles of Prosecco with the girls. It's been an exhausting week but the party never stops.'

Maisie wished she had a fraction of the social life her sister did but consoled herself with the knowledge she had an immaculate, chocolate-box house – albeit rented. Shame she didn't have more people round to appreciate her top-notch domestic skills. Lisa might have bombed academically but there was no denying she'd soared professionally. Whatever it was Lisa actually did, she was moving in exalted media circles and every member of the Meadows family was proud of her.

'Yes, I need to make a move.' Maisie looked anxiously at her dashboard clock, as being late was not something she allowed herself to do. She didn't elaborate on her agenda, however, as Lisa wouldn't be quite as dazzled by her plans to spend her Saturday evening hanging out with octogenarians and drinking tea.

A week later and Maisie felt she'd undergone a second settling-in period at work. Just when she'd got things at Gildersleeve's sussed, a new staff member had been thrown into the mix. Johnny conveniently forgot to mention she'd have to defer to Theo as well and she felt uneasy that the pair of them might be discussing her performance together at home of an evening.

'Excuse me, Maisie,' Arthur said, knocking respectfully on the office door, even though it was wide open. The week had seen the whole spectrum of weather from wet and windy to dry and crisp – sometimes within the space of minutes, but at that moment bright sunshine was forcing its way into the dim room, shooting a heavenly beam of light down to spotlight Johnny's desk where she was sitting with her boss.

'I know you're terribly busy and whatever you're doing is probably far more important and urgent than my silly prattling, but I wondered if you'd got a minute?' Which invariably meant fifteen, bless him.

She'd actually spent the last hour teaching Johnny how to use his smartphone and done barely any productive work all morning – whilst important to Johnny, it hadn't diminished her ever-increasing workload. He insisted that if Theo consistently refused to grasp the internet nettle, he would be the one to rise to the challenge. Like a kitten in a wool shop, he was positively bouncing about in his chair when he realised the tiny rectangle of glass and metal did so much more than make phone calls. Between them they'd installed a selection of apps – news, weather, banking – he'd even insisted she set him up on Facebook. Johnny was delighted, although his sausage-sized fingers struggled with the minuscule keyboard.

'Of course, Arthur. I've fried Johnny's brain sufficiently for today. What can I do for you?'

'It's more a case of what I can do for you. At least, I hope I'm doing you a service. I spotted some cups and saucers that looked rather like that curious teapot you bought the other week. I know how delighted you were with the purchase and wondered if you'd seen them. It's amongst the lots from a house clearance Johnny did a couple of weeks ago – some old dear that's gone into a care home. And I thought perhaps you'd be interested?'

'Really?' There was a slight quickening of her heart and a flutter in her throat. 'I'd love to take a look. Thanks, Arthur.' Maisie handed Johnny his phone and slid her chair out from his desk. The biggest grin spread across Arthur's face.

'You want to look *now*?'

'If it's convenient?'

'Yes, yes, I'm not busy but I rather thought you would be. I know you important office staff always have deadlines and targets and spreadsheets to, erm ... spread out. I didn't intend to take you from your work.'

As they walked through the front office, Maisie tried to make eye contact with Ella again but she turned her head and started scribbling away in a notebook. She didn't take it personally. Ella didn't talk to anyone unless she had to – and instead glided around the office like a silent, pale and beautiful ghost.

As Maisie stepped outside the reception, Arthur pointed out a tiny patch of snowdrops under the gnarly sweet chestnut that stood at the edge of the car park.

'I'm always cheered when the first blooms of the year appear,' he said.

Although pretty in their way, they were too delicate and colourless for Maisie. 'It's the vibrant purple crocuses, the bright orange centres of the daffodils and smudges of yellow primroses I adore most,' she said. 'Brightening up those gloomy areas and damp, dark spaces winter has overpowered.'

Colour was everything, even though she'd bitten back this passion when executing her home décor. One simply did not paint rainbows of colour across the walls of a room – far too uncontrolled. Although her landlord was generally delighted with her requests to redecorate, a full-height mural of random shapes, paint dribbles and brilliant colours might be pushing it.

'Yes.' Arthur paused, seemingly and unusually lost for words. 'I'm partial to primroses too.'

They walked into Saleroom One and came across Theo hanging pictures from the long steel pole running along the back wall. Last week it had been put to good use displaying a small selection of Turkish rugs. He put down the framed print he was holding.

'I'm not stealing it. Don't hit me. Or pelt me with sexually deviant gnomes.' He put up his arms and cowered as if Maisie was about to attack him. She put her hands on her hips, tipped her head to one side and out-stared him.

'Very funny, I'm sure, but I genuinely thought you were stealing from the cabinet the other day.'

'Chill, I'm teasing. I'm not used to women throwing themselves at me. It was fun.' Hmm, was that an invitation? She was tempted. And then maybe afterwards she could offer to run the iron over his clothes and sew up the rip on the cuff of his shirt. 'Although, as well as assaulting staff members, I see you've been playing dolls' houses with my salerooms,' he said, over his shoulder.

'What?' She was confused.

'Getting out the dinner services and laying the table? Filling up bookshelves with rows of books? Shall we make the beds up and tuck a teddy in between the covers?'

'Sorry. I thought ...'

'Don't look so worried.' He shrugged. 'I'm teasing. Again. Let's see if it makes a difference.' He sloped off to a table of household electricals on the other side of the barn, exaggerating the limp and throwing a pained look back to gauge her reaction, but the joke was no longer funny.

'It was here somewhere.' Arthur was tugging out boxes and scratching his thinning hair. 'Aha! Thought I was going senile there for a moment. I saw the cup nestling on the top of the box and thought to myself young Maisie fell in love with a similar teapot. I might be wrong, I usually am, but I thought it was worth mentioning.'

'Thank you, Arthur. It's clever of you to remember.'

She walked over to the box at his feet, and there, in amongst some heavy Denby plates and a couple of cut glass vases, was a teacup that perfectly matched the black and white almost-jigsaw scribbles of her teapot. She'd felt tingly following him up the aisle but assumed it was the anticipation of a potential match giving her goose bumps. Now she wasn't so sure. She bent down and lifted out the cup, which she was surprised to find was painted black inside.

'There's more in there. I'm sure of it. I didn't like to poke about too much because I'd probably break something. I'm such a clumsy old bugger. But I definitely spied a saucer or two.'

Three cups, two with black interiors and one with white, and three matching saucers were located. Excited by the find, Maisie tried to hide her disappointment it was an odd number of cups, the others doubtless broken over time. Odd numbers sat uneasily with her and her need for order.

'Well done, Arthur. A perfect match. Fancy you remembering.' She smiled up at him as she slid the box and its contents back under the trestle table. Arthur puffed out his chest and grinned. 'I'll place another written bid and, if I get them, how about you come over one Saturday afternoon and road test them with me?' A written bid was a safer bet than attending the auction again. Not only was she rushed off her feet with the website now but she didn't want to end up accidentally bidding for a lifetime's collection of plastic dinosaurs, a trailer-load of poultry incubators or more stupid X-rated gnomes.

As she made the offer, Theo looked up from a battered leather suitcase of old photographs he was cataloguing. He studied her face intently for a moment or two and she caught his eye, before his gaze returned to the task in hand. How could a look from her out-of-reach boss so casually flip the trip switch to her dormant erogenous zones?

'You mean come around for a cup of tea?' Arthur asked, his inflection indicating his disbelief.

'Sorry, perhaps that was a bit presumptuous of me.' She tore her eyes from Theo and returned her attention to the conversation.

'No, no, I'd love to. Pam's always saying I need to get out more to make up for the fact she can't. I'm generally busy pottering about, fixing stuff at the weekends and getting a bit of shopping in, but I could pop by on my way into town.'

They agreed a day and Maisie turned back to the box containing the teacups, trying to ignore the weird sensation dancing up her arms.

They're coming back to me, she thought. Meredith said this would happen.

Chapter 13

Maisie's mother had been to see a solicitor. It was two months since she'd discovered her husband's lads' weekend away had actually involved a lass. The shock had now subsided enough to spur her into action and things were moving quickly.

'What with all the stress and then bumping into him in town, I don't mind telling you I've been weeping swimming pools-full, never mind buckets. So I thought I'd pop by for one of your cuppas, Meredith. Don't know what blend you use but it's incredibly calming.'

'It's just supermarket tea,' her neighbour replied.

'I bet it's the magical-ness of the teapot,' Maisie said, looking up from her jigsaw puzzle.

'I'm not so sure. I think a good old cup of tea has merely worked its way into the psyche of the British people,' Meredith said. 'There's a placebo effect at work. We think a cup of tea will solve everything and so it invariably does. I'm fairly certain tea got the British population through two World Wars and the Thatcher years.'

Meredith handed Maisie's mum a dainty cup with matching saucer and Maisie a plastic tumbler of weak orange squash. Maisie didn't mind because the old lady always had an exciting biscuit tin to make up for the blandness of the drink. Would it be sponge fingers, with one side coated in glorious granulated sugar, pink wafers that dissolved in your mouth, or sticky Jammie Dodgers with jam so thick and solid it was impossible to pull the two biscuit sides apart without serious crumblage? She peered in the tin and helped herself to four chocolate chip cookies, tilting her body so her mother couldn't see, and returned to the floor to look for more pieces of edge.

'He was with that ... that woman. In public. All bosoms and low-cut tops. I should have known – he was never short of female admirers. I used to think how lucky I was he'd chosen me. He was such a good-looking man, with those perfect teeth and twinkly eyes ...'

A quiet child, as it wasn't worth trying to compete with the general level of noise in the household, Maisie was often forgotten and consequently privy to many inappropriate conversations. She sat silently in the corner or tucked herself behind the sofa and learned far more about life than many children her age. Only the other day she'd been colouring in butterflies under the dining room table and overheard Lisa talking about doing stuff with her boyfriend in the back of his Fiesta. The 'stuff' wasn't specified but Lisa's friend got very excited about the announcement they'd got the third base. Maisie knew about Ben smoking weeds (was that dandelions? Stinging nettles? Or that stupid sticky stuff that clung to your clothes like Velcro?) and her mother's anxiety over flushing hot things and lots of early men on pause.

Maisie was the forgotten child, watching from the wings, absorbing the atmosphere and listening as rowdy voices carried up the stairs or doors slammed – all the time wondering why everyone was so unpleasant and shouty. And then she would close her bedroom door – assuming Zoe wasn't sprawled across one of the twin beds, headphones on indicating she was off-limits for conversation – and play with her Sylvanian Family to reassure herself this was how it was supposed to be. They never threw their Sony Walkmans across the bedroom, burst into tears for absolutely no reason or slammed down the remote control, storming out the house saying 'the oestrogen levels in this house are suffocating'. And Mummy Cottontail rabbit would never launch Daddy Cottontail's belongings out the window of Rose Cottage and make him live somewhere else.

'Little ears,' reminded Meredith, and Maisie's mum glanced across at Maisie, having momentarily forgotten her youngest daughter was with them. 'Don't let your tea get cold, Bev.'

Meredith returned the teapot to the tray, pulled the suction lid from a metal biscuit tin decorated with a Victorian ice-skating scene and offered it to Maisie again as her four cookies had mysteriously disappeared ... She abandoned her puzzle and skipped across to see what other exciting treats lay within. Bourbons – yummy. Unlike the Jammie Dodgers, these would pull apart and she could lick all the chocolaty scrumminess off before devouring the crunchy biscuit bits.

'You know you said your mummy split up the tea set between your sisters?' Maisie asked her elderly neighbour, thinking of her Sylvanian families. The Cottontail family had a miniature tea set that was made of actual, real china. All the pieces were white, and every single cup and saucer was carefully returned to the miniature dresser after she'd finished playing. Since Daddy had moved out, she'd become obsessed with keeping things together.

'Yes.' Meredith settled into her dark green velvet easy chair.

'Can't you just put it all back together again?' Maisie paused to lick her Bourbon and then scrunched up her face. 'Ask your sisters for the cups and saucers back and have it all in your house? It's what your granny wanted.'

'If only it was that simple, but you know what sisters are like.' Meredith rolled her eyes and gave Maisie a conspiratorial smile. 'They'd rather force down the last cream bun and make themselves sick than share with a sibling. Besides,' she continued, 'Gamma used to say it was the sort of tea set that would always find its way to the right person and I spent so many years hoping that person was me. I asked my sisters from time to time if they were willing to part with their pieces but Essie wanted to pass her cups down to her own children, not that she had any in the end, and Irene took great pleasure in announcing she'd given them away. So I guess it wasn't meant to be.'

Maisie felt for the old lady. It was horrid when you couldn't get things to stay together. And, yes, she understood all too well that sisters – especially big ones – could be mean and uncooperative.

'You know we were talking about how the pattern sort of doesn't look finished before?' Her thoughts were jiggling about but they kept returning to that funny old teapot.

Meredith nodded, smiling at the talkative child and adjusting the crocheted circular cushion behind her back.

'I was wondering what it was *supposed* to be. It's just squiggles and lines.' Maisie stepped forward and traced a sticky finger across the stark black jaggedy outlines of shapes that made no sense to her.

'Ah, that's the joy of the thing. It can be whatever you want it to be. Just because an object is designed to be a particular something, doesn't mean your brain can't interpret it as something else.'

The weird things that Meredith said really made you think. Maisie liked the idea of things being what *you* decided they were. After all, the fluffy green rug between her bed and Zoe's was actually a magic carpet but she hadn't told Zoe.

'Have you ever seen an abstract painting?' Meredith asked the inquisitive girl. Maisie shook her head and Meredith leaned forward and pulled a book from the slatted shelf under the oval coffee table. It was called *Finding Joy in Modern Art*. She opened the book and flicked through the pictures. They were a miscellany of colours and shapes. Maisie took a few tentative steps towards her and peered over the top of the book. Nothing was actually anything but Maisie thought she glimpsed a face or an animal lurking in the muddle.

'I'm sure the artists had something very definite in mind when they created these images, but when I look at this picture ...' Meredith tilted the book in Maisie's direction, '*On White II* by a very clever and innovative Russian artist called Kandinsky, I see horses and a bird in the sky, a stopwatch and a chequered racing flag – so to me as a young woman this was a picture about horse-racing, maybe at nearby Newmarket. But when I was older and read more on the subject, I learned it was supposedly about life and death. In the end, does it matter what he intended when he painted it or what I thought I saw? It made me think and looking at it made me happy because it reminded me of a special day I had at the races with a young gentleman I knew at the time.'

Maisie could tell the memory wasn't *really* a happy one by looking at the old lady's face. It was like when Mummy said to Grandma how delicious her fruit cake was and then put the whole foil-wrapped loaf in the pedal bin as soon as they returned home.

'I admire the skill in a Gainsborough or a Turner, but I do so love the challenge of a Dalí or a Klee.'

Maisie studied the curious picture – noting the sharp black lines, slicing across the canvas, the jumble of colour and the tiny chequerboard patterns. For a few moments she was reflective, then she looked back at the teapot.

'I think it's jigsaw puzzle bits,' she said. 'All floating around the teapot, needed to be put back in their puzzley holes.'

'I think so, too,' said Meredith, and Maisie gave a gap-toothed grin. 'Keep the book, sweetheart. I know you'll treasure it.'

Nigel was clinging to the door of his cage as soon as Maisie approached the sideboard. He wasn't daft and always began to hare around the bottom floor of his cage when he heard her return from work, occasionally optimistically launching himself at the small, square door that opened like a wire drawbridge to the outside world. Maisie pulled back the hook and the door fell forward as he waddled towards her, ever hopeful of a tasty treat. She scooped him up and he nestled happily in her soft, warm hands, munching on sunflower seeds, as she sat recounting the events of the day.

After he'd finished his seedy snack, she placed Nigel carefully in his clear plastic ball and let him explore as she went into the kitchen to unpack the china, mindful that working at the auction could lead to all sorts of impulse acquisitions. Colour co-ordinated ones only, of course.

The box had an unpleasant stale cigarette odour and most of the contents were stained yellow but after a good soak the cups came up shiny and clean. There wasn't much else of interest inside so she lugged it into her petite garden shed with the other boxes – the rosy, bearded faces of the naughty gnomes still laughing at her every time she entered.

She sat down to a quick spinach omelette and then remembered she hadn't taken her phone off silent since the auction. She found a missed call and a text from Zoe – both from earlier in the day.

BIG news but don't want to put it in a text. Skype tomorrow around ten GMT? Zoe x

It would be the early hours for Zoe now but she texted back in agreement and wondered what the news could be. Perhaps a baby. That would be exciting. Their mother was desperate for a grandchild and Lisa had made it clear babies weren't part of her life plan – too selfish and demanding – which everyone decided was rich coming from her. Oliver and Zoe had been together forever and, although Zoe had never mentioned children, perhaps she'd changed her mind now they were in the land of milk, honey and the perennial outdoor barbecue. And at thirty, Zoe's biological clock would be counting down that final decade in readiness to sound the alarm.

'Maisie!'

Zoe's beaming face appeared on Maisie's laptop, slightly glitchy as the signal sorted itself out, and resplendent in mammoth sunglasses, and a floppy raffia sun hat wider than the screen. While Maisie was still de-icing her car every morning and bemoaning the winter weather, her sister was basking in a gloriously hot Australian summer.

'Look at you – all tanned and sun-bleached. It's about two degrees outside and a smattering of the white stuff is forecast for this weekend. If ever you want to swap lives, I'm sure I could make the sacrifice – but only because I love you so much. It would be a purely selfless act on my behalf.'

Zoe adjusted her hat and the smile crept further towards her ears.

'Funny you should say that; I'm coming home.'

'Oh wow.' So that was the news. A UK vacation, and looking at her sister's beaming face, perhaps a sizeable one. 'How long for? Does Mum know? Give me the dates and I'll book some time off work.'

'No, sweetheart, not for a holiday. For good.'

Chapter 14

For a moment Maisie didn't know what to think. She missed her sister terribly since she'd emigrated two years ago but it had been Zoe's long-held dream and it hadn't been an easy one to achieve. Oliver and Zoe had spent several years saving up, applying for visas and jobs, and finding somewhere to live. Her physiotherapy qualifications and Oliver's accountancy career made them eligible for the skilled migrant visa – but now they were telling Maisie it was all for nothing.

'It's not working out,' Zoe continued. 'We've been thinking about it for a while and I guess we both accepted the dream didn't live up to the reality. Now we've made the decision, I know it's the right thing to do. I've really missed you. And Mum. And Dad ...' There were no more Ands.

'I don't understand. Your jobs? The lifestyle? The sun?'

The miserable British weather had been the killer for Zoe. Fair, like all her siblings, but able to take a tan, she'd been a sun-worshipper and outdoorsy girl since childhood. Oliver had a sedentary and staid career – his idea of kicking back was settling down in front of the television with a large glass of Merlot. Zoe, on the other hand, had been known to stride up a mountain to unwind. It was a miracle their relationship had endured for nearly fifteen years.

'Everyone thinks Australia is just a hotter version of the UK but it really isn't. It's been a complete lifestyle change – even the language is different, if you can believe that?' Zoe said, shaking her head. 'It's all so laid-back and in many ways in a bit of a time warp. You go to a party and the men and women stand in different corners – and the men swear *all the time*. Oliver found it hard to integrate into their sport and gambling culture. I'm convinced he was ostracised for not drinking lager.'

'Philistines,' a disembodied voice mumbled.

'Sometimes it was the silliest thing that made me homesick – not being able to buy brands I recognised in the supermarket or pop in on my sis when I'd had a bad day ... We didn't make many friends, are still seen as interlopers, and we've both missed friends and family so much.'

Maisie contemplated their bickering family but perhaps when your relations are thousands of miles away even the bad things seem appealing. Her heart lifted at Zoe's words. Family was important and Zoe recognised this too.

'In the end, I can't even properly define it. If you've got the money, you can get hold of all the material things you miss – Marmite, British TV programmes, *proper* Cadbury's chocolate and Monster Munch. But you can't buy the atmosphere – the pubs, the shops, the English sense of humour and, I never thought I'd say this, even the weather – which at least gives you a conversational starter in awkward social situations.'

'Plus, you can't get Cumberland sausages for love nor money,' grumbled Oliver, still off camera and out of sight.

'Sorry we've kept it to ourselves, but we didn't want unhelpful opinions either way. It suddenly seemed the right time to tell everyone.'

It was bittersweet news: the end of Zoe's dream but also the return of a lost sheep to the fold. Maisie had missed her sister so much after she'd left. The age gap that had mattered when they were smaller had become less significant as the years went by. And the move from Hickory Street, when Maisie, Zoe and their mother shared the bijou two-bedroom Tattlesham flat, had been happy times. As soon as the Sylvanians had been relegated to the top of the wardrobe and Maisie began to understand the appeal of kissing boys, the girls had quickly bonded.

After the call, Maisie's mind inevitably returned to Hickory Street and Meredith. She walked over to the three cups and saucers standing in a line on the kitchen windowsill. For the first time in a while she felt upbeat and positive about the future. Putting the odd cup and one of the saucers in the high cupboard over the kettle, she stood the remaining two either side of the teapot on the display shelf and narrowed her eyes as she focused on nothing in particular.

'Split the set; split the family,' Meredith had said all those years ago. And Maisie knew in that moment, as sure as she knew Johnny would never be seen dead in a pair of pink Crocs and that Theo didn't own a suit, that she had to find a way to reunite Meredith's tea set.

March arrived but winter refused to budge. The pure white duvet of virgin snow that had fallen on the Sunday night was quickly reduced to grubby banks of grey on the verges and diminishing patches of white under the shade of the trees. The nasty weather hadn't prevented people from turning up to the auction house on the Monday though. Johnny explained the 'increasingly glacial meteorological climate' rarely affected sales, as he undertook a supervisory role in the clearing of the car park and gritting of paths – lamenting the fact Theo wasn't out there with them wielding a spade as he had 'muscles to die for'.

'We will doubtless be as busy as usual,' he said, leaning on a shovel that hadn't done much shovelling in the last twenty minutes. 'If not busier.'

'Really?' Maisie was heaving a bag of grit off a sack barrow. 'The snow won't stop people coming to the sale on Friday?'

Unfortunately, snow was forecast on and off for the remainder of the week. Not enough for anyone north of Leeds to fret about, but the bottom half of the country tended to get in a complete flap at the first sign of a snowflake. Long-life milk would be stockpiled in abundance and garage forecourts would be cluttered with de-icer and, rather more optimistically, brightly coloured plastic sledges.

'The reverse is true, my dear. They tend to be of the mind that no one else will undertake the perilous journey, so there will be no competing bidders and they will thus secure themselves a bargain. And because they've made Herculean efforts to get here they are bloody-minded enough not to make the return journey empty-handed. Although logistically a nightmare for us, with all the heavy snow-shovelling and icy paths, bad weather days are often surprisingly lucrative.'

Not that Johnny was doing much snow-shovelling, she noticed.

Ten minutes later, out of the biting wind if not the arctic temperatures, Maisie was preparing the Saleroom One barn for valuations. A queue had already formed and Johnny was right – it was surprisingly long, even if most of the public were wrapped up like knitted Egyptian mummies. The industrial heaters were on and it wouldn't be long before the core temperature was up to habitable levels – aided by the myriad of sweaty bodies.

Working alongside Theo as he valued people's possessions, she realised Arthur was right; he really did know his stuff. She marvelled how he could tell that a shoddily made three-legged milking stool was circa 1820. Or that in amongst a box of costume jewellery was a delicate mid-Victorian turquoise and seed pearl brooch that would fetch upwards of two hundred pounds.

'Are we having the vicar for tea?' Theo joked, as Maisie spread out a cloth on a spare trestle table she'd set up in the valuation area. He was sporting a splendid fur-lined trapper hat and the dangly ear flaps hung down each side of his face. Tempted to grab the plaited tassels and tie them in a bow under his chin, she resisted.

Theo was easy-going and without edge, and reminded her of Oliver. She felt at ease with him. Never having had a gay friend before, she realised that once sex was taken out of the equation, much like with her relationship with her brother-in-law, the friendship was natural and uncomplicated. And then she lamented the possibility she was destined to be one of those women who had lots of male friends but never managed to attract a half-decent romantic prospect. Perhaps she should be more like Lisa and try her hand at something totally off the wall, like speed-dating.

'I'm trying to save time by taking photos as we accept the items,' she explained. 'If everything goes to plan, I'm hoping to go online with the catalogue soon. This is a trial run.'

One of his eyebrows did a little jump. Was she pushing her luck, introducing all these new things when she'd barely been here five minutes? And then she reminded herself Johnny was the big cheese and he had complete faith in her. Theo might have a good-natured grumble about her improvements but even he was ultimately answerable to Johnny.

'I was warned you were anti-internet but the company has to move with the times or we'll get left behind,' she persisted.

Theo leaned back in the chair, the front two feet lifting from the floor, and stroked his clean-shaven chin. He seemed very lackadaisical when it came to personal grooming; shaving about once a fortnight, almost as if it was just something he did when he remembered.

'You have me pegged all wrong. I fully understand the online catalogue will reach a wider customer base – I'm merely wary of over-reaching ourselves. Hats off to you – the new branding is very classy. You've understood the family feel of the company – even though none of us are technically family – and embraced our rural and friendly nature. But let's not alienate our traditional buyers, most of whom are local and support us on a grass-roots level. The atmosphere and vitality of the place is directly linked to the people turning up every week and creating the general buzz.'

'But serious collectors will pay premium prices to get their hands on the things we have to offer, and the internet facilitates this.' They were bickering like extremely polite siblings and it was apparent neither was prepared to give way.

Theo wrinkled up his face and tugged at a dangly plait, letting the chair return to four legs with a bump.

'Not everything in life is about money, honey,' he said, pulling off the statement because he had the air of a vagrant about him.

Before Maisie had realised Theo was not another

sixty-something Johnny clone, she'd assumed his aversion to technology was age-related, but he was her generation. Surely he'd be all over social media like a virulent rash? He hadn't mentioned the Twitter page to her, which was up and running, although not as successful as she'd anticipated as retweets tended to be by the same small handful of people. But there might be people in the queue who'd seen Gildersleeve's online and come along for the very first time. The impact of a Tweet was difficult to gauge.

'Let's aim high and make Gildersleeve Auctioneers a global phenomenon.' Maisie indulged in a sudden burst of enthusiasm and then reined herself in. 'Well, national at least.'

She knew Theo was smiling inwardly at the bouncy, over-enthusiastic new employee in front of him because an eyebrow bopped up.

'Do we *need* to be a global phenomenon? I don't want our loyal customers drifting away because everything is conducted online. You'll lose the vibrancy of this place,' he warned, reiterating his earlier point and shaking his head as the tassels swung from side to side.

How could she take him seriously in that hat? In fact, it was time for a friendly tassel-tie. She ducked down in front of his chair and deftly tied a bow under his chin. Theo jerked his head up sharply and she wondered if she'd overstepped the boss-employee line. He performed a lock-down on her eyes with his – something he kept doing. She couldn't move them for a moment. Her heart, on the other hand, had bolted out her chest and was galloping across the barn.

'Don't you think your TV appearance is going to have the same impact?' she asked, now embarrassed by her childish action and taking a step backwards. Interestingly, Theo didn't untie the bow. He genuinely didn't care what people thought and she admired that, especially as she'd been known to return to the house and re-iron a blouse after spotting a crease of a morning. 'It will be screened in a couple of months. People will see you on the television and overzealous fans will rush to the auction rooms in their thousands to stalk you until the end of your days,' she said. 'I don't see why the TV is an acceptable form of exposure but the internet is not.'

She looked at his earnest face and how the light caught the flecks of green in his eyes and decided she wouldn't blame anyone for becoming a fan. He was the Tom Hanks of the auctioneering world. He had time for everybody and was an approachable figure, even if he was digging his desert boot heels in about being online.

He shrugged. 'Hey, I'm not saying we shouldn't be on Twitface. I'm saying let's be careful what we are putting out there.'

He was teasing her with his deliberate misnaming of the social media platform, she knew. She held the camera up to take a photograph of the item he'd just valued.

'You're just grumpy because you don't understand it,' she said. 'You like old things and are stuck in a time warp. Johnny told me you were a closet Eighties fan and that you embrace the decade in all areas of your life. Do you even own a computer? And if so, is it a Commodore 64?'

'I don't know how you think I got my degree without one. But you're quite correct – I listen to vinyl, watch Betamax tapes – far superior in quality to VHS – and don't have a smartphone. When I go out to a restaurant, I enjoy the ambience, the food and the company, without feeling the need to photograph my plate ninety times whilst my food gets cold, and slap it all over Instagraph. If I attend a concert, I watch the band with my eyes, not through a tiny screen. And I certainly don't spend every spare second updating Facepage.'

They would have to agree to disagree, she thought, as a mutton-chop-whiskered gentleman approached the table with an old Olympus 35mm camera. Theo appraised it and then placed it on the tablecloth for Maisie to photograph.

Despite the odd snowflake nonchalantly fluttering to the ground, the heaters – combined with a sea of bodies and the sun making a bold appearance – meant the barn was now quite toasty. Lifting her fleecy jumper over her head she removed it. Her new thermal top was doing its job and she felt warm.

A dark-haired young woman placed a small piece of studio pottery on the table and Theo gave it a cursory glance, his eyes pulled back to Maisie's chest, as she neatly folded the jumper and smoothed her static-infused hair.

'The bowl,' she reprimanded, indicating to the table in front of him.

'Erm, yeah, nice example but nothing unusual. Twenty to thirty.'

'Oh. Okay,' the lady said, as Maisie logged the details and moved it to the table to photograph.

'You're brave,' she said to Maisie. 'Advertising them like that.' She nodded to Maisie's chest.

And there, lodged between her breasts, was a dark circular retailer's sticker, announcing what lay beneath was Soft to Touch.

Chapter 15

One of the porters was off sick so Maisie was asked to be the show-er for the following Friday's auction. It was easy enough in principle: listen to the lot number, locate the item by its numbered sticker, and either hold it *carefully* aloft, or point to it in a magician's assistant, look-at-this way – but without the sequinned outfit or jaunty feather sticking out the top of her head.

The other porter was dashing about, running between the reception and the saleroom with completed auctioneer's sheets to be inputted into the system and helping buyers who had paid for their lots to retrieve them discreetly while the auction continued. Arthur, however, was just standing around chatting to people. He seemed particularly engaged with one young couple and Maisie could hear snippets of their photography-based conversation, as Arthur thoughtfully highlighted the Olympus to the young man.

It was the first time Maisie had heard Theo conduct an auction and his style was considerably different to Johnny's. He was less insulting, for a start, and quietly spoken, which had the effect of lowering the general volume of chatter in the room. Johnny's banter relied on saying *exactly* what he thought about everything, whereas Theo was flattering about the items – even those Maisie knew he didn't like. And despite looking like a financially challenged student in his baggy loose-knit jumper and a black beanie hat, he had the respect and attention of everyone in the barn.

'Ladies, gentlemen and gender-fluid members of the room ...' only Theo, with his easy-going, no-edge style could get away with that comment '... up next we have a quaint studio pottery bowl with a delightful blue glaze. Not for any old snacks but for your dry-roasted, lightly toasted, sprinkled with salt from the bottom of the clearest crystal blue oceans and harvested by flaxen-haired mermaids *M&S* snacks.' His audience were rapt – even those who had no interest in studio pottery were now craning their necks to see lot 303. 'Do I have twenty to start?'

Starting in increments of ten, Theo was soon jumping up in fifties. There was a buzz about this item and not simply because of the eloquence of the silver-tongued auctioneer.

'Three hundred and fifty with you, sir.' He nodded to someone standing at the front, but Maisie couldn't pick the person out. They must be communicating telepathically again. Chattering bystanders stopped their idle conversations as the bidding went up and up.

And up.

'Eight hundred. Do I hear nine?'

In fact, Theo got nearly double that with the unassuming bowl going for a spectacular one and a half thousand pounds. His usually cool and relaxed demeanour changed subtly as the bidding reached its heady climax, despite the ripple of gasps that filtered through the barn as the lot was finally sold, and he brought the gavel down with a fierce wallop. Her heart gradually slowed to a more sedate pace. Wow – he had a point, she thought begrudgingly, you wouldn't get that atmosphere and tension online.

After the auction, Maisie was at her desk when Theo sloped through the office door. The baggy jumper from earlier had been abandoned revealing a crumpled denim shirt that had been buttoned up incorrectly – one button out all the way up.

'What are you like?' She laughed. 'Come here.'

She stood in front of him and began to undo the shirt as the temperature in the room jumped a couple of degrees. Good job he wasn't a hot-blooded heterosexual male or he'd be paranoid she was making a move on him – especially as she'd had her hands all over his tassels only a couple of hours earlier.

'What are you doing, woman?' he huffed. He placed his hands overs hers for a moment, the warmth of it seeping into her fingers and up her arms. 'I know I'm irresistible but this is the second time you've manhandled my wardrobe today.' Their eyes met and then he removed his hand, as if to give her permission to continue.

Her eyes dropped to the task in hand and she gave a tiny cough.

'I'm sorting you out. Honestly, Theo, four-year-olds misbutton their shirts. Grown men have no excuse.'

His top lip curled lazily as she yanked down the left-hand side of his shirt and started again from the bottom. It was difficult not to get side-tracked by his honey-coloured skin and the handful of straggly chest hairs poking out the gap in the denim.

'So, is it the hair that's the problem?' she asked, glancing up at the beanie as she popped another button through. Her own blonde curls kept falling forward and getting tangled between her fingers and the buttonholes.

He threw her a confused look.

'The reason you wear the hats? I noticed you have thick hair, which must be difficult to manage.'

'If I felt hair management was a massive priority in my life, then I'd be totally shafted. I can no more manage my hair than a mother can manage a hyperactive child who's binged on Haribo and is experiencing a massive sugar rush. I told you before, I wear a hat because my head is cold. I like my hair as it is.'

'So do I.' Maisie looked at his distinctive mane. 'It's really ...'

'Flocculent?' he volunteered, then taking in her expression, he clarified. 'One of Johnny's poncy words. I love that man so much; his flowery vocabulary being part of his appeal.' He looked at her face. 'Don't worry, I had to look it up too. It means wool-like.' He took the hat off and rubbed his hand backwards and forwards through the springy mound of fuzz on his head. For a second, she wanted to reach up and do the same. The sandy brown afro-hair sprung back to its default position, the follicle version of memory foam. 'There's some Nigerian in the bloodline somewhere – a few generations ago. The only genetic remnants being what I like to call my FUN hair, and my enormous—'

'Yes, thank you. I've got the picture.' And then she shuddered and flushed slightly. 'Not a mental picture, obviously. Oh, you know what I mean.'

Theo's lopsided grin came out to play. 'I was going to say stamina. I used to run cross-country for the country when I was a teenager.' He looked straight at her and Maisie felt her breath catch in her throat for the briefest of moments. Where were these mutinous thoughts coming from? Or was it precisely because she knew he was unavailable that her libido was playing up? She focused intently on his odd socks (today's delight: a stripy orange cartoon sock with huge boggly eyes and a thick ribbed black walking sock) and the moment passed.

'So – a real treasure earlier. Who'd have known?' She was desperate to change the subject.

'I should have,' he sighed. 'It doesn't affect the seller – she's delighted – but it affects my professional integrity.'

'Oh, turn that frown upside down,' she said. 'You can't know everything. And we get a massive commission. The seller is happy, the buyer is happy and we've made good money. I don't understand your grumpy mood.'

'I should have investigated the pottery mark more thoroughly. My mind was elsewhere.' She blushed at the memory of the stray sticker. 'Unusual not to have some commission interest, which might have made me pop back and reassess my initial estimate.'

'When the online catalogue launches, people worldwide will be able to view the auction. Any sneaky little treasures that slip past you will soon get picked up by an eagle-eyed collector, and this won't happen again.'

One point to me, she thought, as she skipped back to her desk.

The following week, as they added numbered stickers to the lots in the salerooms, Theo asked if Maisie would mind fetching Johnny over to reassess a necklace. As she neared the door to the back office, she realised Johnny was on the phone. Not wanting to interrupt him, she stopped just outside.

'Indeed, it's a relationship I fear has run its course but how does one break that sort of unpalatable news? Especially when there remains a great fondness – how could there not be after so many years together? Having separate houses has helped. There won't be so much to sort when our ways finally part.'

Maisie's eyes widened. Was Johnny about to finish with Theo? Was that why his face had been longer than Naomi Campbell's legs all day? Now that she thought about it, he'd been distracted recently – forgetting things and short of patience. This was exactly why workplace relationships were a bad idea. If he was about to dump Theo, how would that affect their ability to run Gildersleeve's together?

'I wholeheartedly agree.' Johnny responded to a comment from the person on the other end of the phone. 'It is unfortunately a universal truth that one person in the relationship is always a little more in love than the other. I was, I fear, more worshipped than I worshipped in my turn ...'

Not able to justify eavesdropping further, Maisie entered the room and then went through the pretence of not realising he was on a call and withdrawing.

'Enter, dah-ling, enter,' Johnny said, standing in the corner with a mobile near his ear and beckoning her in. 'My colleague has returned to the office so I shall make an emphatic pretence of working, even though my heart is heavy and my mind is in turmoil. I promise to get over soon and value that bronze. Stay as seraphic as you've always been. Kisses, dah-ling.'

'Sorry to interrupt,' Maisie said, as Johnny sighed and slumped into his chair, not having the energy to scoot it anywhere. 'Theo wanted you in Saleroom Two.'

'Apologies. I fear I have allowed domestic issues to invade the workspace,' he said, heaving himself immediately out of the chair again and shaking his head. 'There are, I suspect, difficult times ahead.'

Yes, for all of us at Gildersleeve's, she mused, following him out the door, especially as she shared an office with them both.

'Why the glum face, mate?' Theo asked Johnny, as the pair returned to the saleroom.

'You don't need to be burdened with my vexations, dear fellow. Now is not the time to confront matters of the heart.'

No, it damn well isn't, thought Maisie. She didn't want to be party to their break-up.

'Come on, mate. You know you can tell me anything.' Theo scratched at his stubble and adjusted his Where's Wally bobble hat.

'Very well – if you force my hand. Although I suspect what I have to say won't come as a complete thunderbolt from the heavens.'

'Erm, perhaps I'll finish these photos another time,' Maisie squeaked, keen to make her escape.

'Nonsense, dah-ling. You may as well be privy to the reason for my tiresome mood.' Johnny did that thing of his where he inhaled deeply and placed a hand on his chest – all very dramatic and very Johnny. 'I have been a tormented soul of late, but the time has finally come to sever myself from the cloying suffocation of my romantic entanglement.'

'Bummer,' said Theo. 'Sorry you don't feel it's working out but I understand your decision entirely.'

Maisie stopped her fumbling and looked up at Theo. There was laid-back and there was horizontal. How could he stand there so calmly and accept the situation? Especially as 'cloying suffocation' was not the kindest way to dump someone. But Johnny had a tendency to inadvertently trample on people's feelings with his blunt manner.

Theo slid open the door to the glass-fronted cabinet. 'I think this Nineteen-Fifties necklace may be worth more than we initially thought ...'

Maisie looked across at Theo with shocked eyes, and Johnny looked slightly crestfallen.

'I had thought to elicit more sympathy from you, young Theodore. After all, you have been aware of my predicament for some time.'

'Yeah, and I told you a couple of years ago she wasn't the right one for you. It's taken you an awfully long time to come around to my way of thinking.'

Chapter 16

'You've got a *girlfriend*?' Maisie couldn't hide her shock, any more than she could conceal the upholstered chaise longue before her in a handbag.

'Lady friend, technically, but it is a situation I am in the process of remedying. Not that the lady concerned is playing ball. She's so terribly awkward and diva-ish.' Johnny's eyes fluttered up to the ceiling in staggered steps like a flitting butterfly, before he noticed Maisie's open mouth. 'But why, pray, should my relationship status surprise you? Do you not think me handsome enough to attract a lady?' he teased, pushing out his chest and preening his tight salt and pepper curls.

'No, I thought you were ... I thought ...' She was on wobbly ground. Was Johnny with some woman as a cover for a lifestyle he feared would be judged? Or had she got everything embarrassingly and horrifyingly wrong?

'Oh! You thought Johnny was gay?' Theo said, as the penny thudded to the ground between them, leaving a small crater. Yup – she'd got everything embarrassingly and horrifyingly wrong.

'Don't be so ridiculous, Theodore. Just because a fellow knows how to wear a cravat, carries himself like a gentleman, and articulates properly, doesn't mean everyone assumes he's gay.' Johnny stated this so resolutely, it was only as he looked between the two faces in the room, he too walked over wobbly ground. 'Oh.' Johnny's tufty eyebrows rose. 'That was your assumption. How intriguing.'

With cheeks flaming hotter than the fires in the belly of Hades, Maisie hung her head.

'I'm sorry. I'm not sure what made me think that.'

'I don't know, mate,' said Theo. 'I don't think her conclusion was that wide of the mark. You do rather conform to a stereotype – however wrong and ridiculously outdated that stereotype might be. I just can't believe she's worked here for all these weeks and not twigged.'

'One doesn't tend to bandy one's domestic situation about. Besides, the first flush of love passed many a waxing moon ago. There was a time we could not keep our amatory hands off each other—'

'Yeah, I remember,' muttered Theo.

'How many times must I apologise? We wrongly believed everyone had gone for the day and she'd always had this fantasy about a four-poster. I was tempted to bid on it but the ceilings at home are simply not high enough.'

'You *frolicked* on a customer's bed?' Maisie was incredulous. 'In the saleroom?'

'Maisie – really? I was not quite so inappropriate. We were merely trying it for size but judge not. One day you too may get swept away with your own libidinous inclinations.'

It was at that point her libidinous inclinations embarked on a frenetic gymnastic routine as Theo rubbed a thoughtful hand across his chin and a slow, lopsided smile meandered across his face.

'I reckon Maisie is the sort of girl who would schedule any

spontaneous frolicking three weeks in advance *and* iron all the bedding beforehand.'

She was about to jump to her own defence until she wondered whether that had been part of the problem with Gareth – her lack of spontaneity. She would never have been amorous in the archives. Too risky. What if her blouse got crumpled? Instead, she smiled, narrowed her eyes and looked at Theo.

'This is the line, mister,' and she drew an imaginary straight line in the space between them. 'And you have just stepped over it.'

'I stand corrected. I'm sure you'd only need twenty-four hours to be spontaneous.' He placed the tray of jewellery on top of the cabinet for Johnny to examine, while Maisie wrestled with another not entirely unpleasant thought.

If Johnny wasn't gay, did that mean Theo wasn't either?

'He told me you were his *partner*,' Maisie whined, as she helped Theo cordon off an area of the car park for the impending building work. He'd taken several opportunities to tease her about her misconception, astounded she'd been in the dark for so long. 'And you said how much you loved him when we were doing the valuations ...'

'I love my car but I'm not having a sexual relationship with it,' Theo said.

Oh, why didn't the English language have an array of suitable alternatives for love, she wondered. It made things terribly confusing.

'But the hugs?'

'Not everyone is comfortable with man-hugs but Johnny and I don't spare it a thought. I ruffle a child's hair, I rub the belly of a friendly dog and I hug my best mate. Quite frankly, I don't care if that's misinterpreted.' And then he paused for a moment, scratching his tufty chin as he too worked through a thought process. 'Hold on a minute there, madam. You mean you thought I was gay?' He swivelled his head in her direction as he placed a traffic cone on the ground. He chuckled. 'It's the hair, isn't it? And the way I'm so immaculately groomed all the time?'

'Oh, stop it.' She shoved him playfully with her elbow as she tied the end of the rope to a fence post – although it felt more awkward than before. All the comfortableness and banter had become something more charged – on her part, at least. 'You can't tell me off for perpetuating stereotypes and then do the same.'

It was more complicated than that though, in her defence. Johnny had told her he had a *partner*, she'd been charmed by his ostentatious manner and quirky dress sense, and he'd taken every opportunity to gush over Theo's good looks, wonderful personality and fit body. Actually – now she came to think of it – what was that all about?

'Interestingly, I've known Johnny a long time and he wasn't always quite so … theatrical. The turning point was pretty much someone commenting on the origins of his surname – which he seemed strangely unaware of. Gildersleeve, or golden sleeve, means flamboyant dresser. Guess he took it to heart and decided to embrace his heritage. He's always been over-wordy and a bit of a dandy apparently, but when he bought out the previous owners fifteen years ago and relaunched the company as Gildersleeve Auctioneers, he really went for it.'

'It still seems odd to me that you *both* own the company.

111

Aren't you a bit young to be a partner in a business?' She knew he was a few years older than her but it was still quite a feat.

'I came into a bit of money when my granddad died – it annoyed the olds that he bypassed them with the inheritance but I think he always felt a bit sorry for me as a kid. Before I knew it, Johnny was offering me the opportunity to be his *business* partner.' Theo deliberately stressed the word, but she got it; there was no need to rub it in so vigorously.

'Isn't it odd to have a friend who's so much older?' she asked, wondering why Theo's granddad should feel sorry for him, but then he never talked about his family or his childhood. 'Do you even have things in common?' Maisie didn't have a huge circle of friends – mainly girls she'd been to secondary school with, or met through college and Wickerman's. Zoe was her best friend and confidante. But all her friends, including her sister, had similar upbringings and points of reference. Theo and Johnny's friendship was curious.

'As opposed to having a sexual partner twice my age? You are a funny girl,' Theo said. 'And actually, we have lots in common, but we are also very different people. It's far more exciting to have a friend who isn't a mirror image of yourself. Think of the things you learn and the experiences you have. Not sure I want to hang out with another thirty-something laid-back bloke who rabbits on endlessly about how MTV shaped the Eighties or his enduring love of the iconic Tulip Chair – the sort of bloke who can't even find a matching pair of socks ...'

'He sounds fun to me,' and she smiled at the higgledy-piggledy man in front of her. 'Just the kind of guy who'd hang out with a hyper-efficient, curvaceous marketing wunderkind who knows how to button up a shirt.'

As Maisie hung a laminated sign over the barrier to request

people didn't block the access, she decided Theo had a point. Friends shouldn't be restricted to the people you drifted through life with. It was far better to seek out individuals who intrigued you and made you think, who had different backgrounds and interests.

'Well, I can honestly say Johnny's widened my horizons. He's taken me to hear Shostakovich at the Barbican,' Theo said, rubbing his hands together and walking towards the offices, as Maisie followed. 'It was fab, by the way, very intense. So I bought us tickets to an Icons of The Eighties gig last year – which he utterly detested. Mind you, he totally adored detesting it – it was all he could talk about for a fortnight.'

That endearing lopsided smile enveloped his face and Maisie's heart popped in a few extra beats per minute. Maybe it wasn't just your friends who should be different to you. The adage opposites attract had come about for a reason, and Theo certainly couldn't be described as a Maisie clone by any stretch of the imagination.

It was time to confront the truth in her heart – Theo's sexual orientation was a total game-changer.

Chapter 17

'Remember you were talking about that funny teapot the other day?' Maisie's mum said to her youngest daughter, her warm breath condensing into a little cloud as she spoke.

They were dressed like Arctic explorers and perched on carrier bags to stop the damp wood on a slightly green park bench from marking their clothes. (Maisie always came prepared.) An elderly resident of Willow Tree House was bundled up in more knitting than Kirstie Allsopp and scattering duck pellets from the local pet store at a collection of honking birds. Chuckling away happily to herself, she rocked backwards and forwards in her wheelchair, totally content. Maisie's mum was a massive fan of getting the residents outside, even in the middle of winter, because, as she often reminded Maisie, they might not make it to the spring.

'I hadn't made the connection before but we had a new resident a couple of weeks back, Mrs Cooper, so the name didn't ring any bells,' her mum continued. 'Poor thing, only in her early seventies, but she's got emphysema and was struggling living alone. There I was, painting her nails, and telling her about our fragmented family – half my kids abroad, Lisa up in York and your father being a total arse and going where the attractive, short-skirted wind blows ...' She paused for effect as she always did when talking about her ex-husband, pulling her coat tighter around her body. 'And she said her sisters, I forget how many, had lived in Suffolk their entire lives, as had she apart from a brief spell in London when she was younger.'

Maisie watched the honking Canada geese mob a happily giggling Margaret as she listened to her mother's words and wondered where this tale was leading.

'Then she said she'd recently lost her eldest sister, Meredith, and despite being at odds most of their adult lives, they'd spent their last few Christmases together at her sister's house in, would you believe, *Hickory Street*? Well, I painted Relentless Ruby right up her finger, I was that surprised to hear the connection.'

A shiver of something trickled across Maisie's shoulders, and not just because it was bone-chillingly cold. It was like that feeling someone was walking over your grave or one of those freaky and inexplicable moments of déjà vu. What an unnervingly small world, because if the cups were from Meredith's sister – the coincidence was beyond incredible. Since her decision to reunite the set she'd drawn a blank, not only with locating the Mayhews, but also finding anything about the design online. Not one of the china-finding sites had come up with a match.

Margaret's bag of pellets was empty, so the geese lost interest and wandered off to see what a young pushchair-wielding mother had for them. The elderly lady looked most forlorn.

'Then this Irene Cooper said she wasn't looking forward to spending next Christmas with a bunch of senile old lunatics, shuffling up and down the corridors and making jailbreaks in their nighties.' Maisie's mum chuckled. 'Her lungs may have packed up but there's nothing wrong with her brain. Or her tongue, for that matter. I had to remind her not to be quite so insulting to her fellow residents, who are a lovely bunch of people. She won't find anyone to sit next to at the sing-alongs if she keeps letting her tongue run wild.'

'Meredith stayed at the house all those years?' Maisie asked, her eyes dropping to the path in front of her. It would have been easy to return to Hickory Street and knock on Meredith's door. Think how pleased their old neighbour would have been to hear that the art book had been so treasured. Maisie's stomach did a vicious little twist and she felt ashamed of herself.

'Seems like it, dear. Now I feel bad I never went back to visit but you lose touch over time. It's barely ten minutes by car but I suppose I avoided the area. Always convinced someone would recognise me as the woman who went loopy and threw all her husband's possessions out the landing window.'

The jibes Maisie endured at school about having a jumble sale in the front garden went on for weeks but she'd never said anything to her mum. And the teasing died down. Eventually. If only her mother had left it at that but hell and the small town of Tattlesham really had no fury like Beverley Meadows; scorned and out for revenge. She even made the local paper after reports of mysterious graffiti appearing on her ex-husband's front door, but her dad never confronted his ex-wife or sought revenge for the revenge. Just as well really. World War Three would have broken out in their small Suffolk town.

'I *really* liked Meredith,' Maisie said, gazing across the mere at the central fountain, water droplets shimmering down like candelabra crystals.

'So did I. She was a real life-saver for me. Such a calm lady, never judgemental or prying. I guess having been through something similar, she understood.'

'I didn't know she had a husband,' Maisie said, turning her head to look at her mum. As a child, she'd assumed Meredith had chosen to live alone. Coming from such a boisterous house, it was a decision that made perfect sense to her. But now, as an adult, she understood very few people actively made that decision. Humans were gregarious creatures and it was often circumstance that obliged people to lead solitary lives. Meredith's situation had never occurred to her before.

'That was the point. She didn't. Her fiancé dumped her shortly before their wedding. It was all the more cruel because she was well into her thirties. Finally found someone after all that time, and then he left her for another woman and I don't think she ever got over it. Love of her life, she told me once, over a cuppa. Now Meredith's tea – that was something else,' her mum said, going off at a tangent. 'One sip and all was right with the world. Reckon she bought it somewhere posh. Like Waitrose ...'

Despite regret still pulling at Maisie's very core, this was positive news. If the sisters were all local, Maisie's plans to reunite the tea set were feasible. Assuming the cups were from Irene (the timing and geography certainly fitted with their arrival at Gildersleeve's), she would seek her out as soon as they returned Margaret to Willow Tree House. She didn't even care about owning the set. It merely seemed important to make it whole again, in whoever's possession it eventually resided.

Keen not to lose another moment, Maisie sprung to her feet and clapped her hands together. 'Home, Margaret?' she asked. The old lady nodded as a strong gust of wind whipped up a whirlpool of dead twigs and lost feathers in front of them and her mother shivered.

'Can't make out Zoe's decision to come back to the UK,' her mum said, changing the subject again. 'I wouldn't choose this—' she waved a gloved hand across the mere '—over a blisteringly hot sandy beach on the south coast of Australia.'

'Oh, I don't know.' Maisie reached out for her mother's hand and gave it a woolly squeeze. 'I'd miss my family too much.'

Her mother's eyes started the familiar build-up of tears – it didn't take much to set her off.

'Oh, darling, you are a sweetheart. It's a lovely thing to say, but we're hardly the Waltons. Even the good times weren't that great.' She tugged at her duffel coat buttons through her mittens. 'Let's get Margaret back before she becomes a human Popsicle. And then you promised her a boxing match on the Wii, remember? Keep it low-key though. Don't want her launching herself out the wheelchair again with those lethal left hooks of hers.'

Chapter 18

Irene Cooper was an interesting woman. And that was being polite.

'What you nosing about my family for?' Her tiny charcoal-black eyes were set in a face rippled with age, tight lips pinched together, betraying a lifetime of their vice-like grip on cigarettes. The oxygen tank next to her chair was a further by-product of that habit. It was difficult not to focus on the clear tubing that ran around her face and over her top lip, administering oxygen into her nose. 'That Beverley woman said you wanted to talk to me about flipping crockery.'

Maisie's mum had shown her to the old lady's room and found them a tray of tea and biscuits, but had to leave abruptly to hunt down Naked Man, whose cries of, 'I've got it. Who wants it?' echoed up the long, burgundy-carpeted corridor.

Walking back to the care home and chatting with her mum, Maisie had learned Irene was a lady bitter with disappointed dreams. Thin and wiry all her life, she'd had a promising modelling career spread before her but had come off the back of a motorbike in the Sixties and ended up with a nasty scar across her face that put paid to it all. Maisie could still see the dent in her forehead and that her left eyelid was puckered into the outside edge of the eyebrow.

'I knew your sister …' Maisie began.

'Oh yeah? I had a few. You'll have to be a bit more specific.'

'Meredith. I lived next door to her in Hickory Street when I was younger.'

'Ah, the sensible one.' Her face softened slightly. 'Always had her head in a book and a mother to us little ones. Invited me over for Christmas Day in recent years. A kind soul – in retrospect kinder to me than I probably deserved. But then when you spend a lifetime being prickly, it's hard to sand down your scratchy bits.' She cackled to herself and let out a wheezy sigh. 'They're all dropping off the edge – the people I grew up with. And now she's gone too and even though she had twelve years on me, it seems I won't be far behind.'

The thought of her own imminent demise led to a prolonged coughing fit. Maisie sat uncomfortably not knowing what to do to help but also not wanting to patronise this spiky lady or attempt some back-patting that would probably only make matters worse. After a few minutes, the baby bird of a woman recovered and took a sip of her tea.

'She's up with the angels now. Reckon I'll be heading south, though,' and she tipped her head to the floor and gave a further chuckle. 'So come on then, what's this all about? Some scam to con me out of my life's savings? 'Cause you're a bit late – spent them on fags and booze. Might as well go out in a blaze of glory.'

Maisie explained about the teapot and cups coming up in the auction and how she remembered Meredith's conviction the set should be together.

'Oh, Verity's set,' Irene said, shuffling in her seat and pulling her thick wool skirt over her bony knees. 'Black and white jiggly pattern?'

'Verity's set?' Meredith had never mentioned a Verity – at least, not that Maisie could remember. 'Was that your grandmother's name?'

'No, might have been my great-grandmother, but I forget now. I don't remember a Verity in the family, but that don't mean nothing. Gamma always referred to it as Verity's though. I lied to Meredith and said I'd given them away because she was always harping on about the bloody things. That shut her up. Feel a bit rotten about it now, though, but then all I had was three sodding cups and saucers. I ask you – what good is that to man or beast?' She looked across to Maisie who was picking at her lip and starting to feel uncomfortable. Her voice became more gentle. 'But it's nice you're trying to get it all back together. Gamma would be pleased. Mother, on the other hand, wouldn't give a flying fig.'

She paused for a few moments, struggling with her breathing. Naked Man chose that moment to throw open the door and give the ladies a clear view of his diminished assets.

'Oh dear, there you are.' Maisie heard her mother's pacifying voice in the distance. 'It's a bit chilly. Shall we find you some nice warm clothes and get back to that game of bingo? You've only got two numbers to go.'

The old man either didn't hear, or pretended not to, as he wiggled his hips and *everything* jiggled about. 'Who's up for a night of how's your father?' he asked, his top false teeth dropping from his gum with a slurp, as he gave an impish grin.

'How's my father?' Irene muttered. 'He's been in the ground forty years. Not going to be in a great state, let's be honest. You'll have to come up with a more interesting proposition than that.'

Naked Man seemed to think about this and tried again.

121

'Let's make the bed rock, thweetheart.' The air whistled through his teeth as he spoke. 'I've got the stamina of a long-distance runner.'

This made Maisie think of Theo's running past and her cheeks flushed scarlet as she linked this to Naked Man's request. The news Theo was possibly on the market had caused restless nights, and any sleep she'd managed was filled with X-rated dreams where Theo's extraordinary hair had proved that no amount of vigorous activity could persuade it to move anywhere.

'I don't think I'll be going the distance with you but thanks for the offer.' Irene dismissed him and returned her attention to Maisie, as Maisie's mum appeared in the corridor, placed a dressing gown about Naked Man's shoulders and steered him away.

'Sorry,' she mouthed, as she closed the door behind them both.

'Totally gaga,' Irene said, her index finger circling her ear. 'I wouldn't mind if he was a bit more with it, but what's the point of all that effort if they don't remember it afterwards?'

Maisie nodded. 'Absolutely.' Mind you, it had been a while since she'd rocked any bed – other than in her Theo-orientated dreams.

'There were six of us – the Mayhew sisters,' Irene clari-fied, returning to the conversation in hand. 'Meredith, Phyllis, Cynthia, me and Joanie, then our little Essie,' Irene was striding down memory lane now that Maisie had opened the gate. 'Gadding about in our lippy and our mini-skirts – beehive hair giving that Marge Simpson a run for her money. We thought we were going to conquer the world but it didn't turn out that way. All full of promise and giddy dreams and then we had this terrible year when every single damn one of us met with some misfortune or another.' Irene tugged at her tube, which was obviously causing her discomfort.

'I'm sorry,' Maisie said.

'No good in you apologising. It weren't your fault. Strange looking back on it all now though. Meredith was engaged, Philly had just met that bastard husband of hers, and poor old Cynth ...' Her voice trailed off, as tears threatened to bubble over.

'Thought I'd escaped it all. Renting a nice little flat in Camden with a girlfriend after this guy swore I would be the next Twiggy – she was nice, by the way, but my legs were better than hers,' Irene said as an aside. 'Starved myself like a sodding refugee but the fags took the edge off and, of course, everyone was smoking back then. Parties every night and the men clamouring to buy you a drink. Ha, should've known it was too good to last. Then this happened.' She reached for her scar. 'Agency dropped me like a scalding hot potato and I had to come crawling home. Boys weren't so quick to buy me a drink when I looked like a battered wife ...'

Not that the scar was horrific but Maisie understood why it had seen the end of Irene's modelling ambitions.

'I'm sorry,' she said again. What else could you say to someone lamenting an unfulfilled and disappointing life?

'Yeah, well, when you're promised the moon and you just end up with a sodding candle, you're gonna wander down a few dark alleys ...' She paused for a moment. Possibly to consider the twists and turns of her sad life.

'So ...' Maisie took a deep breath. '... I was hoping you could put me in touch with your sisters so I could try to gather Meredith's ... or *Verity's* set together again? It's something I want to do for her even though she's not here to appreciate it.' The guilt of not contacting her neighbour since moving away was weighing heavily on her shoulders.

'I can give you a number for Essie. Not sure I've got a contact for Joanie because we haven't spoken in donkey's years. Funny really, you expect twins to be thick as thieves but we never were. Opposites, you see? I was the one putting it about like a trollop, reckoning I was about to be the next big thing on the catwalk and glad to escape this rural hellhole. And Joanie was the quiet one – the stay at home, butter wouldn't melt, daren't even make eye contact with a boy kinda gal. But who got herself up the duff out of wedlock?' She cackled. 'Not sure Mother ever forgave her for that.'

'And the remaining two?' Maisie prompted. With her mother telling her all the sisters were within the county, even a surname or idea of their last known location would be helpful.

'Ha, good luck with that,' Irene snorted. 'Poor old Cynth, after years of carting her poo around in a bag and outliving all the doctors' predictions, went just after the new millennium started, and our Phyll went the year before last.'

As Maisie digested the news that the oldest three Mayhew sisters had passed away, she realised reuniting the set wasn't going to be as easy as she'd hoped.

Chapter 19

Unlike Maisie's mother, who often popped in on the off-chance, Maisie's dad usually met up with his children in locations where he was unlikely to bump into his rampaging ex-wife – presumably to avoid any unpleasant confrontations and the potential loss of his dangly bits. Her mum had form when it came to her dad, especially if he was flaunting a new paramour about town. Maisie recalled her mother's embarrassing announcement via the Tannoy of a large department store asking David Meadows to report to customer services as Lydia (his then girlfriend) needed a grown-up to collect her. And her advert in the local paper: *For Sale – one really used husband. Unreliable, needs constant servicing. Several careless owners –* where her mother listed his mobile number. If she'd had access to his curtains in the aftermath of the divorce, she would have sewn prawns into the hems.

On this occasion, Maisie's dad offered to shout his youngest daughter lunch at a quaint pub just outside Bury St Edmunds; all low beams, open fireplaces and, much to Maisie's horror, an enormous dribbling dog wandering loose in the bar area.

'How's Donna?' Maisie asked, as her dad broke into one of his glorious smiles that made you feel you were the most important person in the world. A slightly stale beer smell hung in the air and the not unpleasant aroma of chip fat drifted from the pub kitchen. With a crackling open fire occasionally spitting out embers onto the hearth, it was the perfect Sunday lunch venue.

'Ah, Donna ...' He gave a ten-thousand-kilowatt smile and a shrug. Maisie's dad had a knack of lighting up every room like a stadium full of powerful floodlights. 'It didn't work out.'

No, it never did, Maisie reflected.

'Maybe, with hindsight, she was a bit young for me. But that woman at the dry-cleaner's keeps giving me a discount on my work suits, so I could be in there.' He winked and his eyes twinkled like a thousand tiny stars in the heavens. She adored her dad unreservedly but was older now and wiser to his faults.

A waitress handed them menus and Maisie scanned it for something that she couldn't produce at home. For her, the joy of eating out was a naughty chip fix because she didn't own a deep fat fryer and oven chips were the work of the devil – on a bad day. She ordered the lasagne *with chips* and then sipped on her pre-dinner soda water as she hunted through her phone for pictures of her recently acquired crockery to show her dad.

She explained how these curious pieces of the long-forgotten tea set had found her again and told him of her decision to reunite it.

'They came from the Mayhew family. Do you remember Meredith, the woman who lived next door to us in Hickory Street?'

'Do I ever? Peering out of her net curtains and sizing me up as I walked up the drive. That woman never did like me.'

'She probably secretly fancied you, Dad. Everyone else over

126

the age of twelve in the neighbourhood did.' Maisie didn't add that as she got older this included half the girls in her class. Joking about it now was manageable but she'd struggled when her pre-pubescent cluster of friends constantly probed her for information about her film-star-looks dad. The urban dictionary definition of dilf was uncomfortably close to home.

'You've either got it or you haven't.' He uncrossed his legs and leaned forward to help himself to an olive. 'Problem is, when you start to lose it, you wonder if you abused it when the going was good.' He ran his hand through greying hair and Maisie let his last statement hang in the air for him to have a jolly good think about. Better late than never.

'So how are you going to hunt down the crockery, Sherlock? Can you get divining sticks for teacups? Walk up and down the streets of Tattlesham until they flick together and then go and knock on the nearest door?'

Given the inexplicable prickles she got whenever she came near the set, he might not be that wide of the mark.

'I've got some leads. It was split between Meredith and her sisters and it just so happens one of those sisters, Irene, has moved into Willow Tree House.'

'One of the sexiest women I ever met,' he said, looking wistfully across at the blazing fire.

'Irene?' Maisie squeaked. Blimey, he really was feeling his age and adjusting his potential girlfriend demographic.

'No – your mother.' David Meadows' train of thought having gone to another station when she mentioned the care home.

'She was saying similar things about you when I saw her last,' Maisie said, being creative with the truth and seizing an opportunity to encourage future reconciliations.

Her dad looked thoughtful, rubbing his chin with his hand.

'They were happy years,' he said. 'I did love your mum but perhaps not in the ways she wanted me to. And somehow I always felt I wasn't enough.'

The waitress reappeared with their meals and Maisie's tummy rumbled as they were placed on the table. Mouth-watering aromas swirled about in the rising steam.

'Surely enough turbulent water has passed under the dilapidated bridge now? Can't you at least be friends?' She stuck her knife into the pasta sheets and a rich, red sauce oozed out. She was hungrier than she thought. 'What's going to happen if one of your children gets married? I don't think we can pull off two weddings in quite the same way as we manage to repeat Christmas Day for the benefit of everyone.'

'It's your mother, not me. It's been nearly twenty years; she should be over it by now. I think you'll find she's the one who's built a solid concrete dam to stop a single droplet of water flowing under any bridges I've tried to erect.'

'So, in theory, if she softened, you'd be okay with seeing her again?' The biggest roadblock to achieving a family Christmas was the point-blank refusal of either parent to be in the same hemisphere – never mind room. Maybe if she sowed the seeds now and nurtured them carefully over the coming months, some sort of truce could be reached.

Instead of answering the question directly, he took a slight detour. 'Highly emotional woman, your mother. When we first fell in love, she loved me with her whole heart, and I suppose I found that suffocating. But when things weren't so rosy, she embraced those emotions equally fervently. I often wonder if she was the one that got away ...' he said, those amazing eyes of his temporarily losing their luminescence.

Maisie shuffled forward and tried not to look too hopeful.

There was a long pause as he fiddled with his cufflinks, picked up his cutlery and subtly changed the subject. 'And you're okay for money? You know, after the change of job?' For all his faults, he'd always been a generous man. Consistently one of the highest earning pharmaceutical reps in the country, he had a healthy wage and a sizeable bonus. It paid for his comfortable home life, subsidised his alarmingly expensive love life and meant his kids had never gone without.

'I'm fine, Dad.'

'You never did tell me what happened to make the brewery job end so suddenly. I thought you'd got yourself a lifelong career there.' He wrinkled up his nose. 'I miss your staff perks. Wickerman's Festival Porter is one of my all-time favourite beers.'

'I needed a change,' she simply said, because answering that her boss was a cheating, can't keep it in his pants, double-crossing flirt to her father would be awkward.

Chapter 20

'Why the glum faces?' Maisie asked, coming through from the back office and perching on the edge of the reception desk. Everyone was clustered together and facing the large front window.

'Have you seen the weather outside, dah-ling? It's positively biblical. Makes it so much harder for us to take the deliveries in and plays merry hell with the lots in The Yard. Arthur went terribly country bumpkin on me earlier, told me "when chimney smoke descends, the nice weather ends" so a storm was on its way.' Johnny rolled his eyes. 'I used that weather app you helped me install and he was only inexplicably correct. All those highly polished mahogany table tops and boxes of paperbacks – not compatible with a deluge of epic proportions.'

'He means they don't like getting wet,' Theo explained and rolled his eyes. 'It's always a pain taking in lots for the outside auction when the weather is bad. Wood and water do not mix.'

Not having a view from the back office, and with it being consistently dark in that room, she hadn't noticed the sudden change in the weather but now she could hear the rain beating against the large glass windows and see the ominous sky.

'I'm sure we can come up with a solution. Anyone got some

big golfing umbrellas? I might have one in the boot of my car,' she suggested, bouncing over to the window.

'Ah, a ray of sunshine on a gloomy day,' Theo said, that wonky smile on his lips.

'Ha – I'm no Mary Poppins, despite my brolly ownership,' Maisie said, knowing it was her work environment making her so upbeat. The other day they'd taken delivery of a coffin and, despite the sombre nature of the lot, there had been a jovial air about the saleroom and an ensuing bidding frenzy – Johnny convinced he'd got a saleroom of closet (or should that be coffin?) vampires. In the end, it went to a middle-aged Goth who announced it would be transformed into a coffee table. How could you fail to be cheered by such amusing interludes? 'Let me see if the brolly is still there from last weekend.'

As she said this, Arthur trudged past in a bright yellow sou'wester with matching waterproof jacket and galoshes.

'What is the temerarious fool up to now?' exclaimed Johnny. 'Honestly, it's like being on the set of *The Perfect Storm.*'

It was as if an imaginary light bulb suddenly pinged above Maisie's head as she jumped up and snatched her phone from her pocket. 'It's fabulous. In fact it's positively inspired! Now THAT'S what we need to kick-start our social media.'

'Please tell me you do not have plans to Twitter Arthur wearing that ensemble?' Johnny asked.

'That's exactly the plan,' and she swept out the main door and into a sheet of driving rain, calling Arthur's name, catching up with him out in The Yard as he heaved a rusty cast-iron garden roller across the gravel.

'Stop right there,' she said.

'Oh, I'm sorry.'

'What on earth for?' she asked.

'For whatever it is I've gone and done now. I do get in muddles and I've probably done something daft.'

'You haven't done anything wrong, Arthur. In fact, you've done *everything* right.'

'I have?' His wrinkled face broke out into a ten-kilowatt smile. 'Well, now. That'd be a first, I reckon.'

Maisie raised her phone and pointed it at Arthur, ignoring the blobby drops of rain running down her face. 'I'm going to take some photos and then with your permission, I'd like to post them online.'

'You want to put *my* picture on the interweb?' His eyes were wide and incredulous.

'If that's okay with you?' For a moment, her heart slowed to a thud. This magnificent idea would be scuppered by Arthur's perfectly legitimate refusal to participate. Theo had already made it clear he wasn't keen on being slapped all over Facebook. Despite setting up the social media sites, engagement was still mediocre. Part of the rural mentality – slow to adapt and embrace new things, she suspected.

'Well, that would just be dandy. Fancy – me on the web. Wait until I tell my Pam.'

Her heart lifted again and she took the picture as a bolt of lightning beautifully illuminated the dark sky overhead. Taking several shots to make sure she had a good one, she finally wiped away claggy knots of hair from her face as a deep rumble of thunder reverberated in the distance.

'Inside, you two,' ordered Theo, appearing from nowhere with a big spotty umbrella. 'You are totally insane to be out here taking extreme selfies, and both far too precious to be turned into blackened and crispy human kebabs for the sake of a stupid photograph.'

He put his strong arm about her shoulders to draw her under the brolly and she felt the heat from his chest as she was squashed up against it. He did have feelings for her, she was certain. The way he held her so protectively, even if it was born of friendship, meant she genuinely mattered to him. They half-walked, half-scampered back to the offices, tumbling through the door as another bolt of lightning lit up the sky like the backdrop to a Gothic horror film.

All three shook raindrops from their bodies like hyperactive wet dogs and wiped sodden feet on the thick coir entrance mat as Ella appeared with a tray of teas. She placed it on the reception desk and floated away again. Maisie noticed Ella often did thoughtful things but went out of her way not to highlight that they were done by her. When the accounts lady had been full of cold the previous week a brand-new box of tissues had appeared on her desk. And when Arthur had ripped his jacket sleeve on a rusty nail, it had been magically repaired over lunch hour – a lunch hour when both Ella and the jacket had disappeared.

'Thank you so much, 'Maisie said, again trying to engage with her. 'This will warm us up. Really considerate,' but Ella was already head low behind the screen.

'Join us?' Maisie pressed and everyone in the office turned to look expectantly at Ella except Theo, who silently picked up a cup and took it over to her. She smiled a shy smile and pushed out a coaster.

'Was it worth it?' Theo asked Maisie. 'Nearly being struck by lightning to get a picture of old Arthur here, in his Norfolk Fisherman fancy dress?'

'It most certainly was,' she replied, holding up her mobile showing the image of Arthur, a jagged bolt of light caught perfectly in the background. As the rain hammered relentlessly on the doors and windows, Maisie uploaded it to their social media platforms.

And within a few moments seven likes pinged through.

By the afternoon, the weather had behaved in a typically British fashion and the sun was out, reflecting its rippled light in the countless puddles that highlighted how badly the car park needed resurfacing. There was a clean, fresh smell to the air, hints of wet soil and traces of plant oils lingering in the atmosphere. Maisie was typing away at her desk when Theo appeared and shuffled his bottom onto the corner of his own desk, nudging the detritus out of the way. She'd been surprised to discover Theo had a desk not far from hers, as it was so hidden under clutter, it had been indistinguishable.

'Okay,' he said. 'You get a gold star.'

'What?'

'Ella's just shown me our Twitter page.' How did he manage to engage with her, when she ran like a frightened rabbit from everyone else? 'That picture of a yellow rain-coated Arthur, with the caption about how a tiny drop of rain doesn't stop Gildersleeve's staff getting on with their work, with a flipping great lightning bolt behind him, has gone viral.'

'Viral?' Maisie had been so busy she hadn't checked since posting it.

'Maybe not viral,' he admitted, 'but it's been retwittered twenty-eight times and had even more likes.'

Their usual retweet rate was about four, if they were lucky. Twenty-eight in the space of a day was incredible.

'People are the key,' she said, putting her best I Am A Wise Marketing Manager face on. 'Put someone in the photo and you get more engagement. The staff here are friendly, charming and quirky – it's one of our biggest assets. We need to use this to our advantage.' She looked up at his mossy eyes and tried not to look too smug. 'Johnny is an adorable if somewhat Victorian character, all smart and wordy – like an auctioneer should be, and Arthur is chatty and game for anything ...'

'And me?' he said, earnestly searching her face in response, like he always did when talking to people. A tightness pulled across her chest and there was a silent beat before he spoke again. 'I've been told the camera loves me.' And then, as if to break the moment, he pulled a ridiculous pouty face, flinging his head back like a diva, with that sheepskin hair of his going absolutely nowhere.

'You? Hmm ...' She considered her response. He was photogenic and unconventional. She understood why the television company selected him. His cockiness was tongue in cheek because he was down to earth, engaging and – if she was totally honest with herself – quite good-looking. Those eyes – whirlpools of green. And, yeah, despite battling the demons of her inner OCD, the odd sock thing was secretly rather endearing.

'You're okay.' She shrugged. 'You know? If there's nothing better available – like a used teabag.'

He punched her playfully on the arm and hopped off the desk.

'Tomorrow,' he said, yanking his crumpled T-shirt straight, 'I might let you show me how to post on our social media platforms.'

How very gracious of him.

Chapter 21

Of all the daft activities Nigel partook in, this was the most bonkers. Maisie smiled as he scampered into the middle of his large ceramic food bowl and fell backwards, effectively doing a backflip out onto the sawdust-covered cage floor. Without pausing for applause, he flipped to his front, and launched himself at the bowl again. This, much like his other gymnastic displays, could go on for several minutes.

The contrast of the frenetic auction house to her silent, tiny terraced house was stark. At least she had Nigel to offload to, even though his acquisition had been forced upon her by a guilt-tripping neighbour. The young family next door had bought a kitten a few months ago and Nigel had proved to be the tempting takeaway treat Minky just couldn't quite get his paws on. After a close shave, the young mum asked her if she knew anyone who would take Nigel on as a matter of urgency because 'the damn cat' had worked out how to open the cage door. Cats were too independent for Maisie's liking and dogs were too messy. A hamster she could just about manage.

'You are such an attention seeker,' Maisie joked, casting an eye over her shoulder, flicking through an *Antiques Trade Gazette*. He was an excellent listener and it was important to have something to talk to, even if it was a four-inch lump of hyperactive fluff that had Olympic-level gymnastic aspirations. He'd been such a life-saver when the whole Gareth thing kicked off.

Her fuzzy orange friend came to the edge of his cage, his tiny paws dangling in front of his splayed white whiskers, and his nose twitching and sniffing the air – ever hopeful of stuffing his expandable cheeks with tasty treats – like fluffy bags for life. Maisie was certain he could smell the lingering aroma of the raspberry and white chocolate muffins she'd baked earlier.

Post the horrifying tonsil-tickling scene in the basement of Wickerman's, an apologetic Gareth had scampered after her up the stairs, words of justification tumbling from his unfaithful lips. Eight months of toying with each other, of shy looks and accidental-on-purpose body contact. And another six months of a burgeoning relationship where she truly believed she'd found someone she had a future with. And then total betrayal. Remaining in the job had been impossible; he was the team leader and their desks were opposite each other, for goodness' sake. No, she'd been right to quit. And as an article about the sale of David Bowie's estate in the *Gazette* caught her eye, the passion she had for all aspects of her new job was proof of that.

The magazine was a couple of years out of date but it mentioned the sale of his extensive late-twentieth-century furniture collection. The pieces were colourful and quirky: clean lines and geometric shapes, in plastics and laminates. It appealed to her, more than the fusty antique furniture that Johnny got excited about – even after he'd explained that the centuries-old ring marks and worm holes were part of the appeal.

'Why would one be tempted to procure antiques if they've been cleaned back and polished to look like new?' he said. 'Because the kicks and scratches, the patina and frayed edges tell of its age and hint of its past life. All part of the charm, dah-ling, part of the charm.'

Secretly, Maisie wanted to say why indeed? Buy new. Cup rings freaked her out and were the reason she placed coasters on every surface her mother night be tempted to rest her coffee mug. But she understood why people wanted their valuable antiques to *look* antique.

'Did you know David Bowie studied art and design before his music career took off?' Maisie said aloud, even though she was the only human being in the room. She was looking at an image of the Peter Shire 'Big Sur' sofa – primary colours, geometric shapes and a curious asymmetry. It instantly reminded her of the Kandinsky from the book Meredith had given her all those years ago, because it wasn't the impressionists that she returned to again and again, it was the cubists and abstract artists. In fact, the spine was creased so definitely down its length that the book fell open at the Kandinsky every single time.

Meredith had assured her young self it was okay not to understand what was going on in a painting and that had been liberating to the point where Maisie actively preferred art when she had no clue what she was looking at and her mind was free to play with and interpret the shapes and colours as she saw fit. What was even more liberating was that one day an abstract painting might resemble a landscape – as the artist intended – but another day, perhaps coupled with a change of Maisie's mood, it would be simply litter on a beach.

The doorbell went and she put the magazine down to receive her guest.

'I'm early, aren't I?' Arthur looked anxious, standing in her fastidiously swept two-metre-square concrete area of front garden, the former flower border now a strip of blue slate with a single low-growing shrub in the centre. His shirt was crumpled and he was clutching a terracotta flowerpot.

'Not at all, come in.' Maisie opened the door to her narrow house, and because the hall didn't give space for her to step aside, she turned and led the way to the kitchen. Without her dad's generous contribution to the rent deposit she would still be living with her mum and knew she was lucky to have this minuscule mid-terrace to call her own.

'This is for you. It's from my garden. I potted it up after you said you liked them.' Arthur held out the flowerpot, which she could now see contained a primrose. 'Before you know it you'll have a nice little patch of them. They're fine with a bit of shade, and like damp soil. The name comes from the Latin, *prima rosa*, meaning the first rose of the year. Isn't that pretty? It will flower in the next few weeks. April the nineteenth is national Primrose Day and we had a little stillborn many years ago in April so we called her Primrose ...'

'How thoughtful,' Maisie said, taking the gift but not knowing what to say about the last piece of heart-breaking information. She placed it on a folded newspaper on the kitchen table. But Arthur wasn't after sympathy and didn't pause for platitudes. She began the tea-making ritual – first swishing out Meredith's pot with hot water.

'When I was a boy, the banks were full of them, especially down by the river. Mother used to pick them – which of course you can't do nowadays – and put them in little green glass vases on the kitchen windowsill. "And in the wood, where often you and I upon faint primrose-beds were wont to lie ..." That's a bit of Shakespeare, that is. Don't reckon you expected a washed-up old boy like me to know anything cultural?'

'You're not washed up, Arthur, or old. Age is merely a number,' Maisie said, this time rolling out a platitude, as the conversation wasn't as delicate. 'You are a very valuable member of the Gildersleeve's team. I know Theo thinks an awful lot of you.'

There was the hint of a smile and he reached out his knobbly hand to spin the flowerpot forty-five degrees, as though positioning the plant just so was the most important thing at that moment.

'We're going to use the black and white cups as you were so clever to spot them,' Maisie said, lifting them down from the shelf and placing them in front of Arthur. The tea had brewed, the muffins were placed on a smaller white tea plate (as she felt it co-ordinated sufficiently with the tea set) and two white napkins were taken from the drawer under the cutlery. She poured the tea.

'To Meredith.' She lifted her cup to toast the lady who had played a small but significant part in her youth, and who had possibly saved her mother from a total breakdown at a difficult time in their lives. 'A good friend to me in times gone by. And to Irene for the cups, even though she doesn't particularly like them.'

'Irene and Meredith?' Arthur's voice sounded unsure as his eyes narrowed. 'Not the Mayhew sisters?'

'You know them?' She jerked her head back, nearly slopping tea into her saucer.

'Everybody about these parts knew the Mayhew sisters.'

He laughed. 'They were a rum lot. I still see Essie about town occasionally, but not to talk to. I feel a bit shy about approaching her after all these years. I'm not rightly sure I'd know what to say ...'

He didn't have that problem with anyone else but she didn't like to point that out. 'You're one of the friendliest people I've ever come across and I've never known you to be backwards in coming forwards.'

'Ah, well, we have history. She was practically the same age as me and I rather set my cap at her when we were younger but never quite got up the courage to ask her out, and then she met Frank and that particular boat sailed far out to sea, with me still standing on the shore.'

This unexpected connection made her feel optimistic about her quest. If nothing else, Arthur knowing the Mayhews was another potential source of leads.

'Went to school with the youngest four,' he continued, 'but there was a big gap between them and the oldest girls – it was the war, you understand? Their dad was on the Western Front. Lucky to come back when so many young men didn't. And them girls were all pretty as postcards, but some more headstrong than a bull chasing a cow in heat through the pasture ...' Which certainly conjured up an interesting image of the sisters.

Maisie explained how the set had been split between the Mayhew girls many years ago, how Meredith had recently passed away and about her visit to Irene.

'How sad. I liked Meredith. Always full of interesting bits of information – you could tell she was a teacher.' He took a long, slow sip of his tea and his eyes brightened up. 'I wonder if Essie and Frank still live on the Forest estate? Maybe I'll pop by one day when I'm feeling brave. And I could get the bus to Willow Tree House to see Irene. Goodness—' he chuckled to himself '—it must be nearly fifty years – always was the rebellious twin. A pretty gal in her day though. Wanted to be a model but a bit thin for my tastes.' It was nice to know there were men out there who appreciated the curvier woman.

'And the other sisters?' Maisie wondered if Arthur had any useful information to impart.

'Phyllis and Joanie were the quiet ones. But Phyllis never stood a chance – picked a bully as a husband. Cynthia got ill, I think, but I don't rightly remember the details. They all seemed to have a run of bad luck, what with one thing and another. And then there was Essie ...' His voice trailed off. Maisie waited but he didn't elaborate. He took a swig of his tea and broke out into another smile. 'But there. Doesn't do to dwell.'

'More tea, Arthur? I know Saturdays are your shopping days and I don't want Pam worrying.'

'You're all right, love. She knows I was stopping to see you before I went into town. More tea would be lovely. It will give me a chance to tell you all about my time at Gildersleeve's and some of the wonderful things I've been learning ...' and he settled back into the chair – clearly going nowhere for the immediate future.

Chapter 22

As the calendar hurtled towards an early Easter, Johnny asked Maisie if she was available to work the Sunday before the bank holiday weekend.

'Are we behind then?' she queried, thinking that between them Gildersleeve's seemed much more efficient and orderly since her arrival in January, despite the imminent online catalogue launch.

'On the contrary although, lamentably, the work I speak of will be unpaid ...' Her heart sank. 'Off site ...' She perked up. 'And I will delve into the deepest pocket of my twin pleated trousers, brush down my calf leather wallet and treat you to lunch.'

It sounded intriguing. 'Okay, you're on.'

The Easter weekend was set to be hectic. Zoe and Oliver were due back and her mum had organised a welcome home party for the bank holiday Monday. She'd also roped Maisie into a myriad of craft activities for the care home when she'd popped round unexpectedly the previous evening – catching an embarrassed Maisie mid-splatterings and forcing her to leap into the shower to scrub away at the lemon-yellow hue from her elbows. They'd made some interesting shapes on the canvas – and let's face it, if Jackson Pollock could walk across his paintings and incorporate a few cigarette butts to connect with his art, her elbows were fair game. Sometimes she got so carried away, with her rock music on full blast, and so swept up with the emotions her art unleashed that other body parts had been employed as well.

Her mum had stopped asking to see her paintings because Maisie continually protested she was still in the experimental stage – they weren't ready to be seen. However, she was pretty sure her mother was expecting twee watercolours of Tattlesham landmarks or beautifully arranged fruit bowls. Not the enthusiastic efforts of a disturbed four-year-old on amphetamines.

'Any chance my clever Mary Berry-esque daughter could rustle up some cakes for the Easter cake sale?' her mother had asked, as she'd scrambled downstairs and into the living room, hair up in a towel turban and mumbling excuses for not hearing her mother's shouts. 'I know it's a couple of weeks away but I'm giving you plenty of notice. And if you're free on the Sunday, I'd love you to judge the Easter bonnet competition? Some of the old dears have already started making paper flowers. They take it all very seriously ...' So, of course, she'd agreed.

Maisie returned her thoughts to Johnny's mysterious off-site work commitment. 'So what will we be doing? A probate valuation?'

'No, you, myself and the Adonis of a man we know as Theodore shall be heading out to the glorious east coast of this fair county to peruse the prestigious Aldeburgh Antiques and Fine Art Fair. I go every year to keep my eye on the current retail prices and to talk to the dealers about shifts in the market. It is always most enlightening and they do serve the most exquisite ethically farmed home-made sausage rolls.'

Maisie couldn't deny a flash of exhilaration when she heard Theo was going to be part of the excursion. Finally – an opportunity to see how the romantic landscape lay.

That Sunday, Johnny drove them to the coast in his sleek but dated Mercedes. An exuberant fair organiser greeted the men like long-lost friends before walking them down a long corridor to an enormous stand-fitted hall in the private school where the event was being held.

Maisie gazed agog at the rows and rows of stands, each with their company name above their allocated six-by-ten-foot space. There was everything from English country furniture to clocks, early metal-ware to erotic art. They wandered around the venue at a leisurely pace, talking to the dealers and picking their brains. Maisie listened patiently to the immaculately turned-out lady complaining she couldn't shift her bow-fronts but had seen a revival in oriental, and to a stout bespectacled man from the television who announced the bottom had fallen out of the cut glass market.

Three hours later, Theo and Maisie sat in the pop-up café eating delicious hot sausage rolls whilst Johnny indulged in the world's most generous slice of coffee and walnut cake at a neighbouring table with the organiser.

'I know he seems to be coping after the split but underneath he's struggling. Seven years is a long time to be with someone,' said Theo, looking fondly at his flamboyant friend.

'It will take him a while to readjust,' Maisie agreed. 'I came out of a relationship at Christmas. It's hard.' It wasn't that she missed Gareth any more, but after all those months of someone to confide in, someone to hold her, she felt a keen loneliness that was almost worse than her single days before she'd been with him. Nigel was a good listener but his scrappy little arms were never going to cut the mustard in the hug department.

Theo studied her face again and scrunched up his brow. 'Yes, I guess time and space are needed after any break-up.'

'He's lucky to have a friend like you,' she said. 'How did you meet?'

'Gildersleeve's were looking for a part-timer and I needed some cash, so I fitted the job around my A Levels. Johnny and I hit it off big time and he gave me holiday work through uni. Any career plans I thought I had were totally banjaxed when I was slowly but inadvertently sucked into this fascinating and glorious world. Fast forward fifteen years and the auction house is my life.'

Theo pulled his gaze away from the animated Johnny, who was turquoise legs akimbo and spouting his usual exotic vocabulary, and locked eyes with Maisie again.

'To be honest, I can't imagine ever working anywhere else. The attractions of Gildersleeve's are increasing all the time ...'

And, at that moment, looking at Theo sprawled across the plastic chair, she felt exactly the same.

The schools broke up for Easter and the auction house was throbbing. Despite a broken china figurine and the not so helpful input of an unsupervised toddler who emptied seven boxes of jigsaw puzzles in the middle aisle of Saleroom One, the staff welcomed the richer diversity of customer: the seasonal tourist who made a visit to Gildersleeve's part of their holiday year on year, the locals who had time off work to coincide with the school holiday and, yes, even the children.

The promised returning snow hadn't materialised and the

fickle British weather managed to jump up about ten degrees in the space of twenty-four hours and then went on to produce more appropriate spring-like weather, at one point reaching a balmy thirteen degrees. Crisp, dry days made life easier for everyone and The Yard sales started to take off, as Maisie was told they often did this time of year. Wrought-iron gates, three-foot-high garden sculptures and outdoor furniture were breeding behind the saleroom barns – although there was a notable absence of garden gnomes.

Johnny bumbled into the front office and announced in a loud voice, 'Why on the earth of our wondrous God has Theodore rearranged all the desks in here? For the love of all that is human, you can't even see Ella. She's stuck up against the wall.'

'I think that's the point.' Maisie tried to be diplomatic, thankful Ella had nipped to the loo.

The penny clattered to the floor. 'Oh. I see. Because of the ...' He waved his hand in a vague circle around the left side of his own face. 'Right. So no one points it out or makes her feel uncomfortable.'

Maisie sighed. Theo hadn't made a big deal of it. He'd simply seen the need to address the situation and dealt with it in his unassuming way. His quiet kindness with outsiders like Ella and Arthur was endearing. She was aware he was growing on her like a woolly-hat-wearing fungus and the more time she spent with him, the more invasive it became.

Later, as she helped out in the front office, she decided to follow Theo's lead. She noticed the fragile pale pink orchid that always stood on the corner of Ella's desk, and seizing an opportunity to bond with her, Maisie slid her wheeled chair across the gangway.

'There are some beautiful botanical prints coming up this week. Are you into gardening? I noticed the orchid.' She waved the photos on her phone at Ella.

'Um, yeah.' Ella barely raised her head and typed faster.

'Did you want to come and have a look at them with me? Johnny has hung them in Saleroom Two. They're beautiful.'

'I'm a bit busy ...' Ella waved a vague hand across her computer screen.

Maisie persevered. 'I can help? It's no trouble.'

'I'll be fine but, um, thanks.'

It was time to step back but she felt it was a shame. There was a real potential for friendship, and she could certainly do with a bigger circle of female friends.

Later, she spotted Ella and Theo chattering away in a conspiratorial huddle and felt rather put out. They were discussing his upcoming Modern Design Sale and he was showing her some of the vintage fabrics that were part of the auction. Twice a year, he put together a sale showcasing modern design at its finest, tacking it on to the end of the Friday sale. It was his expertise in this field that the *Wot a Lot!* team valued so highly. He was an expert in post-war art and artefacts; studio pottery, Scandinavian glass and Danish furniture amongst his specialist areas. Thanks to Meredith's treasured gift, Maisie could hold her own in the art-based conversation, although she'd never divulged her messy hobby to him. Maintaining her professional and organised persona at work was more important than anywhere else.

Ella giggled and put a delicate hand out to Theo's arm. She didn't look so shy and uninterested now, Maisie thought, uncharitably. And for a few moments there were two people in the room with vivid green eyes.

Chapter 23

Maisie's mum had six party poppers clustered in her left hand and the moment Zoe and Oliver stepped through the front door they were greeted by a loud explosion and showered with a hundred multicoloured strips of curly tissue paper.

'Welcome home, my darlings,' she sung, before stretching out her arms and bursting into tears.

Lisa had been invited but couldn't *possibly* make it down to Suffolk due to manic work commitments. Ben was also a no but thoughtfully sent a bottle of Bollinger in his stead. So Maisie's maternal grandparents, some old school friends of Zoe's and a cluster of neighbours came to welcome the adventurers home.

Maisie was in her element having spent a carefree Sunday (either side of the Easter bonnet judging) baking a variety of finger food for the occasion. Because her mother was flat out with care home shifts she'd taken over the food preparation and the subsequent lavish display. She tried hard not to mind when her exhausted mum dumped a pile of pre-packaged food on the end of the table – all jumbled up and still in the packets. Surely her blueberry muffins would win out?

The guests of honour were mobbed by inquisitive hordes and Maisie and her mother stood back, knowing they would get the couple all to themselves later in the day.

She handed her mum an aromatic cheese and fennel scone on a tea plate with a pretty paper napkin tucked underneath. The napkin was ignored, as her mother started nibbling at the scone and dropping crumbs left, right and centre.

'Dad was talking about you fondly the other day,' Maisie said. 'We took a little trip down memory lanc.'

'Hrmph. He should have stayed there then instead of getting on a bus to Affair Street and Lying Bastard Avenue.'

'He was saying how in love you'd both been in those early days and reflected whether you were the one that got away ...' Maisie persevered.

'Was he now?' Her mother's eyes narrowed. 'Great scone. Love the fennel.'

'He's dumped Donna. I think he realised she was a bit young for him. Perhaps he's finally growing up?' It was her last verbal offering in an attempt to find a chink in her mother's anti-man armour.

'Hmm ...' Her mum balanced her empty plate on the arm of an easy chair and dusted her fingers off – Maisie biting her lip as microscopic crumbs were sprayed over the carpet. 'Doesn't Zoe look well?' Her eyes looked over to her middle daughter. The subject was changed and Maisie left it at that. Softly, softly, catchee monkey.

Zoe bounced around the room, shaking people's hands and hugging old ladies who couldn't believe how healthy and young she looked; all tanned, with her white-blonde hair wild about her shoulders. She looked more stereotypically Australian than most Australians but Britain had forced her into a thick cashmere jumper and knee-high boots.

'I've got two pairs of socks on. I can't believe how cold and miserable it is here,' Zoe said, bounding over and giving her baby sister a bosom-flattening hug.

'I don't know what you're complaining about. You missed all the snow. It's positively balmy compared to a couple of weeks ago,' Maisie pointed out. 'Besides, the UK knocks Oz into a cocked hat every time because it has the biggest attraction of all – me.' She grinned.

'Aww, I missed you so much,' Zoe said, giving Maisie a slurpy kiss on the cheek.

'I'm sorry for your sakes it didn't work out but for selfish reasons it's good to have you home,' their mum said, joining them and brandishing a half-opened packet of Tunnock's Tea Cakes, still with dabs of poster paint in her hair from the previous day's Easter egg painting with the residents. 'And I include both of you in that.' She turned to Oliver, who was now beside his wife. Much to Maisie's horror, he accepted the proffered packet. 'I always said you were like a second son.'

Zoe and Oliver exchanged a look Maisie couldn't decipher.

'As for the ghastly weather – I thought that was the whole point of you emigrating,' continued their mum. 'Why you've come back, I don't know.' She glanced out the window as spits and spots of rain dribbled down the glass and she shook her head.

Oliver shook a foil-covered cake out from the upturned box.

'It's not all sun, sea and barbies, Bev,' he said.

'But you've come back to lashing rain, ferocious wind and broken brollies. I know which I'd prefer.'

'How's tricks, Maisie?' Oliver asked, looking over to her and moving the conversation on. 'Zoe said you had a new

151

job? Bit gutted you've left the brewery. I enjoyed the freebies.'

Maisie rolled her eyes. Wickerman's had made her predictably popular with the men in her life. Pointing out second-hand washing machines and a few pairs of good condition Laura Ashley curtains coming up at auction wasn't going to cut it with the menfolk in quite the same way.

'Yes, at an auction house. No more discounted beer but a world of undiscovered treasures,' she offered.

'As long as you're happy.' Oliver pulled her close with a huge arm. 'Glad you've got rid of the sleazebag. You deserve better. Need me to thump him for you?'

She shook her head and smiled. Oliver might be built like a gorilla but she'd never seen him so much as thump a calculator.

'At least one of my children managed to find themselves a decent partner.' Their mother rested her hand on Oliver's barrel-like biceps.

'About that ...' Zoe began as she exchanged another anxious look with Oliver. 'When I said things weren't working out, I didn't just mean on the job front. Oliver and I are getting divorced.'

Chapter 24

Her next free weekend, and using the number Irene had passed on, Maisie arranged to visit Essie Mayhew, Meredith's baby sister – if she could still be considered a baby at nearly seventy. There were only two years between Essie and Irene but it might as well have been twenty. The slightly older Irene looked like a desiccated nonagenarian, not helped by the medical equipment and proliferation of wrinkles, doubtless accelerated by the smoking. Essie, on the other hand, could have passed for a woman a decade younger than her years. With chestnut hair only faintly brushed with grey, and wearing smart black trousers and a floaty blouse, she looked about the same age as Maisie's mother.

'I have cake – I hope you like cake?' Essie's eyes looked so hopeful that Maisie nodded. She adored cake, being a baker herself, but she'd just eaten the last of her recent batch of flapjacks before leaving the house. There was love and there was gluttony.

'Oh goody, because I've baked two.' Maisie's heart sank.

They sat either side of a low coffee table in Essie's cosy living room. As soon as Maisie entered her bungalow the familiar prickling began. She was a tea set radar – able to verify its presence without even seeing it. Essie placed an open shoebox on the table and the distinctive black and white swirls poked out from scrunched-up sheets of the *Tattlesham Echo*.

'Here they are – damn ugly things. I only kept them because they were of great sentimental value to my grandmother and I thought it would be nice to pass down to my ... Oh well, never mind. Life doesn't always pan out the way you hope.' Essie sighed and blinked rapidly before dragging a reluctant smile across her face. 'But you said on the phone you'd bought Meredith's teapot and Irene's cups from the auction, so I guess you think differently?'

'I love them. I think they're quirky and unusual.'

'So is Trump's hair – stupid man – doesn't mean he's on to a winner. The youngsters aren't all queuing up at the barber's asking to look like they've got a guinea pig balanced on their heads.'

Essie seemed to perk up after this observation and she unwrapped one of the saucers and placed it on the table.

'Gamma was incredibly fond of this tea set. *Very* peculiar about when it was used though. I remember Meredith asking if we girls could have a little tea party with it when we were younger but she said it wasn't appropriate. And then Mother laughed and said with them old dreary colours the only appropriate occasion would be a funeral.' She giggled to herself. 'Forever rabbiting on about it being special, although according to my neighbour's son, *special* is a bit of an insult now.'

'Special in what way?' Maisie asked. Meredith had hinted there was *something* about the set but no one could give her any indication what that might be. It wasn't that Maisie needed conformation the set was an oddity, more that she needed to know why. Was it designed by someone famous? A one-off design? Perhaps a prototype that had never made it into mass production? That would explain why she couldn't find it anywhere.

'Blessed if I know but she used to say odd things, like it needed to be supervised – guess she was worried we'd damage it. You're welcome to them. They never brought me anything but heartache.'

Knowing full well an inanimate object couldn't influence someone's happiness, Maisie picked up one of the cups and noticed two had white interiors – one had black. That the six cups were now back together made her inexplicably happy.

'If you're sure? But I insist on paying for them.'

'Nonsense. They aren't worth the loose change in a tramp's upturned cap.' She tutted the offer away, so Maisie decided to buy her a bunch of flowers as a thank you. 'Besides, I know Gamma is smiling down from the heavens and willing you on.'

Essie cut a gigantic slice of the second cake and Maisie gave a weak smile as the waistband of her jeans strained at the thought of more calories. She told Essie of her plan to reunite the set and asked about Phyllis and Cynthia, hoping against hope they'd left their pieces to one of the remaining sisters.

'Phyllis lived out towards the coast. Poor thing. I felt right rotten flaunting my happiness in front of her when Frank and I got together, what with that bastard of a husband of hers, and the son not much better. He used to hit her, you know? Her old man.'

Maisie didn't know, but both Irene and Arthur had hinted the husband was a bully.

'I reckon she married him because he was the only person

to ask. The son never touched her, but he was a verbal bully, and he got that from watching how his old man disrespected her. Poor woman spent her life rushing around after the pair of them, never saying boo to a tea towel, never mind a goose. The grandson was all right though. Can't say he's a particular favourite but she was fond of him. At least he visited her, which is more than her own son ever did.'

'Oh dear. That's a dead end then,' Maisie sighed.

'You might be lucky. She left everything to the grandson, which wasn't much to be fair, but I do have a number for him because he sorted the funeral.' She rummaged in a small drawer under her television and wrote a number down, handing a slip of paper to Maisie. 'Joanie's number is there as well – another quiet one – but she's away at the moment. Her son-in-law pays for a Mediterranean cruise every year. Give it a couple of weeks. She'll be back by the end of the month.'

'Thanks,' said Maisie. She would try the grandson first. If he didn't have any of the tea set her quest would be over anyway.

'Things turned out okay for Joanie in the end I guess,' Essie mused. 'But I don't think she ever got over the shock of finding herself pregnant by a married man. Poor girl cried oceans. Never talked to me about it though – knowing Frank and I were struggling to have a babe of our own. Course I never fell, but that's another story ...' Her voice trailed off again and she wiped away a tear from under her eye before taking a fortifying sniff.

'Do you know anything about the history of the tea set?' Maisie tried to distract Essie from her unhappy memories. 'I've looked online but drawn a blank. My boss said it was Nineteen-Eighties but if they were your grandmother's it must be considerably older than that?'

'Nineteen-Eighties my backside. I was born in 'forty-nine and I can remember them in Gamma's glass-fronted cabinet. 'Bout the only thing they have going for them – their age. Funny how life goes: age is the one thing I don't have in my favour any more. Guess it's different with possessions – even wine. Nobody's celebrating my vintage any more ...'

'Surely your husband—'

'Cancer took him. Eighteen months ago.' Maisie felt her cheeks go hot. She was sure Arthur talked about Frank as though he was still alive. Perhaps he didn't know Essie had lost her husband, but then she had her suspicions he'd been avoiding his childhood friend in recent years. So Maisie told Essie about her connection to Arthur. After nearly choking on her tea, Essie insisted her number be passed on to him – saying she always had baking on the go and remembered him being partial to a bit of fruit cake.

'We had a good forty-eight years together, me and Frank.' Essie circled the conversation back. 'Nearly made it to the golden. It's the cooking for one I find hardest – seems a bit odd boiling up three diddy new potatoes in a great big soss-pan. And he used to love my baking. Can't touch any of it because I'm diabetic. Eat up,' she chastised. 'You haven't taken one bite of that lemon drizzle.'

'Mmm, my favourite.' Maisie tried to sound enthusiastic because lemon drizzle *was* her favourite. After taking a small mouthful, she reached for one of the cups, turning it around in her hand.

'Irene said it was Verity's set. Who was Verity?'

'I'd forgotten that. It was a wedding gift so perhaps Verity was the name of the person who gave it to them? But Gamma got married in the lead-up to the Great War so it's at least a hundred years old and I'd be too young to know any Veritys from that era.'

So Johnny had got the date wrong but valuing such a wide spectrum of objects was an onerous task. How could you possibly know everything about everything? Armed with an idea of its age now, perhaps she would take a piece in to work and ask Theo's opinion.

'To be honest,' Essie continued, 'I've always felt a bit peculiar having them in the house. They unsettle me slightly – probably all Gamma's nonsense – so they've been shoved away in a back cupboard for over forty years.'

'I promise to take good care of them,' Maisie said.

'Mind you do, young lady, because what you don't understand is it's irrelevant who owns the set – the key is it shouldn't be split. Mother paid no attention to Gamma's wishes and now it's too late. The damage was done to the Mayhews a long time ago.'

As Essie's cups and saucers, undamaged and unblemished, stood on her draining rack Maisie noticed, for the first time, a tiny black mark on the bottom of one of the saucers. She peered closer. It was a symbol or letter of some kind, so she turned over all the cups, including the ones on her shelf, and realised they also had similar, but not identical, symbols on the bottom. If they were a maker's mark, surely they would match? Perhaps it was a batch number or something. Did china even have batch numbers?

Maisie horseshoed six cups around the teapot and stood back with a satisfied sigh. The doorbell buzzed and she skipped down the hall to see who it was, not expecting anyone, but always happy to receive guests. Quite frankly, not even

158

a three-month written warning could have prepared her for the sight that greeted her when she swung back her glossy Oxford blue front door. Because there on the doorstep stood her parents.

Together.

Chapter 25

There were no weapons of mass destruction, no obvious hostage situation and no UN peacekeeper hovering in the background ready to take down the first aggressor. In fact, both parents were smiling; her mum still with the name badge pinned to her bosom from her last shift and her dad, as ever, dripping charm and charisma like a melting ice cream in the hot summer sun.

'Surprise,' they choroused.

Hashtag *massiveunderstatement*. She couldn't have been more surprised if she'd opened the door to Meredith – and she was dead. Maisie stood in silence, unable to articulate anything coherent, as she waited for the catch.

'Aren't you going to let us in, love?' her dad asked, arms across his chest and rubbing fiercely at his bare upper arms. 'It's a bit nippy out here and we didn't want to freak you out by letting ourselves in the back.'

Still silent, she headed towards the kitchen, allowing her parents to follow.

'Now, don't be getting too excited,' her mother gabbled, as she followed her daughter into the kitchen. 'We're not a couple or anything, but I thought it was time to bury the hatchet, and this time not in his head, like I've been threatening to do these past few years.' She tossed her coat over the back of a kitchen chair and Maisie resisted the urge to pick it up and hang it on a coat hook in the hall. How hard was it to put things in their proper place? She'd walked right past the hooks, for goodness' sake. Her mother pulled the chair out and slipped into it, as Maisie's dad stood behind his ex-wife in an unnervingly protective way. She was hardly the threat here.

'We bumped into each other by the mere ...' he began.

'Quite literally.' Her mum gave a girly giggle that wasn't age-appropriate as Maisie still struggled to find any words for the astonishing situation. Instead, she slid into the empty pine kitchen chair – Verity's tea set catching her eye as she did so.

'Your mum was reversing a lady up the low steps in a wheelchair and I was hurrying down, glued to my iPhone, and we collided. Luckily the little old dear didn't roll out and into the water ...'

'And he was so kind and charming that he quite won her over. And then he manoeuvred the wheelchair to the bottom for me – which was hysterical because I was actually trying to get her to the top – but he did it in such a chivalrous manner that I couldn't bring myself to be cross,' added her mum, continuing this game of verbal ping-pong.

'So we stood there chatting and giggling like a couple of loons and it felt like we'd been transported back in time.' Her dad looked down at his ex-wife, his eyes glued to her soppy face.

'And then we both stopped, didn't we, David?' He nodded. 'And there was this moment of silence, and I said, "It's lovely having our Zoe back. Family is important," and *he* said, "Bev, despite the cock-ups I've made in my life, I do consider my family as my one great success." We both smiled, acknowledging that truth if nothing else. And then he asked if I wanted to grab a quick drink after my shift. We've been sitting in the Tattlesham Arms for three hours. I don't know where the time went.'

No wonder they both looked so rosy-cheeked if they'd been necking alcohol since mid-afternoon.

'We've talked some things through and decided no recriminations, no point-scoring. We're grown-ups. We can do this.' Her dad's hand gently squeezed his ex-wife's shoulder and she put her hand up to enclose his.

'Life's too short to bear grudges. I should know, I witness the regrets of the elderly all the time at work when they realise it's too late to rectify the wrongs of the past. I don't want to die a bitter old woman.'

And this from the lady who wanted to sprinkle grass seed over his carpets when he took his first post-divorce holiday, but the house had a security alarm. Maisie was bemused.

'We wanted you to be the first to know we've built our bridges. What do you think, love?' her dad finished.

Two heads looked across at Maisie expectantly. There was a long pause. Not one word had passed her lips since she'd opened the door and she was still amazed her parents were in the same room and both were breathing. Of course the bridges were impressive – they'd have to be nothing short of miraculous to traverse the violent and stormy waters that had rampaged down the valley between them. She knew her mum had even written instructions in her will forbidding her ex-husband to attend her funeral. The bitterness had curdled, and turned ever more sour – at least on her mother's part. (To be fair, her dad had always been relatively philosophical about his ex-wife's revenge campaign.) And now they were in her kitchen looking like two tipsy teenagers on a first date – whatever protestations of mere friendship came from their lips.

'Tea anyone?' Maisie finally found her voice, as her mum gave a giggly hiccup. 'Or *really* strong coffee?'

'Tell me about it,' Zoe huffed. 'They sat in the flat giggling like schoolkids.' She bent down to pick up two turquoise, four-kilo dumbbells – one for each hand – and began a series of bicep curls as she listened to Maisie retelling the recent turn of Meadows' family events. Both parents had visited daughter number two as well. 'It was nauseating.'

A panting Maisie turned the treadmill down to its slowest setting, hoping this was the equivalent of dawdle on the dial. Two minutes of running had nearly given her heart failure. She was at the gym to spend quality time with Zoe – getting fit was an unnecessary by-product. As were her knee-length Lycra shorts and double-layered sports top.

Although the sisters had talked every few days when Zoe had emigrated, there was nothing like a face-to-face chat – conversations where you didn't need to finish sentences and an eye-roll said everything you needed to say. Maisie wiped the back of her hand across her hot forehead and stepped off the machine.

'I was as shocked as you, but surely it's a good thing? Perhaps we can start to be a proper family again. Perhaps when Ben's tour finishes in Croatia, Lisa could pop down?' After the shock had worn off, Maisie tried to focus on the benefits of the unexpected situation. This time a couple of months ago she couldn't have envisaged not only would she be hanging out with her youngest sister again but also that her parents

163

would be talking to each other like rational human beings. Perhaps this Christmas wouldn't be as dismal as her last.

'I feel uneasy. It's too much, too quickly. Apparently they are going to see a film together at the weekend *as friends*.' The more agitated Zoe got, the faster she curled those biceps.

'Stand still and stop bouncing about,' Maisie said. 'I'm trying to talk this over sensibly.'

'I need to be active when I'm stressed, because I don't believe all those years of animosity will fade into the background. Remember when Mum made that three-foot scratch along the side of his company car after seeing him with someone at the posh restaurant in town? How he didn't throttle her, I'll never understand.' She placed the dumbbells on the floor, grabbing at a bottle of energy drink and flipping the top.

There were good and bad sides to having a highly emotional mother. She was the best at celebrations – you only had to announce a two-pound lottery scratch card win and she would be cheering and whooping, swiftly followed by all-embracing hugs and unbridled tears of joy. It could make you feel on top of the world in an instant. But over the years, on the odd occasions she stumbled across her ex-husband, her more primitive emotions won out. It was all small stuff, no actual death threats or physical violence – just some minor criminal damage, a degree of public humiliation and a touch of trespassing.

'So ... you and Oliver then?' Maisie asked, changing the subject and daring to mention the impending divorce. 'I'm desperately hoping you'll remain friends.'

'Of course. I told you at the party, there's been no big fight, no illicit affairs. Poor Mum was inconsolable all evening – I knew she'd take it badly. He's a great bloke but both of us recognised the romance element had dwindled away. We'd inadvertently slipped into more of a brother-sister vibe in the last few years.'

Maisie took her sister's calm resignation over the situation as a good sign. Unlike Lisa, who could make a drama over slightly over-cooked fried egg, Zoe was pragmatism personified. Perhaps this was why her sisters clashed so badly; Zoe analysed the facts and worked out logical solutions, whereas Lisa had inherited a more emotional response to situations, where facts came quite low down the list.

'Talking of siblings, I'm thinking of organising a family get-together,' Maisie said.

Zoe choked on her drink and embarked on a minor coughing fit, as Maisie leaped from the treadmill and gently rubbed her sister's back.

'And you think getting our dysfunctional family together is a good idea because ...?' Zoe spluttered.

'Come on. We're not that bad. We lived together in the same house for a number of years. Blood is thicker than water and all that.' The bickering environment of her childhood had been stop-start, with some brief flashes of hope – that last Christmas Day together being a good example. Maybe without the teenage hormones and the enforced confinement, they could come back together as adults and re-create the good times. Maisie wanted to feel at the centre of something whole, not the overstretched bungee straps holding the fragmented pieces of her family together.

'Why? We made a pretty shoddy job of it first time around. Leave it, sis. The logistics alone make it an onerous task, and then there's the L factor ...'

'She's not so bad.'

'Not so bad?' Zoe squeaked. 'Maybe she didn't set fire to your Sparkle Eyes Barbie or out you to your first serious crush, but there's a lot she's done I find very hard to forgive.'

'It's hard being the eldest,' Maisie said. 'People expect things from you and she's under a lot of pressure at work. That can make you snappy and I'm sure she doesn't want to let people down.' She wanted to find legitimate reasons for her oldest sister's reluctance to visit.

Tipping her head to one side and giving her younger sister a You've Got To Be Yanking My Chain look, Zoe snorted.

'Her social media posts are full of her floating around life, attending glitzy work functions, pulling ridiculous pouty selfies, always with a glass of fizz in her hands, rubbing shoulders with well-known actors and name-dropping left, right and centre. Oh yeah – she's got it so tough. Boohoo for Lisa. She's not been down to Suffolk for months. Face it, Maisie, she's moved on.'

'A month ago, I would have said getting Mum and Dad in the same room would be harder to achieve than an Ann Widdecombe/Kim Kardashian girls' night on the town, but now look at them.'

'Rather not.'

Maisie persevered. 'In theory though, if I could gather everyone together, would you come?' She dug out a pleady face, one she had occasionally employed as a child when asking her dad for a tongue-staining cup of blue raspberry Slush Puppie – something her mum point-blank refused to buy her.

Zoe shrugged.

'Thanks, sis,' said Maisie, giving her sister a squeezy, but slightly awkward hug as Zoe's arms hung limply by her sides, refusing to let the energy drink go.

'Lisa better behave ...' Zoe warned. 'Or I'm ramming this right up her—'

'She will, I promise. And anyway, it's only an idea at the moment. But you, me, Mum and Dad – that's a start.'

Zoe grabbed the dumbbells and began pumping her arms up and down with renewed vigour.

'Start of what though?' she said, looking uneasy.

Chapter 26

'Hi, Mum.' Maisie skipped through the back door, which was always left unlocked if her mum was home. They were a back-door kind of family. It was only the vicar and meter readers who used the front door.

She hung her damp quilted jacket on the coat hooks in the utility and walked towards the living room, recognising a familiar voice, and her heart soared.

Oliver stood up as she entered. His good manners had earned him a whole heap of potential son-in-law points when her mum had first met him all those years ago. Some of the men Lisa had brought home over the years had been ... less well-mannered. But then compared to Ben, even a postbox was sociable.

'Maisie! Always good to see you.' Taller than her by well over a foot, and very broad across the shoulders, Oliver gave her the most bone-crushing embrace, and then ruffled her hair as he stepped back. Maisie slumped as he let go, her ribcage and lungs recovering from the hug, and tried not to mind about the ruffling. She'd only been eleven when he started dating Zoe, so always felt like a schoolgirl in his eyes. She adored him then, secretly hoping she would one day have an Oliver of her own, and adored him still.

'He's popped around to reassure me that the divorce won't be the end of everything,' said her mum. 'I got overly emotional the other day but then we've known him fifteen years. He's practically my second son.'

Crikey – had she really known this hulk of a man for over half her life? As for the second son thing, there were times she'd have gladly swapped her brother for Oliver. Although, with hindsight, she felt for Ben, realising he'd been outnumbered by hormonal women for most of his childhood. Their father worked long hours and her brother had often been the only male in the household, drowning under an unstoppable tide of pink and mindless chatter. No wonder his music was so alpha male and macho-sounding. The band's first hit, 'Suffocation', always made her feel guilty as she'd long suspected he'd written the lyrics, wholeheartedly embracing the phrase 'write what you know'.

'It's an amicable separation so I can't see any reason I'd lose touch with you all,' Oliver said. 'No big dramas, I guess we've both changed in subtle ways since we were sixteen, and being together in a foreign country, with only each other to rely on, we simply realised we had nothing in common any more.' Zoe had said much the same.

He waited for Maisie to take a seat and then sat back opposite them both.

'Zoe gets the Norwich flat – glad we kept it now – and she'll buy me out. I felt sorry for the tenants, but they had several months' notice ...'

'Oh, you knew months ago then?' Her mum huffed, pulling up her shoulders ready for an outpouring of emotion. Oliver coloured, realising his error a fraction too late.

'Zoe didn't want to worry you but we've been thinking about it for a long time. I think she missed her mother too much.' Maisie's mum slumped slightly at Oliver's attempt to appease and Maisie was pleased her sister's need for family was as deeply embedded as her own. 'We wanted to sort everything before we made any big announcement. So I'm shortly to be homeless and furniture-less, and flat-hunting as we speak.'

'That's heartless of our Zoe,' said her mum. 'Chucking you out.'

'She isn't – not really. I need to be further south for my new job and it's a long commute. Fingers crossed I might even have found somewhere. I'm going back for another look tomorrow.'

'A couple of trips across to IKEA will soon have you sorted,' her mum offered helpfully, piling more Hobnobs onto his plate, despite his shake of the head.

Oliver groaned. 'Oh God, I'd rather eat my own internal organs. No offence, Bev, but visiting the store is a trauma in itself. I'm not even one of those compliant husbands pacified by the meatballs. And then there's the queues, getting it all in the car, the assembling ... I have many strengths, but DIY isn't one of them.' Oliver was indeed less practical than a Frank Spencer/Chuckle Brothers combo. He could work out a household budget spreadsheet in the blink of an eye but glossing a skirting board – not so much. Zoe always said he was so perfect in every other way, she could forgive him this one deficiency.

'Or,' said Maisie, realising there was an alternative for her impractical brother-in-law, 'you could come to the auction and pick up some cheap bits and pieces. We often have decent second-hand furniture come in. If you're not in a hurry and don't mind pre-loved, I'm sure you can accumulate enough to furnish a flat over a few weeks. We get in all sorts – from washing machines to bunk beds.'

Oliver put his spade-like hand to his dimpled chin. 'Hmm ... might take you up on that. Although, despite entering singledom again, I'm not sure how bunk beds would go down with any future lady friends, Titch.' He picked up a Hobnob but put it down again.

Urgh, that nickname proved he definitely still thought of her as about eleven.

'Dare I ask how David is doing?' he said, turning to her mother and moving the conversation on. 'Zoe was pleased to hear you were on speaking terms again.' Maisie would bet Nigel's favourite bag of sweetcorn nibbles those weren't Zoe's exact words. It annoyed her slightly – almost as if Zoe wanted any reconciliation to fail.

'It's time I let all that go,' her mum replied. 'I held on to the bitterness for too long, but he really broke my heart. I can't begin to tell you how much I loved that man. I could barely even look at him in the early days without wanting to rip off his clothes with my teeth and pin him naked to the floor.' Maisie winced at the graphic image. 'He'll always be my one true love. I would have scaled the Empire State Building for him – blindfolded. Life has a funny way of taking you full circle,' she pondered.

'And Lisa? Is she still ... unsettled?'

Maisie glanced over to her mother. It was nice of Oliver to ask after Lisa but she'd caused him endless trouble in the past, flirting with him from the very first day Zoe had dragged him through the front door. (Despite moving out, Lisa had often crashed at the Tattlesham flat when its proximity to town suited her needs.) Her actions were not enough for Zoe to slap her but enough to make people feel uncomfortable – asking him to zip up her minuscule dresses, wandering around the flat in a bath towel, that sort of thing.

'She's still at that big television studio outside York. You know? The one that makes the gritty detective series and that rural vet thing. Not quite sure what she does, it's all very technical, but she's worked her way up,' her mum said, positively glowing. 'Made quite a success of her media career, by all accounts. Certainly too busy to come home and visit us but if you were ever up that way, I'm sure she'd love to see you.'

'Erm, yeah, maybe,' said Oliver noncommittally, curling his top lip.

'You never stop worrying about them though,' her mum conceded. 'I always said to David she was too pretty for her own good. She never had to try, that was her problem. Her dad spoiled her rotten from the off. All she had to do was look at him with her saucer-sized crystal-blue eyes, twirl a strand of golden hair around her little finger, and he'd mortgage the moon for her. And it was the same at school. She didn't have to work at being popular – she just was. Scraped through academically and lived off her looks ever since. Heaven knows what will happen when they desert her. Poor baby.'

'I'm pleased she's come good,' Oliver said. 'She drifted for a while there.' He turned to Maisie. 'And I'll take you up on that offer. I've never been to an auction before so it will be an experience.'

'Great, and if you behave I might even make you a cup of coffee. Google Gildersleeve's and see what lots are coming up this week – we're *so* all over the internet, it's unreal. I understand they have a breathtakingly talented marketing whiz working for them who has quite revolutionised the company.' She gave a Colgate smile. 'We'll be giving Sotheby's a run for their money before the year is out.'

172

Chapter 27

Maisie's head was in such a spin that if anything else nudged into her tiny brain, it would lift from her shoulders like a helicopter. She had some serious thinking to do with regard to Theo. The attraction she felt was undeniable despite the fact, on paper, he was everything she wanted to shake by the scruffy shoulders. She had to face it, her previous methods for selecting romantic partners (largely relying on commonalities) had met with disaster. Most of her relationships had been short-lived and unfulfilling. Sometimes because the man concerned hadn't lived up to her expectations and sometimes because she hadn't lived up to his. Perhaps she should ski off piste and embrace this antithesis of herself.

Adding to her muddle-headedness, Verity's tea set (it would always be Meredith's teapot, but the sisters were adamant the set was Verity's) was pulling her family back to her – the evidence was almost irrefutable. Perhaps Zoe's Skype call coinciding with her purchase of Irene's cups could be considered a coincidence, but her parents' unnerving truce after her visit to Essie was fate – and the tea set was the master. Who would be next?

As visitors began to arrive for the afternoon viewing, she wandered outside to find Arthur posing for selfies with several people in The Yard. He never had any trouble finding someone to talk to, even if the people concerned didn't particularly want to talk, but there he was in the middle of a swarm of buyers jostling to get near him. He stood by a collection of mushroom-shaped objects that were the draw for this week's sale. Wandering towards the buzzing little group, Maisie noticed he was sporting a Harris tweed flat cap. He saw her approaching and doffed it.

'A good morning to you, miss,' he said. And then conspiratorially, as she got closer, 'Seeing as they loved the sou'wester, I rootled around for something else to woo the crowds.' He turned his attention back to the customers. 'And these would make splendid garden ornaments,' he said, to murmurs of agreement. 'Staddle stones,' he said, stressing the 'T'. 'I remember seeing them supporting haystacks out in the fields when I was a young boy. Them mushroom caps stops vermin from climbing up, you see?'

It was another light-bulb moment for Maisie and it was wonderful. Arthur understood. Why hadn't she seen it before? He was basically the auction house tour guide and she realised this skill could be channelled to great advantage.

She wandered over to the salerooms, excited to see a buzz of people viewing the Modern Design Sale. The online catalogue had attracted a good deal of interest and they already had some sizeable bids on the books.

Theo had been off site most of the day but she was determined to work out whether there was any attraction on his part. Thinking back over the last few months, she was sure there'd been some tingly moments before her stupid misconception had been corrected but she needed to be certain. Then again, he was like that with everyone. Ella was a prime example – unless there was more to that relationship than met her jealous eyes. She certainly couldn't blame him if he was attracted to her slender, ethereal beauty.

She caught sight of him across the barn and he caught her eye and broke into one of those asymmetrical smiles. Yes – there was *something* in that look. She was certain of it. Her peripheral vision blurred and all she could see was the green of his eyes as they held hers for a fraction too long.

'Maisie.' Oliver's booming voice broke her from the trance-like state. 'What a phenomenal place. Can't believe I've not visited before. All sorts of things you never knew you wanted and a blast from the past everywhere you look. Simply fabulous.'

'Oliver, you came.' She walked over to her enormous brother-in-law and threw her arms around him as he bent forward to kiss her head – it was easier than trying to negotiate a friendly peck on the cheek with their twelve-inch height difference.

'Look at you, all grown-up and official.' He nodded to the clipboard she was holding.

'I've been grown-up and official for years. You just haven't noticed.'

'Fair point. You'll always be eleven to me though,' and this time he really did pat her on the head. 'Making me play with your Sylvanian Hazelnut squirrels and Cottonbud bunnies.'

'You were just trying to impress Zoe by humouring her little sister. There was no real dedication,' she teased. 'You were forever posting them down the chimney or using the pram as a race car. You couldn't even remember their names – as you've just proved.' Cottonbud bunnies indeed, she had to bite her lip from correcting him, especially as eleven was probably a bit old to still be obsessed by the Cottontail Rabbit family.

'Bet you've still got them somewhere? All neatly tucked away in a carefully labelled box in an old wardrobe?' She blushed. 'Ha-ha. Knew it.'

'They're very collectable,' she said, putting her right hand on her hip and clutching the clipboard closer to her chest with the other.

'Only messing with you. Right, let's see what you've got to help turn my poky two-bedroom flat into a salubrious residence fit for a footloose and fancy-free bachelor.'

'Goodness, you're keen to get back on the dating horse. You've only been separated for two weeks ...'

Oliver scrunched up his nose but didn't say anything. She knew that expression of old. It was the one he wore when Zoe asked who'd been at the biscuit tin, or why there were wet towels across the bed.

'Ah, longer?'

'We've not been a couple – if you know what I mean – for over a year.'

'You don't need to explain anything to me. It's no one else's business.' And she looped her arm through his as she embarked on a tour of the Gildersleeve's empire.

They wandered together up and down the aisles, Oliver noting various lot numbers in a tiny pocket-sized notebook he produced from his jacket pocket. She wouldn't be surprised if there was a calculator in there too – accountants were notoriously organised people.

'I picked up a new bed and fridge yesterday as they're pretty essential. And the dining table came from my parents, but I'd like to get a sofa and some storage. My clothes are still in packing boxes.'

'There's a nice pine chest of drawers over the other side and it won't go for much,' Maisie suggested, so they ambled across the barn, stopping to look at the things that caught Oliver's eye as they went. Eventually he had a list of items he wanted to bid on and Maisie took him into the reception to help him sort a bidder's number.

'Anywhere on site we can grab a coffee?' he asked.

'Hopefully soon. The builders have started on the footings for the café and once the building is up it won't take long to get it running. Johnny's all for making viewing the auction an experience. The longer you hang around, the more you see.'

'I'm sure he's right.' Oliver glanced at his watch. 'I want to have another quick look at the bookcase I noticed on the way out – as long as I'm not holding you up?'

'Not at all. It's good to have staff wandering around chatting to the public on viewing days. Anything we can do to add to the personal touch.'

They walked back across the forecourt and she looped her arm into Oliver's again. She'd really missed him these past two years. He'd been in her life a long time and they'd never had so much as a cross word. The times he'd snuck her a bag of sweets to make herself scarce when he wanted some alone time with Zoe in the girls' shared bedroom. And the occasions Oliver had stood up for her when Lisa had been on the warpath. It was a solid friendship and one she hoped wouldn't be affected by his move.

As they re-entered the barn, she noticed Theo lurking at the back, throwing glances their way. She would make a point of going over and speaking to him as soon as she'd finished with Oliver.

'I don't know why you want a bookcase. I don't remember

you being a big reader – I thought numbers were more your thing.'

'I'll be back in the dating game at some point so I'm planning ahead. I'm thinking of getting some classics in to impress.' He pulled his cuffs down and tried to raise a James Bond eyebrow, but it didn't quite work.

She gave him a friendly thump and he caught her arm. With his spade-like hands holding her tiny wrists, she wriggled and squealed as she tried to break free.

'You rotter,' she said, the biggest grin across her face.

'You never could beat me in a fight but I still think the world of you, Titch. The divorce won't change that – promise. Right, I'll put these written bids on and then I'd better get back and give Zoe a ring. Is it sad we still chat every day?'

'Nah, it's great. Everyone needs an Oliver in their lives. Agree with Zoe though, being married to one might be a stretch too far. You can't even change a light bulb.'

'My skills lie in other areas; household budgeting and selecting the best wines in a given price range. There must be someone out there who appreciates that?'

Her heart broke a tiny bit and she stood on tiptoe and kissed his cheek. 'I hope you find someone soon. You deserve to.' She gazed at him fondly and he reciprocated.

'I'm in no hurry. Enjoying the lie-ins without a ball of energy zipping around the bedroom telling me the best of the day has gone. I'll always be fond of Zoe though.'

Oliver walked back to reception and Maisie made her way across to Theo. The warmer weather meant he was hatless and she was almost sad to see the assortment of weird knitted headgear consigned to the cupboard until the autumn. They were part of his charm.

He was leaning against the wall watching her intently as she approached. Was it her imagination, or was there a waft of Old Spice floating across the gap between them? It was a bit retro and one her dad had favoured years ago, but whatever it was, it made her feel slightly giddy.

'Friend of yours?' he asked, his eyes dropping at the last moment to the floor.

'Who? Oh, Oliver? He's much more than that,' she said. Oliver was practically the fifth Meadows sibling.

'Yeah, I could tell,' Theo muttered. Oh dear, had she been larking about too much with her brother-in-law? Theo looked cross – no, he didn't do cross. Disappointed? She'd try to behave less flirtatiously in the future, especially as Oliver was the last person on the planet she would ever flirt with. It was part of the unspoken code; you don't mess with your sister's man, even when he's no longer her man.

All this small talk was by the by. She'd walked over to ascertain if there was any romantic potential between them.

'I, erm, wondered if you'd like to come to mine one day for dinner? I do a mean risotto. And there are some curious marks on that tea set of Meredith's that I'd like your opinion on.' She was skirting around the issue but could hardly come straight out and ask, 'Do you fancy me or not?'. It was the dance of the dating game – like two birds of paradise hopping around in circles on the forest floor.

'As friends?' he qualified, looking up.

'Yeah, erm, as friends.'

'Right, that's what I thought. That would be good. Any day works for me except Friday when Ella is coming over. Just let me know.'

Maisie's heart stopped. Ella? Since when were they hanging

out? That niggling suspicion lurking in her brain was right. Now she understood why he'd so carefully specified friends.

'Oh, okay, I'll get back to you,' she said.

Waiting for further comment, which didn't come, she fiddled with her pen. Theo appeared engrossed in something on the other side of the barn, so she pretended to jot something vitally important on the clipboard and wandered back to the main door.

That was her answer then; there was no chance of romance. But wasn't that what she'd wanted from this job back in January?

Chapter 28

'Hello, I've been given this number by your great-aunt Esther and understand you're Phyllis's grandson?' Maisie hoped she'd dialled correctly because Essie's ones and sevens were really ambiguous.

'If you're trying to get hold of her, you'll need a medium ...' The voice on the end of the line seemed disinterested and bored. ''Cause the old bird died two years ago.'

'I heard and I'm *so* sorry.' She cleared her throat. 'This might sound odd but I'm trying to track down some plates of hers. It's rather a long shot but your great-aunt Esther said you'd inherited all her possessions.' In fact it was such a long shot, she'd need telescopic binoculars to focus on the target.

'Yeah, I got her stuff. Most of it's long gone but she left everything to me because I was her favourite, see? Backfired a bit though. Don't get me wrong, I was fond of the old girl – but she thought I actually liked all the books 'n' shit. There are some boxes of tat left. Been in the garage for far too long: ornaments, kitchen stuff and clothes.'

Hmm ... possibly not sentimental about a few black and white plates then. Trying to rein in her excitement, she took a measured breath.

'I have some pieces of a tea set that belonged to her sisters.

It's a hip-hop black and white Eighties set,' she said, going with Johnny's description, rather than admitting it was older than it should be. 'I thought I'd try to make the set whole again, if the plates were still lurking about.'

There was a loud snort down the line.

'I would pay you for them, naturally ...'

He hesitated. 'Not sure I can be bothered, to be honest, but you can have a look if you want.' He gave her his address and they arranged to meet later in the week.

That Friday evening Maisie drove up to Norfolk to investigate Phyllis's plates.

Her satnav guided her into a modern housing estate on the outskirts of Norwich and, as she pulled up in front of a row of Georgian-style new-builds, the lilting Irish voice gleefully announced she'd arrived at her destination. The symmetry and uniformity of that architectural period appealed to her. The house had a large central front door, a glazed fanlight above and matching long windows either side of two faux-Grecian columns. She pressed the plastic bell and the door swung open to an indifferent face.

'Hi. We spoke on the phone.' She stuck out her hand, which was studiously ignored.

'Right – the woman nosying about Granny's stuff.' The wiry man stepped outside and pulled the front door closed behind him, his black hair matching his black eyes.

'I don't want to pressure you in any way. But if they are still around and you don't want them, I'll gladly compensate you.'

'So ... worth much, are they?' He took a cigarette from a pack in his polo shirt breast pocket, tapped the end on the back of his hand and lit it.

'Not especially. It's probably not even that old and it's not fine bone china or anything. I've been assured the set as a whole would only be worth about twenty pounds.'

'But it's worth something to you, right?' His top lip curled slightly, as if he had a smirk itching to get out, and his eyes narrowed. He took another drag on the cigarette and blew it out excruciatingly slowly, watching the smoke curl and dissipate before him.

'I wanted the set to remind me of your great-aunt Meredith. I knew her when I was little but it doesn't matter if I can't find all the pieces.' She was lying. It mattered more than anything. And if this overtly suspicious man withheld the plates from her, especially if he didn't even like them, it would be beyond frustrating.

'I'd say a fancy lady like you, spending all that time tracking down a bunch of old women from years ago, and taking the time to contact their family in the hopes they've got a few poncy bits if china – I'd say it matters *a lot*.'

Maisie shrugged. 'I'm happy to give you something for them, I said that from the beginning, but we don't even know if you still have them. Equally, if you don't want to sell, that's fine. They are heirlooms, things to remember your granny by, and you absolutely can't put a price on that.' There was something about this man she didn't trust and she wasn't interested in playing his silly games. She made to turn back to the car.

'Fifty,' he said.

'Fifty what?'

'Pounds. For the plates.' He dropped the butt and ground it into the gravel of the driveway with his heel.

'Fifty pounds for three plates? I'm sorry but that's absolutely ridiculous.'

'There ain't three – there's a big one an' all. Like a dinner plate with ears.' So he did have them. She felt excited and angry all at once.

'A cake plate?'

'Yeah. One of them. So, it's fifty.' Maisie shook her head – his price was too high – and turned to the car for a second time. 'Wait. You ain't even looked at them yet. Let me show you.' He rummaged in his trouser pockets for a bunch of keys and walked to the up-and-over garage door, unlocked it, and stood back as it disappeared into the roof. Inside, it was like a scene from Storage Hunters; packed full of cardboard boxes but the contents a total mystery.

'All her bloody crap. Been there for nearly two sodding years. The missus said she were going to boot fair the last of it, might as well get all the cash we can, but it's still sitting here. Now, which box was it?' he muttered to himself, as he began to pull open flaps and peer inside.

Maisie could have told him. She could have walked straight over to the left-hand side of the garage and pointed. The prickling was back and it was intense. Instead, she waited patiently as he worked his way down the row until he stumbled on the plates.

'There. Look. No chips or nothing. Lovely pattern – all squiggles and stuff. Look great with anything. And here's the big one – just like I said. Gotta be worth it, especially if you've got the other cups 'n' stuff?'

Maisie didn't have money for non-essentials, especially since the salary drop working for Gildersleeve's and her acquisition of a dubious collection of garden ornaments, but she was torn. He didn't want his granny's belongings. They meant nothing to him. She might as well have left them to a charity. But he was trying to extort an unreasonable amount of money from her for something he realised she was interested in.

On the other hand, if she walked away, that was it. She couldn't reunite the set. There was no doubt he'd sell it just to spite her. And it was about so much more now. It was calling to her and she couldn't let it down.

'Twenty?' she offered. She wasn't so green she'd pay his initial asking price. He looked at her, his slitty little dark eyes weighing her up again.

'Fifty. And you can take the whole box. Take it or leave it.' Perhaps she'd made a mistake by haggling. It indicated she was keen. 'It's a now-or-never offer. I'll get our missus to shift 'em next week. 'Bout time we got shot of it all anyway.'

'Twenty-five?' she squeaked. Why was she even bothering? He'd worked out she wanted them now.

'Fifty-five. The price just went up.' His lip curled again and he picked up the plates and held them at waist height in front of him.

'You can't do that. That's not fair.'

'I can do what I like, lady. In fact, I can go all Spanish and start chucking them at the goddamn garage wall if I feel like it.' Correcting his cultural reference would not endear her to him, so she said nothing. 'Well?' he said, lifting them and pulling his arm back as if he was about to launch them at the brickwork.

'Okay, fifty but there's no way I'm letting you put the price up. That's just mean.' Her eyes fell to the floor. 'They really aren't worth that much,' she whispered. 'I just like them.'

'Yeah, the wife is the same about handbags. She can put this towards another one now. I'll treat her. Right, get your banking app up and I'll tell you my account number.'

Maisie transferred the money, wondering how much his wife's handbags cost if fifty was just a proportion, then she picked up the plates from where he'd put them down to sort the money.

'Oi, hold on, missus. You've gotta take the whole box. That was the deal.'

'I really don't want—'

'Take the damn box.' His voice was loud and intimidating. 'I want my garage back. Even if I have to do it one box at a sodding time.'

Maisie stood back from the small circular dining room table in the corner of her living room and smiled. Arranged in trios, with the cake plate and teapot in the middle of the table, the tea set looked stunning. As soon as she'd returned from the grasping grandson she was desperate to see the pieces together and discovered the tea plates all had little symbols on the bottom as well, tallying up with three of the cups and saucers.

It was lovely, she thought, that Verity's set was being reunited alongside her efforts to get her own family back together. If she could achieve both, it would truly be a year for reunifying.

Nigel was trying to squeeze his fluffy pompom of a body up the tube that led to his sleeping level but because he had a cucumber baton in his mouth, he was considerably wider than the tube. The doorbell went and he turned to look at Maisie.

'No idea.' Maisie shrugged at Nigel and skipped out to the hall.

As the door swung inwards, Maisie was greeted by a slender, elegant and slightly older version of herself – but then what's a decade between sisters?

'Aren't you going to ask me in?' Lisa asked.

Chapter 29

Maisie's eyes dropped to the collection of bags at her sister's feet. This wasn't a flying visit. Her scattered family members really were catapulting themselves back into her life at an alarming rate.

'Chillax, sweetie. I just want a decent bed for a couple of nights – preferably memory foam but sprung at a push. York is so hectic and I need some time out to reconnect with myself. I haven't eaten so whatever you've got in will be fine but I'm gluten-free now.'

Lisa squeezed past her sister, planting a huge kiss on her cheek as she did so, and disappeared into the house, leaving her luggage on the doorstep.

'Come in, why don't you?' Maisie said to the empty hallway as she bent down to gather her sister's belongings, only to hear a shrill scream as Lisa scurried back into the hall moments later.

'You've got a mouse in there.'

'A hamster.'

'Get rid of it.'

'No.' Maisie's voice went up an incredulous octave and they stood looking at each other like some sort of Mexican stand-off.

'You know I'm scared of rodenty hairy things with tails.'

'Nigel doesn't have a tail.'

'Nigel?' If Lisa was the sort of person prone to humour, she might have accompanied that with an incredulous laugh. Instead she snorted. 'I'm not going back in there until he's gone. Put him in the garden or something. He might get out and—'

'And what?' Maisie laughed. 'Savage you with his teeny-tiny teeth or pin you to the floor under his microscopic two-hundred-gram frame? *You* sit in the garden.'

Lisa huffed. 'Can you at least move him somewhere I don't have to look at him?'

'How about you face the other way so Nigel doesn't have to look at your sour, pouty face?' It wasn't something she would have dared say to Lisa when she was little but she felt braver on her own turf.

Realising her baby sister wasn't going to bend to her will, Lisa stomped back into the living room. Although Maisie was delighted to have another family member close, albeit temporarily, she drew the line at evicting Nigel – this was his home, after all.

'How are things?' Maisie asked a few minutes later as she cracked open a bottle of chilled Chardonnay she kept in the fridge for emergencies. The unexpected arrival of Lisa, with her innate ability to turn her ordered life upside down, definitely qualified. Maisie took one look at the abandoned shoes, the jacket slung across the back of the sofa and the trail of charger leads and clothes from her sister's luggage, and hastily downed her first glass.

'Good. Honestly – good.' Lisa was shoulders back and chin defiant, but Maisie gave her a penetrating look. Lisa was not the sort of person who dropped in on family with no notice if things were 'good'.

'I wanted to get away for a bit, that's all. Got someone bothering me. Needed some air.'

She avoided eye contact, stared intently at her lap and then promptly burst into tears. Maisie looked across at her sister, open-mouthed. The thing about Lisa was, however dramatic her actions, it was always a strong, angry, totally indignant drama, not a vulnerable, pity-me drama. Maisie sidled closer and placed a comforting hand on her sister's shoulder.

'You can always get help. Talk to the police if it's harassment?'

The hand was immediately shrugged off.

'I'm perfectly capable of sorting my own life out. It's just a friend who wants more than I'm prepared to give – honestly, you go on a couple of dates and blokes think you owe them the moon. Not sure where the tears came from. Guess I'm overtired. It's been a long drive.' Lisa carefully wiped under her eyes with her beautifully manicured index fingers so as not to smudge her perfect make-up. She gave a fortifying sniff and tilted the defiant chin back up.

There was so much about Lisa's life Maisie didn't know. The impersonal was posted on social media for all to see but the things that really made her sister tick were not discussed and never had been. Perhaps some quality time with Lisa would bring them closer. The ten-year age gap meant Lisa had left home by the time Maisie was nine – so desperate to escape Hickory Street that she'd moved in with a biker boy she'd met online. Mum was traumatised and rung her about four times a day to check she hadn't been raped and murdered by this mysterious man but the relationship hadn't lasted long. He was merely the springboard into the unsettled and hedonistic life that Lisa had led for the last fifteen years.

'For goodness' sake, stop looking at me with those anxious

eyes,' Lisa muttered. 'It's like having Mum here. I'm totally fine. PMT and two hours' sleep would even break Genghis Khan.' And the old Lisa was back in the room.

Great, so her sister was bossy, premenstrual *and* overtired. Maisie picked up the bottle and refilled her glass.

'So, you're here for the weekend? Or longer?' Maisie tried to plan life around her unexpected guest. Theo was coming over Saturday night to look at the tea set and she didn't want the glamorous Lisa wafting about in the background, half-dressed and fresh out of the shower, when he did.

'Maybe a few days or so but I won't get in your way. I know you've got a spare room so I can tuck myself out of the way.'

'I'm afraid it's out of bounds. I have, erm … things stored up there.' She didn't want Lisa nosing about and scoffing at her artwork. The room had a key so she would lock it. Her paintings were private and she wanted to keep them that way.

'Can't the things be moved? Honestly, Maisie, that's what a spare room is for – guests.'

'If you'd given me more notice it would be different but there are personal items up there and I've got nowhere else to put them. Stay for a couple of days, by all means, but you'll have to crash on the sofa. Mum's got a guest bed and Zoe's back at her Norwich flat. Share the love?' Maisie knew from previous experience, Lisa's idea of not getting in the way was sprawling across the living room furniture expecting everything to be brought to her.

'Oh, come on. You know Mum fusses and completely over-reacts? And Zoe and I have never got on.' And then Lisa shifted to flattery. 'I need to be with someone who's not going to get on at me, who is kind and understanding, and who can give me some space to recharge …'

And Maisie realised her big sister was moving in with her for a while, whether she liked it or not. And knowing Lisa, that 'while' was unlikely to be as brief as a few days.

Maisie began to prepare for Theo's visit. Lisa's clutter was returned to her overnight bags and stood at the foot of Maisie's bed but it would doubtless be scattered across her living room again by the end of the following day. Then she paid her sister to be elsewhere – Lisa complaining she was short of funds as there had been some mix-up at the bank. Clutching two twenty-pound notes, Lisa decided to head to Norwich to clear her head and why didn't Maisie join her?

'Because I've got my boss coming round.'

'Yeah – this evening. It's lunchtime. Come and catch a matinee with me?'

'Films are more your thing than mine.' Maisie found it impossible to sit still for that long. If she had two hours to kill, she knew where she'd rather be – and it was a solitary activity. 'I need to tidy up.'

'You are joking? This bloody house is immaculate. Always was your problem, Maisie, too obsessed with the irrelevant minutiae of life to get out there and live. Honestly, you're so tightly coiled that if anyone springs your release catch you're going to ping over the moon.'

It wasn't fair; she was organised, not uptight.

'Have you even got back out on the dating scene? It doesn't do to dwell.' Lisa peered into the large white-framed mirror above the mantelpiece and applied a generous layer of strawberry-red lipstick, blotting her lips together and then winking at her reflection.

'I don't need a man to be complete,' said Maisie.

'No, but you need to get laid to feel alive. There must be someone who gets your heart racing?'

Maisie couldn't stop her face colouring up and she focused intently on rug tassel-alignment and didn't comment.

After Lisa had left, Maisie continued to restore order to her tiny terrace. Nigel followed her around in his plastic ball, always curious to oversee the domestic chores. She let him clatter over thresholds and bump into furniture as she carefully carried the tea set through to her tiny circular dining table in the far corner, ready for Theo's knowledgeable pronouncements. Finally, with a few minutes to spare, she returned the hoover to the understairs cupboard, only to be greeted by two open halves of plastic ball in the hallway, and not a stumpy hamster tail in sight.

As she scrabbled around on all fours, desperately trying to locate her tennis ball-sized companion, the doorbell went. It was Theo. 'Quick. Come in. I need to close the door,' she gabbled. 'Nigel's gone missing.'

'Nigel?'

'I know.' She rolled her eyes. 'It's an old-fashioned man's name but I didn't name him and those older-generation names are in at the moment; one of my old schoolfriends called her son Wilberforce. I've looked everywhere – in the cupboard under the stairs, behind the sofa, at the back of the television cabinet ...'

'Those are some pretty tight spaces. How old is Nigel?'

'About eighteen months.'

'Okay,' he said, tossing his jacket towards the bannister rail. It slid down the final foot, but failed to stop at the newel posts and tumbled to the floor. 'Any chance he could have got outside? Near the road?'

'Possible but highly unlikely. It's hardly like he's tall enough to reach the door handle,' she said, eyeing the creased pile of jacket but not making a fuss. Nigel was more important.

'Where did you see him last?'

'He was following me around as I hoovered, and I was half chatting to him about my day, but when I came back to the hall I found his ball and he was nowhere to be seen.'

Theo frowned and scratched his bouncy hair. 'Okay, okay, don't worry, we'll find him.' He put a comforting hand on her shoulder and an involuntary ripple made her quiver. 'He'll have to come out eventually, even if it's just to use the loo or because he's hungry.'

'Knowing him, he'll wee on the carpet ... more mess for me to clear up.'

He gave a half-smile. 'And you don't do mess, do you?' They were by the living room door now and he glanced into the room. 'No wonder you keep huffing at the state of my desk. Do you actually live here? Or just levitate above the furniture?'

He ducked into the room and began peering behind the sofa and opening cupboard doors, calling Nigel's name and working around the room in a methodical fashion.

'I'll carry on down here and you look upstairs – I'd feel uncomfortable being in a lady's bedroom – and we'll meet in the middle?' he called over his shoulder.

'Okay,' she said, and scampered up the stairs. Could Nigel really have climbed them? But then she'd seen him scale the side of the sofa before, his little claws digging into the fabric as he heaved his fluffy, bulbous body upwards.

She gave her bedroom a thorough search and then closed the door when she was satisfied he wasn't in there. Theo bounded up the stairs.

'He's not in my bedroom,' she said. 'I'll try the bathroom.'

'How about in here?' Theo said, going for the handle of the spare room.

'He won't be in there. It's locked.'

'Oh yeah – got a secret you don't want anyone to know about?' There was a mischievous look in his eyes and a curl of the lip.

'Something like that.' She couldn't prevent a flush of red creeping across her cheeks.

'Don't tell me you've got a kinky Christian Grey red room?' he teased. 'Somewhere you can control things other than your pencils?' Deliberately not answering, she went into the bathroom and got down on all fours to peer behind the basin pedestal and heard the familiar scratching of claws. Nigel was casting his knowledgeable eye over the pipework.

'I've found him,' she called to Theo, who was still staring at her locked spare bedroom door, clearly itching to know what lay behind it. There was nothing more intriguing than an unanswered question.

'Thank goodness. Where is he?'

She opened her hands to reveal a cradled Nigel, bright eyes like jet beads and, unusually for her immaculate house, cobwebs hanging from his whiskers.

'He's a hamster?' Theo looked horrified. 'I thought we were looking for a child!'

Chapter 30

Nigel was so exhausted by his impromptu expedition that he trundled into his tiny plastic house for a sleep whilst Theo examined the tea set.

'Love the pattern,' he said, turning a cup around in his hands. 'I'm all for the asymmetrical, and challenging traditional design. I agree with Johnny – quirky but not old. I would guess at Eighties as well. The little symbol is curious. Not a factory mark or artist's monogram because each one is different.' He turned the cups and saucers over and started to match the symbols. All the cups had a matching saucer and the tea plates matched three of those.

'Are they numbers?' Maisie said.

'I think it's the Theban alphabet – you might know it as the witches' alphabet? I recognise the little m shapes because we've had jewellery pass through our hands with these symbols on before.'

'Witches' alphabet? You are winding me up?'

'Someone's little joke, for sure. Wiccan symbols on a hip-hop design tea set, in a low-grade china that no one can trace. Something a modern potter knocked up when they were bored – a total mishmash of nonsense.'

'But it's over a hundred years old,' Maisie insisted.

'Nah. Eighties – maybe Seventies.'

'This set is pre-World War One. Irene, Meredith *and* Essie all said so.'

Theo pulled his phone from his trouser pocket and with a lazy flick of his thumb he called up the Wiccan alphabet. His eye flicked between the black marks and his screen. 'It's just random letters that don't make any sense,' he said. 'Collectable for curiosity value though. I'll see what else I can find out. So ...' He flopped onto her sofa, dislodging her perfectly positioned cushions. Leaning back and lazily crossing one leg over the other, he asked, 'What's really going on in that spare room of yours?'

'Never you mind,' she said. 'Let me pour you a drink whilst I start the food.'

There was now quite a lot of alcohol in the house. Lisa had persuaded her to add several bottles to the weekly shop, saying they could bond over a drink or two. They'd be cemented together if she wasn't careful.

'The Modern Design Sale was a great success,' she said, deftly changing the subject. 'I noticed the Mdina glass vase sold for two hundred – beautiful aquamarine blues and earthy browns swirling around in a bubble of clear glass – very reminiscent of the ocean.' She handed him a glass of red.

'Ella grew up by the sea and she said the same. Her tiny flat is an homage to the coast. Out of her price range though,' Theo said, as Maisie tried not to mind that he'd been socialising with her elegant colleague outside work.

Maisie had noticed, however, Ella successfully bid for a couple of Nineteen Forties wooden armchairs in the sale, the backs and seats upholstered in awful bobbly grey fabric. Nothing about the chairs had a coastal connection and

Maisie wondered what Ella could possibly want with the ugly old things. If she could only get her colleague to engage in conversation she could ask, but every attempt was met with a panicked look and a mumbled excuse to be somewhere else.

'I think the new series of *Wot a Lot!* airing last week has helped numbers through the door. Several people turned up eager to hunt you down,' she said, pouring herself a small glass.

'Yeah.' Theo shrugged. 'Three ladies asked for selfies. I refused, naturally, but I did sign two Gildersleeve's leaflets and a woman's arm.'

Maisie was irrationally jealous to hear he'd been scribbling all over some lovesick groupie and took an extra big gulp of her extra small wine.

'And it's two gold stars to you now,' Theo said. 'Some of the highest bidders were online. Mind you, some posh woman Johnny knows from Norfolk had her nose put out of joint when the competition pushed up the prices of the vintage fabrics. She's used to getting the curtains for a steal.'

'But the lively atmosphere was down to the locals and specialist dealers you'd contacted ahead of the sale,' she conceded. 'And possibly the breathless groupies.'

They exchanged a smile, happy they could be accepting of each other's point of view.

'A few of the pieces were from Meredith Mayhew's estate,' he said. 'Arthur told me about your connection with the teapot. I held them back for this sale; the Danish teak cabinet and the Ercol dining chairs.'

'Johnny's fusty country-made antiques and twiddly, over-fussy Victoriana are delightful in their own way, but I'm postmodern all the way and enjoy artists and designers who challenge tradition,' she admitted. 'I like the way an abstract can screw with your head in a way that something like a Stubbs never could. He painted a horse and it looked like a horse – there's no room for any other interpretation.'

'Really? I didn't have you pegged as that sort of girl at all. You seem too ordered and tidy-minded to appreciate a canvas splattered with random dribbles of colour – Johnny's take on modern art, by the way, not mine.'

Maisie gave a smug smile. She liked the thought she wasn't totally readable and could surprise people. It was easy to label a neat freak as boring and she was far from that.

'Meredith showed me a Kandinsky many years ago and it was the first time I'd seen art that didn't look like a recognisable object and it stuck with me – probably even subconsciously influencing my chequerboard kitchen floor. I've really enjoyed learning more about twentieth-century design since working at Gildersleeve's. But then, it's all about context and setting. The simple lines of Meredith's G Plan furniture never struck me before because her house was so cluttered that the objects were lost. Take a few statement pieces and arrange them in a tidy, ordered space and they can really shine.'

'Yeah, I had noticed you were a bit OCD. Can't find a darn thing in the office now you've started fussing around the place.' He smiled to reassure her he was teasing. 'As for some great post-war design – you must come to my house one day – it's crammed full of interesting bits and pieces. I buy things because I love them and then find I don't have anywhere to put them.' He rolled his eyes.

If Theo lived in a cluttered postmodernist house and Johnny, who she knew from snatched conversations, lived in a period thatched cottage in a tiny village on the outskirts of Tattlesham, full of Georgian dark wood country furniture and dripping with Victorian artefacts, then their friendship, as well as their working life, would be all the richer. She could see that now.

'Don't you find it comical,' she continued her musings, 'that Johnny is the one embracing technology when, by rights, he should be listening to a wind-up gramophone and walking about with a Wee Willie Winkie candlestick holder, and you're the one who struggles with it.'

'I'm just wary of it, that's all.'

'You watch too many dystopian conspiracy films,' said Maisie. 'Probably on an eight-millimetre cine film reel.' She was slipping back into the easy relationship she'd had with her boss before her world was nudged by the revelation he wasn't Johnny's boyfriend. And it felt fantastic.

'Actually, I love a good film. I spent a lot, and I mean *a lot*, of time watching TV as a kid. Mum's idea of a babysitter, I guess. I'm currently re-watching my entire Eighties Betamax collection.'

'So why the Eighties? I know it's your favourite era but you weren't born until the end of the decade.'

'I guess because it was when my parents did their living, before they were lumbered with a kid, so I was heavily influenced by the Eighties growing up. I'm all-embracing when it comes to that period – even my house is 1985. A typical half-timber clad box with an integral garage – what's not to love? And it's full of funky furniture in bold primary colours. Can't be doing with this modern trend for shades of grey ...'

'Indeed, at least fifty different shades, I'm reliably informed.'

Theo groaned. 'You know what I mean.'

Maisie wiggled her eyebrows. 'I suspect I do.'

She began the risotto, Theo following her out to the kitchen and leaning against the doorframe as she tossed a large knob of butter in the pan and added a splash of extra virgin.

'We now have nearly a thousand Twitter followers,' she said, as the rice slid into the pan and the creamy smell of melted butter curled around the room. 'And Arthur is going down a storm.'

'Don't push your luck, young lady. Still not convinced about that one. I'm all for fun but let's keep it professional, eh? I have to look out for the old fella. He gets enough stick from Johnny, who between you and me was never happy about his appointment in the first place.'

'Then why on earth did he get the job?' Maisie was confused.

Theo looked down at his feet and let out a long breath, shrugging his shoulders in resignation. 'Because he desperately needed one.'

Maisie frowned, stirring the rice and adding the first ladleful of hot stock. Theo looked up.

'I've lived around the corner from Arthur for a couple of years now. Lovely chap, worked at the foundry all his life. No trouble to anyone and always happy to help shovel snow from a neighbour's drive, or rummage through his shed for the right-sized washer to mend a leaky tap – that kind of thing. He retired not long after I bought the house and I used to stop and chat to him as he pottered about his front garden. He would talk about his life, always cheery and positive, never self-pitying. But I noticed his non-stop chatting could come across as an ambush – especially to those rushing past on their way to work, or busy young mothers with a trillion and one demands on their time.'

Poor Arthur. He was so desperate to make friends but his

need for conversation was such that he often forgot to let the other person contribute.

'I've seen passing neighbours call out a cheery hi and find themselves sucked into a forty-five-minute conversation,' Theo said. 'You've seen him do it at work. It took me a while, but eventually I realised he was pottering out the front on purpose. The flower beds were so over-tended that weeds didn't bother to try. The gardening didn't need tending – the old man did.'

'I don't understand. He's got his wife and his hobbies.'

'But after his retirement, I guess she needed space too. And Arthur is a proud man. His job kept him going, made him feel useful and gave his life a purpose. When that finished he was lost.'

'I agree, he doesn't look for sympathy. He told me they'd had a stillborn but barely paused to acknowledge it,' Maisie said.

'He only mentioned Primrose to me once and that was because he was dead-heading some at the time, but he gabbled on, like with you, and there wasn't an opportunity for me to offer any words of condolence. Their tale had a happy ending, however, because I happen to know Pam spends a lot of time with their surviving daughter.'

Maisie was beginning to understand. Theo had offered Arthur a job, even though Gildersleeve's didn't technically need him. It made her like him even more.

'But don't think for a moment it's a one-way street. He may not be productive in terms of wardrobe lifting or organisation but Arthur has other strengths. When he chats to customers, he remembers what they are looking for and is able to point out items of interest in the sale. He's also quite knowledgeable and either answers their questions or finds someone who can. Gildersleeve's would be lost without him – as would I. He's like a surrogate dad to me.' It was another indirect reference to a family life Theo never elaborated on.

'You really are as lovely as Johnny says you are,' and she gave him the biggest, widest smile, briefly resting her hand on top of his warm fingers. The delicious smells weren't the only thing circling the space between them. There was an invisible mist of pheromones that were equally enticing. Neither of them moved for a moment until the sizzle from the pan reminded her that the meal needed her attention.

Maisie focused on her culinary efforts and within a few minutes Theo was making appreciative noises as he scooped up forkfuls of risotto, the tea set returned to its shelf as they sat at her tiny dining table.

'Do you always eat in here – setting the table with five-star restaurant pretensions? The only thing missing is the fish fork,' he joked.

'That's because there is no fish course.' Her face was inscrutable. She didn't mind him teasing her because there was no edge to his comments, and so she played along, enjoying their gentle teasing. 'Quite frankly, I'm surprised you knew what the napkin was for.'

He broke first, unable to stop a smile creeping out from the edges of his mouth.

'Yeah, well, my childhood was more food on the go. I was one of those kids who appreciated the leak-proof inner of the Coco Pops packet because it meant less washing-up.'

'Seriously? Oh, Theo. You need a good woman to take you in hand.'

'Are you offering?'

And there it was again – the pheromone-thick atmosphere making it hard to focus on anything other than his aftershave and those mesmerising green eyes. There was silence as she contemplated her response. The more she thought about it, the more she was convinced they would be a good fit.

'I'd quite like—'

There was a crash as the front door was flung open and Lisa tumbled into the room. Theo stood up immediately and Maisie didn't get to finish her sentence.

'Sorry to interrupt the shagging but I ran out of money. Settle the taxi for me – there's a doll,' she said to Maisie, before sliding onto the sofa and beaming at Theo. 'It's about time my little sis got back on the horse after that two-timing rat cheated on her. You must be the mysterious bloke she won't talk about.'

Maisie's insides imploded. Lisa wasn't particularly tactful at the best of times, but slightly intoxicated all discretion went out the window.

'Theo is my *boss*,' she emphasised.

'Oh,' Lisa hiccupped, 'so it's someone else you've got your eye on?'

Maisie let her sister's misconception hang there. She'd deal with her feelings for Theo in her own way and in her own time. Perhaps it would keep Theo on his toes if he thought there was competition.

As she pondered this, an angry taxi horn pipped in the distance. Lisa looked expectantly at Maisie, who huffed out to the hall to locate her purse.

Chapter 31

Lisa politely refused Maisie's invitation to join her at Willow Tree House on the Sunday afternoon – she didn't *do* old people apparently, but Maisie knew she was missing out. The residents were always interesting to talk to and many had led fascinating lives. It was all too easy to look at a worn-out body and forget there was still an active mind and vibrancy within. Plus, Naked Man was stalking Irene and their interchanges were highly amusing. His puppy-dog adoration of the sharp-tongued old lady also had an upside for their mother, as she no longer spent half her shift chasing him down. As long as she knew where Irene was, Naked Man was invariably close by.

Lisa chose instead to visit their dad – greatly amused by the mystery reconciliation between her parents. She returned with several bags of shopping, undoubtedly funded by their father, and all of which were promptly scattered across the living room.

Maisie wanted to scream and shout and give her sister a hefty kick up the backside. She sighed as non-matching towels were pulled from her airing cupboard and used with gay abandon. Things weren't returned to their rightful places, and if they were, they were returned carelessly; books in the wrong order (yes, there was an order to where they lived on the shelf), and cutlery thrown in the drawer and not placed in the correct compartments or even the right way up. She grumbled a couple of times to Lisa, who nodded and said 'absolutely' a lot, but still did very little. Ultimately, it was easier to clear up herself.

By the end of the weekend, Maisie's adequate two-bedroomed mid-terrace felt more like a tiny one-man tent, and judging by the state of most of the rooms – a tent at a particularly debaucherous music festival. Returning from the care home she'd also detected a suspiciously festival-like odour drifting from the bathroom and spotted an empty vodka bottle in the rubbish. Her sister clearly felt she was on holiday and was determined to kick back and enjoy herself.

As she sat at her desk that Monday, a million thoughts tumbled around in Maisie's head and were, apparently, equally visible across her face; from the frustration of her scattered family to the worries about her parents' truce, from her concerns about Lisa's real reasons for descending to the turmoil her visit was bringing into Maisie's ordered little life.

'Come on – spill.'

Theo leaned a lazy arm up against the back wall of the office and grinned at Maisie as he ripped open a packet of cheese and onion crisps and started to toss them into his open mouth. She knew she was bringing her grumpy mood to work with her but couldn't help it.

'Spill what?'

'Whatever's got our sunny Maisie all gloomy and intro-spective.'

Maisie shook her head and straightened the papers in front of her so the bottoms were parallel to the edge of the desk.

'We can do it in the abstract if it helps,' he offered. 'You know? "I have this friend whose chaotic sister has descended ..." But you seriously need to offload to someone. You're giving off the vibe of a coiled spring that's been stood on by an elephant.'

He'd been understanding about Lisa's dramatic appearance on Friday night, discreetly excusing himself not long after she'd tumbled into the room. Maisie suspected Lisa's tactile nature, and the silky dress just about clinging on to her body as she pawed at him, had hastened his decision to leave. But then he'd eaten the meal and cast his eye over the tea set, so what reason did he have to stay?

'I'm fine. Honestly.'

Theo studied her face for a while and then shrugged his shoulders as he tipped his head back to pour the crisp crumbs into his open mouth. He screwed up the packet and tossed it onto the corner of his desk. Maisie looked at him, deliberately not focusing on the abandoned litter. A whole five seconds ticked by, Theo clearly trying to process why Maisie was giving him the eyeball, and then, without breaking eye contact, he reached for the packet and bent down to place it in the waste-paper basket she'd optimistically placed under his desk the week before. The tiniest flicker of a smile played with the corner of her mouth.

'That's more like it,' Theo said, sensing a small but significant change in her mood. 'Right, grab your bag, missus. You're coming with me to the experience the unbridled joy that is a probate valuation.' He pulled his faded denim jacket from the back of his chair and slung it over his shoulder.

'I've got this update to finish.'

'It can wait. I'm your boss and it's an order.'

206

Gildersleeve's was often engaged to produce a declaration of the value of someone's estate on the date of their death – the probate valuation – for which the company charged a fee. After probate was granted, the inland revenue swooped in and collected the relevant tax. Sometimes the auction house would then be instructed to clear the property and items would end up in their sales. It was a time-consuming task and the thing that took Johnny or Theo off site the most, so Maisie was curious to see exactly what this process involved.

With one elbow sticking out the window of his vintage Ford Capri and an audio cassette of The Jam's 'The Eton Rifles' thumping out of the crackly car sound system, Theo looked totally at ease. He was particularly excited about this visit, not only because it was in a glorious part-Tudor property in the middle of the Suffolk countryside, but also because the deceased gentleman concerned had run a successful antiques business for many years and had lived amongst the residue of his stock. Maisie understood that just because his personal preference was twentieth century, it didn't mean he couldn't get excited about the wonderful history of everything that had gone before.

'Families, eh?' he said, in between watching the road and turning to study her face when he thought she wasn't looking.

'Is it that obvious?'

'I've met your sister, remember?'

'Mmm ... we're quite different people. I'd forgotten how different until she was around me twenty-four/seven.'

'I'm not a fan of houseguests either. You have to pretend to be all neat and stuff. Too stressful.'

Maisie put her hands to her head and rubbed ineffectually

at her temples. Her problem was the exact opposite; she wasn't the one making the mess.

'It's more complicated than that. I've lumbered myself with a hefty dose of be careful what you wish for. My mission to gather my fragmented family back together has led to repercussions I hadn't anticipated.' Theo looked over to her as he waited at a junction so she explained in more detail.

'My parents divorced when I was seven and my older siblings ended up strewn across the globe. I had this grand plan to organise a reunion and it was starting to come together. Unfortunately, there are unanticipated side effects. My youngest sister has returned from Australia but her marriage is over. My parents are speaking again but it's all too much, too soon. And Lisa has driven down from York, dumped herself on my doorstep and as lovely as it is to see her, she shows no sign of leaving. She's crashing on the sofa and her stuff is everywhere. From the tidy house you saw on Saturday, I'm now living in a refugee camp. Honestly, I walk in and I could cry.' Then she remembered Theo was hardly Hyacinth Bucket.

'You stress about things too much. A coaster out of place is not going to lead to the collapse of the international stock market or speed up global warming. I bet you're the sort of person who gets out poncy matching guest towels when someone stays, irons the bedding and plans the whole week's menu in advance?'

Maisie looked into the foot-well and didn't answer but noticed his smile out the corner of her eye. How could he be so relaxed all the time? It didn't take much for him to wear that easy-going, all is good with the world face. Here he was, in a beat-up old car, listening to his favourite music and grinning from one side of his frizzy head to the other as if he'd won the lottery. Perhaps she needed to be less uptight about things that didn't matter. Chill more. Not stress out if she accidentally stuck a stamp on the envelope upside down. Try to enjoy her time with Lisa instead of rushing around after her to reassemble the neatly ordered life that her sister was carelessly cluttering.

'I've so got you pegged, lady. No wonder you look traumatised. So, if she's on the sofa I'm guessing the Red Room of Pain is still barricaded shut? Why don't you bung the handcuffs and whips in a cupboard and throw a dust sheet over the red leather Tally Ho chair? At least that way you can keep your sister contained.'

She refused to rise to the bait. 'But then where would I take my lover for our nights of unbridled and risqué passion? I get ratty when I've gone too long without my S&M fix.'

'Ah, yeah, forgot about him,' Theo appeared to go along with the joke but he suddenly looked more serious and his smile slid down into his lap.

Despite the fast beat of the music, everything in the car seemed to slow to a halt as their words drifted around the interior and gave them both too much to think about. She cleared her throat and Theo appeared to give himself a mental shake. The moment passed and he found his trademark smile again.

'You're not going to tell me what's behind that locked door, are you?' he said.

'No,' she replied. 'But only because you want to know so badly.' They both chuckled and the awkward atmosphere dispersed. She looked across at this kind man, affection born of friendship, even though her erogenous zones were crying out for more, and she reconsidered. 'Tell you what – follow me home after this and I'll let you see inside the room.'

'Really?' he said, leaning forward and more animated now.

'Really,' she said, her stomach giving a nervous roll.

Theo changed down through the gears and turned into a quiet lane, dappled by shade from the overhead trees.

'Hey, don't stress about all that family stuff. Not worth it. Personally, I can't be doing with the guilt it brings, not that my family is the size of yours. I don't have siblings and my parents live abroad, which they have done since I was eighteen, so I don't see them very often. They put the house on the market as soon as I went to uni.'

Maisie was horrified. 'They just left you?'

'It's fine. I knew it was coming. They kinda did what they were legally obligated to do when I was little and then moved on. Don't pull that face – it's not like they don't love me, but I guess I was either an inconvenient mistake or more of a responsibility than they'd bargained for. They are free spirits and me coming along put paid to their itinerant lifestyle. Let's just say I was never the centre of their universe.'

Maisie glanced over to him as he concentrated on the road and the music switched to a Police track. Poor Theo. Not having siblings was one of those things but for your own parents to make you feel you were an inconvenience was sad. He noticed her concerned expression.

'I was a latch-key kid as soon as I could reach the door handle,' he said, 'with a mother who kept disappearing to the shed to express herself through her pottery and indulging in Yoga retreats in isolated locations. My father worked away a lot, popping home occasionally to ruffle my hair – although my hair is pretty ruffle-resistant, but you know what I mean.'

Theo grinned. 'He occasionally chucked me the odd tenner but that was pretty much the extent of his parenting skills.'

Thinking of her own childhood, Maisie realised that even though her dad wasn't on the scene on a day-to-day basis, he was a good father. Dropping whatever he was up to and focusing on his kids when they visited, always generous with his bottomless wallet, and still being a big part of their upbringing. Even now, he was always keen to hear what was happening in their lives and offer support and advice where he could – although he was always the first to acknowledge relationships weren't his strongest suit.

'Mum was never one for ironing or cooking,' Theo continued. 'The plus side is I was more independent for my age than most of my mates. If I wanted something doing, I had to do it myself – including my laundry. Guess that's where the odd sock thing came from. An angst-ridden thirteen-year-old doesn't have time to pair socks.'

Was that why he was so laid-back? He'd never had anyone on his case? And whilst he probably benefited from the enforced independence (Ben spent most of his first year away ringing up Mum in the early hours asking if he could cook chicken from frozen or how long it took to boil an egg), he also had no one looking over his shoulder, guiding him and telling him that matching socks and a clean-shaven face were a good idea every day, not just when he stumbled across two socks vaguely the same colour or a razor.

'So you're not a huge fan of the whole marriage and kids thing then?' she concluded.

'You misunderstand me. It works well for some people – my parents' marriage is rock solid. That is almost the problem; they love each other so much they don't need anyone else.

I'm quite a fan of that particular institution myself – with the right person, of course.'

Such a shame, she reflected, as he pulled up outside a glorious L-shaped red-brick country house, she clearly wasn't *his* right person.

Chapter 32

After a fascinating day at the Hall, Maisie felt her friendship with Theo had returned to the level it had been before her silly crush made her feel uncomfortable and awkward. The crush hadn't gone anywhere, but her sensible head had returned – it always won out.

Theo complimented Maisie on her efficiency as she trailed behind him, studiously noting everything down, and they worked their way around each of the twenty-three rooms in the house (even the boot cupboard counted but then it was bigger than her bedroom). The son of the recently deceased owner kept them supplied with hot cups of tea and chocolate digestives and by the end of the day they had a complete schedule of all the items in the house.

Expecting Lisa to be lounging about at home, Maisie was surprised to find a hastily scribbled note propped up against the kettle to say she'd gone to visit their dad – doubtless having run out of money again and hoping for a top-up. Not much tidying had been done, she noticed, and she apologised to Theo for the mess.

She politely offered him a drink but he declined and she could tell he was itching to enter her spare room. Now he was metres away from her alarming compositions, she felt anxious and embarrassed. Perhaps it hadn't been such a good idea after all. He still occasionally teased her about the gnomes; there was no way he'd let a comedy opportunity like this pass him by.

Maisie retrieved the key, turned it in the lock and swung the door inwards, watching as Theo's eyes scanned the utter disarray before him.

'What the fu—'

'Don't make me regret bringing you up here,' she warned.

'Sorry.' He looked abashed.

Before them was strewn a clutter of colour and mess: huge six-foot canvases leaning against paint-spattered walls, the floor covered in swathes of plastic sheeting, rows of acrylic paint tubes neatly laid across high shelving – the only ordered aspect of the space. Drippy tins stood around the edge of the floor and a mop and bucket were propped up in the far corner.

'Blimey, woman. I really want to say this is a load of Pollocks but I'm betting that joke's been made before.'

'You're the first person I've shown these to,' she said. 'Ever.' It didn't matter to her what he thought of her dubious master-pieces but it did matter that he appreciated what a big deal this was – she was sharing a tiny piece of her soul.

He gave her one of his trademark looks – the intensive, Your Words Are The Most Important Thing To Me In The World At This Moment look.

'Don't tell me you're embarrassed by all this, um, whatever it is?'

She shrugged and didn't answer. Instead, she stepped gingerly onto the sheeting. It was her way of inviting him in. Theo paused at the door. Clearly he'd been expecting many things to be revealed behind her locked door but not this.

'So, I … erm … paint,' she mumbled.

'Yeah, the bloody walls and ceiling, by the looks of it. Are you an interior decorator and these huge, white canvases got caught in the fallout, or were you trying to paint the canvases and you catastrophically missed?'

That lopsided smile sat lazily across his face, eyes twinkling like hyperactive fairy lights as he continued to assess the room with all the wonder of an awestruck child.

'It's abstract,' she explained.

'Sure is.' He looked at the largest canvas, resting against the side wall: great looping smears of purple and green, flicks of bright orange, and perfect circles of bright white shining through everything.

'Do you even use a brush?'

'Not often,' she admitted. 'I dribble the paint, or squirt it when I'm feeling particularly emotional. Mostly, I use my hands and sometimes ... other things.'

Theo stepped into the room, a curious eyebrow dancing along his forehead, as he bent down to peer at two round imprints at the left-hand side of the picture.

'I'm not even going to ask,' he said.

'Good,' she said, fidgeting from foot to foot. 'But the acrylics are water-based so as long as they don't dry, they come off with a good scrub in the shower.'

Theo, who rarely looked anything other than totally chilled, let his mouth drop open and squirmed uncomfortably at her last comment.

'Not the kind of hobby I would have pegged a neat freak like you for. You're expressing a side of you that you keep buried. VERY buried – mineshaft deep underground, only accessible by highly trained underwater divers and experts in potholing.'

'Yes, I get the point.' She knew her painting was the antithesis of everything she stood for. It's why it felt so decadent, so naughty, so deliciously forbidden. And so right.

'So?'

'So what?'

'What's the story? With these, erm ... paintings?'

Maisie leaned her bottom on the cool metal of the radiator under the window and exhaled slowly; in for a penny, in for a pound.

'Remember me telling you about the art book from Meredith?'

'Teapot lady?'

'The very same. When I got older I would flick through the book and see reflected in the jumble of the shapes and colours, my jumbled, uncontrollable life. It's hard for kids when parents separate. I was only little and I didn't really understand the art in the pages of that book, any more than I understood why my mum threw my dad out of the house. I guess the art grew out of that. I didn't do it to be seen by anyone ...'

'Thank God for that,' Theo muttered. 'They're enough to send persons of a fragile nervous disposition completely over the edge. In fact that one at the back makes me feel quite nauseous.'

He was joking, she knew that, but any illusions she harboured that perhaps she was an undiscovered genius were quickly dispelled.

'It's a kind of therapy, I suppose. I get totally lost when I'm creating them. Nothing outside the room matters and I feel free and unencumbered.'

'What I don't get is why you control everything in your life apart from what you splatter on these canvases.'

She sighed and turned her face from his. 'This is why I don't talk about it. I know people won't understand. The physical act of painting is cathartic and mentally liberating, I suppose.'

'And then you lock it all up in your spare room like a guilty secret?'

'Pretty much.'

'You really are a surprising girl, Maisie,' he said.

And a smile that had been dancing at the corners of his mouth for some time finally stopped flirting with his face and embraced it.

Chapter 33

Later in the week, Maisie's landline (which came with the house and Maisie hardly ever used) rang only for the caller to hang up as soon as she answered. The caller ID was withheld – not a drama in itself but that was the third time that week, including a mumbled, 'wrong number – sorry' and it was starting to unnerve her. She mentioned the call to Lisa – still lounging about the house and still very much in residence. Zoe had given Maisie a wide berth since Lisa's arrival, saying work was hectic, but Maisie suspected she had other reasons for not stopping by. She'd met Zoe at the gym again but the novelty of exercise had worn off quickly for Maisie. Perhaps all three sisters needed a bit of time to adjust to their proximity. She was astute enough to realise forcing relations too early might backfire.

'Oh, I've had that,' Lisa said, her feet on the coffee table, foamy separators fanning out her toes as the first coat of Sable Shimmer dried. 'I thought you'd got a stalker or something. I'm sure there was a bit of heavy breathing the last time.'

'What makes you think some creepy stalker is ringing for me? You're practically living here at the moment. Perhaps it's someone fixated on you?'

'Oh no, he's not got my ... I mean, no one knows I'm here.

I'm keeping a low profile – remember?'

'Yeah—' Maisie gave a chuckle '—the loud music with all the living room windows flung open, catwalk strutting up and down the road in gravity-defying outfits and the regular social media posts. Really off the radar, sis. Practically underground.'

'Stop getting on at me. You don't know the pressures I'm under.' Lisa blinked her watery baby-deer eyes as she gave a dramatic tilt of the chin. Maisie, who'd been flitting around with a duster and tidying up chocolate bar wrappers, paused to look at her sister.

'Truth is, I've been signed off work with, um, stress,' Lisa said.

'Oh, sorry. I didn't realise. I was unforgivably flippant.'

Maisie put the duster down and walked over to the sofa, bending down to give Lisa a hug, as a couple of tears dribbled down Lisa's immaculately made-up face. That certainly explained the vague, open-ended visit. She would try to be more understanding and kinder to her sister. Poor love was burning out and she felt guilty she hadn't spotted the signs. She must be really struggling because tears weren't Lisa's thing – launching random objects at people's heads and slamming doors was her preferred form of emotional release.

'My GP is really worried about me,' she whispered. 'Says I've been working too hard, pushing myself, constantly running around after other people. You mustn't tell anyone – especially Mum – it would worry her too much.' Maisie nodded in agreement. Their mother didn't need anything else to tip her seesawing emotions. 'I came here to recharge. I was hoping you'd understand ...'

'Oh, honey. Sorry if I haven't been very supportive. I didn't know what was going on, but it's been lovely having you stay and sharing some sister time.'

'Sister time?' Lisa sniffed. 'You hardly do anything outside of work apart from endless cleaning and hanging out with old people. Every time I've suggested going for a drink at a pub or hitting the cinema you've moaned about how much housework you've got to do. In fact, I've been so bored I've even considered stopping in to see Mum at work, hoping she could make me a cuppa and take my mind off things.'

'I think you'll find she's far too busy to stop and chat about your latest lip balm. Do you have any idea how hectic her job is? Why don't you go along and offer your services for a couple of hours instead?'

'Hmm ... anyway, the point is I shouldn't be reduced to hanging with a bunch of pensioners.' She shuddered. 'You're my sister and I've come to spend time with you. The muddy floor and dirty laundry will always be in your life. I'm only here for a short while.'

She was right, Maisie realised. The more time she spent with Theo, the more she understood he would never allow other people's expectations to pressure him into lifestyle choices. Or wardrobe choices, come to that. Perhaps the world wouldn't stop spinning on its axis if she left the washing-up and went out for a drink with Lisa. It was even more important now that she realised her poor sister was struggling so badly.

'Oi, watch the nails,' Lisa huffed as Maisie gave her a squeeze. She dropped her arms. Her big sister didn't really do affection – even though she was probably the person who needed it the most.

Maisie collapsed into the sofa and tried not to focus on all the things in the room that were out of place.

'Talking about phone calls and before I forget, you had a

call from some woman called June, Jane, or something,' Lisa said, returning to the nail varnish and sweeping all previous emotions and vulnerability aside. 'Forgot to mention it. It was about that teapot of yours.'

'Joanie? When?' She must have returned from her cruise. Maisie sat up straighter and subconsciously tweaked the cushions.

Lisa shrugged. 'I don't know. I'm not your secretary. Last week sometime? But she wasn't the pervert because I asked.'

'You asked her if she was a *pervert*?' Maisie squeaked.

'Doh. Of course not. I'm not stupid. I fished around to see if she'd tried your number before. Wasn't her. Said Bessie had mentioned your visit so was getting in touch.'

'Essie,' she corrected and retrieved Joanie's number from her bag. Fifteen minutes later she had an appointment for afternoon tea at a posh hotel the other side of Bury St Edmunds the following Saturday.

Highbury Hall was a glorious Georgian country house converted into a five-star hotel just off the A14. Nestled in a cluster of tall trees with open fields spread around like the flowing skirts of a fairy princess ballgown, it was an impressive venue. Wondering if she should have dressed up a bit more, Maisie pulled into the sweeping gravel driveway of the hotel. The rows of new Mercedes and Audis, all chamoised to a high gloss, suddenly made her feel self-conscious. She tucked her hair behind her ears and smoothed down the front of her casual cotton dress.

After clip-clopping across an echoey entrance hall to a discreet desk between two imposing Grecian pillars, she was directed to the sumptuous restaurant. There, behind a pristine cream-coloured tablecloth, was an Essie lookalike. There were enough similarities between Irene and Joanie to see they were family, but it was Essie and Joanie who looked like twins: height, body shape, even hairstyle. Joanie, however, was the Essie upgrade; with a pale pink cashmere jumper and tailored Paul Smith trousers compared to Essie's M&S jeans and soft cotton T-shirt. She put out a bejewelled hand and invited Maisie to take a seat.

'We shall have high tea – on me, naturally. Well, my son-in-law actually. The hotel belongs to him.' She gestured for Maisie to take a seat and smiled.

Wow, Joanie had climbed several rungs higher than her sisters in her journey through life and she could quite understand how her path had diverged from Irene's. With her career hopes so cruelly dashed, it was easy to understand the burning resentment that exuded from the jealous Irene.

'Esther mentioned you knew Meredith?' the elegant older lady asked, settling herself back into the burgundy upholstered dining chair and catching a passing waiter's eye with a half-nod. Within moments a white bone china service arrived, complete with a three-tier cake stand, overflowing with dainty mouth-watering treats; from uniform triangular crustless sandwiches and perfectly baked vol-au-vents, to fancy cakes and pastries, and on the top tier small glasses of sorbet and individual mini trifles. The smoked salmon aroma made Maisie's nervous tummy grizzle in anticipation. A waiter offered the ladies a selection of loose-leaf teas and they settled for a simple English Breakfast, which he dutifully poured before silently retreating – and then reappearing periodically throughout their conversation to top both ladies up.

'Which means apart from Phyllis and poor darling Cynthia,

you've met us all now. What do you think? Peculiar lot, aren't we?' Joanie raised the delicate cup to her lips, peering over the top to assess Maisie's reaction.

'As I explained on the phone, I knew Meredith many years ago but it's been interesting to meet more of her sisters.'

'Interesting? Now there's a polite and evasive answer, if ever I heard one. Irene is certainly interesting.' She smiled to herself. 'I'm sure she wasted no time telling you that I was an unmarried mother?'

Maisie looked down at her hands. 'She mentioned it briefly but we talked about many things.'

Joanie gave a disbelieving huff. 'How she crowed when she realised I was pregnant – guessing before I was even certain myself. I felt sorry for her really. She had a certain reputation and was teased for it. So when it was quiet little Joanie who messed up, she enjoyed her moment and I don't blame her. Of course, it frustrated her no end that I never told anyone who the father was – even the father himself. I just slipped into the background and got on with it. I was very good at that.'

'Because he was married?' asked Maisie, Irene gleefully having told her that much.

Joanie looked thoughtful, sizing up the young woman before her with narrowed eyes and taking her time to respond. For a moment, Maisie thought she'd offended the elegant older lady, but Joanie carefully placed her cup back on its saucer and smiled across the table.

'I'm going to tell you something now that is not common knowledge. When I told everyone all those years ago that the father was married, it was a fabrication – a story I came up with to avoid awkward questions, but it wasn't true. Even my mother finally let it drop because I told her he was a

223

professional man with a career and a young family to think of. In a strange way, it pleased her to think her granddaughter was possibly the daughter of a high-ranking politician or an investment banker – whereas in reality he was no such thing. Just an ordinary guy, a sweet man, with no ties, and most definitely not married.'

'I don't understand.' For Joanie to launch straight into something so personal seemed odd to Maisie. After all, she was nothing to her.

'The sad truth was the gentleman concerned was utterly and totally in love with someone else – someone I knew. I was a temporary stopgap. Sometimes though I wonder ...' She shrugged, and let the sentence trail off. 'You can be happy without necessarily being in love. And maybe he would have learned to love me. But there. I made the decision and I stood by it, throwing all my energy into bringing up my little girl.' Her eyes scanned the room. 'I'm hoping she'll join us presently. I'd like you to meet her.' Joanie's eyes returned to the table and she sighed. 'Funny thing was he never did get the girl and by the time I realised it wasn't going to happen for them and thought about approaching him with the truth, he'd found a different kind of happiness with another woman. I couldn't do it to her.'

'Why are you telling me all this?' As fascinating as Joanie's life story was, Maisie thought as she selected a couple of sandwiches from the bottom tier, she was here to discuss the tea set.

'I wanted to warn you, I suppose. You see, it all hinged around that damned ugly crockery of Gamma's. She told Mother time and time again to keep it all together, and it's only as I've got older and looked back at the paths my sisters and I took, I realised not one of us was particularly lucky in life.'

Watching this gracefully, immaculately turned-out lady select a shiny, mint-green macaroon, her manicured fingers dotted with gemstones, she decided Joanie's definition of lucky differed somewhat from hers. Joanie noticed Maisie's expression.

'Ah, you are looking at my material wealth and wanting to chastise me for being spoiled and ungrateful?' Maisie stared intently at her tea plate. 'The truth is, my dear, I would trade this all in an instant to have had someone by my side this last fifty years. My daughter became my life – my focus. And for twenty years she was my everything. A bright girl who despite her unfortunate beginnings, studied hard and became a success. She married a property tycoon – lovely fellow, if somewhat up his own backside – and she has paid me back tenfold for all the sacrifices I made over the years. I am very close to her but it's not the same. I've lived a terribly lonely life. You can give all your love to a child and for those first formative years it's returned in equal measure. But as they get older, you are a less significant part of their life – and that's how it should be. Meanwhile, you get into bed every night alone. No one to help you make life decisions or laugh with through the good times ...'

Maisie was still feeling lost. 'But what does all this have to do with Verity's tea set?' she asked.

'Because all the disasters that befell the carefree, optimistic young Mayhew sisters; Meredith's fiancé dumping her two days before her wedding, Cynthia's illness being diagnosed, Irene's career-destroying motorcycle accident, Essie's inability to conceive, my unplanned pregnancy, and Phyllis meeting that abusive husband of hers – it all happened in 1969.'

Maisie looked blank, her eyebrows dropping together as she tried to work out why this year was so significant.

'The year Gamma died and Mother split up the tea set.'

Chapter 34

Joanie had the jug and sugar bowl with her, neatly wrapped in silver tissue paper and in a Fortnum and Mason's bag, handing it to Maisie after her shock announcement. But then Maisie had known Verity's set was in the restaurant the moment she'd walked through the door.

'I insist you take them, and can only hope I'm not passing on something that will cause you or your family any misfortunes in turn. Perhaps bringing them together will undo some of the damage.'

Maisie was sceptical. Even if she did successfully reunite it, nothing could bring three sisters back from the dead, make Irene's lungs magically healthy again, or give Essie the much-longed-for child.

'Please let me give you something for them,' Maisie offered, always feeling guilty when she acquired more of the set.

'Nonsense, child. Money is one thing I have plenty of. And my daughter, Clare, feels no attachment to them. She's more than happy for me to pass them over.'

For all her wealth, there was something about Joanie that betrayed the emotional poverty of her life. Her eyes didn't sparkle like Essie's or even study you as acutely as Irene's. They were lost eyes – lonely eyes. Perhaps that's why she wore all the jewellery, Maisie thought, to add the sparkle she knew she was missing.

'Ah, talk of the devil.' Maisie followed Joanie's eyes and saw an equally elegant middle-aged lady saunter towards their table. After brief introductions, Clare pulled up a chair and the omniscient waiter appeared with extra crockery.

Joanie introduced the two ladies.

'Do excuse me briefly, my dears. I need to powder my nose,' and she dabbed delicately at the corner of her mouth with the linen napkin and then slipped away from the table.

Casting a cursory glance at the Fortnum and Mason's bag, Clare selected some of the dinky sandwiches and then looked across at Maisie.

'Mum always thought that set was trouble,' she said. 'She pretends not to be superstitious but secretly I think she feels splitting it did something wafty and mysterious to the universe. Load of old tosh but I'll be pleased to see it go.'

If she was totally honest, Maisie wasn't sure where she stood regarding Verity's set. In her heart, she knew gathering a few old cups and saucers together couldn't possibly determine someone's actions, but all the Mayhew sisters had been troubled by their grandmother's warning words.

'Mum feels she failed me – not giving me a father – and somehow blames the tea set,' Clare continued. 'Maybe it was easier than admitting she'd messed up. I want to say that you don't miss what you never had but I sometimes wish she'd be honest about who he was. All she'll say is he was a kind man, a man who never let his tough childhood keep him down. But ask her any details, like a name or a profession, and she clams up. It's weird to think he might still be out there, walking around, and that I could pass him in the street and not know. I love my mother so much but there is a part of me that is angry with her for not telling the poor man he'd fathered a child – not letting him make the decision whether to be part of my life or not.'

'I guess she has her reasons,' Maisie said, knowing from her conversation with Joanie that they were unselfish ones, but equally, looking across the table, her heart went out to this fatherless woman. Maisie simply couldn't imagine life without her dad, for all his faults.

'If you did ever find out who he was, what then?' she asked.

Clare looked into the middle distance and considered Maisie's question.

'I guess I'd start with the fifty years of hugs we've both missed out on,' she said.

Back in her silent house, Maisie placed the newly acquired milk jug and sugar bowl on the shelf with the rest of the set. It had been a wonderful afternoon and every time she encountered a Mayhew she felt she'd made another friend. In spite of her prickly nature, or maybe even because of it, Irene had stolen the top spot in Maisie's heart, but she knew Essie and Joanie would also be part of her life from now on.

Maisie stood back to admire her display, thinking about Meredith and her sisters, as her brain began to link the tea set to the return of her own family. Zoe's text message had been sent the day she bought the first three cups, even though they hadn't been able to Skype until the following day; her parents had overridden twenty years of animosity when Essie's cups had been given to her; and Lisa had turned up the day she'd visited the grabbing grandson. Did this mean Ben was about to make a dramatic return to the UK? Was she about to have her Christmas Day wish after all?

Returning to the living room, she poked a raw carrot stick through the bars of Nigel's cage, as something out the front window caught her eye. Nigel was delighted and managed to stuff it into his ever-expanding cheeks lengthways. If she'd given him two, he'd resemble a catamaran.

She looked across at the long bay window and a figure strode past. A tall man, possibly in his thirties, with fair straggly hair and a familiar jawline. Her heart thudded so violently it physically jolted her forward.

It was Ben. And he was back.

The doorbell buzzed and Maisie raced down the hall to throw wide the front door and embrace her brother.

'Ben! How did ...?' Her words died in her mouth because the man standing before her was a total stranger. She was so desperate for Ben to come home, for Verity's stupid tea set to have the power to do something she couldn't do by herself, she was seeing what she wanted to see. Ben was still in Croatia and there would be no family reunion until the tour was complete, when the logistics of gathering them all again would be difficult. Her parents' truce was fragile and Lisa would undoubtedly return to York long before Ben returned.

'Good afternoon,' the man said, and nervously adjusted his tie. She could see now that although he was similar in build and colouring to her brother, his face shape was different and his eyes were a dark chocolate brown. All the Meadows family members had blue eyes – her dad's being the bluest and most hypnotic of them all.

'Yes?' Perhaps he was a Jehovah's Witness – all smartly dressed in a suit and beaming at her like he was her best pal.

'I've recently moved in a few houses down and I've got a wiring issue. I wondered if you had a number for a local electrician?'

'Of course. Come in and I'll fetch you an old parish magazine.'

He ran a shaky hand through his mousey hair and stepped inside. Maisie disappeared into the living room, expecting the stranger to wait by the door, but he followed her down the hall.

'Erm, my sister is down from York and crashing for a few nights,' she said, to explain the state of the room. He wasn't supposed to be in here and she was dreadfully embarrassed by the chaos but the young man didn't seem fazed. 'She's rather ... disorganised.'

'What's a bit of mess between family? It must be fun having her stay – like a student sleepover? Bet you're getting up to all sorts of sistery things together?'

'Um, yeah.' She began to flick through the tray of neatly stacked paperwork as a whirring noise came from the sideboard.

'What's in the cage?' the man asked. He was a bit over-friendly for her liking.

'My hamster, Nigel.'

'They make great pets. I had hamsters when I was little. And rats. And stick insects. And cockroaches. And a corn snake ...'

'That's a lot of pets,' she said, thinking only the hamsters really appealed in his extensive list.

'Only child so I guess my mum overcompensated.'

She handed over the April issue of the Tattlesham magazine, which he barely looked at.

'Keep it. There's lots of useful numbers at the back.'

'Thanks. I'm Josh, by the way,' and he stuck out a hand.

'Maisie. Have you moved far?'

'Essex, so not a million miles. Just outside Braintree. But I like it here. Much more peaceful.'

'You won't be so enthusiastic when you're stuck behind a tractor doing about ten miles an hour down the A140. Or when a stream of low-flying aircraft set off from one of the airbases. Or when they spread muck over the fields at the back and we get invaded by a biblical plague of flies.'

'Duly noted,' he said, with a mock-serious face.

Her mobile started to ring so she grabbed it from the circular dining table as she showed Josh out, telling him to ask if he needed anything else. Ben's name flashed up as she closed the front door. Aha. The stranger had been a false alarm but Ben was about to break exciting news to her; perhaps a tour date had been cancelled or he was squeezing in a trip home because he'd realised the importance of family after all.

'You're coming home?' she gushed, heading back to the living room. Maisie bent down to pick up a stray thread of cotton from the carpet, then looked across at Lisa's bags and rolled-up bedding and let the thread drop from her fingers. What was the point? She knew Josh was right. She should be focusing on her time with Lisa instead of stressing about the chaos her visit had caused. Nigel was swinging from the top of his cage by his back feet, tiny arms waving about in the air like a rodent gymnast. He plopped to the bottom, waddled over to the side bars, climbed up to the top and proceeded to hang from his toes again.

'Nope. Ringing about Mum,' Ben said.

'I've never seen her happier. She's bouncing about like Tigger, has renewed her wardrobe and even had her grey coloured.'

'Then you get why I'm worried?' Ben muttered.

Maisie nodded slowly, even though Ben couldn't see her. 'Yes. If it all comes crashing down she'll be inconsolable.'

'*When*, you mean, not if. But you've got her back, right?' he asked.

'Of course.'

'Cool. Just checking.' Typical Ben. Intermittent and brief contact but often coming from a pure place.

'Perhaps if you're worried about Mum you should make the effort to visit? Even for one night. You know I'm keen to organise a get-together and the Mum-Dad window could be microscopic.' All the siblings felt uneasy about the reconciliation. It wasn't that anyone wanted it to fail, it was more that the oil and water combination that was their parents was always destined to separate.

'No can do, sis. The tour's been extended and then I'm house-sitting in Helsinki for the winter. Sorry, but count me out of your plans because I won't be back in the UK until early next year.'

Chapter 35

It was fascinating to Maisie that you could follow the changing seasons through the salerooms. Now that summer was stalking the tail end of spring, DIY enthusiasts and outdoorsy people skipped from the woodwork and the items coming up in the auction adjusted accordingly. Sets of garden furniture and assorted ceramic plant pots made a steady appearance, along with rusty tools and the contents of musty garden sheds. She found it odd that someone might want items in less than perfect condition but Arthur explained there were people who made a good living from selling reconditioned lawnmowers and resharpened shears.

'A lick of paint and a whetstone across the blade and that there scythe'll be swinging through the summer meadow like new,' he assured her, wearing a sun hat and Hawaiian shirt he'd dredged up from somewhere. It was a bit early to be sporting tropical attire but too warm for the woollen. Theo had equally embraced the better weather and was in khaki knee-length shorts. Maisie could now fully appreciate his firm calf muscles, like steel nutcrackers, the by-product of his running days.

'Isn't he just adorable?' Johnny mused, as Theo strode across the forecourt in a lurid orange and blue tank top over a crumpled beige granddad shirt. Maisie nodded a quiet acquiescence. 'Quite muscular under those shapeless shirts of his, like Michelangelo's David. He used to run for the county, don't you know?'

Maisie nodded again even though she still struggled with the notion that Theo had a sporty side. He seemed too lethargic to motivate himself to even play dominoes. She imagined him running over hill and dale, nonchalantly gazing at the wildlife around him, surprised as the next man that he was first to cross the finish line. But yes, she mused, as his fuzzy head bobbed down to help a porter lift a tin bath across The Yard, he was adorable.

A little while later she found herself alone with Theo in the back office.

'I appreciate this is short notice but would you like to grab some dinner tonight?' he asked. His eyes dropped away and he started fiddling with a jumper he'd flung across the back of his chair the day before, rolling it up in an attempt to tidy. It needed a good shake, one of the arms pulling through and folding properly, but Maisie didn't interfere. 'I mentioned coming to mine before, as you've shown an interest in modern design. No funny business – just friends,' he stressed.

It was fine. She got it. He wasn't interested romantically but it was great he wanted to be her friend outside of the auction house. That was good enough. Almost.

'And Ella?' she asked, braving the subject she'd avoided for so long. Was there something going on between her colleagues or not?

'I could ask her, I suppose, but our relationship is a separate thing. And anyway, I'm seeing her Friday. Such an exceptional and beautiful young woman, but a little lost – like most of us.'

Maisie meant would Ella *mind*, not did he want to include her in the meal, but regardless, it seemed her suspicions were right. There was something going on and she really couldn't blame him.

'No, just us is fine. Shall I follow you back after work?' she said, never having been to his house before.

'Great plan. I'm dying to show you my spider chairs,' he said. Maisie wasn't sure she liked the sound of them, being an arachnophobe, but she kept an open mind.

'Sorry, I should have given you an hour and followed on later,' Maisie said, casting her eye over Theo's living room. Abandoned T-shirts and socks were strewn over the floor, and the sofa cushions were lopsided and squashed out of shape. Food debris littered the surfaces, and there were enough pint glasses to open up a small pub. Books and magazines were balanced open in haphazard piles on the floor. Whatever type of gathering he'd had, his houseguests hadn't been particularly considerate.

'Not at all,' Theo said. 'Take a seat.'

What seat? Not one of the chairs was available for immediate bottom placement.

'If you'd told me it was a post-party night, I would have happily satnavved after you'd got yourself sorted.' She began to gather up a few of the glasses by the rims.

'I *am* sorted. Will you put those glasses down? I wouldn't come to your house and start tidying up. You are implying my lifestyle isn't up to your inflated standards.'

She blushed. 'Sorry, I thought ...'

'What? I'd had some sort of wild rave last night?' He snorted. 'Chance'd be a fine thing. I'm so busy at the moment,

I barely have time to have a wild cup of tea, never mind a rave.' He pulled a crumpled jumper out from the seat cushion at the end of the sofa and gestured for her to sit.

Looking about her, she could see Theo's passion for modern design reflected in his furnishings and décor. A framed Andy Warhol poster of a young Elizabeth Taylor hung above the mantelpiece and an awful lot of primary colours jostled for dominance in the room. The simple elegance of the Danish teak furniture was complemented by his eclectic possessions: a tan leather landline, an orange mushroom lamp and two red and black mini trampoline-like objects either side of his wooden-clad stereo system.

'What do you think of the spider chairs then?' Theo asked, launching himself into the nearest trampoline. The criss-cross of web-like elastic that stretched inside the black metal circular frame moulded to his body as he landed. 'They're surprisingly comfortable and were a snip at two-fifty.'

The G-Plan-style furniture and pop art she could appreciate. The chairs – not so much, despite their quirkiness. Problem was, you had to look hard through the clutter to see the brilliance of design beneath. Her fingers were clenching and relaxing in an effort not to close the books lying open on the ceramic-tile-covered coffee table or to pick up the empty crisp packets.

Theo noticed.

'Is the mess making you uneasy?'

'Not at all,' she lied. 'It's very ... cosy.'

'Good, that's what I think too. It's where I live, not a show home. It reflects my personality ...'

He left the statement hanging there. He didn't need to finish the sentence. She got it. Lisa's visit aside, her house was sterile,

236

her desk at work was sterile, bloody hell – after six months without a boyfriend, she was sterile.

'Right, I promised you dinner but I didn't promise I would make it. I'm going to ring for a Chinese. You said you weren't a fussy eater.'

'Not at all. Shall we set the table? I'm starving.'

'If we must. And if I can find it,' Theo mumbled.

Theo passed the crispy seaweed as Maisie struggled with the revelation he didn't possess two matching plates. Or two matching anythings, come to that. Even more horrifying was this was deliberate. He liked bold colours, offbeat items and clever design. But assembling them randomly, she was bemused to discover, was his idea of interior décor. The table was a mishmash of crockery styles and colours, including the large ceramic cabbage-leaf-shaped bowl containing the sweet and sour pork balls.

'Bordallo Pinheiro,' he said, as she ran her fingers over the bumpy surface, tracing a line down the stalk. 'A master of the rustic and the unusual. I don't like all his stuff, but I do hanker after the pineapple pitcher if I ever have a spare hundred lying around.'

It wasn't something that would grace her table but she got it. 'So you like this because it's tactile and a break from the traditional bowl shape?'

'Yeah and I adore cabbage.' He grinned. 'Should have put the crispy seaweed in it really – if I wanted to be pedantic. Talking of ceramics, Arthur tells me you've only got one Mayhew sister to track down?'

'It's not going to happen,' she sighed, her heart heavier than it should be. 'Cynthia died a long time ago.'

Maisie knew in her heart the tea set was unlikely to ever be reunited. She'd spent hours online looking for matches and – after learning Cynthia lived and died near Bury St Edmunds – had popped down to Bury several times to scour local charity shops and antique emporiums on the microscopic off-chance she'd stumble across her pieces.

None of the sisters had talked much about Cynthia but Maisie had finally broached the subject with Irene the previous weekend, as they played cards and Maisie studiously avoided looking at Naked Man. He had a tendency to leap out of his seat when he won a hand and Maisie was seated directly opposite.

'Poor Cynth was only twenty-three,' Irene told her. 'Dating some lad from the airfield when she was diagnosed with cancer, but Father warned him off. Told him she wouldn't have much of an existence and he should cut his losses. Bloody interfering old bugger. I think the young man would have stuck by her and she could have had a half-decent life. Instead she sort of pulled out of the world and sat on the sidelines, watching it play out for others. People nowadays lead completely normal lives with ileostomies. Makes me want to spit feathers.'

'Poor girl,' Maisie said to Irene, amazed that three of the sisters had never married. Irene's own marriage to the never talked about Mr Cooper had been short-lived. Only Essie had been lucky in love but even her life was cast in shadow.

'These things are discussed more now,' Irene said. 'Everything is splashed over the telly and then that Jeremy Kyle does a show about it. But going back fifty years you drew your front blinds and kept your business to yourself – excuse the pun.' She'd cackled and coughed in equal measure, as Maisie sat squirming uncomfortably in the red vinyl wing chair. 'So

Cynth devoted her life to her damn cats. Don't suppose they cared about her bodily functions as long as she chucked food at them. Seven of the little blighters she had at the end. Talk about cat lady – she left the rescue centre *everything* ...'

Maisie relayed the conversation to Theo and sighed. 'I may have to accept my quest is over.'

'Yeah, my research drew a blank too. Meredith's set is quite the mystery but you can use odd plates to replace the missing ones.' He shrugged.

'Some of us like things that match,' she said, comfortable enough with this easy-going man to pull his tatty denim leg. She looked pointedly at the items on the table.

'*Some of us* place more importance on sentiment and artistic merit than making sure everything in our life conforms. All my possessions have memories attached to them and therefore an emotional significance, or they are items I simply love and must have. Pretty much my guiding criteria for everything in my life.' He gave her a funny look that she couldn't quite decipher and then carried on talking. 'The Pinheiro was my grandmother's, as were some of the plates. Sometimes friends buy me quirky pieces and I'm always on the lookout for odd bits and bobs at boot fairs or artisan markets. It doesn't matter who the manufacturer is, how old it is or, to some extent, the price. What matters most is that I like it.'

Despite finding the concept charming, the idea of uneven-sized plates stacked inside a kitchen cupboard was almost enough to bring Maisie out in hives, but she paused to consider his words.

'I wish I was more like you,' she said. 'Not worried about what people thought – flinging on the first thing that came to hand in the morning—'

'Oi, are you implying my dress sense is random?'

She tipped her head and gave him a knowing stare.

'Yeah, fair enough,' he conceded.

'And I love that you surround yourself with an eclectic group of friends: Johnny, Arthur and, I hope, me?'

'Of course you're my friend. I find you fascinating,' and he broke into a David Attenborough voice. 'And here we see the Maisie in her natural habitat. Watch as she fusses about her nest – not a twig out of place. But later, out in the wild, she becomes restless due to the disorder around her. Her feathers are ruffled and she paces endlessly in the undergrowth ...'

'Ha-ha.' Her tummy rolled and not just because the sweet and sour sauce smelled heavenly. 'Can we do this again?' she asked, hopefully.

'Oh, a second date,' Theo teased, helping himself to the last of the beef chow mein.

'Stop it with the dates. You'll upset Johnny if he thinks his right-hand man and left-hand woman are conducting some sort of love affair in the back office.' She rolled her eyes.

Theo's eyes flicked briefly up from the forkful of noodles making their way mouth-ward. 'It's fine, there aren't any no dating policies at Gildersleeve's.'

'Well, there should be,' she said firmly. 'It's all very well while everything in the garden is rosy, but when it all goes bottoms up, the fallout is immense. Believe me – I speak from experience.'

'Right, well that's me told then ...' Theo mumbled to himself.

And then she blushed as she realised he was possibly already one half of a staff couple.

Chapter 36

'W ho's the guy hanging about in Saleroom Two?' Maisie asked, as she sauntered into the back office the following morning. Sighing inwardly, she lifted a bundle of papers and a dirty coffee mug from her desk and placed them firmly on Theo's teetering pile of carelessly abandoned belongings.

Johnny leaped up from his desk, his chair smacking the wall behind.

'You're here at last. Thank all that is good and light,' he said. 'We have been graced by a visitation from some televisual fellows.' He looked even more flamboyant than usual in an iridescent peacock-feathered waistcoat and a red velvet tie. And she could swear he'd dabbed some rouge on his plump cheeks. Either that or his burgundy tweed trousers were too tight.

'No one told me they were coming,' she sniffed, thinking she would have made considerably more effort if she'd known. Her pale green cotton summer dress might be suitable for the weather, but with no public on site that day, and intermittent access to her own bathroom, she hadn't worried too much about accessorising.

'More to the point, my little genius marketing whiz, no one told *me*,' Johnny replied. 'I confronted Theodore this morning, and he gave me a shrug and informed me it was, and I quote, "no biggie". Of course I rushed immediately homeward and reassessed my wardrobe for the day. I don't want them thinking Gildersleeve's is some provincial indecorous establishment. Imagine – I didn't even have a handkerchief about my person.'

'Please don't tell me they're about to whisk Theo off for more filming? We really could do with him here whilst the builders are in.' She slumped into her chair.

'They are researching possible filming locations for the next *Wot a Lot!* series, and as Theodore has proved such an exceptional hit with the female contingent of the audience, they thought we were worth investigating. I can only thank the heavens and the deities that reside therein that we got you on board when we did. In a few short months you've smartened up Gildersleeve's beyond my wildest imaginings.'

'It's not all down to me. I think the three of us are heading in the same direction, even if Theo and I occasionally bicker about the best way to get there.' She'd been given the job at a pivotal point in the company's evolution. Johnny and Theo were expanding and had the funds to do so. The planned café and insulation of the barns were in motion long before she'd arrived.

'And how *are* you two meandering along now, dah-ling? I know you've had some vexatious moments, but I do so want two of my favourite Gildersleeve's colleagues to adore each other as much as I adore each of them in their turn.'

Maisie felt a glow in her chest. These past few months she'd grown particularly fond of Johnny – who was always supportive and full of praise for her work. It was nice to know he felt the same.

'We're good. He's a genuinely likeable person.'

Johnny smiled and gave a happy sigh. 'Most excellent news. Now to more pressing matters. I fear we need to instigate an expeditious plan.' He jerked his thoughts back to the immediate crisis. 'An impromptu staff meeting in five minutes, to show this fellow what the Gildersleeve's establishment is made of ...'

The morning proved to be, as Johnny later put it, 'triumphant'. The researcher seemed impressed with the venue, commenting on its quirkiness. From her own marketing background, she knew he was coming from the same place as her. Its rural charm, the eclectic staff and the haphazard nature of it all made for an interesting and appealing mix. Johnny, Theo and Maisie gathered in their dim back office after the researcher had left.

'He was worried about refreshment facilities for his team but I said the building work for the café was nearly completed,' Theo said.

'But that's just the structure. How about the interior décor? The equipment? The staff?' Maisie squeaked. 'We're not exactly "good to go".'

'Stop getting your knickers in an unnecessary twist.' Theo gave Maisie his wonky smile. 'We'll put you on the case and it'll be fine. Organisation is one of your strengths.'

'A great man once said, "Beware the flatterer, for he invariably wants something he is not capable of achieving himself,"' Johnny said, scooting across the office on his wheely chair as he gathered some papers together.

'Churchill? Wilde?' Maisie ventured.

'Gildersleeve.' Johnny's unruly eyebrows bounced up and down his forehead.

'I don't know why you two are stressing. They loved the place. And anyway, it's hardly like they're turning up tomorrow.'

'When are they hoping to start filming *exactly*?' Maisie asked.

'July.'

'That's less than six weeks away. Honestly, Theo, I despair of you.' She thwacked him with her ruler.

'I'm efficiency and organisation personified,' Theo said, as a pile of reference books on his desk chose that moment to topple to the floor with a thud.

'Dah-ling Theodore,' Johnny said, 'you really are most vexatious at times. Endearing but vexatious.'

That weekend, Maisie and Lisa had a sisterly breakthrough. It was brief but it was fun. Midway through a second shared bottle of wine, Lisa persuaded her sister to play an impromptu game of charades using some app on her phone that flashed up a variety of film, book and TV suggestions. Lisa was a natural with her dramatic leanings but Maisie soon got into the swing of it. Lisa's *Chitty Chitty Bang Bang* had Maisie in stitches and she realised a good belly laugh had been woefully overdue.

'How come you are so good at this game?' Maisie asked, reaching for the Prosecco.

'I watch a lot of ... I move in these circles, remember?' Lisa said, handing Maisie her phone with the next charade. Maisie pressed the screen and 'Rapunzel' appeared. Her heart sank as she wondered how she was going to approach this one – she couldn't even do a sounds like.

'So, what are you working on at the moment?' she asked, keen to engage and mindful her sister had chastised her for focusing more on the housework than their relationship.

'This and that. Can't talk about it. You know how it is?' Lisa was always evasive about her life unless it was a topic she wanted to talk about. Maisie could almost feel the shutters being pulled closed.

'And this man who's bothering you?' Maisie asked, hoping to draw her sister out.

'Not tonight, Maisie.' Lisa began biting her nails but realising it would spoil the manicure she let her fingers drop. 'But thanks,' she finished.

'For what?'

'For letting me crash. For caring enough to ask. And for putting up with all my crap over the years.'

'No one is perfect and everyone has redeeming features. We all know Dad's moral compass is glitchy, especially in the monogamy region, but look how he's supported us all over the years, financially and emotionally, without question.'

Lisa glanced at the pile of shopping bags and sighed. 'Yeah, Mum was the one who suffered there. I guess we didn't do so badly from the split.'

'And Ben pretends not to care about anyone but himself but he truly does – underneath everything. He notices the little things and they bother him, even if he doesn't have the social skills to deal with them.' Maisie topped up both glasses and sunk back into the sofa, feeling more relaxed than she had a right to be, considering the state of the carpet.

Lisa thought about this for a moment and frowned as she cast her mind back. 'When I moved out with Biker Boy, Ben used to cycle up and down that damn road about twenty times a day – especially in the beginning. I'd forgotten that. At the time I thought he was just being a pain in the arse but perhaps he was looking out for me.'

'See? And I know I'm full-on with my Little Miss Tidy freak-outs, but I've been told my Christmas presents are the best.' She smiled and Lisa raised her glass.

'Cheers to that. You're the best of the bunch. I honestly expected you to be a little brat when you were born but you never were. Always tucked in a corner of the room, just getting on with things. I guess you were just outnumbered.'

'You weren't so bad yourself,' Maisie insisted, wondering what positive example she could cite to make Lisa feel good about the past. 'You, um ... well, you ...'

They exchanged a look – a long look where they both reflected on Lisa's history. Maisie narrowed her eyes as she searched for an example. The pause stretched out like an empty highway and they both started giggling all over again.

Chapter 37

The following Thursday late-night viewing, Oliver made a second visit to the auction house. He looked exceptionally smart in his charcoal-grey work suit and greeted her with another lung-squashing hug. Now the evenings were lighter, it didn't feel such a long day when Maisie worked late, especially with surprise visits from a beloved brother-in-law to lift her spirits.

'You liked the tie then?' Maisie asked. It had been Oliver's birthday the previous week and she'd stopped by to see his new flat with Zoe and drop off a couple of gifts. Maisie bought presents when she saw things she knew the recipient would like and never left shopping until the last minute. The silk tie had been purchased in the January sale and was accountant-appropriate as it was covered in pictures of fifty-pound notes.

'Unfortunately, dealing with everyone else's millions doesn't mean I have bundles of my own stashed away. I fear this is the closest I'll ever get.'

'You're welcome to come back for a drink later,' she offered but Oliver shook his head.

'Not if Lisa's still crashing. She scares the hell out of me.' Oliver actively avoided Lisa and Maisie couldn't blame him. Despite their minor breakthrough, Maisie still found her scary.

Arthur ambled by. He always had a smile on his face, she noticed, even when he was on his own.

'This is my friend Arthur,' Maisie said, introducing Arthur to Oliver. 'He's our head porter. And this is Oliver – a very good friend of mine.'

'Very, *very* good friend,' said Oliver, stressing the second very and wiggling his eyebrows.

'Right you are, sir. Well, she's a special girl, our Maisie. Mind you take great care of her ...' Arthur's smile wobbled but he managed to stop it falling from his face altogether.

'I always have.' Oliver grinned, putting a large arm around Maisie's shoulders and pulling her in tight. 'Isn't that right, Titch?'

Uncomfortable that Oliver's familiarity with her might be mistaken for something more, she wriggled free and cast her eyes about the barn. She didn't want Theo witnessing the hug.

'As lovely as it is to meet your nice young man—'

'He's not my—'

'I actually came over to let you know that Ella's on her own in the front office,' Arthur said. 'I'd offer to help her out but as you know I'm not very good on them computer things, and the poor love always acts a bit awkward around me. Not sure she appreciates a boring old man chatting away. She's a quiet one and I don't like silences so I always fill them with rambling nonsense. Perhaps you could nip over for a bit? Or I could ask Johnny?'

'I'm happy to help her through the rush, although I'm not sure she's any more enamoured with me than she is with you, Arthur.' She made her excuses to Oliver and headed over.

'Would you like a hand?' Maisie asked, peering round the front office door.

'Um, actually, yeah.'

'I'll issue the bidder numbers, if you input all the information?' Maisie offered, knowing full well Ella would prefer not to deal with the public. She seemed more comfortable since Theo had moved her desk but not everyone was a natural with people and Maisie understood that.

'Um, thanks,' Ella said, vacating the reception chair.

There was a rush of customers, including Oliver leaving a bid on two kitchen chairs and a TV cabinet, but it calmed down in the last hour. With the office quieter Maisie tried to strike up a conversation with Ella.

'That's a pretty dress,' she ventured. 'Boden?'

Ella blushed and looked down at the olive and cream linen smock dress she was wearing.

'Yes. Thank you.'

There was a pause. 'Going somewhere nice after you finish here?'

'Oh, I'm not a very sociable person.' Dragging her for an impromptu after work drink wasn't going to work then. Ella's head was down again, and her fingers bashed away at the keys in a nervous blur.

After a few moments, Maisie tried again. 'I know it's none of my business, but what do you do with the chairs you buy?' It was her last attempt to engage her colleague. She'd made it clear she wasn't sociable, so bombarding her with questions wasn't her best approach.

'I sell them,' she answered. It was a whispered response and, intrigued as she was, Maisie decided to leave the poor girl alone. Even she knew when it was time to quit.

Maisie prepared to head back over to the salerooms now reception was empty but was surprised to look up and find

249

Ella at her side, pushing a mobile phone in front of her face. On the screen was a beautiful Nineteen-Forties wood armchair upholstered in a bright fabric of purple and yellow flowers.

'Wow. That's beautiful. I love the pattern.'

'They're crocuses. My design.' There was a tiny smile from Ella.

'You designed the fabric?'

She nodded. 'It's easy; there are lots of companies that print fabrics to order. You upload your design to their website, choose your repeat and then select the size and type of material. I use a polyester canvas for the chairs – it's more durable and easier to clean than cotton.'

'You've done more than one?'

'Erm, yeah, I've done about six now. Each chair goes for about four hundred.' She swiped her phone and another chair appeared – this time pale yellow and tangerine coloured tulips in a smaller repeating pattern. 'Keep swiping left,' Ella urged, moving from foot to foot, her arms hanging limply by her sides. And then she looked down at her shoes as Maisie flicked through several shots of stunning pre-loved but totally transformed chairs – a dramatic aqua blue chair covered in starfish catching her eye.

'Sometimes I make commission when other people buy my fabric designs. It's not a fortune but enough to make it worthwhile. It's why I prefer the older wooden-armed chairs – less fabric, less cost, more profit.'

'Honestly, Ella, these are amazing.' As someone with an eye for colour and design, she appreciated Ella's fabrics were brilliantly executed and highly original. 'I had no idea people could get their own patterns printed up. Don't you have to order roll-fulls?'

'No, it's by the metre, although I always order a sample piece first to check I'm happy with it.'

'You certainly have a talent for it.'

Ella looked up from the floor. 'Um, thanks. I grew up by the sea and particularly loved painting nature when I was younger: seascapes, flowers, seashells ... I've always enjoyed drawing.'

'Me too. Or rather, I love the idea of drawing but my still life isn't up to much. Quite enjoy splashing a bit of paint around though.'

'There's a still-life class starting at the community centre soon,' Ella said, dropping her eyes again. 'Um, I might go. The teacher is someone I knew at school. He's rather ...' She dropped her head again.

'Hot?' Maisie said flippantly and then, looking at the panic in Ella's eyes, realised she was right.

'I was going to say talented. Do you think you might like to come along with me? Don't feel obliged or anything ...'

'Ooh, yes please,' Maisie said. 'My art teacher at school always said I needed to focus on my line, shadow and form – her way of saying she didn't recognise a damn thing I drew.' Ella smiled at her and Maisie wheeled the office chair backwards to face her. 'It's why I veered into graphics and marketing – I get to manipulate other people's images. Never could master a nose.' She rolled her eyes. 'So how did the upholstery come about?'

'I did an evening course a couple of years ago because I wanted to restore a special but somewhat battered armchair from my childhood. Arthur mentioned that these older chairs often went for next to nothing because of the dated fabric, and I'd so enjoyed designing the fabric for my own chair, I thought perhaps I could make some money restoring them. If the framework is sound and they predate the fire regulations, I bid for them. Arthur even introduced me to the woman who I sell through. He's a very thoughtful man.'

He was, Maisie acknowledged, and she could see what Theo had been getting at when he said not to underestimate Arthur's strengths.

'But I, um, don't always know what to say to him. He's quite ... wordy.'

'To be honest, I think if you can stop and give him some of your time, you'll find you have to say very little at all.'

The two girls exchanged another smile. It was a start and a positive one. Perhaps Ella would open up to her a bit more now. At the very least it had given her the encouragement she needed to pursue a friendship. And Ella could draw – really draw – a useful friend to have if she was ever to refine her daubings.

With her colleague promising to let her know further details about the art class, Maisie headed back to Saleroom Two. She scanned the barn for Theo, wanting to let him know she'd had a breakthrough with Ella. He was at the back, behind the glass cabinet, so she made her way over. But when she was almost there, an unwelcome figure caught her eye. He was walking up the centre of the barn and made her heart rate triple.

It was Gareth. And he was with the willowy, treacherous girl from HR.

Chapter 38

Gareth did a double take when he noticed Maisie. He stopped to say something to his companion, who scuttled off in the other direction.

For a moment all Maisie could think of was his face stuck to Twig-Girl's and it wasn't a pleasant thought. She put out an arm to steady herself on the glass cabinet and briefly closed her eyes.

'Are you okay?' Theo asked, sliding a tray of watches out so a gentleman could look at the vintage diver's watch. The interested party picked it up and began to inspect it through a small folding magnifier.

'Yeah, someone I know,' she said, dropping her eyes to the concrete floor.

'But who you aren't particularly pleased to see, I'm guessing?'

Gareth's face was all smiles as he came striding towards her with a familiar bounce. Theo edged away slightly but his body remained tilted towards Maisie's as he returned his attentions to the man's question about the damaged bezel.

'Maisie, how fabulous to see you. What are you up to now?' Because she was standing at the end of the cabinet, it wasn't obvious she was staff. 'I know you didn't move to any of our rivals – I checked. You went totally off radar.'

How had she ever found this man attractive? That wasn't a smile, it was a smirk.

'I work here,' she said. 'I'm head of marketing now.' *Head* as in the only member of the marketing team but she prayed Theo wouldn't feel the need to point that out.

'Here?' He looked confused. 'Bit of a tinpot outfit. You should be in a bigger organisation; a national concern, somewhere you can shine and climb the career ladder. Truth is, we've really missed you at work. The new lad isn't anywhere near as competent as you – doesn't know his curly speech marks from his feet and inches and you know how that bugs me. Won't you consider coming back? We can be grown-up about the whole thing.'

'I don't think so,' Maisie said, smiling sweetly and feeling in control of the whole Gareth situation for the first time.

Gareth leaned in a bit closer and lowered his voice. 'I can give you a pay rise. Seriously, you were bloody good. I'll match whatever you're getting here, plus ten per cent.' What Gareth didn't know was that her salary here was substantially less than at Wickerman's but she wasn't about to tell him that.

Theo, only half a metre away, returned the tray to the cabinet. He froze for a fraction of a second.

'Thanks for the offer, but I'm happy here,' she said. '*Really* happy.'

And Theo placed the tray onto the bottom shelf, slid the door closed, and turned the key with a satisfying click.

Three drinks in and Maisie's head was spinning. Lisa, on the other hand, looked as sober as an abstemious judge.

Finally persuaded by her socialite sister to let her hair down outside her own living room, and on the back of their charades success, Maisie decided she could hardly preach about the importance of family relationships if she wasn't prepared to make an effort herself. Lisa suggested a wild night out and, although she thought it was an odd choice for someone professing to feel fragile and struggling with work stress, Maisie agreed.

Maisie's need for order was usurped by the realisation she'd got her priorities skewed – even her new neighbour, Josh, had assumed her sister staying involved lots of girl time. Still waiting for Lisa's bank to sort out the unspecified catastrophe that had left her low on funds, and feeling guilty she hadn't spotted any sign of her sister's overload, the night was on Maisie. Lisa may have a glittering career but it had obviously come at a price. A night out would do them both good – although she hadn't dared mention the planned evening to Zoe.

Lisa winked at the bartender collecting empties from nearby tables and then returned her focus to Maisie.

'You'll never get a man if you spend your evenings hoovering the carpet to within an inch of its life. You need to stop being such a control freak,' Lisa said. Conversational topics had so far covered work, family and had now moved to boyfriends – or lack thereof.

'I'm not. I'm tidy-minded.'

Lisa rolled her eyes and downed her remaining drink in one. They were at a trendy wine bar in Norwich, full of young, suited work-types who Maisie noticed had come in, shoulders hunched and the stresses of the day etched across their faces, but who had begun to unwind and embrace the noisy atmosphere and the end of their working week.

'Tonight is about setting you free. For a start that's the

last boring vodka and tonic you're having. We're moving to cocktails and finishing the evening in a club.'

'I'm too old for nightclubs,' Maisie whined. 'I'm not you, Lisa. I don't lead a socialite life.'

'Yeah, but look where it got me? I'm a shell of my former self,' she sniffed. 'It's such a nightmare – working all the hours God sends. You don't understand how ... stressed I feel all the time.'

'Then talk to me about it.' Maisie leaned over the sticky table towards her sister. 'What can I do to help?'

For a moment her sister looked vulnerable and Maisie wondered if she was about to break through Lisa's veneer of independence. It was as if her sister felt she had to trail blaze. From the moment she left home she could never admit failure or seek comfort from her family, even that first misguided adventure when things went pear-shaped with Biker Boy, Lisa Meadows had pulled her shoulders back and strutted confidently through life.

'Not tonight ...' Lisa paused, studied her glossy nails and wrinkled up her nose. 'It's too raw. And work has sucked the life from me.' Her eyes avoided Maisie's as she suddenly rocked back on her chair. 'It's hard being so ... in demand. I had no one and I needed support. I even went to church looking for answers, if you can believe that?'

'But that's what family is for. Why didn't you come and see us sooner? We're all here for you. Mum would have loved an opportunity to help – she worries about you.'

Lisa sighed. 'She asks too many questions.'

'Then talk to me,' Maisie begged. 'It's what sisters do, after all – share.'

'Huh – like you and Zoe? Closer than layers in a damn

onion and always shutting me out.' Lisa's demeanour changed slightly.

'We *don't* shut you out.' It was quite the reverse. Lisa chose to distance herself.

'You won't even tell me what's in the spare room. That's not sharing. Unless you're either growing cannabis in there or have a leather-clad sex slave chained to the radiator, I don't see what the big deal is. Don't you trust me?'

Maisie crossed her arms and felt the tips of her ears glow, as she prepared to lay her soul bare. If she was honest about her hobby, perhaps Lisa would trust her more.

'It's where I paint.'

Lisa looked disappointed. 'Is that it? I thought it was some deep, dark secret. Something you were ashamed of.'

'Not ashamed – embarrassed maybe. You haven't seen the paintings. They're a bit ... random. I'll show you when we get home but you're not allowed to laugh,' she warned.

Several colourful cocktails and one throbbing nightclub later, Maisie kept her word.

Chapter 39

The following morning, Maisie moped about the living room with a nasty headache. She had drunk enough the night before to forget how many she'd had – though it was obvious now that it should have been considerably less. The pain was worth the gain, however, as it had been a memorable evening. She felt totally reckless that the washing-up from the night before was still on the worktop, and strangely elated that they hadn't been the oldest people in the club.

The bonding element, though, had been a limited success. Maisie had opened up to her sister but her sister hadn't reciprocated in equal measure. Lisa wouldn't talk about work or her needy admirer and Maisie felt she was hiding something connected to this mysterious man. Perhaps, she pondered, he was someone famous.

There was a knock at the front door and she was bewildered to find Theo on her doorstep. He'd featured heavily in another muddled and overtly sexual dream.

'What are you doing in your pyjamas at eleven o'clock?' He looked genuinely surprised but her head was a little too thumpy to give a detailed explanation.

'Come in,' she mumbled, shuffling back down the hall and wishing she'd removed her make-up the previous evening, as she was fairly certain it was still on her face but perhaps not in the specific areas she'd initially applied it.

'Good grief,' Theo said as they entered the living room. 'Have you actually been living a life, Maisie? The house is a mess – and that's not a criticism, more of an accolade.'

'Whaaa ...?' Lisa's head popped up from the bundle of bedding on the sofa – a scrunched-up sock stuck to the side of her face. She peeled it off and sat up. 'Bloody hell, sis, you didn't tell me your boyfriend was dropping in.'

'You know full well Theo is my boss,' Maisie said, feeling the temperature in the room jump a few degrees.

'Poor man. If you don't want him, I could give him a test drive?' Lisa offered. 'How about it, Theo? You, me and a Sloe Comfortable Screw Against the Wall?'

'It's a cocktail,' Maisie gushed, anxious to clear up any ambiguity. 'With sloe gin. We were out clubbing last night. And drinking cocktails ...'

'I'm not on the market but thanks for the offer,' he said to Lisa and then flicked his eyes to Maisie and rubbed his hand slowly over his stubble. Ella was the beautiful yet meek elephant in the room – although as members of the animal kingdom go, she was distinctly more gazelle-like.

'Oh, your heart is taken?' Lisa pouted.

'Afraid so,' he said, 'and as lovely as the offer is, I'm not on the lookout for anyone else.'

'Shame.' Lisa collapsed sideways back into the pile of bedding.

'And as for you, young lady,' he said, turning to Maisie. 'I didn't have you pegged as a clubber. You keep surprising me.'

'Good,' she said, hastily grabbing crumpled clothes and dirty cups in an attempt to tidy up. 'Now we've satisfactorily established the complicated relationships within the room, how can I help?'

'Right. Yes. I'm nipping into town to get some flowers for Pamela as Arthur let slip it was her birthday when we were locking up the barns on Friday night. I wondered if you'd like to come back with me? I know you are as fond of him as I am,' said Theo. 'Although looking at your pale face and state of undress, perhaps it's not a good time.'

'I'd love to come,' she said, tugging at her top. 'Just give me five minutes ... maybe ten. Lisa can keep you entertained.'

He raised an eyebrow and took a step back. 'Right. Be quick,' he said, eyeing Lisa suspiciously as she mumbled something into the pillow.

'Just flowers?' Maisie asked, exactly seven minutes later as she slumped into the front seat of the Capri.

'Apparently they are her favourite thing and the reason he grows so many in the garden. I guess as you get older you don't want to keep acquiring possessions. I need to remind myself of this or when I'm ninety I won't be able to get through my front door.'

'What's she like – his wife?' Maisie imagined her to be a cheery but firm lady. She was always encouraging Arthur to get out and about, although she gathered Pam wasn't terribly mobile herself.

'I've only been in his house a couple of times and on both occasions she was with the daughter. He's obviously fond of her but they do a lot of things independently. She's never been to any staff get-togethers, for example, but from everything he's said about her, I gather she wears the polyester print trousers.'

They stopped at the florist in town and Theo selected

a beautiful bunch of roses, lisianthus and eucalyptus, and the young aproned lad wrapped them in pretty pink tissue paper and tied a huge raffia bow around the stems. Maisie wanted to buy Pamela something as well and tried to rack her brains to recall conversations she'd had with Arthur, but the problem was a lot of what he said was lost in the rolling river of words. He'd mentioned she liked pretty bits of china from when they'd talked about the tea set, but she wouldn't presume to know Pamela's tastes. In the end, she bought a potted begonia and a card.

Arthur was delighted to see them, opening the front door in his vest and trousers.

'Flowers for Pam's birthday,' Theo said, passing over the bouquet to a watery-eyed Arthur.

'Oh, how embarrassing. I didn't mean for you to—'

'I know, Arthur. I know.'

'Well, it's right kind of you, sir. She'll absolutely love them.'

'I've got her a little something too,' Maisie said, handing over her gift.

'Well, bless you both. I'll take the flowers down to her in a few minutes. I was just ironing a shirt but it takes me an age. Women are so much quicker at jobs like that and I've never properly got the hang of it. Perhaps you'd both like to come with me?' He looked hopeful for a moment.

'Ah, she's with your daughter,' Maisie said.

'Yes, it's only round the corner but I expect you're busy. I know you youngsters are always rushing about. This non-stop modern life is exhausting to witness. Not like in my day. We had all the time in the world to enjoy the simple things; sitting in the long grass, watching Holly Blues and Red Admirals flutter around us in the meadow, a lazy Sunday lunch that would stretch well into the afternoon, and an evening simply sitting outside watching the sun as she slipped below the horizon.'

'I'd love to come, mate,' said Theo. 'About time I met the lovely Pam.'

'Absolutely,' Maisie agreed. 'I'm in no hurry.'

'Oh, she will be pleased. Give me two minutes.' After disappearing briefly to collect his shirt, he picked up a door key from the shelf in the hall, and locked the front door. 'I've told her so much about both of you and she knows how kind you are. Not everyone makes the time to chat with me but you two always do and I appreciate it.'

They followed the old man down the road and turned into a quieter lane dotted with traditional Suffolk cottages set back from the road. Most were rendered and painted in sunny yellows or the more traditional pink. At the far end of the lane, at the top of the gently sloping hill, was Tattlesham church. Maisie could see its flinty walls and imposing round tower as they turned the corner. The sun was on her way up, rising through drifting blobs of marshmallow cloud, and as they followed behind, Arthur maintained a happy chatter about his morning's activities – managing to make getting up and having breakfast sound like a full day's work.

Maisie assumed they were going to the daughter's house but as Arthur swung open the low wooden gate to the church she realised, as it was Sunday, the ladies were probably engaged in something church-related. She could imagine Arthur's wife being the sort of lady who gave up her weekends to arrange flowers or bake cakes in support of the local vicar.

She stood and held the gate for Theo, as he was starting to lag back. Arthur continued to stride across the churchyard so she let the gate swing shut and trotted behind him – not wanting him to disappear from view. Theo had all but stopped. Wuss, she thought, he can't be out of breath, unless it was an anti-religion thing.

Arthur stopped by the low flint wall on the south side of the churchyard and rested his bottom on the edge, putting up his hand to shield his eyes from the sun.

'So where exactly is she, Arthur?' On such a glorious day, perhaps she was outside tending to graves or cutting back unruly brambles. Everything had shot up in the past few weeks with the warm, wet weather. Maisie looked around for any sign of life in the peaceful but unnerving place of death.

But something didn't feel right. The church and churchyard were silent. A blackbird landed on the top of the wall near Arthur – a fat pink worm hanging from its bright yellow beak. It studied the pair of them, now both at a standstill as dappled light from the lofty canopy of the trees danced across their faces.

'There's my birthday girl ...' he said, with a grin, a shaky hand rising slowly. And in that moment, when time was split into fractions of indeterminable length and that one second took ten times longer than it should have, between focusing on his raised hand and turning her head to see where it was pointing, she suddenly knew.

She knew why this dear old man talked so much every time he came across people – desperate for human contact and to pass the time of day with another living soul. She knew why he gabbled on, not pausing for questions or sympathy when he opened up his heart a tiny bit to the tragedies or bleak things that had happened in his life. She knew why his shirts were creased and his socks occasionally had holes, why he took odd jobs home over the weekend to keep him busy and leaped upon every social invitation that came his way.

Her stomach folded in on itself as she questioned how she could have been so stupid.

Maisie allowed her gaze to shift slowly from the end of his finger, across the recently mowed grass of the churchyard, and rest upon a large white marble headstone – a piteously smaller stone in its shadow, topped with a delicate carving of a weeping angel.

'... With Primmy, our daughter.'

Chapter 40

'You knew, didn't you?' Maisie whispered, as she carefully arranged Theo's flowers in the stone vase at the foot of Pamela's stone. 'When we came through the gate – you knew?'

'Yeah, a few things suddenly dropped into place,' Theo admitted, pulling up the tiny weeds that had germinated at the base of the headstone. 'He's a proud man, and one who goes out of his way not to inconvenience or elicit sympathy from others. I remembered his words more clearly as we approached the church. "Flowers are the only thing I can give her now." And I realised they are one of the few gifts we give to the dead.'

Arthur reappeared from behind the west tower, where he'd trundled off to fill up a watering can from the churchyard tap.

'Well, now, I'm thinking that from the way all the colour drained from young Maisie's face, that perhaps I hadn't made it clear that my lovely Pam was no longer with us. And now I feel right bad that I prattle on about her the way I do.'

'Maisie and me both, to be brutally honest, Arthur,' Theo said.

'Really?' Arthur sounded surprised as he topped up the water.

'How come no one in the neighbourhood mentioned it? I'm mortified. I've lived around the corner from you for nearly two years.' Theo stood up and brushed soil from his fingers.

'I don't think there's anyone left in our road who remembers her, if I'm honest, and in many ways, she isn't gone to me. She's the first person I speak to when I wake, and the last person I tell my troubles to when I sleep. I know she can hear me, and she's always been that calm, steady voice in my ear, guiding me through the difficult times and telling me off when I've mucked something up.'

'You talk to her – like *out loud* talk to her?' Theo was frowning and scratching his springy hair. 'Oh, Arthur, my dear fellow.'

'Well, yes, and it don't seem weird to me so I forget people might misunderstand. But when she passed and I was so alone and lost, I began talking to her to help me cope. "*Now* what am I going to do, Pam?" "How the hell do I load this washing machine, woman?" – that sort of thing. And it made me feel like she was there with me and helping me through the muddle.'

Maisie's heart went out to this vulnerable old man who had allowed a mask of coping and a barrage of words to shield his misery and loneliness.

'Has she been gone long?' Maisie asked, still playing catch-up with this unexpected turn of events.

'Now, let me see,' and Arthur scratched his head as he did the maths. 'It will be twenty years this autumn.'

And her heart, which had already taken a battering on this old man's behalf, crumpled even further. Twenty years, reflected Maisie, was an awfully long time to live alone.

A week later and Maisie was back at Willow Tree House with a slightly less suspicious but equally blunt Irene. She took a large bunch of yellow tulips to thank the old lady for all her help with the tea set but they were greeted with the mumbled aside that a couple of packs of Benson and Hedges would have been more useful.

Much to Maisie's surprise, Lisa tagged along, muttering that she was so bored it was either eat her own head or slap some nail polish on the quavery hands of a few old dears – the latter being the most appealing option by a smidge. Maisie reminded her sister that those 'quavery hands' mercilessly thrashed her at Wii Sports and knitted the most delicate baby clothes in a blur of fingers and clicking needles. Their mother was beside herself when her glamorous eldest daughter appeared in reception and she whisked Lisa down to the salon to work her magic on the residents – clearly expecting Lisa to transform them all into Hollywood superstars.

Maisie was heavy-hearted, and still hadn't got over Arthur's tragic revelation. She'd had a long conversation with Theo, both racked with guilt and thinking how awful it must be to have no one. At least Irene had Essie and, if she sanded down her jaggedy bits, possibly Joanie.

'I have most of the set now and am only missing Cynthia's plates,' Maisie said to the wheezy Irene. Naked Man was sound asleep in the corner chair, covered with a crocheted blanket. 'But with everything you've told me, I can't imagine tracking them down so I guess this is where their story ends. But I will use the pieces I have and think fondly of Meredith when I do.'

It was frustrating to be so close yet so far away. She was convinced Verity's tea set had been the key to reuniting her own family and that it had chosen her, all those years ago in Meredith's front room.

'I suppose I'm pleased you're pleased,' said Irene, tutting at the tulips for the umpteenth time. They'd been unceremoniously dumped in a vase, still in their cellophane and not so much as a 'How kind'. Some people were simply not flower people.

There was a knock at the door and Maisie's mum popped in with a tray of tea and biscuits.

'Thought I'd join you for a cuppa on my tea break. Lisa has a queue halfway down the corridor so I daren't hold her up or she'll be here until one or both of us turn into pumpkins. Aren't you interested in a make-over, Irene?' she asked, sliding the tray onto the table between them.

'Had enough make-up slapped over my face to last a lifetime. Besides, not over keen on being sat in front of a mirror, staring at a reminder that ton-ups in the dark, without a helmet, high on drugs wasn't my finest hour.'

'Ton-ups?' Maisie's mother enquired.

'Hitting a hundred miles an hour on the back of a lad's motorbike. You had to get your thrills where you could in them days.'

'Anyone for a Jammy Dodger?' Maisie's mum asked, as she settled into the spare chair next to her daughter. Irene grabbed a handful. 'Don't let me forget the time, though. I have a meeting at eleven with a gentleman interested in initiating an Adopt a Gran scheme.'

Irene embarked on a prolonged coughing fit. 'Adopt a Gran? Bloody bonkers, if you ask me. Adopt something useful, like a puppy or an elephant in Sri Lanka. We're all past our prime. It would be like adopting an empty tube of toothpaste. We all know we're here to die.'

'Come now, Irene.' Maisie's mum jollied the old lady along. 'Everyone is going to pass away at some point. No need to get maudlin about it. Some of our residents have been here for years, enjoying a rich and fulfilled life. Just because you need a bit of help to get about doesn't mean you're no use to anyone.'

'Rubbish. I'm not going to be doing any enjoying of anything any time soon. And I don't count endless games of stupid bingo or sticking paper flowers on Easter straw bonnets fulfilling. Much rather be nursing a bottle of gin or playing poker for fags. I don't even have the energy to take advantage of my naked stalker.' She nodded over to her sleeping boyfriend. 'Besides, the sodding tubes and bottles would only get in the way. Fancy that,' she mused, 'never thought I'd be too old for a no-strings offer of sex.'

'Some of the younger generations don't have older family around, Irene,' Maisie's mum chastised, ignoring the sex reference. 'There are people out there who have lost parents and grandparents and are looking to fill that gap in their lives. It's not all for your benefit, you know. You have a wisdom and a life experience that could benefit those prepared to listen. Just because you can't cartwheel down the corridor, doesn't mean you aren't useful.'

'Hrumph,' muttered Irene.

'I'm genuinely excited by the scheme,' her mum said to Maisie. 'We've got several residents who never have visitors and it breaks my heart when they don't get so much as a Christmas card.' There was a familiar moistness around her mum's eyes and Maisie wondered if she ever made it through a whole day without crying.

'I think it's a lovely idea,' said Maisie, thinking of Arthur.

Still relatively young and sprightly at seventy, would there come a time when he found himself in a care home with no family to visit? Perhaps before he'd met Theo and her this might have been his fate, but she knew neither of them would let that happen now. Poor Theo, she'd never seen him look so upset – blaming himself for missing the signs and lamenting the loneliness of old age.

After a few minutes of tea and chatter, there was a knock at the door and it swung open to reveal a slim girl in a navy blue and white care home tunic.

'Your appointment has arrived, Beverley.'

Maisie and her mother walked together down the long, carpeted corridor towards the main reception.

'I'll drop Lisa back later,' said her mum.

'Really? I don't think she was planning on staying for long.'

'It's her idea. She doesn't want to disappoint anyone.'

Maisie shrugged. She knew Lisa was struggling, rattling around the house all day, but had rather expected her to find a more self-serving outlet for her energies.

'And it's kind of you to visit Irene. She's not the easiest person to get along with. There are so many chips on her shoulder you could serve them with a nice piece of battered fish.'

'I don't mind. I find the history of the Mayhews both interesting and terribly sad, and she did give me her cups and saucers for nothing. I feel sorry for her and wonder how her life would have turned out if she hadn't come flying off the back of a motorbike and lost her promising career. I saw some of her modelling photos. She was very pretty, in a gawky, baby-owl-eyed way. Fancy having it all snatched away.'

'You can't spend your time thinking about what ifs, love. Maybe she'd have been picked up, been the next Twiggy, led a hedonistic life and ended up dead of a drug overdose at twenty-five.'

It was true. You couldn't regret the might have beens because there was no certainty the outcome would have been any happier.

They rounded the corridor and her mother typed a four-digit combination into a tiny keypad to allow them access to the reception area.

Maisie looked over to the corner seating where a scruffy young man was sprawled across the sofa, one leg flung carelessly across the other.

'Theo, isn't it?' her mum said, extending a hand. 'Come through.'

Chapter 41

'Adopt a Gran?' Maisie placed a steaming, smoky-smelling mug of hot coffee on her desk, as she spoke to the top of Theo's springy head.

He didn't look up from where he was countersigning a pile of cheques and broke out in a broad grin.

'No thanks. I've just got myself a shiny new one.'

'Shiny maybe. New? Old Mrs Leggit is ninety, if she's a day.'

'I had no idea of your connection to Willow Tree House, by the way. It was just after Arthur and everything ...' He looked lost and Maisie wanted to scoop him up and hug him.

She slipped into her swively chair and nudged his elbow. 'It's sweet. I think it's a great idea. Mum is always desperate for visitors to help with activities at the home. She's even managed to rope Lisa in.'

Theo scratched his head with the end of his Biro. 'Yeah, one of my better ideas. Mutually beneficial though; she's an amazing old bird. Lived a colourful life. Grew up in the west country and mixed with some of the great post-war potters, including Bernard Leach. Thought I might get her pass stamped and bring her to an auction viewing. Women love poking around other people's possessions and reliving memories.'

'Let's hope it's not a week when we have another coffin in then, or the poking might lead to premonition rather than a memory.' Theo gave her a mock-stern look. 'I was joking,' Maisie said hastily.

'Pretty sure the coffin was a one-off.'

'Like me – I'm a one-off,' she said, tossing back her head and pulling a playful pout.

'Yeah,' Theo said, and then cleared his throat. 'Arthur said you've given up on the last of the tea set. That's not going to sit well with the lady who broke out in a cold sweat when she saw that chess set was missing a bishop last week.'

'I like things to match and be whole. It's not a crime.'

'You do know that that's the joy of antiques?'

'What is?'

'Their imperfections. If they all survived beautifully intact and looked as good as the day they were made, not only would people not believe their age, but they would also lose something. Think of a highly scrubbed pine refectory table or a well-thumbed book. They've lived a life and been appreciated.' He looked at her intently for a few moments and then lazily shoved his chair back. 'I want to show you something. Come with me.'

They walked over to Saleroom Two. Now that summer was heading their way, each trip to the barns was a sunshine-soaked joy. Her vitamin D levels had definitely increased since her time at Wickerman's. Every breath in this rural idyll was clean and somehow green, even when combined with dubious odours from the countryside.

'This is a set of harlequin chairs,' Theo said, as they walked inside, pointing to a set of six chairs that she now recognised were peculiar to East Anglia. Several had gone through their hands since she'd been working at Gildersleeve's: square-backed, elm or fruitwood, with wooden concave seats.

'Pretty chairs but not a set,' she said.

'That's what the term means,' Theo explained. 'It's rare to find a complete set from this period because they were often split up or broken. People buy the same quality, period and style and they work well together. These are all Suffolk Ball Back chairs – see the row of turned balls along the cross rail? These chairs at the front only have two, the rest have three – with this odd chair here having grooves in the turnings. But they're all elm, and all from about 1840. And in some ways nicer than an identical set.'

She'd heard the phrase harlequin set bandied about by Johnny before; now she understood and the concept did have a certain appeal.

'To me, the fact they've come from different places makes them more interesting – they each have a story to tell. And even though I'm more twentieth-century in my personal tastes, the patina and wear on these chairs add to the charm. If they didn't have these knocks and bumps, if they were in perfect condition, no one would believe they were nearly two hundred years old,' Theo finished.

She couldn't explain to him that the tea set was about so much more. That without all the components her family might never reunite. He'd think she was daft. And he'd probably be right.

Arthur ambled up to them in a black fedora, looking rather like Frank Sinatra, and waving a sheet of paper.

'Johnny asked if you could photograph these items to show-case on the website,' he said.

'I'll leave you to it,' said Theo, 'but remember, not everything has to be pristine or matching to be perfect.'

But she'd already learned that during her time Gildersleeve's, because she was watching a battered, scruffy, less than pristine man walk out of the barn and into the blinding sunshine and he was perfect to her.

'Lot 67 ...?' Arthur muttered to himself, scanning the numbered stickers. 'Well, now, here's a rum fella and no mistake,' he said, standing next to a medical skeleton. 'This skinny little chap will sell well. I can feel it in my *bones*.' He bent down to a stuffed otter on the trestle table. 'Whatcha think? Is it me or is it getting *otter* in here?' With his rich Suffolk accent and the incongruous fedora, it was like watching an impromptu comedy skit.

'Say that again, Arthur,' she said. 'All of it.' She held up her phone to take a short video clip. They played it back, Arthur peering over her shoulder, and she knew it was social media dynamite.

'With your permission, can I put this on Facebook?' she asked.

'Well, now, do I really sound like that? Well, there's a thing. Of course, my dear, you post away, but I don't imagine you'll be getting many of them likes for it. Just a silly old boy prattling on.'

'I think you'll be pleasantly surprised,' she said.

By the end of the afternoon, the silly old boy prattling on got more retweets than her usual social media posts and a lot more interaction. Over the next couple of days, she experimented with further clips where Arthur came out with some comedy classics like, 'Do anyone out there like sitting in their garden and admiring their dahlias? Well, it won't be long until it's that time of year again. Jugs of Pimm's and some factor ten.

Git yourselves along to our Yard to see a right nice section of garden furniture.'

The public response was overwhelming. In the space of a week, Arthur became even more of a local celebrity than he'd been with the hats. The in-house response was less enthusiastic.

'What do you think you're doing?' Theo sounded unusually irritable as he came striding in to the back office, tossing a clipboard across his desk and sending a cascade of papers and empty drink cans onto the carpet. 'Slapping Arthur all over FaceAche like some circus sideshow. Yes, we're getting a lot of social media coverage, but it's at the expense of a dear old man, who you're using as a stooge. We're trying to present a professional façade to the world, as we deal in antique artefacts and high-end jewellery. Don't turn us into some kind of joke.'

Maisie was taken aback by his ill temper as Theo was generally so easy-going but then he'd been unusually grumpy of late. Things with Ella were clearly in those tricky early stages.

'Arthur knows what I'm doing. I always ask, and I *always* show him afterwards. You're not his guardian and he's not a child. Arthur is perfectly capable of making his own decisions.'

Maisie was equally riled. It was as if every step forward she took with the company, Theo was there peering over her shoulder and pulling her two steps back. Johnny, on the other hand, never checked up on her. If he commented at all it was only to give praise.

'We're raising the company profile and giving people a laugh,' she added.

'People are laughing *at* him, not with him.'

A movement caught the corner of her eye and Maisie looked up to see Arthur, who had clearly been standing in the open doorway for some time.

'Well, now, I think it's a lovely thing to have lots of people looking at our little videos, and watching me talking. And if they're laughing at the silly old bugger, in the daft hat, who has an old Suffolk boy way of speaking, that's all right by me. It's helping Gildersleeve's, and we have fun doing it, don't we, girl?' He winked at Maisie. 'And I'd rather do something that makes people smile, even if it's at my expense, than makes people cry or, worse still, suffer indifference. As much as I appreciate your concern, sir, I can probably speak up for m'self if I need to.' He nodded deferentially to Theo. 'Anyhoo, I just popped in to speak to Maisie ...'

Knowing her cheeks were aflame, Maisie was pleased to see Theo also looked uncomfortable.

'I'm sorry, Arthur,' Theo said, gathering up handfuls of papers and, to Maisie's annoyance, stuffing them higgledy-piggledy into the seat of his desk chair. 'We shouldn't have been talking about you behind your back. But you are quite correct; I shouldn't speak on your behalf. I apologise.'

'That's all settled then, because I saw all that there play-ground equipment come into The Yard yesterday, and I was wondering about some video of me going down the slide – head first?'

'That lovely young man of yours was in again yesterday to visit Mrs Leggit.'

It was the following week and all her mum could talk about was the Adopt a Gran scheme – which had now made the local newspaper.

'He's not my young man. He's my colleague and technically my boss.'

'Lovely-looking chap,' her mum reflected. 'Surprising hair though. Bet it's the devil to wash. Wouldn't have wanted to be his mother trying to comb it out for head lice when he was little.' Her mum really came out with some odd observations – but then she guessed it went with the motherhood territory.

Lisa appeared in the doorway to the living room, her hair spun up into a towelling turban of pale blue and wearing Maisie's silky bathrobe. She'd been in the bathroom for nearly an hour. This wasn't unusual but jolly inconvenient when the house only had one loo.

'What's for tea?' asked Lisa.

'Oh, I'm going out. Sorry. I'll order you in a takeaway. Not sure what gluten-free options will be available though,' said Maisie.

Her mother's mouth dropped open.

'Surely Lisa is capable of getting herself a meal?'

'I don't think she feels great today and I don't mind,' Maisie said, as her sister sauntered towards the kitchen and out of earshot. She was mindful Lisa didn't want her work struggles flagged up to other family members.

'You run around after her too much,' her mum chastised, patting Maisie's knee. 'Anyway, I only popped by to let you know your father and I are going to see a live band at the Tattlesham Arms together this weekend. I can't remember the last time I listened to live music. I've missed him, sweetheart. We used to have so much fun when we first started going out. I'm not blaming you kids in any way, but things change when you become parents.'

'But not for the worse?' Maisie asked.

'No, you get a lot of joy from your children but there is also a lack of energy and weariness from the role that seeps into your very bones. Honestly, every day with you four was such an emotional roller-coaster of a ride; from the delight of a home-made pasta necklace and being told you are the best mum in the world, to doors slammed in your face and the diplomatic negotiations to avoid World War Three breaking out in the back seat of the car. By the time your dad got home from work I was emotionally spent. Perhaps it was all my fault. Perhaps I had nothing left to give and he sought comfort elsewhere ...'

She decided not to comment on her mother's misplaced guilt. It really wasn't her business. They were grown-ups and they had to sort this thing out for themselves.

'Talking of family, I've set a date for my family meal. I'm not holding out for Ben any more but gathering five of us together would be a coup of sorts. With Lisa staying it seems like a good time to organise something,' Maisie said.

'Good luck getting your bickering sisters together.' Her mother rolled her eyes. 'Those two never did get on. I would have put it down to the age gap but you always seem to bring out the best in them. Different personalities, I guess. So what's the plan? And will there be bouncers on the door to intervene if they start clawing each other's eyes out?'

That was rich. A few weeks ago it would have been her parents who needed supervision.

'A low-key Sunday lunch with all fire exits clearly marked, and life jackets and oxygen masks under the seats,' Maisie joked. 'Surely everyone can be civil for a couple of hours and if it proves a success, I wondered about a family-orientated Christmas.' She paused. 'Do you think I'm being too optimistic?'

'Not at all, love. Let's aim for the stars. I wouldn't start planning anything as adventurous as a six-week family holiday halfway up a mountain in a three-foot-square bivouac, but things with your dad are ... developing. We've been reminiscing about the old days, and we have great affection for each other. It was only a couple of meaningless flings and perhaps I did inadvertently push him away. Four is a lot of children to manage and very draining on any relationship.'

Maisie was feeling increasingly uncomfortable with her mother's excuses for her dad's behaviour so moved the conversation on.

'I've decided on the sixteenth.' Maisie lowered her voice. 'As much as I love Lisa staying—'

'We both know that's a very generous choice of verb,' her mum interrupted. 'And it's not like I haven't offered to have her at mine.'

'I think she needs to head back to York and face whatever it is she's running away from,' Maisie said. And get the help she won't let me give her, she thought.

'Funny you should say that,' said her mum. 'I got the impression she's hiding something, too.'

Chapter 42

Gildersleeve's were riding the crest of a very high wave. The auctions were now more popular than ever and it was often a struggle fitting everyone in the barns. Theo's *Wot a Lot!* episodes were generating local interest and Arthur's video posts were garnering hundreds of likes – way beyond Maisie's wildest dreams. Two local newspapers picked up on the videos and ran a further story. The county loved nothing more than a 'Suffolk old boy'. On the back of all that, Theo was giving a late-afternoon radio interview in Bury St Edmunds and invited Maisie along for the experience. She was delighted and curious in equal measure so accepted his offer.

The radio DJ, who had the requisite sexy rumble to his voice, ushered Theo through to a side room with a huge illuminated On Air sign. She waited in an anteroom, sipping tea that tasted as if it had been swept from a warehouse floor, and listening to the show go out live from a ceiling-height speaker in the back corner.

Theo was funny and charming and had a great rapport with the interviewer. He talked about his TV appearances but always managed to bring the conversation back to promoting Gildersleeve's. Sitting by herself and clutching the plastic cup of tepid tea, Maisie closed her eyes and let his voice stream into her head and realised how precious his friendship had become. Would she have embraced it quite so easily if there had been sexual undercurrents? Her initial belief romance was not on the agenda had enabled her to be relaxed and open with him but it had also drawn him dangerously close to her thumping heart. As if on cue, Ed Sheeran's 'Perfect' played from the speakers as the interview ended and shivers ran up her arms, bristling every single hair along the way.

'You have a great radio presence,' she said, as he ambled out the studio after the broadcast and her heart returned to its normal rhythm. 'You're a natural.'

'Nothing to it. It's just a conversation in a room with some bloke about things I love.'

'Not sure I'd be so chilled.'

'No,' Theo agreed. 'You'd be more of a multiple cue cards kinda gal, I imagine. But then I tend to wing life generally, whereas I suspect you have a ten-point life plan, with a list of potential husbands, seven possible wedding locations lined up, and the names already picked out for your two perfect children – one of each, naturally.' His lip curled upwards and she silently added his name to the potential husband list.

'Nothing wrong with being organised,' she said. 'Whereas you will amble through life, bump into someone and just know she's the one.'

'Probably,' he admitted. 'You can't overthink these things.'

'Unless, of course, you've already met her?'

It was like picking at a scab. She couldn't help herself – returning to the Ella question time and time again. He'd quite clearly been referring to her when Lisa had asked if his heart was taken. 'A colleague perhaps?' She pushed for confirmation.

'Okay, you've sussed me out.' Theo gathered his man-bag from the table where he'd left it with her for the interview, yanking forcefully to adjust the strap. 'But let's not have this conversation – it's awkward for me. It's embarrassing having feelings for someone when it's not an equal attraction.'

The little she knew about Ella, she guessed she wasn't the kind of girl to launch head first into something. He'd have to be patient.

'Give it time,' she said.

He looked cheered by her words. 'Are you saying I need to back off a bit? Perhaps let things develop more slowly?'

'Women don't like being rushed. They take relationships very seriously. When we give our hearts, we give them completely. Sometimes we need to explore our options—'

'I'd noticed,' he muttered.

She didn't immediately understand the reference but then remembered Ella's crush on the art teacher. It was very unfair that some people had several potential romantic prospects when all she wanted was the one standing in front of her, tugging at his faded T-shirt and totally unaware the laces on his scuffed brogues were undone. Determined not to be churlish, and instead supportive of this embryonic relationship, she smiled. 'A girl's got to try on several pairs before she buys the perfect shoes.'

Theo scratched his extraordinary hair and frowned. 'But I haven't been rushing anyone. If I'd taken this whole thing any slower, we'd be going sodding backwards.' He looked at her face, doing the deep, staring thing again. 'But okay, I'll apply the brakes,' and he put up his hands in capitulation. 'Wouldn't want to rush anyone whilst they *explore options* ...'

*

'Stop,' Maisie said, as they walked in the cool late spring air and back to his car. The shock she felt was overwhelming and she hardly dared believed the truth. After all, she'd been down to Bury St Edmunds several times already in her futile quest.

'What is it now, woman?' Theo joked, back to himself now that the conversation wasn't so personal.

'I'm not sure.' She crossed her arms and rubbed her hands over the tingling.

Sauntering down this side street her mind had been on a billion and one things, only to have Verity's set violently dragged to the forefront. She was being called again and had to answer.

'Don't tell me you're cold? It's a lovely evening.'

'No, it's not that.' She walked a few steps further and the feelings intensified. Glancing up she noticed they were opposite a junk shop, and not one she'd visited before, so she headed towards it. Theo trailed behind, as a tinkly bell on the door jangled. There was scant light inside, in contrast to the brightness of the afternoon, and she squinted to make out the shapes before her.

Like a cornucopia for dusty old things no one really needed, the shop was piled high with bric-a-brac and stacked furniture – rather like the Gildersleeve's salerooms before she got her hands on them. As she shuffled through the narrow aisles of precariously balanced plastic boxes, a singsong voice drifted from the shadows.

'Afternoon. Feel free to browse.'

Nearing the counter at the back of the shop, Maisie could see a pair of spectacles and a sleek bob – all very Mary Quant, except the hair was a violent pomegranate red.

'I'm looking for black and white china,' Maisie explained.

'Specifically plates. Abstract in style.'

'I'm not sure I have anything like that,' the woman said, rising to her feet and walking around the counter. She peered in glass cabinets and over the piles of clutter.

You jolly well do, Maisie thought. I know it. Instead she followed the woman as she wove up and down the shop.

'If you're looking for more of Verity's set, it's going to be a needle in a haystack job,' Theo whispered. 'You could scour all the antique and collector shops in the country and not find any more. You already know it's pretty scarce from your online searches.'

'Hmm ... I have these?' the woman said, holding a black and white cup and saucer aloft. 'Four Royal Albert Night and Day trios and a solitary sugar bowl.'

It was pretty enough; black exteriors to the cups with white ferns, and the reverse image on the saucer and plate. But it wasn't part of Verity's set.

'Are you sure you don't have anything else? Out the back maybe?' Maisie asked, trying to look pleady without being pushy.

'My stockroom is a nightmare,' the sleek-haired lady replied. 'It would take weeks to sort through it.'

Maisie's heart fell. 'Let me show you what I'm after, and I'll leave a contact number in case you ever have anything like it pass through your hands.'

She slid her phone from her pocket and looked through her photos until she found one of the tea set she'd taken for research purposes. 'I collect it and I'm only missing a few tea plates now.'

She twisted the screen so the tiny lady could get a better look.

'Oh, *that* pattern,' she said. 'You aren't going to believe this, but I own some of that – a tiered cake stand and three matching tea plates I bought donkey's years ago from a jumble sale. They're in my flat upstairs. How odd.'

'How odd indeed,' said Theo, giving Maisie the most piercing, mossy-green stare.

Chapter 43

Maisie and Theo stood outside the junk shop, the low sun basking them in a warm light. The temperature had dropped slightly and the previously bustling street was almost deserted, as it was now nearly six o'clock. Food aromas drifted past on the breeze as the various take-away establishments opened their doors for the evening trade.

'I've done it,' Maisie said, with the biggest grin on her face. 'I have the complete set.' If she was more like Zoe, she would be physically bouncing up and down and possibly performing an impromptu triple front flip.

'At last – now you can have a decent night's sleep after months of pacing in front of your mantelpiece and wringing your hands over the incompleteness of it all. Don't forget—' he raised an eyebrow '—I know you.'

'I'm not that bad.' She playfully punched his shoulder with her free hand, the other still clutching the handle of the supermarket bag for life that contained her newspaper-wrapped purchases. 'In fact, since Lisa's arrival I have taken a step back from my inner control freak. However, I won't deny it feels good to be holding the last pieces. I'm so lucky the shop owner was happy to part with them.'

'Once a dealer, always a dealer.' Theo smiled. 'As long as

the price is right, most of them would happily sell their left kidney. And well done for haggling. I didn't want to interfere, but I thought she was going to shaft you with her initial price.'

'Yeah, I'm learning,' she said, thinking back to Phyllis's grabbing grandson.

'How *did* you know, though?' he asked.

'Know what?'

'That the plates were in there?'

'I didn't.' She gave him her best innocent face, the one she'd perfected as a child when Zoe asked what had happened to her favourite sparkly top.

'Well, there's something going on.' He eyed her suspiciously. 'There we were merrily walking down the street and you took a sudden detour into a random shop and insisted she hand over your missing pieces.'

'No, I didn't. I popped into a likely-looking shop because I've been scouring junk shops and charity shops for weeks on the off-chance. I was lucky, that's all.'

'Hmm ...' He was clearly unconvinced. 'You unsettle me, Maisie Meadows. In lots of ways ...'

'Good,' she replied. 'I wouldn't want to be predictable.'

'So, I think your *extraordinarily* lucky find—' he glanced at her through narrowed eyes '—calls for a celebration. I know how much Meredith meant to you. Let's put the bag in my car and I'll take you for a drink in this idyllic little courtyard restaurant I know.'

The evening was glorious but the company was making her nervous. How silly to have a hundred flapping butterflies in her chest when all she was doing was grabbing an after-work drink with the boss. They dropped off the plates and walked to a huge Georgian-fronted pub at the far end of the city.

The setting sun cast her embers of light across the cobble-stone courtyard. They were surrounded by high flinty walls, edged with a beautiful Suffolk red brick, as the clatter of her shoes and the squeak of the metal chair legs over the cobbles echoed around them. It felt a safe and comforting space, shutting them off from their work lives and just letting them be.

A tight-trousered waiter shimmied across the courtyard, a black circular tray balanced across his arm, and heavenly wafts of garlic and lemon floated past.

'Let me buy you dinner?' Theo offered, as Maisie pulled her gaze away from the waiter's firm buttocks and took a sip of her Prosecco. Theo was on the non-alcoholic beer as he was driving but insisted she had something suitably celebratory and bubbly. His gaze was intense and made her feel uncomfortable. She knew he stared at everyone like that – one of his endearing features, that he was truly engaged in what you were saying and gave you his full attention. Perhaps it was those first two mouthfuls of Prosecco, zipping down to her knees and making them feel disobedient, or perhaps it was because she wanted there to be more to those simple words, but his eyes had a further reach than hers. They had positively dived into her heart and made everything whirly and wobbly.

'Okay, but we go Dutch,' she insisted, the lingering smell of citrus and apple from the Prosecco making her stomach flip. What with everything that was going on, her insides were more tumultuous than a spinning drum of tumble-drying towels.

'Tulips in a cheesy Edam sauce?' He leaned back in that relaxed manner of his, one leg tossed carelessly across the knee of the other, and gave her a friendly wink. She rolled her eyes.

Fifteen minutes later, and with the conversation strangely more formal and awkward than it had been in recent weeks, the alarmingly close-fitting trousers of the waiter presented themselves at eye height to the pair. A plate of mushroom ravioli was slid in front of her and steak-frites were presented to Theo.

'Here's to you.' Theo lifted his beer and clinked her glass with the edge of his. 'Gildersleeve's is all the better for your input.'

'Even when I prostitute us on social media?'

'Yes, even then. I ... *we* would miss you terribly if you left.'

'I'm not going anywhere for a while,' she said, adding the 'for a while' to keep him on his toes.

'I heard that bloke trying to lure you back to Wickerman's the other day.' He began to cut into his steak, dropping his eyes.

'Then you also heard me say I was happy where I was.'

'Even though we are a disorganised shambles?' It was a phrase she'd used a couple of times when she'd first started.

'I find the less formal atmosphere of Gildersleeve's endearing. And I'm learning to chill about these things. I had some serious childhood control issues to work through but I'm getting there.' He looked quizzical. 'My parents' divorce,' she reminded him. 'I hadn't realised until recently it was something I had no control over and it naturally turned my life upside down. In the following few years when my siblings started to disperse, I guess I focused on things I could control. When you gather up inanimate objects and arrange them how you want them, neat and orderly, they stay there. People don't behave in the same way – rather frustratingly.'

Theo rested his fork on the side of his plate and stroked his stubbly chin. 'Okay, I understand where your happy-families vibe comes from. But as I explained, my own lack of family and parental disinterest had the opposite effect.'

'But you're a more chilled personality than me.'

'If you can't control it, why stress over it? I'm not going to be playing happy families any time soon and that's fine. Family can be a drag as well as a blessing. The old "you can choose your friends …" adage is true. I choose my "family" and it's made of friends. Hey, I even started up a scheme so I could pick my own grandmother.' He grinned. 'And I'd much rather spend time with an interesting man like Johnny than my own father. For all his bluff and big words, Johnny's a fun and generous man. Taking a chance on a struggling auction house was the best thing I ever did. I can't imagine being stuck in a desk job. It's the variety and people that bring my day alive.'

'And the stardom? And the hundreds of sexually ravenous fans throwing themselves at your feet on a daily basis?'

'Yeah, and that.' That grin accentuating the asymmetry of his face was balanced by a flick upwards of the opposing eyebrow and Maisie nearly launched herself across the table-cloth to offer the very same services as his imaginary groupies. She let out a long, slow breath to rein in her inner emotions and the low candle flickered horizontally between them, nearly going out.

Thinking of women offering Theo sexual services, she said, 'I'm pleased Ella has started to come out of herself now – largely due to you. I realise now I was too pushy, whereas you had her back the whole time.'

'I agree, it's wonderful to see her blossom. I like spending time with her. Plus, she doesn't try to tidy up my house when she comes round …'

Looking at him across the table, her internal organs still merrily tumble-drying away, there was a poignant pause. Eyes locked, she prepared herself to say something. She wanted to make a comment about how great he looked. It wasn't exactly top-level flirting but it was a testing dip of the toe in the potentially romantic waters in case the thing with Ella didn't last. She wasn't trying to seduce him, just let him know that she found him attractive should he ever come back on the market.

As this flitted around in her conflicted mind, her phone started to ring and shattered her thoughts into a starburst of unspent sexual frustration. It was doubtless her mum updating her on the night out with Dad. She could do without more misguided gushing because she knew her mother had purchased new underwear – the relationship was no longer platonic. Besides, she wanted to give Theo her undivided attention so she ignored it. The teenage yearnings of the middle-aged could wait.

Her courage silently slipped away from the table and didn't even nod as it left. She knew these growing romantic feelings for Theo were wrong. A relationship with the boss turning sour would be an opportunity for another life-altering double whammy. She needed to pull back now before everything went down the Gareth route – not that Theo was anything like her ex.

An hour later, as they left the soft glow of the courtyard and walked back towards Theo's car, the tension returned. She looked across at her springy-haired friend, striding into the night and towards the car park. His jaw was resolute and his eyes serious. They stood in front of his battered car and he paused.

'Maisie?' he said. 'I know we said earlier that I should apply the brakes ...'

Theo took a step towards her under the street light. The

gentle hum of the town traffic filled her ears, and the sweet smell of a late honeysuckle blooming in a nearby tiny edge-of-town garden drifted past. She'd had such a lovely evening and didn't want to spoil it by handing out further relationship advice to someone when the devil on her shoulder was ready to sabotage the whole damn thing for her own devious ends.

'Please stop,' she said. 'I don't want—'

'Maisie!' A raucous shout cut through her words and Theo immediately took a step back, his shoulders slumping and his eyes dropping. A rumble of footsteps approached. 'You little minx. What are you doing in Bury? If you'd said, we could have rendezvoused.'

Oliver bounded over, a small crowd of suited men lagging back. He threw a brotherly arm about her bare shoulders and ruffled her long fair waves. If she'd had short hair he might have got away with it, but his vigorous rub gave her a windswept tramp look and she had to sweep the straggly bits from her eyes.

Feeling patronised, she glared at him. 'Oliver, this is Theo – my *boss* from the auction house?'

Oliver stuck out his hand and Theo gave a quick sigh and the fakest smile Maisie had ever seen him give. Theo was nothing if not genuine.

'All right, mate?' Theo said, and they shook hands.

'I won't stop you. I'm out with friends making up for lost time.'

'Don't overdo it,' Maisie warned. 'You know it doesn't take much to get you tipsy.' He was so far removed from the blokey drinking culture he'd need a satnav to find it. One glass of Merlot and Zoe said he was anybody's.

'Ha, yeah, I'll take it steady. And whilst I remember, you left some girlie pink cardie at mine the other week.' Ah, she'd been missing it and had forgotten she'd worn it to see Oliver on his birthday.

'It's not important. Give it to me when I see you next.'

'Okay,' Oliver said. 'Say hi to the wonderful Bev from me and I'll catch you soon. Better go. We're hitting a few pubs around town so I'm hoping the house reds are up to par ...' And with that, he disappeared as abruptly as he'd arrived.

'My mum absolutely adores Olly,' she explained, as she turned back to Theo. 'The very first time she met him she had him marked up as suitable son-in-law material. He had her wrapped around his big, manly fingers from the off.' There was a pause as their unfinished conversation hung in the air. 'Are we done? Shall we go home?'

'Yeah, we're done,' huffed Theo. His mood became darker and he was quiet for the entire journey home. And because she didn't feel like talking any more either, that suited her just fine.

'What time do you call this – you dirty stop-out?' Lisa asked, lounging across the sofa with a glass of sparkly white in her hand.

Maisie slumped into the nearest armchair, not even bothering to move Lisa's scrunched-up laundry to the side. She was too tired to answer. And anyway, she assumed it was a rhetorical question.

Lisa tried again. 'You'll never guess where I've been?' So Maisie, still feeling flat, didn't try. 'I've spent the day at Willow Tree House. That Irene's a character but, bloody hell, the stories she can tell. She partied with some big names in the Sixties.

Not sure about the boyfriend though. He kept winking at me. Didn't help that I was staring at his face the whole time, but then, where *do* you look?'

Maisie shuffled up the seat. 'I told you they were a great bunch. I enjoy volunteering and I know Mum appreciates extra visitors.'

'Yeah, it was more fun than I expected. So, did you get laid tonight, Mrs Neatly-Pressed-Knickers?' Lisa returned to one of her favourite subjects; Maisie's lack of love life. Her other hot topic was herself and it seemed that had been dealt with satisfactorily for the time being.

'Actually, I've had an amazing day,' and she told her sister about acquiring the last of Verity's set.

'Whoopie-do. Perhaps you can stop rabbiting on about the damn thing now.' Lisa drained her glass and reached for the bottle. 'This'll cheer you up; I'm heading back to York after your family thing. Time to face up to some things. Irene was a big help, actually. Old people know some surprising stuff.'

'I'll miss you,' Maisie said, because she genuinely would. 'And if the meal is a success, perhaps you'll consider coming back for Christmas? I know it seems a long way off but I'd like to sort something. It will be fun. We can play games and have a good giggle. Just like old times.'

'Maybe,' said Lisa, clearly not over-keen to commit.

'Great. It's a shame Ben can't make the meal. I'd linked it all to Meredith's teapot in my head – as if reuniting the set would bring us back together, but nothing happened when I got Joanie's pieces, and now I have Cynthia's plates and we're still scattered ...'

Lisa frowned. 'You mean he didn't get you?'

'Who?'

'Ben. He rang this afternoon and I suggested he tried your mobile. Mum pulled out all the emotional stops and all but threatened to hire an assassin apparently, so he's flying back for the weekend of your blasted meal.'

Chapter 44

Finding herself in Essie's neighbourhood the following Saturday, Maisie stopped by to let her know that against all odds she'd gathered Verity's set together and to thank her for her help.

'Such wonderful news – I know Gamma would be pleased. I was going to contact you soon to say I'd been digging through our family tree but there was no Verity – not that I could uncover anyway.'

'Don't worry, I don't expect to solve that mystery. The important thing is it's reunited. It was quite a moment when I assembled it on my tiny kitchen table. Please come over and use it with me soon. I don't want it to spend its life on a shelf.'

'I'd love to. I would ask you in but I'm just in the middle of icing a birthday cake and it needs to set before my guests arrive.'

'Ooh, someone's birthday?'

'Mine, actually. A few friends and family are coming over shortly. Can't believe I'll be seventy.'

'Seventy is hardly old,' Maisie assured her. 'Many congratulations.'

'Thank you, my dear. And do wish Arthur the same when you see him. He's still not been in contact but I guess he's busy.' She shrugged her slender shoulders. 'Fancy still working at his age. You'd think he'd be content to put his feet up and watch the world go by.'

'It's Arthur's birthday?' An uncomfortable feeling flooded her body. Why hadn't he mentioned it when they'd visited him that day with the flowers for Pam? Or said something at work? Maisie felt she'd let him down enough by not realising he was a widower and now she hadn't even acknowledged his birthday. Theo should have told her.

'Tomorrow – the day after mine. That's the only reason I remember. We used to joke about it growing up, how we were practically twins like Irene and Joanie. It's the big one for him as well. Can't think of him as a man of seventy. He'll always be in his twenties to me, but then I haven't seen him properly for such a long time. We sort of lost touch after I got married. You know how it is.'

'Perhaps you should be the one to break the ice? I think he feels equally awkward getting back in contact after all this time. The number seven bus stops at the end of his road,' she added, helpfully.

'Oh no, I wouldn't want to turn up without giving Pam notice.'

Maisie was once again shocked how the death of Arthur's wife had gone unnoticed by so many people. Tattlesham was hardly a throbbing metropolis of nameless thousands.

'Didn't you know? He lost her twenty years ago.'

'Twenty years? How sad. And he never remarried?'

Maisie shook her head.

'The job makes sense now. Never was any good with his own company, even as a young man. Said it gave him too much time to dwell on things. He didn't have a nice childhood but then things were different in them days. You could whack your kids and get away with it. Always put on a brave face though.'

Not able to make any comment about Arthur's dreadful childhood without the possibility of unleashing emotion, Maisie summoned up a smile.

'I'll let you get on with your icing,' she said. 'Have a wonderful day.' The tragedy of Arthur's life just got worse and worse.

'Thank you. Both my sisters are coming – if you can believe that? Someone from Willow Tree is kindly dropping Irene off – oxygen tanks and all. Don't think they've been together in a room for thirty years. Strange to see them reconnecting out of the blue like this.'

Was it? Because to Maisie the explanation was black and white.

'Happy birthday!' Maisie sung, as Arthur pulled back his front door.

'Well now, what a lovely surprise. Come in, come in,' he pleaded and Maisie followed him into a disorderly living room that was in a bit of a time warp.

It was as if the house had stood still for a couple of decades and Maisie guessed that would coincide with Pamela's death; lace antimacassars on the backs of chairs, a dado rail running around the living room with green stripy wallpaper above and mint green emulsion below. But more poignant was a half-finished cross-stitch embroidery on the side table and a pair of beige fluffy slippers paired together under the sideboard – dusty and unworn for decades.

As Maisie handed over her gift, she noticed a large framed photograph propped up next to the television. Pam – she presumed. A pale, freckle-faced lady with a long nose, offset by two charming dimples either side of a wide smile. She looked friendly and fun.

'It's terribly kind of you to come out this way to see me.' He took the proffered parcel – a little something she'd picked up after speaking to Esther the previous day. 'How did you know? I don't advertise my birthday. Look, Pam,' he said, turning to the photograph. 'Young Maisie has brought me a gift. Isn't that thoughtful? After all, we're only work colleagues and I'm nothing to her outside of the auction house.' His eyes were watery and his voice cracked slightly as he spoke to his long-departed wife.

Maisie felt a lump rise in her chest. This dear old man, who was so keen to make friends he sometimes overwhelmed people, had been living alone all this time, unable to let his wife go and, looking around at the clutter, struggling to manage. Arthur followed her eyes.

'Don't look sad, love. These things happen. And I don't mind so much as I used to. It was hard at first. I didn't even know how to work the washing machine – her domain, see? And I'm not rightly sure I'm properly on top of everything even now. We had separate roles but I expect that's old-fashioned nowadays. She did all the home-making and I did the garden, and the fixing and mending.' He cast his eyes around the room, looking at things as if through Maisie's eyes. 'I know them curtains are shabby but the truth is, even if I bought new, I wouldn't rightly know how to hang them ...'

'Oh, Arthur. I can always help with anything like that. All you have to do is ask.' She gave him an encouraging smile, determined he shouldn't feel maudlin on his birthday. 'Come on, open your present.'

His bony fingers tugged at the pretty paper to reveal a book of British wild flowers, the primroses on the cover had caught her eye, and a small box of chocolates.

'How thoughtful, although I'm not sure I want to be thinking about turning seventy. Everything is slowing down, wearing out and dropping off. I don't know how much longer I'll be useful at Gildersleeve's.'

'Nonsense. You're in the prime of your life and a valued member of staff – we'd be foolish to part with our Twitter megastar.'

The old man's eyes began to look suspiciously watery again so she moved the conversation on. 'I won't hold you up on your special day. I expect you've got things planned?'

'Not exactly. Although I've got a smashing piece of fish for my supper, and there's some good things on the telly later ...'

'Arthur, please don't tell me you're spending your birthday *alone*?'

He looked abashed and started to mumble about people with busy lives and not having the time to sit around with a silly old bugger on such a glorious day, so Maisie decided to take things into her own hands.

'Are you about this afternoon?' she asked.

'Well, yes, I've got lots to catch up on; there's several episodes of *Gardeners' World* on iPlayer and I told Theo I'd have a go at mending the dodgy wheel on one of the sack barrows. He asked if I could have it done for Monday, so plenty to keep me busy. In fact I'll be so rushed off my feet, I won't have time to feel sorry for myself.'

He was a proud man, and she understood he didn't want sympathy, but a bit of gentle intervention wouldn't do any harm. She could nip to Theo's and see if he was free to help make Arthur's day a bit more special.

'If you're happy to dig out some cups and plates, and you don't mind me inviting myself, I think we should have a little celebratory afternoon tea. I'll be back in an hour.' After I've reprimanded Theo for keeping me in the dark, she thought.

'Fancy giving Arthur a sack barrow to mend on his birthday weekend,' Maisie said, hands on hips, to a dishevelled Theo, as he opened his door.

'It's his birthday?' He sounded genuinely surprised.

'Seventy today.'

'I had no idea.' He tugged at his faded Rolling Stones T-shirt, and she noticed for the first time that he was in boxer shorts. Her cheeks grew warmer and she focused intently on the Jagger lips logo to avoid her eyes dropping to his bare legs.

'How can you have known him all this time and not know when his birthday is?'

'He never said.' Theo sounded defensive. 'And if you knew, why didn't you tell me?'

'I only found out yesterday,' she said. 'I bumped into Essie again and it came up in conversation. I've just dropped him off a present but it would appear he's spending the day alone.'

'Then we need to remedy that. No one should be alone for their birthday, least of all a lovely old fella like Arthur.' Maisie's heart lifted. She loved that Theo was on the same page. Laid-back and underdressed he might be, but he was also incredibly thoughtful and compassionate.

'Actually ...' Her thoughts turned to Essie and despite learning the salutary lesson from Jane Austen that interfering in other people's love lives never ended well, she toyed with an idea. 'I might rope Essie in. He keeps talking about going over to see her but still hasn't made it. I could call by on my way to the supermarket for party supplies. It's about time the two childhood friends were reunited.'

'I'll throw on some jeans and join you,' he said, and she felt relieved that he wasn't quite laid-back enough to hit Tesco in underwear.

Ten minutes later, she was wandering around the supermarket with Theo, tossing assorted cakes, sausage rolls and even pre-made sandwiches, into the trolley. As much as she'd enjoy rustling up some home-made goodies, there simply wasn't time. Especially as a frantic phone call meant they were now collecting Essie in half an hour.

'As I live and breathe – Essie Mayhew.'

Arthur could hardly get her name out, he was so overcome with emotion. Perhaps Maisie had been mean not warning him she was bringing a former sweetheart into his home, especially as she suspected he'd spent the last few years ducking into doorways and behind postboxes to avoid her. Because the more she thought about it, the more she decided the excuses he gave for not calling had been his way of putting off a reunion that was too scary. After all, halcyon memories have a way of disappointing when confronted in later life.

'Happy birthday, Arthur, you old devil. It's been a while.' The pair locked eyes and seemed to have a whole conversation telepathically.

Maisie knew, for that brief moment, that she and Theo were totally superfluous to the proceedings. Two pairs of wrinkled hands reached out to each other, both slightly trembling as they gripped fingers. They bent forward to exchange a tentative kiss and then Essie rallied.

'Are you going to invite us in, Arthur? Or are we having this party on the doorstep?'

The four of them congregated in Arthur's small kitchen and it was as dated as his living room: orange beechwood cabinets, brown and cream floral blinds, and Tupperware containers on every surface. The black vinyl-seated kitchen chairs were strewn with laundry and floral threadbare tea towels were draped over the oven handle but it was a cheery room. There was a vase of freshly cut flowers on the windowsill, probably from his stunning front garden, their delicate floral scent jostling with the faint whiff of burnt toast.

Not expecting the extra two guests, Arthur rummaged for more plates and everyone helped to set out the buffet food on the yellow and black Formica table in the corner. In pride of place stood a hastily iced fruit cake from Essie.

Maisie's inner events organiser had won out in the supermarket. They'd purchased balloons, candles, a bottle of fizz, pretty napkins and a bag of party poppers. Theo, amazed by her organisational skills, had insisted on paying for everything – probably feeling guilty that he'd not noticed Arthur's birthday in the two years he'd known him as an employee and friend.

There was a satisfying pop of the cork from the Cava and they toasted Essie and Arthur's landmark birthdays before devouring their fill from the buffet.

'This is the best birthday I've had in many a year,' Arthur said, licking icing sugar from his lips. 'Probably since my Pam passed away.'

'Maisie told me you'd lost her. I'm sorry. She was a kind lady,' Essie said.

'She was,' Arthur confirmed. 'I still talk to her, you know, tell her about my day, ask her advice ... Pathetic, isn't it?'

'Nonsense,' said Essie. 'I still bake for our Frank. Can't seem to get out the habit. You've no idea how much I throw away. But it sort of helps. Keeps me busy.'

'Arthur adores cake, don't you?' Maisie said, unleashing her inner Emma again and getting a stern Mr Knightley look from Theo.

'Then he'll have to come and visit me now we've re-established contact, won't he?' she said, turning to Arthur. 'You'll be helping me out. I can't bear the waste. Plus, we have so much to catch up on after all these years. I can't believe we were both still living in Tattlesham and haven't bumped into each other more. But then I often think you're more anonymous in a bustling town than a quiet backwater – everyone so protective of their forty square foot of land that they scurry into their houses and shut their front door on their little kingdom without so much as a How Do You Do?'

'That would be lovely,' Arthur said.

Maisie caught the lingering glance between the two old friends. My work here is done, she thought to herself.

Chapter 45

After a couple of hours of chatter and merriment, Theo and Maisie discreetly left Essie and Arthur alone. Theo invited her back to his.

'Do you think they've even noticed we've gone?' she asked.

Theo chuckled. 'It's kinda sweet. Gives you hope.'

'Hope?'

'Yeah, that everything in life comes together in the end, whatever obstacles are thrown at you along the way.'

He opened the door to his living-cum-dining room, which was distinctly less cluttered than when she last visited.

'Ooh, had a tidy-up?'

'Yeah.' He shrugged. 'There's this neat freak at work and she's like an earworm, telling me things are easier to find if they have a proper place. Drives me nuts but it's like trying to run away from the wind.'

'And are they? Easier to find?'

'Maybe.' He still tossed his front door keys onto the sofa though, she noticed, as they slid down the arm and into the gap next to the seat cushion.

'Where do you put all your auction purchases? The house seems less cluttered than before, when by rights it should be chock-a-block with late-twentieth-century nostalgia.'

'Ah, well, since I've been doing more entertaining ...' there was a little knife wound to her heart as Maisie realised he was referring to Ella '... I've needed more space. Ella suggested the garage, actually. Seeing as I never quite get around to putting my car in there. I even dragged some stuff down from the bedrooms. Enough room to swing a Houdini hamster around by his stumpy little tail up there now. Let me show you my treasure trove.'

They stood together in his suburban garage as she surveyed an Aladdin's cave of retro collectables: G Plan furniture, boxes of LPs and various vintage household items, framed prints stacked against a wall and a stylish sage-green enamelled appliance that resembled a small Dalek with droopy weapon attachments.

'What on earth is that?' she asked, pointing to the curious machine.

'A Nineteen-Fifties Hamilton Beach 40DM Triplehead milk-shake machine – *obviously*. I've even got the stainless steel cups, erm ... somewhere.'

'Oh yeah – the 40DM model. Silly me. Does it still work?'

'Makes the best milkshake this side of the twenty-first century.' He wiggled his eyebrows.

'And a jukebox? And all those framed posters? What are you going to do with all this stuff?'

'Nothing. I just like it.' He shrugged, reaching for a Specials LP. 'Gotta admit – it's kinda cool.'

'Yes,' she admitted. 'I see the appeal of the post-war era. Great period for design and innovation. I might start to collect some pieces myself. I love vintage kitchenalia.'

'But it would have to match, right?' Theo smiled.

'Naturally. Monochrome or red, and it absolutely can't upstage Verity's tea set.'

'I've been thinking about those marks,' he said. 'Do you suppose they might spell a word – like an anagram? I know craftsmen and artists have had fun in the past with symbolism, hidden messages, puzzle boxes and the like.'

'I did work out what they all represented,' she said, reaching for her phone and scrolling through the gallery for a screenshot of her results. 'Six letters for each cup, saucer and tea plate: T, I, Y, E, R and U, or possibly V – the alphabet has one symbol for both. Great for Scrabble perhaps but not much help to me.'

He was looking over her shoulder, the warmth of his breath and a waft of his pine-scented soap giving Maisie more pricklings than the tea set ever had.

Saying the letters over to herself, they suddenly fell into place. Her body went totally rigid for a second and she had a much-longed-for answer to one of her burning questions.

'Of course – *Verity*!' she said. 'Irene referred to it as Verity's set when we first met but Essie was adamant there was no one in their family by that name. Does that mean this mysterious lady commissioned it? Or it was the name of the artist and she popped her name on the bottom – like a puzzle?'

Theo frowned. 'Possibly, although I've not seen someone split their name up into individual letters before ... but it's a pretty name. It derives from the old Latin word "veritas" – meaning truth. Your run-of-the-mill Eighties set gets curiouser by the day.'

If only he knew the half of it.

Maisie decided it was difficult being super lovely to someone when they had something you wanted – rather like heartily congratulating someone for winning an award when you were on the shortlist – although she doubted she was ever

308

on Theo's shortlist, but still. She was determined not to let jealousy spoil her relationship with Ella.

The shy girl with the hidden talent for fabric design really was starting to bloom – clearly Theo's input. Still often head down, or with the left side of her face tilted slightly away from people, she engaged more with her colleagues. And although Maisie didn't have Theo's easy-going way with her, the two girls were forming a tentative friendship.

Maisie was in the Tattlesham Community Centre car park, about to attend the still-life class. It promised to cater for all abilities – a bonus because she suspected her years of splodging paint about in hidden rooms was rather childish and she was keen to refine her hobby. Her love of colour and design had never been in doubt but her eye for still life or portraiture was questionable. She could still remember the teacher at school holding her drawing of a majestic and graceful Black Beauty aloft and asking, 'But what is it, Maisie? A cat or a poodle?'

When Maisie undertook something, she liked it to be done properly. People always wrongly assumed if she was a competent graphic designer she could draw. She most definitely could not. Perhaps if she became a better artist she would be more confident showing people other than Theo and Lisa the paintings she produced so recklessly during her quiet evenings.

A middle-aged couple walked past the window of Maisie's car, hand in hand, and carrying sketch pads and pencil cases. She waited a further five minutes for Ella but she was a no-show so she collected the leather document wallet containing her bits and pieces and made for the double doors in the industrial-looking brickwork building. Her hand went up to the handle at exactly the same time as a long-haired, unshaven lad dressed completely in black appeared beside her. He was barely twenty if he was a day.

'After you,' he said, holding the door.

'Thanks. Are you here for the still-life art class?' she asked, as she slipped through and into reception.

'Totes,' he replied. 'Because I'm, like, the teacher.'

Despite the shock she was older than him, the class was more of a challenge than she'd anticipated. Ella snuck silently into the back of the room at the last minute and Maisie moved to join her. Despite the youthful Tristan predictably enthusing about line, shadow and form, Maisie's pathetic effort at a simple apple was uninspiring. It was all very well learning to use a 4B but the complete lack of colour in her little sketch left her feeling flat. Especially when compared to Ella's triumphant drawing. She could see the object in front of her clearly but when her hand tried to execute the image there was a serious breakdown of communication. It was no good. She simply couldn't do it but Tristan was eternally optimistic.

He leaned over her and took the pencil from her fingers. 'Soft, small lines,' he purred. 'Don't commit to the paper. Feel your way around the curves and then stand back and see where the line needs to be.' With a few deft strokes of the pencil her apple looked less like a meteorite and more like an edible fruit – even if it was difficult to be specific about which one.

After the class, Maisie waited outside for Ella, who had stayed back for a quick chat with Tristan. She was clearly weighing up her options, much as Maisie had suggested to Theo, and if the admiring glances Tristan was throwing her earlier were anything to go by, the lucky girl now had two potential suitors. When Ella finally appeared at the door, a pink flush to her face and her long, loose hair about her shoulders, Maisie decided to broach the subject of Theo with her. Working out where he was coming from was like playing blind man's buff. She thought she'd sussed him, stumbled around to reach out and was then metaphorically poked from behind. She was spinning in circles without direction.

'How do you feel about Theo as a romantic prospect?' she asked, as they sauntered towards their respective cars. Was Ella interested in the man or not? If not, she knew someone who most definitely was. The night was warm and it was still light, but it wouldn't be long until those glorious evenings – bathed in the low, setting sun – would start to get shorter again. 'Hypothetically, of course,' she added.

'Oh yes,' Ella gushed, coming to a halt and grasping at Maisie's arm. 'He's *wonderful*. Have you noticed his sincere and mesmerising eyes? And he's so kind, especially to people on the sidelines – like Arthur and me. He is going to be the most thoughtful and amazing boyfriend,' she said. 'Plus, he's got a cute bum and *very* toned legs.' She gave a shy smile.

'Right.' Maisie kicked at a loose stone in her disappointment. 'And you don't think workplace relationships are a bad idea?'

'I think love is a very precious thing and you should grab it when it comes along, wherever you find it. He's been a bit down recently, misreading signs and getting himself in a stew, but the more I think about it, all that's needed is a conversation where both people are honest about their feelings. There is so much room for misunderstanding when people skirt around the issue. Sometimes it takes someone to be bold and lay their heart on the line. Not that I'm one to talk. I've spent a lifetime hiding in the shadows.'

'But it's lovely to see you finally peeping out from them,' Maisie said.

'That's down to people like you. Friends are so important and Theo's helped me step away from destructive relation-ships – I'm not close to my mother. He's right – you should choose the people you want to be with and not waste your time on those you feel obligated to.'

All very well, reflected Maisie, unless the person you wanted to be with was falling in love with someone else.

The following day, the Gildersleeve's staff were rushing around more than usual because both Theo and Johnny were off site – so naturally it was the day *everything* went wrong. The builders had encountered delays with vital deliveries, one of the porters had back issues and couldn't lift anything, the ladies' toilet was blocked and everyone was looking to Maisie to steer the ship. By lunchtime she had the mother of all headaches.

'Arthur mentioned a shabby Forties upholstered cocktail chair was dropped off a while ago – they don't have arms so it wouldn't need much fabric. It's in Saleroom One. Want to come and have a look with me?' Maisie offered Ella. 'I need to clear my head, even if it only involves the short walk over to the barns. I've been so busy I've forgotten to photograph some items dropped off this morning.'

'Ooh, yes please,' she said and they walked over to the saleroom together.

The chair, Ella announced after sitting in it, was perfect and she noted the lot number.

'What's this?' she asked Maisie, holding up a Gothic-inspired lamp where the plastic skull was the shade and the vertebrae formed the lamp stem.

Maisie looked up from where she was squatting to get a good angle of an embroidered fire screen.

'It's a bedside lamp. Not to my taste but maybe one for the guy who bought the coffin.'

Ella nodded and continued to inspect it as Maisie snapped away. Peering at Ella through the camera lens, she took a photo of the girl, holding the lamp, her face full of wonder.

The photograph was perfect. Ella looked beautiful, giving an unguarded smile that made her gentle brown eyes come alive. She was stunning: long lashes, a blush of pink across her apple cheeks and glossy chestnut hair framing her delicate face.

It was only later, after Ella had gone home, and Maisie was in the back office uploading her other photographs that she came across the picture again. She manipulated the image, cropping it slightly, but there was no need for filters or adjustments. The builders kept popping in to ask her questions she didn't know the answers to, and Arthur said there'd been an accident in Saleroom Two and a Royal Doulton figurine had 'come a cropper'.

'Okay, I'll notify the customer,' she said, aware she was now running late for her evening out with Zoe – they were making the final pans for the big family meal that Sunday. On top of everything at work, the pressure of pulling off the perfect meal was immense and it was all her brain could focus on. The photo of Ella and the unusual lamp was still on her phone so she hastily posted it to Gildersleeve's various social media platforms, adding a LookingForSomethingaBitDifferent hashtag and pressed the blue tweet button for it to go live. She turned her phone to silent and headed out the door to meet her sister.

*

Skipping into work the following morning, Maisie was pulled aside by a worried-looking Johnny. His brow was more furrowed than a recently ploughed field.

'Oh, dah-ling, I fear you may have incurred the wrath of our most un-wrathlike Theodore. I do not think I can recall ever seeing him so tempestuous. He's positively a force twelve. My advice is to hastily right the horrendous wrong and apologise, although it may be a case of latching the stable door long after the mighty stallion has bolted into the wilderness.'

Maisie hung her handbag over the back of her chair and frowned. Not sure what she'd done to incur Theo's wrath, at least she now understood the anxious face of the accounts lady as she passed through into the back office.

'Careless, dear Maisie, but I'm certain not intended. Least said, soonest mended. Although speedily deleted, soonest mended would be preferable.'

'I have no idea what you're talking about,' she said. 'I can't think—'

'Delete it immediately,' Theo shouted, storming into the office and throwing back the office door so hard it bounced off the rubber stop and nearly swung back into his face. Only the quick raising of his arm stopped him from getting a face-full of door. 'How dare you post a picture of a member of my staff without asking their permission and then add such a hurtful hashtag. Ella rang me in tears last night, and will certainly not be in the office today, *if ever again*.'

Chapter 46

A horrible churning sensation began inside Maisie. Slowly at first, like an engine turning over, it gained momentum and began to invade her whole body. She knew in her heart she should have double-checked Ella was okay with her post but it was such a stunning shot, and her colleague had been gaining so much confidence recently. What harm could it do?

'Don't stand there gawping. Remove it. I would have done it myself if I knew how. Every minute it's on there, it's attracting more attention. For God's sake, Maisie, you've really over-stepped the line here.'

Opening up the laptop and sinking into her seat, the true horror of what she'd done unfolded before her eyes. Never post in haste, Gareth taught her at Wickerman's after a campaign with the OneDrinkAndImYours hashtag for a new beer had rightly led to a huge backlash from irate women across the nation. Social media at its worst – people swooping on innocent posts and tearing them to shreds. Initially assuming Theo's reaction was disproportionate to her crime, and seeing a healthy number of retweets and likes, she suddenly realised the enormity of her actions.

Scanning down the comments, her stomach crumpled as she realised how her LookingForSomethingaBitDifferent hashtag underneath Ella's photograph had been deliberately and unkindly leapt upon by cruel-minded people – with several nasty comments implying as long as she functioned like a woman, they didn't care what she looked like.

The repercussions were immense.

'DELETE IT,' Theo shouted, and she hit Delete Tweet, quickly logging into the company's other platforms to do the same. 'If it wasn't sale day and we weren't so busy, I'm not sure you'd even have a job. You can do your work and hers today, while I think about the consequences of your thought-lessness.' He stormed out of the room and an uncomfortable silence followed.

'Oops a daisy. Tweet in haste, repent at leisure,' said Johnny. Then taking in her distraught face, he added, 'He'll calm down. Theo is not a man to do angry and unreasonable for long. It will all die down over the weekend.' He put a comforting hand on her shoulder and then bowled out the room to begin The Yard auction.

After a frantic morning, Theo walked into the back office, glared at Maisie, and slumped into his chair.

'I'm sorry,' she whispered.

'You have no idea what you've done,' he muttered. 'That poor girl has spent her life feeling unwanted and awkward. Every day she is convinced people are looking at her face and laughing on the inside – from wandering around the supermarket, to being in the office with her work colleagues. Even leaving the house takes enormous courage. Do you know how often she sat in front of her mother's dressing table mirror as a child and worked her way through a packet of wet wipes trying to remove the mark? You've undone years of confidence-building in an instant.'

The look on Theo's face crushed her on the inside.

'You are absolutely right. I should have checked.'

'Too damn right. What were you thinking, Maisie? You're not an unkind girl – I only have to watch you with Arthur to see that. All I can think is your unhealthy obsession with social media outweighed any scrap of common sense or consideration for the feelings of others.'

'It wasn't like that.' Although her voice was level and controlled, her eyes betrayed her. A swelling of tears finally spilled over her bottom lids and trickled down her expressionless face. 'You're assuming I shared her picture conscious of her birthmark. The truth is I hardly think of it. She's such a beautiful girl and it's a part of her, like having red hair, or particularly long legs. I took a charming photograph of a pretty girl holding a lamp and posted it. I should have asked her permission – absolutely my mistake and I can't apologise enough. I know that's the first rule of sharing on social media. My only excuse is I was so busy I didn't stop to think. I need to make my apologies to her and explain. You can sit there and tell me how angry you are all you like, but that's the truth.'

Theo shook his head slowly from side to side and rubbed the back of his neck. Unusually, he did not meet her eyes when she was talking. He can't even bring himself to look at me, she realised.

After Gareth told her about Wickerman's embarrassing publicity campaign, she'd always triple-checked anything she'd posted or written, fully aware the saying 'there's no such thing as bad publicity' didn't take into consideration the feelings of those innocents caught up in the mess. When you knew real people had been adversely affected, the increased exposure

317

offered no consolation.

Perhaps the success of Arthur's video Tweets had given her an arrogant air. At Wickerman's she was part of a team. Gareth monitored them all and reined them in if they overstepped the mark. She'd been foolish to think she was ready to head up a marketing department, even a department of one.

'I understand if you wish me to resign,' she said.

'I was hasty this morning and irrationally angry.' Theo started to sort the piles of papers and pulled the waste-paper basket out from under the desk. It was much tidier and you could even see areas of the scuffed mahogany top. 'Your job isn't on the line but your friendship with Ella most certainly is.'

Chapter 47

'I can't believe you've actually pulled this off,' whispered Zoe, as she stepped through Maisie's front door, giving her baby sister a crushing hug. Those bicep curls were paying off. 'I know the menu will be fabulous because I helped you choose it, but let's hope the guests don't let us down.'

'You're the last to arrive. Even Ben made it before you, although he's a bit quiet,' said Maisie. 'Mind you, he's exhausted. He only landed this morning.'

'Conversation was never his forte. That man is a perennial teenager.'

Maisie had temporarily shelved her catastrophe at work to focus on the meal but her heart wasn't in it. Ironic that she'd been careless in her job because she was focusing on the meal, and now the meal was happening, all she could think about was her job. She cared about her work colleagues more than she'd realised and their inevitable and justifiable disappointment was painful. Even Arthur had mumbled something about how upsetting the whole affair was. Despite leaving numerous voicemail messages for Ella, she'd heard nothing back.

As they joined the rest of the Meadows family, Maisie's eyes swept the living room and she allowed herself a moment of hope to combat her current self-loathing. Her mum was squashed up on the sofa next to her dad and they looked for all the world like newly-weds. Lisa had claimed the large armchair that faced the TV, her legs elegantly crossed, and was blowing on her freshly painted fingernails. The nail-varnish pot was balanced precariously on the wide arm of the chair, sending a ripple of anxiety through Maisie should it topple over and spill onto the carpet, but she bit back any negative comment, not wanting to spoil this much-longed-for day.

Ben was sitting on the floor, earbuds in as he listened to something on his iPhone. Perhaps only there in body and not spirit, but it was a major coup to have him there at all.

She *would* make this work – she had to.

Lisa had helped move the sofa earlier and there was just enough room for six around her dining table, providing no one wanted to rest their elbows on the edge, so after mumbled hellos, they all squeezed into their allocated chairs.

The first course of watercress soup was largely a silent affair but Maisie noticed people were starting to open up by the time she served the artichoke, aubergine and lamb moussaka. The wine helped, enabling people to relax and drop their guard. Her parents insisted on sitting together, and judging by the tiny squeaks and giggles from her mother, there was more going on under the table than there was above it. Friendly chatter began to fill the room.

'When do you return to work, love?' David said to his eldest daughter. 'You must have used up your annual holiday.'

'Soon – they've been lost without me,' and her eyes flicked to Maisie's, a signal to keep up the charade that all was well. Lisa turned to her brother. 'How's the band doing, Ben? Gone platinum with the album yet?'

It was unusual for Lisa not to take an opportunity to talk about herself, and more unusual for her to show an interest in others, but then Lisa had been on the wine before any of the family members had even arrived. Still, it made her more sociable and gave Maisie small hope that the meal wouldn't end in tears.

'S'all right,' he mumbled. He wasn't going to get away with that response. Everyone else around the table was making an effort.

'Will you return to the UK after the Helsinki house-sitting job?' Maisie pushed.

'Maybe. The lads are fed up of living on a tour bus. The lead guitarist is expecting a baby in February. Not sure how that'll affect things.' There was a pause. 'The food is good, Maisié. You always were an excellent cook.' High praise indeed, from the man who by his own admission lived off tinned beans and Mars bars. 'And how's the move been, Zoe? Slotted back in okay?'

Zoe smiled at her big brother. They'd always clashed over his total inactivity and her pursuit of exercise.

'Thanks for asking. I love the new physiotherapy practice I'm at – great bunch of people. I miss my Australian colleagues but it was the right decision. Dreams don't always match up to the reality. I'm happy to be back and can't say I didn't try.'

'What a lovely bunch of kids,' her dad said, surveying the faces around the table. 'I may not have got everything right in my life, but I'm proud of each and every one of you.'

Their mother reached her hand across to his and gave it a squeeze.

'We need to be thankful we have family,' their mother agreed. 'So many of the old dears at work have no one, especially those who were never blessed with children. Thanks to your friend Theo, we now have two other residents adopted.'

'Naked Man?' Maisie asked, hopefully.

'Actually no but his attachment to Irene is quite endearing. They almost don't need anyone else. She asked me to get hold of some *Carry On* DVDs and the pair of them chuckle away together – happy as Larry. He's usually starkers but she doesn't bat an eye. What with that and their shared love of card games, they keep each other occupied.'

'If it's strip poker, he'll be at a massive disadvantage,' piped up Ben, who had actually removed his earbuds and was continuing to make an effort.

'I've worked it all out and when I'm in a care home, you can take it in turns to come and visit each weekend. That's only once a month and twelve times a year,' their mum said.

'I'll visit you loads, Mum,' Lisa said. 'I've realised care homes aren't the scary, dull places I thought they were. I'll miss Willow Tree House when I go back to York – particularly Irene. I fully intend to be as outrageous as her when I get that old.'

'You can always pop in when you're down in Suffolk,' their mum replied. 'Which will hopefully be more frequently?'

'That would be good,' said Lisa, which was so much better than her usual outright refusal to commit.

Maisie's thoughts returned to Arthur. He'd had no children to visit him for the past twenty years. How his life would have been different if his little Primrose had survived. If there had been a daughter on the scene. Look at the sad state he'd got himself into – so lonely he'd carried on as though nothing had changed and so few people suspected it had. Family was a blessing, she reassured herself, even if you had to work at it.

'I'd like to host Christmas Day this year,' Maisie ventured.

'I know Ben won't be around but you're all invited. We could try to re-create those fun Christmases from years ago. There were good times before ... you know?'

'Hrmph,' mumbled Ben, taking a hasty swig from his glass. 'Not quite how I remember them.'

'Oh, come on,' she persevered. 'The mountains of food, the Christmassy smells and cheesy music, playing games and, even though most of us were too young to drink, the flowing wine and late-night brandies?'

Eyes met furtively across the table.

'I suppose Dad was a pretty funky dancer,' Ben said.

'And Mum – I mean Father Christmas – was always spot on with our presents,' Lisa admitted, helping herself to yet another brim-high glass of Burgundy.

'I miss the sprout cricket we played in the back garden Christmas morning,' said Zoe. 'Launching Brussels at each other, whacking them with the wrapping paper tubes and running to the water butt and back.'

'I wondered why I always seemed low on sprouts.' Their mum laughed. The wine continued to flow and the room was filled with happy chatter and tasty aromas as Maisie silently toasted Verity – whoever she was – and her simply marvellous, if slightly unnerving, tea set.

This Christmas, even if Ben couldn't make it back, was going to be the best ever.

'Right, guys,' Maisie announced, 'I know you should finish a meal off with coffee but I'm desperate to try out Verity's tea set. It's over a hundred years old and I want to christen it today, surrounded by my family. I didn't think I'd get you all here but somehow everything has fallen into place. Let's raise a glass to Meredith, because finding her teapot was the catalyst for this meal.'

'Great speech, sis,' said Lisa, swinging her wine glass up in the air, some of it sloshing over the edge. 'To family.'

The assembled guests raised whatever they could find and joined in, their mother bursting into tears as soon as everyone's glass was in the air.

'Now, now, sweetheart,' her dad said, throwing an arm around his ex-wife and gently dabbing at her tears with his napkin. 'We've talked about reining in those reckless emotions. Enjoy these moments and don't overanalyse everything.'

Zoe set out the cups and saucers whilst Maisie went into the kitchen for the miniature double chocolate muffins she'd baked for the occasion. They were presented on the cake stand, all very *Great British Bake Off*, and a selection of after-dinner mints were arranged on the large cake plate.

After allowing the tea sufficient time to brew, Maisie filled everyone's cup and passed the milk and sugar around in Joanie's jug and bowl.

'It doesn't look a hundred years old,' mumbled Ben. 'But then, what do I know about teacups?'

'I agree but I can assure you it is,' said Maisie. 'And I think it's particularly apt that we use it today as it's been reunited after fifty years and we've been reunited as a family for the first time in nearly twenty.'

'Cheeerrsss,' Lisa slurred, raising the dainty cup in the air.

And then there was silence as everyone took a sip and stared at each other across the table, not knowing quite what to say.

It was a moment of calm before the almighty thunderclap announced the mother of all storms.

Chapter 48

'I paint,' announced Maisie, shocked by her own admission, as the hot tea slid down her throat and all her worries about her family's reactions to her secret hobby no longer seemed important.

'Sorry?' Zoe queried. 'Paint what?' Maisie's comment was a complete random tangent to the conversation.

'Huge abstract canvases, smaller random dribbles and a few smears and smudges that I lose myself in. Not proper painting, just ... stuff.'

'Don't be silly. All art is valid,' Zoe said. 'Is this connected to the still-life classes you started recently?'

'Sort of. I want to hone my talent – or lack thereof.'

'Yeah – I've seen them – they're awful,' said Lisa, chuckling to herself. 'A blind chimpanzee could do a better job.' She caught Maisie's face and coughed. 'But I guess it's a kind of therapy.'

'You've shown them to Lisa and not to me?' Zoe voice was quiet and steady but the hurt was apparent. 'Oh my God – she's nudged her way between us, hasn't she? Staying here and pretending to be all vulnerable. You said I was your closet sibling ...'

'You've been playing favourites?' Lisa squeaked. 'Charming.

And there was me thinking we'd made progress in our sisterly bond. Have you two have been laughing behind my back and—'

'Children. And Bev ...' Their father cleared his throat and a puzzled look flashed across his handsome face as he intercepted the escalating hysteria of his daughters.

'I wasn't going to do this today, in fact I wasn't going to say anything at all, but as we are acknowledging the importance of family ...' he swallowed '... not quite all my family is around this table because you have a half-brother.' He beamed his hundred-kilowatt smile, Maisie half-expecting a dazzling chink of light to bounce off his perfect teeth.

'Pardon?' their mother said, her own smile sliding down her face and into her lap. 'Are you saying you have *another* child, David?'

David was less sure of himself in that moment. What had seemed a good idea, was possibly a massive miscalculation. He gazed at the five stunned faces semi-circling him.

'I erm, well, it's not like it's a recent thing, Bev. It was a long time ago,' he blustered. He started to back-pedal so fast his legs were a blur. 'We've talked about the affairs. You said you understood. That's all behind us now, love.'

He reached out for her hand but she pulled away and stood up, throwing her napkin to the table and stepping back from her husband – unable to control the erratic swingometer of her emotions.

'You have another child I know nothing about? And to think I let you back in my M&S high legs,' she screamed.

'TMI!' said Ben, shaking his head and glaring hard at his tablemat. 'You always did overshare in front of your kids.'

'Well, these knickers are securely padlocked from now on.

You won't be getting your wandering fingers anywhere near them again in this lifetime ...'

'MUM!' all four children shouted in unison.

'And telling me it happened years ago doesn't make it better. That makes it WORSE. Before or after we were married?' she demanded.

David once again circled the bemused faces of his family and swallowed slowly. 'During,' he finally admitted.

'Oh. My. God. *When?*' Tears billowed at the edge of her lower eyelid as she took a step away from the table, and her deceitful husband and four grown-up children could only watch as their mother had her heart broken a second time.

Even if their dad was too stupid to see it, every single sibling knew there would be no going back this time. There simply wasn't a wallpaper in existence thick enough to paper over these yawning cracks. Tears fell from their mother's dumbfounded eyes in rivers. She clasped her hands together to stop them from shaking and the children sipped nervously at their tea, waiting for the tale of their dad's misdemeanour to unfold – a tale that could never have a happy ending.

'Someone from work not long after Ben was born. I have a son a year younger. He's recently come back into my life and I thought ... I thought ...' He trailed off.

'You really are a massive waste of space, Dad,' said Ben, pushing his chair up against the wall and standing up. 'You all look at me and criticise my reluctance to be part of this family but what kind of role models have I had growing up? A man who couldn't keep it in his pants for two minutes, and a mother who can't hold it together when she so much as drops an egg on the floor. No wonder I've never wanted anything to do with you all.'

'That's not fair,' said Zoe.

'No, you're right, I adore Mum – emotional maelstrom that she is – and I don't particularly have a problem with you or Maisie.'

'Meaning you DO have a problem with me?' Lisa spat, moving to pick up her wine glass and knocking the stem with her hand, sending a stream of red wine sloshing across the pristine white tablecloth. With a gasp, Maisie ran to the kitchen to get a cloth and some stain remover, dashing back in to the room and mopping at the purple stain through the continued disquiet.

'Everyone has a problem with you, Lisa.' Ben laughed. 'The spoilt little girl who got whatever she wanted if she made a big enough fuss.'

'Pretty spot on,' Zoe agreed. 'Daddy's little girl from the off. The rest of us never got a look-in.'

'Rubbish.' Lisa stood up but staggered to one side, missing her footing, as a frantic Maisie continued to scrub away at the stain. 'I was the one pushed aside. My life would have been perfect if you lot hadn't come on the scene. I don't even know why our parents had so many children. It always made me feel I wasn't enough.'

'Oh, you were, darling, you really were. I suppose with hind-sight, I wanted to keep David from straying, and I thought if we had lots of lovely children he wouldn't leave me. Especially my little Maisie – a last-ditch attempt to save the marriage.'

'You what?' shouted her ex-husband. 'Maisie was planned? You told me she was an accident.'

Shocked to discover she was an attempt to patch up a failing marriage and not a longed-for fourth child, Maisie stopped scrubbing, throwing the cloth onto the table, and abandoning all attempts to rescue it.

'I wasn't wanted?' she whispered.

'Of course you were, sweetheart – you were always my favourite.' David Meadows' eyes flashed wide as his own words echoed through his ears.

'That's it, I'm outta here,' said Ben. 'And you wonder why I pretend I have no family.'

'Oh, darling, please say that's not true,' said their mother, the tears still flowing.

'Sorry, Mum. Makes life easier.' That was a yes then, they all realised. 'I only took up the drums as a way of drowning out all the quarrels and to justify thrashing something really hard without getting arrested. Quite frankly, there were times it was either the snare drum or your face, Lisa.'

Joining her mother in mass tear production and still absorbing the shock news, Maisie sunk back into her chair.

'Please don't say harmful things. You don't mean them. Lisa is the biggest success of us all and sometimes you have to be a bit selfish to make it to the top. She loves us all – don't you, Lisa? It's hard being the oldest child,' said Maisie.

'Oh, honey, you're sweet but you're totally misguided.' Lisa hiccupped and stared intently at the stem of her empty glass. 'I was fired eighteen months ago for continually turning up late. I live in a crummy bedsit in a dodgy part of the city. I'm broke and I'm so terribly lonely – probably because I'm a total cow and just don't know how to stop being one. And then I drink too much and feel worse about myself. It's a vicious circle.'

'You're unemployed?' their mother asked. 'Oh, darling ...'

Ben looked at Lisa, his head shaking slowly from side to side. 'Why I thought it would be a good idea to come back for this, I don't know. Nothing has changed. Put us together and the sparks fly.' He manoeuvred himself out from behind the table.

'You never could cope with emotions,' Lisa said. 'I always suspected you were on the spectrum and now I see it's true.'

'Take that back, you bitch.' He lurched towards his sister, their dad intercepting him at the last moment.

'Just go, son,' he said. 'Before you do something you regret.'

'Like fathering an illegitimate child, you mean? Doing it in the first place is bad enough, but keeping quiet about it for thirty years wins you the biggest tosser of the year award. I'm outta here.' And with that, Ben grabbed his bag and stormed into the hall. Seconds later the door thumped shut and a second eerie silence descended over the room.

Calmer now, their mother turned to her ex-husband and demanded the truth of his extra-marital affair.

'It was someone from the office. It didn't last long. You were so tied up with Lisa and the baby. I wanted—'

'You wanted to get laid,' slurred Lisa. 'Good old Dad, putting himself and his needs first.'

'Don't you dare blame me for this, David,' Maisie's mum said. 'I need to stop making excuses for your unforgivable behaviour. You're like a stick of Blackpool rock, David Meadows; cut you open and the word selfish is written through your very core.'

'But it was over barely before it begun,' he blustered. 'She meant nothing but I tried to be there for the lad, even after they moved away. I supported them properly and made sure they never wanted for anything ...'

'Huh ... You always were generous,' said their mother, slumping back into her chair. 'Your *only* redeeming feature.'

'It was a long time ago, Bev.' He put his arm on her knee and she stared at it as if it he'd placed a hand grenade there with the pin removed. 'We can make this work. You forgave me once, forgive me again? You're the only woman I've ever truly loved.'

'It's not the affair, it's the lying. All this time you had a son I knew nothing about. I want you to leave, David, and I NEVER want to see you again. Because if I do, and there's anything pointy nearby, my javelin-throwing arm will be getting some serious exercise.'

It was with an eerie calmness and control, possibly because she was totally sobbed out, that she instructed her ex-husband to go. Maisie briefly closed her eyes as she anticipated the instigation of a whole new revenge campaign.

Her dad's shoulders slumped and he stood up once more, preparing to depart. 'By a strange coincidence, he only lives a couple of doors down from here, Maisie,' he said, collecting his jacket and turning to the door. 'Don't blame him. It's not his fault. His mother passed away recently and he's moved back into the area. He'd like to meet you all, when you're ready.' Maisie's heart had begun to quicken, because she knew what her father was about to say before he said it. 'He's called Josh.'

Chapter 49

With only the ladies left, Zoe began to pace the room and Lisa poured herself another glass from the bottle in the middle of the table.

'I'm disgusted with Dad. All this time we had a brother we knew nothing about,' said Lisa. 'We could have swapped him for the irritating one we did have.'

'I'm disgusted with *you*, Lisa. You're still the same selfish, calculating cow of my childhood,' Zoe said. 'Look at you: totally off your face and expecting Maisie to run around after you. Sponging off her for weeks and not doing a goddamn thing to help. I don't care if you've lost your job – it's not about money, you could have done more about the house. You really think you're lady muck, don't you?'

'It's okay, Zoe. You don't understand.' Maisie's tears were still plopping onto her lap. 'She's not well and suffering from stress ...' Although Maisie knew the truth about the job now, she was still protective of her oldest sister's state of mind. In fact, the unemployment explained her struggles even more.

'No, no, I'm not actually.' Lisa's voice was quiet. 'You were being so lovely to me and I couldn't face telling you the truth. I'm broke and don't know what I'm doing with my life but I'm not ill.'

Maisie's sadness morphed into anger.

'How could you lie to me like that? You have no idea how worried I've been. Making excuses for your behaviour and trying to be a caring sister ...'

Zoe shook her head. 'Unbelievable. No wonder you dumped yourself on Maisie. Mum would have asked too many questions and I'd have sussed you in minutes.'

'At least I didn't break my mother's heart by emigrating to the other side of the world.' Lisa placed her wine glass down in front of her with extreme care.

There was a moment where Zoe contemplated the fact her decision to live in Australia had impacted on people other than herself.

'You buggered off to York and practically never came home. It's the same thing.'

'Girls ...' their mother warned.

'Oliver is a rubbish kisser.' Lisa spat the last comment out – designed to wound and shock. It did both.

'You'd better be joking ...' Zoe began to suck in a very long, very slow breath, her eyes not leaving her oldest sister's face for a second.

'Oh no, we snogged – not long before the wedding. Perhaps he was double-checking he'd plumped for the right sister. Y'know, sussing out his options?'

No wonder Oliver avoided Lisa at all costs. They had history and not in a good way.

There was no stopping the physical violence this time. Zoe ran up to her sister and slapped her so hard across the face that Maisie and her mother sucked in long breaths through their teeth, almost able to feel the sharp sting on their own skin. Maisie slid between them before chunks of hair were ripped out or long, painted fingernails did long-term damage to delicate skin.

'Stop it. Stop all the nastiness, girls. I can't bear it.' The sisters moved apart and their mother gave a pathetic sniff. 'I'm *so* disappointed in Oliver. I never thought he'd turn out to be one of *them*.' Everyone in the room understood she meant their dad and any man with similar behavioural traits.

'Nor did I, but guess that goes to show you never really know someone.' Zoe turned to Maisie. 'I'm sorry your meal turned out to be such a disaster, honey,' Zoe said, deliberately turning her back on Lisa – who was clutching her pink cheek, 'but I can't stay here any longer. Nice idea but wrong crowd. I tried the whole blood thicker than water thing. She may be my sister but it's in name only.' Zoe gave Lisa a withering stare and left quietly, gliding out the room, her earlier anger dissipated through the slap.

The third awkward silence descended as Lisa picked up her teacup and swigged the last of her tepid tea.

'To make me think you were suffering from stress ...' Maisie said.

'That wasn't a kind thing to do, darling. And all those posts?' their mother added.

'You see what you want to see, Mum,' Lisa sighed. 'Standing in front of a beautiful York-stone block of flats and saying I was off out for the evening wasn't technically a lie. Selfies of me in front of a crowd of partygoers talking about so-and-so's launch doesn't mean I'm actually there. I messed up and tried to hide it because everyone was waiting for me to fail – well, newsflash, I did.'

'But we would have been here for you whatever, darling. You could have come back at any point, instead of continuing such an elaborate charade. There was always a bed for you – for any of my children.'

'I didn't bloody know how to.' Lisa, on the back foot, was coming out fighting. It was easier than accepting unconditional love, especially as she didn't feel she deserved it. 'It was like you'd all given up on me. I was never wanted. Even as a child. I had to move over for the rest of you. Why you had so many bloody kids, I don't know. It was like ...' she paused, searching for the right words '... you needed more than me. And that made me feel a disappointment from the off.'

Was this what it was all about? Some irrational jealousy that her parents had more children? It really was all about her, Maisie thought.

'How about the friends that follow your online blog?' Maisie asked, embarrassed to have been sucked in by Lisa's lies along with everyone else.

'Of the three hundred, do you know how many I know in real life?' Lisa said. They both shrugged. 'Excluding family – four. Four sodding people. And I don't even like two of them. I have few friends and a family who couldn't care a toss about me.'

'We all love you, Lisa. I'm your mother – I would die for you – but sometimes you are a really difficult person to like.'

'So it's all my fault, is it?'

'Yes,' Maisie and her mum said quietly in unison. 'You've been fighting everyone for as long as I can remember,' her mum continued. 'Why don't you let us in? Why don't you embrace the love, instead of pushing it away?'

The three women all looked at each other, tears falling from every pair of eyes in the room. Sometimes no further words were necessary. Lisa couldn't justify her actions, and Maisie and her mum had said everything they needed to.

'I can't do this. I'm outta here,' Lisa muttered, grabbing her keys from the end of the sideboard, and swiping her handbag from where she'd dumped it earlier in the middle of the floor.

'You seriously aren't about to get behind the wheel of a car?' Maisie said. 'You've been drinking.'

'Watch me.' And Lisa walked out, as every other member of the family had done that afternoon, slamming the front door so hard, the house shook.

Chapter 50

Lisa tumbled into the driver's seat and turned the wheel away from the kerb. The vehicle in front was parked uncomfortably close. She knew her judgement was off and toyed with abandoning her dramatic flit, but the anger was bubbling inside and it needed a release. Mixed with several glasses of wine, it was a dangerous cocktail. She had to get away and, anyway, it wasn't like she was the first one to storm out.

The car bumpers missed each other by millimetres as she slipped into second gear, upping the revs and pulling into the road. Her head was starting to thump from the tension and the wine. All of those vicious truths that tumbled out around the table. She was angry with so many members of her family: her dad for keeping such a massive secret, her mother for spreading her love between too many children, Ben for giving up on them all, and Zoe ... She'd never worked out why she was so angry with Zoe all the time – it had simply always been that way.

A blaring horn pierced her thoughts and a furious driver waved a fist at her. She wasn't even sure what she'd done.

Sod them. Sod all of them. And sod Craig perhaps most of all.

She accelerated onto the main road out of town and

thumped the steering wheel. How dare they judge her all the time. The need for speed was like a drug. Pressing the electric window, she allowed a gush of cool air to enter the vehicle and whip through her hair. The headache was building and somehow this rush of wind and mounting speed was a form of release. Flicking the radio on, she turned the volume up and let a pop song belt out as she headed into the countryside, down a long straight road, lined by occasional trees and low banks.

It came from nowhere. A darting shape across the road; low and quick. She turned the wheel too sharply to avoid it and the car started to skid. Overcompensating and not fully in control, she spun it back just as sharply the other way. The car snaked and left the road. Its front nearside tyre dropped down into the shallow bank and she no longer had any control. She panicked. The car flipped – a terrible cacophony of noise as metal buckled and glass smashed.

The shape didn't look back as it pelted into a dense hedge of green, leaving the groans and hisses from the smashed vehicle in its wake. Imagine dragons played 'Sucker for Pain' at full volume to an empty road in the middle of the Suffolk countryside – a haunting finale to the events.

And across the deflated airbag, hanging limply from the dashboard, was a bloodstained Lisa – face down, eyes closed, and with no obvious signs of life.

Chapter 51

Maisie, wrong-footed by the speed of Lisa's actions, hurtled through the front door, only to hear a crunch of gears and see the car disappear into the distance – a little cloud of exhaust fumes slowly dispersing where it had stood moments before.

She slumped back inside and found her mum with a mobile phone to her ear.

'It's going straight to voicemail, love. I'm not sure what more we can do.' Her voice wobbled as she put the phone back on the table.

'Hopefully, she'll park up out of sight and calm down. We both know Lisa is all about the dramatic gesture and there's no way she'll be outdone by a flouncing Zoe.'

'She's not safe to drive.' Her mother was wringing her hands again. 'What if she crashes?'

Maisie was torn between concern for her sister and anger that she might endanger others, but there was nothing they could do except hope she returned soon. And safely.

Trying to refocus, Maisie cleared the table. Domestic chores usually helped her deal with stressful situations and there was something soothing about putting things in order and tidying away. She needed to be in control of an activity right now – even if it was only where the cutlery lived.

'Let me help,' her mum offered.

'No, I've got this.' She collected the teapot and stacked some of the side plates but her mother began to silently shadow her. There were no words left. Their anxiety over Lisa and the painful revelations of the afternoon filled their heads. There wasn't space for anything else coherent. They worked methodically, clearing the table, putting uneaten food back in the fridge, and wiping the surfaces. Lastly, Maisie returned Verity's set to the display shelf, carefully lifting up each piece and positioning it just so.

As she reached up to place the final cup on the shelf, her mobile buzzed, startling her. Her sleeve caught on a cupboard door handle and the cup fell from her hand, bouncing off the edge of the worktop and landing with a smash on the floor. There was a pull in her chest – real or imagined, she couldn't tell – as she stared at the jagged pieces of black and white china, playing hide-and-seek on her black and white chequerboard floor.

'Noooooo ...' she cried. It was the straw that snapped the back of the fragile, limping camel and she knelt by the pieces, her sobs coming out in painful rasps.

Her mum came rushing in from the living room, where she was returning the tablemats to the sideboard, and looked at the fragments scattered across the tiles.

'Oh, darling. Your lovely tea set. Such a pity. Never mind. Here, let me get the dustpan while you take your call.'

Maisie glanced at the screen in case it was Lisa's number, but it wasn't. Her gaze returned to the smashed cup, as her mother began to sweep the pieces into the dustpan and walk towards the swing-top bin.

'No!' she squealed. 'Don't throw the bits away. It has to stay together.'

'Don't be daft. What are you going to do? Keep them in an envelope? It's beyond repairable, love. Chuck them out.'

'You don't understand,' she sobbed. 'Bad things will happen.'

Her mum looked at Maisie's distressed face and sighed. 'It's just a cup.'

'No, Mum. Meredith said, "Split the set; split the family". I know it sounds ridiculous but as I've been gathering the pieces, we've all been coming back together. I thought it was all coincidence at first, but now I look back, every time I located more of Verity's set, the scattered Meadows family began to reunite – even a half-brother I didn't know existed until today turned up on my doorstep the day Joanie passed over the jug and sugar bowl.' In fact, the realisation Josh's first visit was on that day was the spookiest of all.

'I never had you pegged as superstitious.' Her mum shook her head but swept up the pieces and put them in a cereal bowl on the side as Maisie stood watching and wringing her hands. 'I hope you know it's all a lot of silly nonsense. How can bits of china possibly influence our decisions? Zoe had been planning to return for months before she called us and you've been talking about a family gathering for weeks. *You* gathered us together. Not an inanimate tea set.'

But it was all too much for Maisie as the floodgate swung open and a cascade of unhappiness gushed down her cheeks. Wordless and zombie-like, she felt her mum's comforting arm guide her back into the living room and they both flopped onto the sofa, Maisie giving the cushion a final adjustment as she did.

And even Nigel, who had been haring around all afternoon,

getting high on the delicious aromas from the meal, was unusually silent and still.

The phone rang late that evening. After her mum had left, Maisie retreated to the spare room and painted lots of angry colours and violent lines to ease her troubled emotions, all the time wondering whether Lisa would return to the house or had bolted for York. Continued attempts to contact her via her mobile had proved fruitless.

'Darling? It's Mum.' From the panicky breaths and emotion-laden voice, she knew something was seriously wrong – like 'my head is on fire' wrong.

'I've just had a call from the West Suffolk Hospital and I'm heading out the door now. Lisa's been admitted and they've asked me, as her next of kin, to get there as soon as I can.'

'Oh my God. Admitted for what?'

'I'm not sure exactly but it's serious if they've rung. I know how it is – we've had it a hundred times with my old dears. You get the relatives there as soon as you can without panicking them. You don't want to end up causing a crash as someone hurtles through the night at ninety miles an hour. They wouldn't give me any details over the phone but I'm thankful I wasn't opening the door to a police officer on the doorstep, because that would have been much worse news.'

She heard a beep down the line as her mother unlocked her car. 'I'll join you as soon as I can,' Maisie said, already grabbing her bag and making for the hallway.

A motorcyclist had seen Lisa's car leave the road and called 999 almost immediately. The ambulance was with her within fifteen minutes, by which time she had regained consciousness.

The priority for the emergency services had been Lisa, and so it had taken several hours for any information to filter down to the immediate family.

Maisie and her mum arrived at the hospital simultaneously and were told by a nurse she had sustained severe bruising, was suffering from whiplash and had a fractured wrist.

Everyone realised it could have been so much worse.

'Does Dad know?' Maisie whispered as they sat by Lisa's bed.

Lisa had been staring at the ceiling when they first arrived and had now closed her eyes. Whether she was actually asleep or just pretending in her continued efforts to shut them out, Maisie didn't know.

'Of course. I rang him first and he's on his way. He may be an absolute shite of a husband but he's always been a good father.'

It wasn't long before her ashen-faced dad joined them, desperate to be updated.

'She rolled the car. Lucky to be alive, they said.' Her mother stood, shoulders stooped and wringing her hands together as if that would mend her broken daughter. 'Thankfully no one else was involved.' It was an unspoken relief to everyone that Lisa's actions hadn't impacted on an innocent party.

David reached for his wife's arm but she turned sharply away before he made contact.

'No, David. Whatever happens with Lisa, this is where our story ends. Fool me twice, shame on me ...'

'I know I handled this badly. When I got home, I realised what a fool I'd been and called Maisie to apologise but you didn't pick up, love.' He looked over to his daughter questioningly.

Maisie's heart thudded out a violent and irregular rhythm. This could not be happening. She put both her hands to her cheeks as she worked through her startling thought processes.

Lisa's crash happened about ten minutes after she'd stormed out from the meal, so roughly when Maisie's mobile rang, but it wasn't this coincidence that upset her. Much more unnervingly, this meant Lisa had crashed her car when Maisie had smashed the cup. Her stomach collapsed like a detonated building.

Some guardian of the tea set she'd turned out to be. She'd almost killed her sister.

Chapter 52

At various points over the next twenty-four hours, every single member of the Meadows family gathered around Lisa's bed. There wasn't much conversation; they weren't there to mend bridges or dissect the events of the disastrous family meal, they were there for Lisa. For most of those visits, she lay, pale and bruised, with her eyes closed. Despite the arguments and the unpleasantness, there was a silent acknowledgement that they loved each other – why else would they be there? – but for that state of affairs to continue it was best that any verbal interaction was kept to an absolute minimum.

With the social media farce at work still hanging over her, but her priority to be with her sister, Maisie tendered her resignation by email on Monday morning with immediate effect. She cited her gross error of judgement and the resulting bad publicity for the company, along with personal circumstances. It felt cowardly not to speak to either Johnny or Theo but, on top of Lisa's accident, she didn't feel strong enough to face them. For the remainder of the week, Lisa was her priority, even though her sister barely spoke during the visits.

After rushing to Lisa's bedside that first day, her parents avoided coinciding visiting times. It was a wise move – no one wanted any more members of the family admitted to hospital. The family juggled visits and a disorientated and badly bruised Lisa started to mend physically and mentally – although the high level of alcohol in her system had other implications. A police doctor had taken a blood sample shortly after she'd been admitted but everyone knew she was well over the limit. Lisa had to get better and then she had to face the consequences of her actions.

As Maisie approached her sister's bed one evening, a middle-aged man she didn't recognise stood from the chair, politely made his excuses and withdrew.

It was the first time she'd seen Lisa sitting up and the first time she'd seen her sister engage with anyone other than hospital staff. Maisie approached the bed but didn't say anything. The bruising across her sister's face was working through the colours of the rainbow but the swelling was down. Lisa's eyes bored into hers. They were both waiting for the other to make the first move.

'I know my behaviour was stupid. I'm sorry,' said Lisa.

Well, that was a first. Her big sister had spent a lifetime turning things around to absolve herself of blame. Whatever the stranger had said to Lisa, he had almost certainly insti-gated this breakthrough. Perhaps some good could come of this awful accident.

'And I understand there will be serious repercussions for this, not least the loss of my driving licence,' she continued. 'But when I think that I could have killed someone, it seems a small price to pay. Imagine if a car had been coming the other way? I can't even begin ...' Lisa's hands went to her face and she let out a couple of soft sobs.

'But there was no other car,' Maisie said. 'Be thankful and move on.'

Realising she wasn't going to get the expected crushing embrace and soothing words, Lisa let her hands drop and nodded.

'I'll try. You'll still be there for me, won't you?' Lisa asked, finally looking up.

'I *always* be there for you,' Maisie said. 'I *always* was. And yet you kept this massive secret from everyone and lived a charade of a life. You must have known it would all come tumbling down?'

'Huh, you're a fine one to talk.' Lisa shuffled up the bed and once again locked eyes with her sister.

Maisie frowned. 'I'm not posting pictures on social media of a fake life or lying about my job. What you see is what you get.'

'Apart from the room you shut away from everyone? I may be a selfish, self-absorbed cow but I'm astute enough to recognise my baby sister has spent a lifetime wanting and creating order, yet one look at your paintings and I'm pretty certain that for most of that time, you've been craving the exact opposite. You're living just as much of a lie as me.'

They exchanged a look and Maisie realised her sister had a point. Why did she feel she had to hide her hobby? Did it matter what people thought about her daubings? The capable, coping person who created and maintained control was still a big part of her, and these skills made her good at her job, but she could be multi-faceted. She could go on a wild rampage with a paintbrush – it didn't make her any less capable.

'To be honest,' Lisa said, 'I loved you a tiny bit more when I found out about them. It made you seem more normal and therefore me less of a failure. It's been hard living up to the perfection you exude.' Lisa crept a tentative hand across the pressed white cotton sheet and Maisie took it in her own.

It seemed to Maisie that everyone's perception of success was different. She admired Ben and Zoe so much for grasping their dreams with both hands and having the courage to leave the country in order to do so. She thought her mum was one of the most amazing and bravest women on the planet, doling out love and care to the people of Willow Tree House, despite the fact it ripped her apart emotionally every single day. And she admired Lisa for being honest and finally asking Maisie for support.

As they sat and chatted, Maisie detected subtle changes in her sister and some new emotions in Lisa's repertoire: humble, thankful and repentant. Whether these feelings would last, remained to be seen, but she had softened – the magnitude of the crash a metaphorical and almost literal slap around the face.

'Your earlier visitor. He's not someone I recognised,' Maisie finally said.

'Yeah. Craig. A friend.'

'But he's a—'

'Vicar. Yes, I do know.' Lisa sighed. The dog collar was the first thing Maisie noticed as she entered the ward. 'I met him when I went along to church a few times. I told you I was looking for answers.'

Lisa was being visited by a vicar? All the way from York? He must have really thought she was about to shuffle off this mortal coil. Dashing down to administer the last rites was one thing, but they were happily beyond that now.

'And did you find them?'

'Maybe. I thought I had. It was starting to make sense, all coming together. I was lost and alone, and church is like a family – a far more functional one than ours.'

'We're not so bad,' Maisie bristled. 'I guess we're like pick and mix sweets – deep down you love them with a passion but you know they're no good for you. We all have our own agendas and our own demons to fight. Perhaps church isn't like that?' Not being a churchgoer, Maisie was grasping at straws.

'No, everyone cares and looks out for each other and I was accepted into the fold and embraced. I felt things, I guess I started to believe, and then things got ... complicated.'

'Theologically?' Maisie frowned. She wasn't sure she was following this conversation. Had Lisa wrestled with deep religious concepts, like hell or forgiveness?

'No, romantically. Craig was the complication.' Maisie was completely lost. 'There was this connection,' Lisa explained. 'We both felt it, but he's a *vicar*, Maisie. Not my style. I backed off. He persevered. And he's so hot – totally wasted on God. We had a thing for a while and then he wanted a happy ever after so I stepped away a second time. After all, it's what I do ...'

Perhaps it was a family trait – bowing out when things got tough. It was what Maisie had done with both her disastrous work situations, after all, and it was starting to sit uncomfortably with her. She reached for her sister's fragile hand again, noticing the chipped nails, and squeezed her cold fingers.

'I'm not good for him. I'm a complete mess,' Lisa continued. 'And I mean, really, can you see me as a vicar's wife? I'd be necking the communion wine behind his back.' It was an attempt to lighten the mood but it didn't work.

'Whoa, steady on. The poor chap was probably thinking a few dates and take it from there. You're jumping ahead a bit. It's not like he proposed.'

Lisa lifted her eyes and didn't break contact with her sister's. 'Oh. When?'

'After the first couple of months. Like I said, we *really* connected. And I felt like I was some bloody project for him. Let's rescue this poor damaged girl and make her whole again. And then what? It wouldn't take him long to realise I was unlovable and he'd walk away.'

How sad, thought Maisie, that her sister couldn't see she was the one doing the walking. From leaving home at the first opportunity, to haring up to York after a half-promised job to escape her tiresome family and prove something no one needed her to prove.

'Maybe you should let him be the judge of that.'

'He doesn't give up. All the time he's in my peripheral vision, lurking like an unidentifiable odour. Even now, after everything I've done, he's here trying to save me, telling me he loves me, and that we can get through this. I don't deserve his love. I've been a complete cow.'

'But do you love him?' It was the obvious question, the one Lisa hadn't addressed.

'Yeah,' she whispered. 'I really do.'

Chapter 53

After submitting her resignation at the start of the week, Maisie switched all notifications on her phone off and focused on her sister. She didn't want to see sunny social media posts, nor did she want to deal with the response from Theo or Johnny. It was easier to shut work out than deal with it, even though she knew she was behaving like Lisa. But on Friday evening, there was a knock at Maisie's door and there stood the joint proprietors of Gildersleeve's.

'We need a little tête-à-tête, dah-ling,' said Johnny. 'Or perhaps, more accurately, a tête-à-tête-à-tête.' She let them follow her into the living room as her shoulders slumped south. She couldn't bear to look at Theo.

'Ah, *Mesocricetus auratus*,' said Johnny, peering at Nigel over his half-moon spectacles as he passed the sideboard. 'Syrian hamster,' he explained.

Maisie gave a half-smile but wasn't in the mood for hamster-related small talk. She wanted this visit over with, so she gestured for them to sit, removing a bundle of her own discarded clothes from the chair. Perching on the arm, she waited for someone to speak, preferably not in Latin.

'You do not appear to be responding to our electronic mail but I'm afraid that we cannot possibly accept your resignation, dah-ling, not only because under the terms and conditions of your employment, you are required to give us a full month's notice ...'

Maisie sighed. 'Of course. I'll work the month.' She'd hoped they wouldn't be petty over details, instead pleased to see her go. Wickerman's let her leave immediately, probably because Gareth didn't have the balls to sit opposite her knowing he'd been such a two-timing snake.

Johnny leaned forward and tried to make eye contact but Maisie's head was low. 'We would simply miss you too much and cannot contemplate the future of Gildersleeve's without you as part of the team. So we shall pretend we haven't seen your initial email and say no more about it.'

Maisie looked up from the intense study of her lap.

Theo, who hadn't said anything since arriving, put a gentle hand on her knee. 'If you need more time, we completely understand. Come back when you're ready.' Those eyes bored deep into her head again and she squirmed under his scrutiny.

'Ella?' She could only summon up one word, but it said everything she needed to.

'Oh, dah-ling, no horrors are insurmountable,' Johnny said, wriggling uncomfortably and pulling a silky balcony bra from behind his back and dropping it in horror. 'And although you deleted the posts faster than an elegantly swooping falcon, our little shy maiden had been alerted to their presence and saw many of the comments. She will, however, survive.'

'Poor girl.' Maisie's stomach rolled. She'd hoped Ella had been spared those nasty posts obliquely referring to her birth-mark and misconstruing her hashtag. 'What have I done?' Her head fell to her hands.

'Indeed. What have you done?' Johnny gave one of his

dramatic pauses. 'For amongst the hurtful snipes, she saw a profusion of posts commending her fortitude.'

Theo leaned forward and his soft voice made her turn her heavy head. 'It's not to say what you did wasn't a terrible misjudgement but it seems some good has come of it. Not only was there an outpouring of love but a birthmark charity even contacted her to ask if she'd be interested in being an ambassador. She's not a stupid girl, just a painfully shy one. She knows your post wasn't intentional, and she also knows the vagaries of human nature. But you do need to apologise to her properly.'

'I fully intended to. She didn't answer my calls and then with my sister and—'

'We never doubted you,' Johnny said, heaving himself off the sofa, the low arms making it difficult for such a rotund man. 'So, with all that silly nonsense dealt with, we expect you back at the office as soon as you feel able.' He ambled to the hallway, Theo lingering behind, as if he had something to add.

She studied his face, her stomach flipping, and knew there was another reason she couldn't continue to work at Gildersleeve's.

'I can't come back,' she said, not prepared to admit she couldn't bear to have the wrecking ball of his relationship with Ella demolish her heart.

'Why? Because it seems to me you find it easier to quit than to stay and resolve your problems. You were out of Wickerman's faster than a scampering hamster, when you had no reason to leave. If anything, Gareth should have gone for putting you in that position. Don't bail again.'

'It's not bailing. There are things going on you don't under-stand.' Her bottom lip started to wobble. Not only was her heart in peril, but also the universe and the tea set were messing with her head. 'I broke one of Meredith's cups,' she whispered. 'A cup from a set that Meredith's own grandmother warned should never be separated. Lisa's accident was my fault.'

'Don't be ridiculous. How can you smashing a cup influence events miles away on a quiet country road?' His voice was gentle but his eyes were serious.

'Because it's a special set. All the Mayhew sisters, with their bright futures, *all of them* suffered life-changing consequences when their mother broke the one promise asked of her; don't separate the set ...' She buried her face in her hands as Theo put an arm out to her shoulders. He pulled her in to him and rubbed her back gently, his soft strokes soothing and much-needed.

'You are a beautiful, wonderful and intelligent girl and I can't believe you think those two things are linked. The only person responsible for that terrible accident is Lisa. She made the decision to drink and then *she* made the decision to drive. No one else.'

'I should have taken her keys ... realised that she was at risk ... I should have ...'

Theo wrapped his arms tighter and let her head rest against his shoulder, soft shushes whispered into her ear. She let his concern envelop her and his warmth soothe her.

Johnny coughed pointedly from the hallway as she choked out quiet sobs and briefly allowed herself to fall a little bit more in love with the man before her.

Over the weekend, Maisie had an unexpected visit from a very nervous Josh. He'd been told about Lisa and was

354

understandably concerned but also knew it wasn't his place to turn up at the hospital.

'Sorry I didn't explain everything when I came around that day. It's hard to find the courage to say, "Hi, I'm the brother you didn't know existed."'

He sat with Nigel on his lap, who was contentedly munching on some peanuts Josh had thoughtfully brought, along with a huge bunch of flowers he wanted Maisie to pass on to Lisa. He really did look like Ben, she realised – it was the nose and the hair.

'It's okay. None of this is your fault.'

'Dad said she'll make a full recovery.'

'Yeah, she's a tough one. And I'm sorry you haven't been part of our lives all these years but we can remedy that. Let's take it slowly though, eh? The Meadows family is still dealing with the cataclysmic fallout from a nuclear explosion.'

'Of course, but to be honest, it's only been an issue since Mum died. She never wanted me to have anything to do with Dad's other family but I thought about you all and Dad let things slip from time to time. I know about Ben's band. I've got all their albums even though it's not really my kind of music.'

'Nor mine,' Maisie admitted. 'It's all a bit shouty and angry. Ironic when you can barely get three words out of him most of the time.' Although Ben's albums often found their way into her spare room on painting days. 'And if you find him difficult at first – persevere. He's got a caring side, buried deep under a stupid wall of indifference. I guess it built up over the years as a form of self-preservation. Families are vicious little devils – we want to embrace them but they snap at us with their jaggedy teeth and scratch us with their sharp claws.

Entering the Meadows family will be like trying to snuggle up to a wildcat.'

'Message received and understood. And sorry about those calls.'

Maisie frowned.

'I managed to track down a landline number for you so I rang you a few times but never had the courage to see the call through. Dad told me to bide my time, things were getting back on track with your mother and there was a lot of pressure for your family meal to be a success. We were planning to come to you first, hoping you'd pave the way for me. I'm still not sure why he jumped the gun and announced it in such a dramatic fashion.'

Ah, so Josh was her mysterious caller.

Chapter 54

After a weekend of soul-searching, Maisie withdrew her resignation and that Sunday she prepared to return to work. She still hadn't spoken to Ella and it bothered her, despite Theo's assurances her colleague was fully aware of her sister's accident. Maisie's decision to quit had been impulsive but Theo was right – she couldn't run away. The past six months at Gildersleeve's had been the best and even though returning in the morning would be scary, she would face her colleagues, knowing that they were all good people.

As she ironed a blouse and rummaged around for her insulated lunch bag in her uncharacteristically cluttered kitchen, she had a late-night visit from Zoe, returning home after an uncomfortable confrontation with Oliver.

'He fessed up about the encounter.' Her sister slumped into the armchair and sighed. 'Wish he'd been honest from the start. Seems he was jumped by an enthusiastic and slightly inebriated Lisa and the actual kiss was fleeting – but it was long enough for him to have told me. I'm done with her, Maisie. I don't wish her ill but we are different people.'

There had been a lot of thinking time sitting at Lisa's bedside. Sometimes the commonality between family members simply wasn't enough to bind them and perhaps it all boiled down to one unpalatable truth: the tea set wanted to be reunited but her family didn't.

'I shouldn't have forced everyone together. I've done so much more damage to the fragile relationships in our family than if I'd left well alone,' Maisie acknowledged.

'It's not your fault everyone decided to have a cathartic truth session out of nowhere, but I told you putting us all together in one house was never going to end well.'

'But we managed it when I was little. That last Christmas, before Dad left, we were so happy – the festive spirit embraced us all. We overlooked our differences and had a great day. I guess I wanted to recapture some of that good feeling and prove we were capable of being a family.'

'If you're talking about the year Lisa started sneaking vodka from the kitchen after breakfast and got so drunk she was inexcusably rude to our grandparents, who left early in disgust, and then she threw up in the downstairs loo and had to go to bed early – you have a skewed memory of the day, honey. Mum was furious when she realised. Lisa was only sixteen and, having worked her way through half a bottle of Smirnoff, lucky she wasn't in hospital having her stomach pumped.'

With her head shaking slightly from side to side, Maisie narrowed her eyes. That couldn't be right. Was that why Lisa had been so pleasant to everyone – *she was drunk?*

'But Dad was on top form,' Maisie persisted. 'I remember him laughing and joking, buying Mum flowers and giving us all magazines and sweets.'

'Oh, Maisie,' Zoe said, inching closer to her sister and putting her hand on her sister's knee. 'You were so young. I guess we shielded you. Truth is, Dad cocked up big time and forgot to get Mum a Christmas present. He was lucky the independent garage on the edge of town literally never closes. He tried to make amends by being generous with his wallet and, knowing what we know now, I wouldn't be surprised if he'd popped in on his second family while he was about it. It doesn't take two hours to take Grandma and Granddad home and grab a handful of chocolate bars. He even paid me to play with you when he returned, making sure at least one member of the family had a good day.'

This wasn't the Christmas she remembered, and Maisie was torn between not wanting that precious memory spoiled and needing to know the truth.

'And Ben?' she whispered.

Zoe shook her head slowly from side to side.

'He was so angry about not getting the PlayStation game he'd asked for, he spent most of the day upstairs in his room taking out his anger on that damn drum kit of his. As for Mum ...' she paused, letting out a long sigh '... after you and Lisa had gone to bed, she practically downed the remaining vodka in one go. She did everything that day – from tidying the house, to preparing and cooking the meal. Even the grandparents sat around like royalty, expecting her to wait on them hand and foot. I look back now and am horrified that we treated her like an unpaid domestic servant – not you, you were too young,' she added, hastily. 'But I've apologised since and tried to pull my weight more when we moved to the flat. I babysat you and often cooked our tea when she got the job at the care home.'

Zoe looked at her younger sister's shell-shocked face and leaned in to give her a hug. 'Sorry, sweetie,' she whispered into her hair. 'Perhaps I shouldn't have said anything and let you hold on to your precious memories.'

'No, it's fine. I don't feel such an abysmal failure now, knowing how outrageously high the odds were stacked against me from the start. I was clinging on to something that wasn't real.'

With everything Maisie remembered crumbling before her like a kicked sandcastle, she realised her family dream was never going to happen, especially as the one she was so desperate to re-create had never even happened in the first place. She had to accept that as much as she loved each member of her family in their own way, they were simply not meant to be together.

Determined to make up for lost time, and justify Johnny's enduring faith in her, Maisie arrived early Monday morning. As soon as she swung open the door to the back office she knew she'd been foolish to contemplate giving up on Gildersleeve's. It was so much more than just a job. She loved researching the quirky items that passed through their hands, or flicking through back issues of the *Antiques Trade Gazette*. And now the company was growing, she'd been thinking about some ways to take it forward and had a head full of ideas to pitch to Johnny and Theo.

Barely had she collapsed onto her chair and started to boot up her laptop, than Arthur knocked on the open office door behind her, with a small, round brown paper parcel in his hands and an enormous grin across his crinkly face.

'Well, now, I don't want to stop you, and I'm sure you've got far more important things to be doing on such a sunny day than listen to me, but I need to put my two penn'orth forward,' he said, still clutching the parcel as she gestured for him to take a seat. 'We missed you terribly last week but I'm glad your sister is on the mend. Gildersleeve's seems so much smarter since you started here and them *Wot a Lot!* people are in later to start the filming. Johnny doesn't think we'll pull it off without you – you're so good at all that. I said to my Essie how the place would be so much poorer without you ...'

Not commenting on the use of 'my' when describing the youngest Mayhew sister, Maisie smiled.

'I needed a little headspace but I'm here now. And the first order of the day is to catch Ella as soon as she arrives and apologise properly.'

'She's tougher than she looks, that one. Having a boyfriend has boosted her confidence no end.' Of course, Maisie thought, anyone dating Theo would feel on top of the world. He had that knack of making you feel as if you were the only person in the room. 'And when you feel loved,' Arthur said, 'it helps you remember your worth in life. Which brings me nicely on to a little bit of news of my own – although I'm sure you've guessed already. And it was, in part, down to you ...'

She couldn't help but smile, as she realised her inner Emma had got it right. 'Essie?'

'I've been in love with that woman for so many years and, although I wouldn't trade my life with Pam, there's something very special about your first love. I grew up with those Mayhew girls and hung around the younger sisters for years hoping I'd catch her eye. Turns out she had a bit of a thing for me back in the day too. Frank was just that little bit bolder, that little bit sooner. But there, we're together now, and that's all that matters.'

A warmth flooded Maisie's heart. It was all coming together nicely. Arthur would have someone real to talk to other than a photograph in those previously lonely evenings, and Essie could bake to her heart's content, knowing her surplus cakes and biscuits would no longer end up in the bin. Actually, Maisie thought to herself, feeling more buoyant after Arthur's words, she might have a chat with Essie about another outlet for her baking …

'Anyhoo,' he continued, 'we've been packing up all her things – my house is bigger – and we came across something we thought you'd like …'

'You're moving in together? Goodness, Arthur, isn't that a bit soon?'

'Nonsense. At our age you might not have a lot of time to play silly games. One of us could be dead before the year's out. You need to grab opportunities when they come along. I look back now and realise I should have said something when she started dating Frank. She thought I wasn't interested – see? And I was too much of a gentleman to step on Frank's toes. But sometimes you have to be brave and at least try. Speak now or forever hold your peace and all that. Anyway, enough of my chatter – this is for you,' and he handed Maisie the brown paper parcel, his eyes anxiously watching her hands as she unknotted the string.

Pulling back the crisp brown paper, she gasped as a small black and white bowl was revealed. It was instantly recognisable as part of Verity's set but she already had the sugar bowl so was confused as to its purpose.

'It's a slop bowl,' Arthur clarified. 'Essie forgot all about it until she was clearing out a back cupboard.' Noting Maisie's blank expression, he explained. 'You tip the cold, undrunk tea into it before you pour yourself a nice fresh cuppa. People don't use them nowadays.'

'Slop bowl? What an unfortunate name for such a pretty thing.'

'Now you really do have the complete set,' he said, smiling. And Maisie wondered if that meant she had another unknown family member lurking in her life, who was about to leap out and unmask themselves.

Thinking about her dad's less than exclusive love life, it was entirely possible.

Chapter 55

'I can't apologise enough,' Maisie said. 'I never put photos of people online without their permission. It was such a stunning picture of you and I was rushing about ... I didn't think. I'm so sorry.'

She was sitting in the front office with Ella and had presented her with the bouquet – not that a bunch of flowers could undo the damage, but it was a start.

'It's okay. And you shouldn't have got me these,' Ella said, lifting them to her nose and inhaling the sweet scent of the stocks, before placing them on the table beside her. 'Although I'm not comfortable going online in the future, if that's okay. Theo went ballistic but he's just overprotective. I'm stronger than I look. And, of course, having a boyfriend has given me more self-confidence. It's early days but he seems genuine enough.'

'Of course he is. He's one of the nicest blokes I know. I hope you'll be very happy together.' Ella looked confused, but Maisie carried on speaking, not wanting to linger over the thought of Ella and Theo being blissfully happy for too long. 'Sorry I let you down. I've not been much of a friend.'

'You've been amazing,' Ella said, moving closer and touching Maisie's shoulder. 'Look how you persevered with me when I could barely even acknowledge you. When you spend a lifetime trying to blend into the background, it's hard to step forward. Social interaction still petrifies me but then Theo and Arthur, in their different ways, don't put pressure on me to be a great conversationalist and I feel enormously comfortable with them both now.'

'Is Theo about?' Maisie asked, wanting to run some ideas past him and prove she was back on the team.

'He's in Saleroom Two talking to someone from the television company ahead of Friday's filming.'

Maisie walked over to the barn as a slight summer drizzle peppered her face. She'd built up the meeting with Ella in her head, but a bit of time and space from the incident had been key – for both of them. How could she have considered resigning over it? Theo, however, was a different kettle of heartache. Perhaps time would help this to heal too.

She heaved back the barn door and immediately spotted Theo's glorious fuzzy head. He was bent forward, setting up the trestle tables for valuing, chatting to a stocky girl with a *Wot a Lot!* clipboard about how they operated. As Maisie walked towards him, all she could think of was burying her face in his hair.

He looked up, hearing her footsteps, and gave her a lopsided grin.

'Glad you're back. You had me worried for a bit there. It's going to be a bonkers week, what with the TV crew descending. Excuse us for a moment,' he said to the young girl, who nodded and announced she'd scrounge a coffee from the ladies in reception to give the pair some privacy.

'Yeah, sorry. Gut reaction. I had a lot going on,' she said, as the researcher closed the barn door behind her.

'How is your sister now?' he asked, giving her an intense stare with concerned eyes.

'She went back to York with Craig yesterday. Early days, but he genuinely seems to care about her. She's been formally charged with drink driving and will have to return for the court case but knows she's probably looking at a twelve-month ban and a hefty fine. And with that on her record, her employment prospects aren't great. With God and Craig on her side, she'll get through it all, but the house seems empty without her. I didn't think I'd miss her as much as I do, although it's amazing what a great companion a honey-coloured ball of fluff is. I guess he's my equivalent of Pam's photograph, but the company of real people wins every time.'

'Bet you don't miss her mess though, Little Miss Spick and Span?'

'Yes and no. Some things are more important than an ordered cutlery drawer.' She smiled and there was an awkward pause. 'Anyway, I wanted to talk to you about the company ...'

'I'm listening,' Theo said, smoothing the tablecloth down, and hitching up his leg on the chair.

'I've been thinking about all the lonely people I know – Arthur, Lisa, the Mayhew sisters, the elderly residents of Willow Tree House, even Ella when I first got here – of course, that's changed now,' she said, avoiding his eyes, and trying not think about how Theo might be helping Ella fill her lonely evenings. She failed. 'The more I thought about your Modern Design sales, the more our auction layout started to resemble the houses of the elderly people I know. The furniture, the coloured glass and the kitchenalia, and it started me thinking. These were people who would appreciate and remember these objects from their heyday, and would these people be a potential market? Or even a potential source of lots?'

'And your genius idea is ...?'

'We have an over-sixties preview for some of our special sales, particularly the modern design, which I think we might even be able to make once a month once we get going with the promotion. Just an hour in the afternoon, maybe before we let everyone else in, where they can wander about and look at the items and support the café. Mum could even get some of the more able-bodied residents down here, as long as we keep an eye on the memory-challenged individuals.' She smiled. 'We might get some good promotion out of it – local newspaper coverage and *carefully monitored* social media.'

It was the nostalgia element, something she'd been pushing in all her advertising. Trying to associate Gildersleeve's with happy memories and halcyon years gone by. The number of times she'd walked around on viewing days and overheard people say, 'My mum had one just like that,' or 'I always wanted one of those when I was little.'

Theo rubbed his unshaven chin and made a hmm sound. 'Like all your ideas, I think it's a bit full-on, but you do have a knack of making things work, even if they take some tweaking. You're too enthusiastic and I'm too laid-back. We make a good team,' he said, avoiding her eyes for a second. 'But don't get hung up on the Twitter fiasco. You were right about pushing our online presence. Johnny and I can see a direct link to our leap in profits and attendance. We might even have to give you a pay rise.'

'We haven't got to the good bit yet,' she said.

'We haven't?' He raised an eyebrow.

'I think Johnny's café should be themed.'

'We are NOT going down the Hooters route,' he warned, totally deadpan.

'Aww, don't dismiss it out of hand – Arthur would look fabulous in stockings and suspenders.' Theo broke out another of his deliciously wonky smiles so she continued. 'I was actually thinking of a simple Fifties and Sixties mix. I know someone who has a garage full of vintage paraphernalia, including a working milkshake machine. Johnny is right; if we make the café as much of an attraction as the auction house, they'll benefit each other. Although not everything we sell is old, the majority of our stuff is. Let's make Gildersleeve's a place people want to come to for an afternoon out.'

'A retro café for a retro company with its retro staff.' He chuckled. 'Great idea and well done for bouncing back. You're one amazing woman, Maisie Meadows.' He was scrutinising her face again, searching for something but she didn't know what.

Now was the time to be brave, she thought, looking into Theo's mossy eyes. She had to tell him everything she said about workplace relationships was purely because she was jealous Ella had pipped her to the fuzzy-headed post. Arthur's words played in her head. How different his story with Essie might have been if one of them had admitted their feelings from the start. Frank and Pam would have met other people and Essie and Arthur would have been together fifty years sooner.

The barn was silent. There was no one to invade this moment with clumping boots or flapping clipboards. Theo's eyes locked on to hers and Maisie felt a nervous lump slide painfully down her throat as she swallowed. Her lips were dry and her head was giddy. Did he feel the same? Sometimes when he seemed to be studying her so intently she thought so. Their bodies swayed a tiny bit closer and she tipped her head slightly to the side, her thudding heart out of control. She saw his tongue moisten his lips and there was no longer any doubt where this was heading. His mouth was millimetres away from hers and she inhaled his spicy aftershave and pine soap. And then she remembered Gareth's unfaithfulness and pulled away abruptly.

'I'm sorry. I can't do this.' How could she even contemplate going behind Ella's back when she'd never been anything other than kind to her? She felt ashamed and disloyal. 'If we were both free it would be different but there are other people's feelings to consider.'

Theo closed his eyes and shook his head. 'You're right. What the hell are we thinking?'

I know what I'm thinking, Maisie thought as she reluctantly turned and began to walk towards the barn door – that I love you and it sucks that someone beat me to it.

Chapter 56

It was a spectacularly busy Friday. The auction house had acquired the estate of an avid militaria collector and had several potentially valuable lots – the showstopper being a pair of early nineteenth-century cast-iron canons. Online bids had given a good indication of the level of interest and several serious collectors had travelled across the country to attend, resulting in a swell of numbers at the salerooms that morning. This was Gildersleeve's at its best: staff milling around, engaged in conversations with the public, and a bustle and energy that was contagious.

The *Wot a Lot!* crew were on site – the overenthusiastic director loving every frenetic minute and following Theo around like a lovesick puppy. Maisie may have got Johnny's leanings wrong but she would stake Nigel's life there was more to the director's close personal attention than being a fan of Theo's extraordinary hair.

The auction got off to a promising start, with the canons going for double the estimate and bringing the atmosphere alive. Maisie was a runner – taking the completed auction sheets from Theo over to the office. It was on her second run that she skipped though the door of the reception to see her long-haired art class teacher, Tristan, kissing Ella behind the desk. They stood facing each other and there was no doubting his arm around her tiny waist was the arm of a romantic relationship.

'What the ...?'

'Apologies.' Ella flushed bright red. 'I know this isn't appropriate at work. He only popped by to drop off my phone because I'd left it in his car this morning. I'm terribly sorry.'

'Of course it's not appropriate,' Maisie muttered. 'You're kissing another man whilst your boyfriend conducts an auction, blissfully unaware of your disloyalty. I can believe you're doing this to Theo.' Tristan took a startled step backwards and Ella frowned at Maisie.

'Tris is my boyfriend.'

'No, Theo is,' Maisie said, quite definite in her statement.

'He really isn't,' Ella countered, just as firmly. 'Theo's a kind man and a good friend but not my type.'

'But you've been hanging out together after work. Theo said you are often over at his house.' Maisie began to feel less certain about her assertion in the face of Ella's denial. After all, she should know who her boyfriend was.

'Yes, I'm upholstering a chair for him – my take on the Eighties, inspired by the Rubik's Cube. It's been fun. Besides, I'm not the one he wants. Surely you've noticed how he looks at you? Everyone else has. Johnny's been hoping you two would hit it off from the start.'

Hearing his name, Johnny appeared from the back office clutching a bundle of papers.

'Am I missing out on some delicious gossip?' he asked. 'Has this wondrous child finally realised what I have been subtly trying to tell her from the very first day she stepped foot in the Gildersleeve's premises? That Theodore would indeed be perfect for her and is undoubtedly the Lancelot to her Guinevere?'

'Hold on one cotton-picking minute, Mister Jonathan Gildersleeve.' Maisie's brain was unravelling the conversation. 'Are you telling me every time you harped on about how adorable Theo was, you were trying to *sell him to me?*'

'I was hardly coveting him for myself. My tastes are decidedly more ... breast-orientated. I rather thought that had been satisfactorily established – admittedly somewhat late in the day.'

She shook her head in disbelief. 'And you wondered why I thought you were a couple. Always telling me what impressive thighs he had and how intense his eyes were.'

'Ah, yes, I do see your point and it was terribly naughty of me to presume to match-make. Planting seeds in your mind and cultivating the delicate plants pushing their way through the soil. I so wanted darling Theodore to be happy and you seemed the perfect person to help with that. Deep in my very bosom, I know I'm right. You need to dump that oversized boyfriend of yours and look a bit closer to home, dah-ling. Poor fellow has been in torment, watching you with another man.'

'But I don't have a boyfriend.' What *was* going on? It was like some ridiculous Shakespearean comedy. 'Where did you get that idea from?'

'The tall chap who simply can't keep his hands off you. We've all seen you flirting in the salerooms, you can't deny it, my dear.'

Ella nodded in agreement. 'Theo's been totally wretched.'

'Oliver? My brother-in-law? Who still ruffles my hair like I'm a child? Seriously?' She allowed her mouth to drop open to drive home her point.

They both nodded and Maisie shook her head to allow muddled thoughts to settle into a more logical order. How had she and Theo managed to get everything so catastrophically wrong?

'But I'm in love with Theo.' Saying the words aloud made her realise how true they were. These few months at the auction house her feelings had been sneaking up behind her and waiting for her to turn around and recognise them. No wonder they'd both pulled back earlier in the week – each thought the other was in a relationship. If she wasn't so full of colliding emotions, she would have burst out laughing.

'Then for all that is righteous and holy, go and tell him that, dear child. Do it. *Do it now*.' Johnny's face was positively beaming. 'There is no time to lose in matters of the heart.'

'Do I hear six hundred?'

Maisie burst through the barn door and waved frantically at Theo, standing behind the oak lectern and looking totally ravishable in a floral open-necked shirt and tatty knee-length shorts.

'An astonishingly keen bidder has entered the room, so it's six hundred with you, madam,' and he gestured in Maisie's direction, gave a cheeky smile to camera one and the camera fell a little bit more in love with him too.

'No. No. I'm not bidding. Unless your heart is up for auction? In which case I'll sell everything I own.' There was nothing like a bold and ill-thought-out statement to really get your heart racing. The fact it was being filmed for national TV wasn't helping.

The room became eerily quiet. That gentle hum of conversation that usually accompanied the auctions dropped away to nothing. Theo stared at the bouncing blonde in front of him, his eyes almost wider than his head.

'I'm mid-auction. Can this wait?'

'Not really ...' She shuffled from foot to foot and an awkward silence followed. 'I think we should deal with this now.'

'Hear, hear.' Arthur stepped forward. 'You go, girl. Tell him how you feel. Do it for me and my lost opportunities.' His voice was cracking and tears swelled in his crinkly eyes. He was alongside her now and Maisie reached for his thin hand, clasping the old man's bony fingers, and gaining some Dutch courage from her friend.

Theo locked eyes with Maisie, above the heads of the assembled crowd. The *Wot a Lot!* director whispered into his headset mic and began frantically directing cameramen to focus on Maisie as the scene unfolded.

What can only have been a few seconds stretched between them like decades. Maisie sucked in a long breath and laid her soul bare, Arthur's last-minute squeeze giving her all the courage she needed.

'I really like you,' she said. 'As in *like* so much I'm almost certainly in love with you.'

Theo blinked once, still staring at her face.

'Oliver?' There was no visible emotion in that question. She was rather disappointed. He was supposed to reply: 'I love you too.'.

There was a cough from somewhere at the front. 'Shhh ...' the director whispered.

'Brother-in-law and lifelong friend. Not boyfriend. Ever. I thought I'd said?'

'Nope – at no point was he ever introduced as your brother-in-law.'

Still their eyes were fixed on each other until Maisie finally blinked.

'Wish you had though.' He shrugged. 'Kinda been in purgatory for the last month. I've had Foreigner on repeat and watched *Casablanca* SEVEN times.'

'Huh,' she snorted. 'Yet you let me think you were dating Ella ...' He needed to know he did not have the monopoly on self-pity.

'Ella? Are you totally mad? She's a friend. I even admitted to your sister my heart was taken ...' There was a pause as he replayed events. 'Ah, yeah. I see where the confusion arose.'

'Don't be a tease, Theo, old boy,' Arthur piped up. 'She's put her heart on the line. Tell her how you feel.' Theo's eyes flicked briefly to Arthur's face and then back to hers.

'I thought it was bloody obvious – I've been gradually falling for you since the day you launched yourself at me like a woman possessed. But you had this "just friends" thing going on, telling me what a bad idea workplace relationships were and thinking I was gay ...' The director looked up at Theo, his shoulders lifting in anticipation. 'But it's been you all the way.' The director shrugged in resignation. 'So, hey, yeah, I'm up for it if you are. As long as you promise you won't make me buy matching dinner plates?'

'Up for it' was possibly as good as she was going to get from Mr Horizontal. The swelling in her chest made her feel light-headed and giddy – like she was a slowly rising Chinese lantern drifting up to the heavens, fuelled by love. She nodded.

'In that case – sold!' he shouted, as he banged the gavel down with gusto.

His asymmetric grin reached both ears and he hopped down from the rostrum and parkoured over the cabinets, striding over to her and taking her head in his hands. One more lingering look – just to make sure – and then he swooped in on her mouth. Maisie was immediately lost in a buzz of chemical reactions that set her body on fire, as her heart joined her knees on the floor beneath her feet.

There was a ripple of applause and Arthur stepped back to mop his streaming tears with a freshly laundered cotton hanky. Essie and he might not have quite that energy any more but Maisie suspected the passion was the same.

Theo pulled back to look into her eyes once more.

'I can add you to my eclectic collection – things that hold great emotional significance, things I simply love and must have,' he said. 'I don't care that you don't match anyone else in my life. In fact, I think I prefer it that way.'

'And yet you're my slop bowl,' she mumbled, smiling at Theo's totally bemused expression. 'Completing my set.' Who said family had to be related to you?

'And that's a wrap,' came a voice from the front as Theo and Maisie's lips collided once more and the camera panned out on their happy ending.

Chapter 57

Two weeks later, on a hot and sticky August day, Maisie organised an afternoon tea party for her friends, with the expectation that it would be a more successful and less explosive gathering than her ill-fated family meal. It would be different this time – this wouldn't be people forced together by a well-meaning if misguided woman, desperately seeking to unite something that had never worked as a whole in the first place. These were people who had gravitated to her, and her to them, through choice. Today, she would celebrate that at least one of her quests had been successful – reuniting Verity's tea set.

Waiting for her guests to arrive, Maisie picked up the envelope containing the jagged pieces of broken cup, still sitting on the worktop since the day of Lisa's accident. Theo was right. How stupid to think a tea set could influence real-life events. It was unusual and quirky and had unleashed all sorts of weird feelings in her because she'd associated it with a troubled time in her childhood. Meredith's misguided conviction that it was in some way special had fuelled the imagination of a small child and nearly twenty years later, that of a desperate woman. Maisie loved it and would always keep it, but the notion that reuniting it had somehow brought her family together was ridiculous. It was a series of extraordinary coincidences, and when she looked back now, she recognised her actions were the catalyst – not the teapot.

She'd nudged Zoe and Oliver into a decision they'd been hurtling towards anyway, made Ben feel suitably guilty about not coming home, and engineered the bridges that made her mum more amenable to overtures from her dad. And it was her friendship with Lisa, however one-sided, that enabled her troubled sister to take refuge with her when life got difficult.

It was possible she would never find out who Verity was, or if she'd even existed at all, but that didn't matter. Inanimate objects couldn't affect people's decisions – real people, with real feelings, made the world go round. The Mayhews had encountered a spectacularly dreadful run of bad luck in a relatively short space of time but it was ludicrous to blame the tea set.

She walked over to the shiny chrome bin in the corner, pressed her toe on the pedal and let the envelope slip from her fingers. It landed with a clunk at the bottom. She lifted her foot and the lid closed.

Arthur and Essie were her first guests – Essie laden with enough freshly baked cakes to feed most of Tattlesham and Theo, Johnny and Ella turning up shortly afterwards in Theo's battered Capri – the strains of Bon Jovi pulsing through the open car window and Johnny leaping from the car almost immediately, to escape the assault on his eardrums.

It was a glorious summer day so Maisie flung open the narrow French doors to her small decked patio and her guests filtered outside. The rich perfume of her neighbour's climbing rose drifted gently into her tiny garden. Verity's set was arranged neatly on her circular plastic garden table and she poured everyone a cup of tea, instructing them all to help themselves to cake.

'To Meredith,' Maisie toasted, wondering if she should perhaps be toasting the mysterious Verity as well, whoever she was.

'To Meredith,' they chorused in response.

There was a moment of quiet as the tea slipped down their throats, the buzz of a fat bumble bee hovering near the trellis was the only backdrop to their silent contemplation until Ella broke the silence by announcing, 'I have a difficult relationship with my mother, partly but not exclusively because she has absolutely no idea who my father is.'

No one knew quite what to say – her statement was so out of the blue, especially as Ella was the last person to draw attention to herself. She dropped her head, allowing her hair to partially cover her face and her flushed cheeks.

Johnny cleared his throat, ensuring all eyes were on him, much to Ella's obvious relief.

'Continuing in the spirit of unanticipated disclosure, dahlings, I've signed up to Tinder and have my first date next week with an intriguing thirty-eight-year-old woman from Belarus who collects Victorian erotica.'

Wow. Giving Johnny a few smartphone lessons had really opened up his world. But why was everyone suddenly making such candid and personal announcements? Maisie's mind returned to the disastrous family meal when equally unexpected truths had tumbled out in quick succession around her table.

She looked down at the cup of tea in her hand and another prickle rippled through her body – the sort you get when you suddenly realise you've left the gas on at home or the person you're talking about is standing behind you. The little symbols on the bottom of the cups spelled out that name danced in her mind. Meredith had told her Gamma was very particular about who used the set – almost as if it needed supervision. And that, coupled with her insistence it was never split, made Maisie wonder.

What if verity had never been a name but a *noun*? What if the consequences of reuniting the set were linked to those innocuous Theban letters on the bottom of each piece of the china? Theo had said something about it meaning truth ...

Maisie felt a rising panic in her chest. Her disastrous family meal suddenly made sense. After all, it had been going swimmingly until she poured everyone a cup of tea ...

'I also have a confession to make.' Arthur gave a nervous cough and his wrinkled eyes scrunched up into a frown, as if he wasn't in control of his own mouth. 'And it's a biggie. I'm not even sure I should rightly be telling you all. Something I did many years ago that I'm not particularly proud of but perhaps now is the time to get it off my chest. It's been a burden to carry around all these years, especially as I never even told my darling Pam. No harm done in the end but I think it's important to be honest with Essie now that I've found her again ...'

He took a deep breath as Maisie tried to attract Theo's attention with a flash of her startled eyes across the decking, but he was sprawled across her tartan picnic rug, the brim of his ridiculous straw sun hat obscuring his eyes. No, this couldn't be allowed to happen. She had to stem the flow of these alarming truths before the afternoon descended into the unbridled chaos of her family meal.

Arthur turned to his lady friend.

'I was so in love with you, Essie darling, but you never gave

380

me a second look. Instead, I spent all those years hanging around your sisters, just to be near you.' He paused. Essie reached out for his knee, her eyes scrunched up in confusion, and Maisie's heart thudded so violently, she half expected it to explode through her ribcage. 'It was bound to happen, I suppose – two lonely souls drifting around the edge of other people's lives ... And Joanie was such a sweet girl ...'

Chapter 58

'This will be awkward,' said Essie, picking at a loose thread in her pale pink cardigan, anticipating the arrival of her older sister and her niece. 'Fifty years she's looked me in the eye and never once said a word.'

Maisie sat next to the youngest Mayhew sister on a wooden bench near the bandstand, overlooking Tattlesham mere. No more secrets, Arthur promised, and insisted Essie came with him. Essie, in turn, insisted Maisie was with her so she didn't feel like the only superfluous wheel on this runaway train that had broken free of the tracks.

It was yet another glorious August day. The weather, for once, abiding by the calendar and delivering an appropriate climate. Maisie leaned forward to unpack the picnic she'd brought, with proper glasses and not a HobNob in sight. Through her dark sunglasses, she finally spied Joanie and Clare, ambling along the path at the water's edge.

Arthur stopped his restless pacing as they approached, and Joanie stopped to face him, her eyes anxious and her hands shaking.

'I'm sorry,' she said. 'It wasn't my intention to cause anyone pain – quite the opposite. But it was never love, was it? How could it be?' Joanie's eyes flicked over to her sister and they exchanged understanding but fleeting smiles, Essie gripping Maisie's hand a little tighter.

'Now, Joanie, don't be fretting. We got there in the end, eh? And I understand your reasons. Think it would have broken Pam, although obviously I've told her all about it now. No point living a life of regrets. Grab the here and now – ask Pam, she'll tell you.' He ran a shaky hand through his thinning hair and swallowed. 'So, who have we got here, then?' And he turned to Clare, lurking behind her mother, her eyes cast to the floor.

'Arthur, this is your daughter – Clare.' Joanie stepped to one side. 'She's got your eyes. And your relentlessly cheery nature.'

Arthur stood in front of the daughter he'd never known – a woman of fifty, who had amassed, over her lifetime, everything she'd ever wanted – except a father.

'Hello, love,' said Arthur. 'I've got so much to tell you, although Pam and Essie both say I chatter too much, so I shan't mind if you tell me to stop talking. I do sometimes get a bit carried away with my—'

Clare rushed forward and interrupted Arthur's speech by clinging to her daddy as if she was eight years old and he was about to leave for the moon – the poor man unable to stop a stream of tears falling from his crinkly eyes and wobbling about as Clare squeezed tighter and tighter.

No one dared speak or break the moment, and Maisie knew this embrace would last some time.

After all, Clare had fifty years of missed hugs to make up for.

Epilogue

Christmas Day – 4 months later

Maisie looked at the myriad of happy faces squeezed around her dining table. Last Christmas she'd been so desperate to gather her scattered family together that she'd made it her mission over the following months to do just that. Instead, through her job at Gildersleeve's, she'd inadvertently assembled an eclectic but much treasured group of friends – friends so dear to her they felt like family.

It was early evening. Theo had told Maisie not to stress over producing a lavish Christmas dinner with all the trimmings for the two of them. Frozen pizza would do and, much to his surprise, Maisie agreed. Instead of a morning slavishly following a complicated schedule of cooking times, she was whisked off for a brisk walk around the mere, leaving a crumpled and unmade pine-scented bed behind. She wore Theo's fur-lined trapper hat because it had special memories, and Theo wore matching socks because they were a gift from Maisie and he was still in those early stages of their romance where he tried to meet his girlfriend's expectations for at least some of the time.

Christmas Eve had been a girlie affair: Mum, Zoe and

Maisie. Lisa rang to wish them all an early happy Christmas because the following day was, after all, one of the busiest days of the year for her boyfriend.

'How's Craig?' Maisie had asked.

'Pushing for counselling to confront the drinking. Telling me how wonderful I am. Sorting out my debts and helping me look for work. God gets a mention now and then.'

'Give yourself a break and let him love you, sis.'

'I'll try. And say hi to Irene for me when you see her. I sense in her a kindred spirit – we're both too spiky for our own good but at least no one can accuse us of being boring.'

Everyone knew Lisa still had a lot of issues and a long way to go but finally letting someone love her was a tentative first step in her journey.

Maisie's mum was working a Christmas Day shift at Willow Tree House. She didn't mind a bit and was looking forward to spending the day with her cherished residents. Every year she put her heart and soul into the day, knowing for some it would be their last Christmas on this earth and so needed to be special.

Maisie finally stumbled upon a use for four boxes of naughty gnomes and they were now a permanent feature in a secret corner of the Willow Tree House grounds. It was surprising how many of the old dears who regularly tutted at Naked Man motivated themselves to get outside for some fresh air since their arrival. Irene thought they were a bunch of hypocrites. 'We all still think about it even if we can't do it any more,' she said. 'Some of us are a bit more honest about it, that's all.'

Sadly, Mrs Leggit passed away suddenly at the end of November but Theo, helping Maisie move the gnomes from her shed, spotted a late Victorian Royal Crown Derby plate in the box of tat Phyllis's grabbing grandson had thrust upon her. There was karma at play because it was put into the auction and sold for several hundred pounds. Maisie donated the entire sum to the Adopt A Gran scheme, knowing Phyllis would have approved. After all, if her grabbing grandson had spotted its value it would only have gone on handbags.

It was early days but Maisie's half-brother, Josh, seemed genuine. They'd met a couple of times for coffee and she was paving the way for a relationship with her more reluctant siblings. Even Ben had shown interest in his half-brother and they'd agreed to meet when he finally returned to the UK. Dad, much to everyone's surprise, had been single since the summer – his longest ever spell as a bachelor. Boxing Day would be Maisie, Dad, Josh and a curious Zoe …

Families, Maisie reflected, were complicated things. A group of people who looked similar but who often had very different personalities. Sometimes this random combination worked and sometimes it didn't. The Meadows were all great people in their own way; they had their virtues and their weaknesses, like every other human being on the planet, but forcing them together was like tossing a handful of magnets into a box. There were strong forces at work, repelling some and attracting others. Maisie accepted, whilst she loved each and every one of them in their turn, they simply weren't a family that worked well when placed in a confined space. Much like the tea set – each component came from the whole, was beautiful and unique in its own way, but alarmingly dangerous when assembled together.

Nigel's wheel was doing four hundred miles an hour. Maisie smiled at her whirring ginger friend as she walked past his cage to put a plate of hot sausage rolls and a potato salad on the table, and surveyed her guests; Arthur and Essie fresh from a lavish lunch with Clare at the hotel, Ella deep in conversation with a velvet-bedecked Johnny, and her own darling flocculent Theo. These people were her harlequin family. Like Theo's chairs, they were all different but similar enough to work. There would be no storming out, slapping of faces or unpleasant scenes that afternoon – especially as her precious tea set was staying firmly on the shelf.

As unhappy as the Mayhew lives had been, sometimes there was no one to blame. It all depended on your point of view. Yes, Cynthia's diagnosis was awful but she had outlived all the doctor's predictions. Meredith had been happy in her way. Her career had been fulfilling and she'd been a positive influence on several generations of young lives – not least Maisie's. Essie had found real love twice, even though she hadn't been able to have children. And Joanie led an extremely comfortable life and successfully raised a loving and caring daughter. Although Joanie never found true love herself, Clare now had the most attentive of fathers. A curious love triangle that had somehow worked out in the end.

Contented guests chatted away with the frenetic whirr of Nigel's wheel a backdrop to their conversation. There followed a gentle thud as he stopped running and the perpetual motion launched him against the bars of his cage.

He shook his little whiskers, dazed and surprised, and trotted back to mount the wheel again, because Nigel knew that whenever life sent you flying, it was best to hop back on and keep going. And Maisie Meadows, watching her fluffy little energetic friend, determined that whatever unlikely things life threw at her in the future, she would embrace her inner Nigel.

Acknowledgements

So that was it, folks. That notoriously tricky second book. I hope I got there in the end and I couldn't have achieved it without the help of the following people.

Thanks to my editor, Phoebe Morgan, who helped me knock Maisie Meadows into shape, and the exuberant team at Avon – who consistently go above and beyond. To my agent, Louise Buckley, for her constant pom-pom waving and calm reassurance. And, of course, much owed to The Brutal One – beta reader of the highest order.

A shout out to Clare who meets me every day in the virtual office and shares her virtual biscuits, and Heidi-Jo who trod this daunting path before me and passes on her wisdom when I flounder. Just two of the myriad of amazing RNA peeps who continue to love, support and advise.

From a research point of view, this book benefited from the expert knowledge of Elizabeth Talbot and James Bassam of TW Gaze (Diss Auction Rooms) – both of whom gave up their time to answer endless questions and give me an insight into the running of an auction house. Only a fraction of the research made it into the book, so maybe there is another book in there somewhere. Gaze's has been part of my life on and off for over twenty years and it has been wonderful to see the company evolve and grow during this time – giving me the inspiration for this story. It really is quite an adrenalin rush to attend an auction and if you have never been to one, I would encourage you to go.

Also, grateful thanks to Lara – antipodean extraordinaire, and Ken Mellor, for the drink driving guidance. As ever, any mistakes within the book are mine alone.

To Sharon, Marcus and Anthony for being so cool when I took my book on holiday to Italy with me. Thanks guys – sorry I missed out on that fab day but the hammock and the manuscript needed me. Besides, you left me with plenty of Puglian wine so all was good.

To family and friends, who put up with me when I'm grumpy and up against deadlines, who avoid me when I'm shouting at my outdated laptop and who wisely leave me in peace when I'm looking dreamily into space. Every day, life presents me with housework and my unfettered imagination. Most days I choose the latter – thank you all for understanding.

Last, but not least, thank you, dear readers, for buying and reading the words I have wrestled with and cried over. When you buy an author's book, borrow it from a library, review it online, or simply contact them to say how much you enjoyed reading it – it truly makes their day.

Do follow me on
Twitter @**JenniKeer**
Facebook **JenniKeerWriter**
Instagram **jennikeer**

Jenni x

If you enjoyed *The Unlikely Life of Maisie Meadows* and would like to read more from Jenni Keer, why not try *The Hopes and Dreams of Lucy Baker* – turn the page for further details ...

Meet Lucy, aged 25, and Brenda, aged 79.
Neighbours, and unlikely friends...

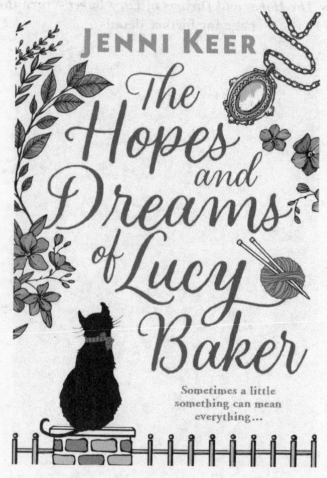

Jenni Keer

The
Hopes
and
Dreams
of Lucy
Baker

Sometimes a little
something can mean
everything...

A charming, heart-warming and feel-good novel,
perfect for fans of **Ruth Hogan** and **Gail Honeyman.**